## *A CALL TO ARMS*

'Mallinson's books are far more than the "rattling good yarns" one might expect – though anyone who does will not be disappointed . . . his tales are not only believable but delightfully informative . . . I read on with increased admiration and renewed enjoyment, for his books wear their impeccable scholarship lightly . . . The tales of "derring-do" are wonderfully vivid. But the real delight of Mallinson's books is their authenticity. His portrayal of his characters, as well as his vignettes of historical personages . . . show a rare and thoughtful understanding of the human condition and the mind of the soldier. It all makes for a thoroughly satisfying and entertaining read'
*The Times*

'Once more Mallinson displays his extraordinary knowledge of military history and practice. Throw in the fact that his usage of English is as pure and precise as Jane Austen's and his imagination as vivid as Kipling's and we have another cracking adventure in what is proving to be an altogether outstanding series'
*Birmingham Post*

'From the relaxed, reflective Roman episodes, to the remustering of the regiment, to the journey to India, the training of the inexperienced troopers, the march into the jungle and the final bloody engagement – the book picks up a pace that mirrors exactly a cavalry charge, from walk, to trot and, finally, to charge . . . Hervey continues to grow in stature as an engaging and credible character, while Mallinson himself continues to delight in the minutiae and arcaneness of military life'
*Observer*

'Thrilling . . . in addition to his exceptional knowledge of history, Allan Mallinson shows his deep awareness of human feelings and failings. This is an exceptional book'
*Country Life*

'Mallinson is a good historian. He gives his people a well-researched hinterland. He knows what it is like to command and to serve. He is as good on the details – and it is detail we historical novel buffs like – of the workings of a cavalry regiment in 1820 as ever Patrick O'Brian was on the workings of an 1820 warship'
*Spectator*

'Oozing action, *A Call to Arms* is a military tale of epic proportions that will leave fans counting the days to the next adventure'
*Ireland on Sunday*

'With each book, Hervey himself is becoming a more complex and interesting character . . . Mallinson writes of his inner questionings with subtlety and sympathy. This series grows in stature with each book'
*Evening Standard*

'Mallinson has lost none of his vigour for writing intense prose; whereas lesser authors might go off the boil slightly four novels into a series, Mallinson patently agonizes over his descriptions, gets the balance right on just how much cavalry information to slip in, and masterfully dovetails historical events to create an excellent balance'
*Good Book Guide*

*Also by Allan Mallinson*

THE NIZAM'S DAUGHTERS
A REGIMENTAL AFFAIR
A CALL TO ARMS

A

Sketch
of the
**BATTLE** of **WATERLOO**,
Fought
Sunday 18th June
*1815.*

FOREST

OF

SOIGNEN

Road to Bruxelles

Waterloo

Joly Bois

le Roussart

les Vieux Amis

Verd Cou

le Strange

le Mesnil

Mont St Jean

A

Merbe Braine

A

Braine la Leude

B

le Haye Sainte

Hougoumont

la belle Alliance

Ophain

de Leaux

Observatory

B

Mon Plaisir

Road from Nivelles

Quatre Bras and Charleroi

Road to Charleroi

Grispontwez

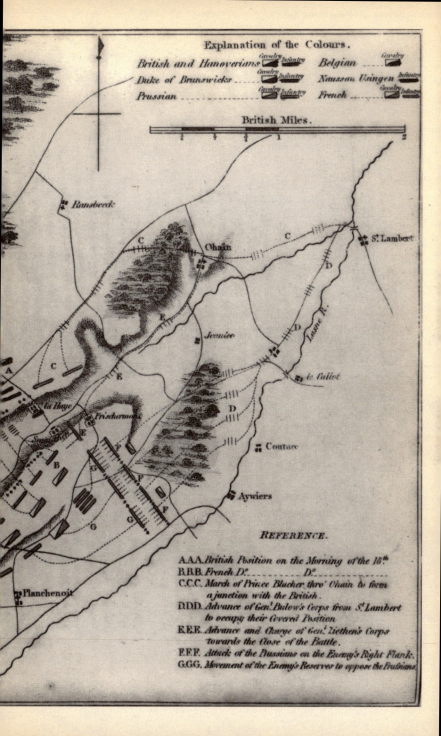

Explanation of the Colours.

British and Hanoverians ____ *Cavalry* *Infantry*     Belgian ____ *Cavalry*

Duke of Brunswicks ____ *Cavalry* *Infantry*     Nassau Usingen *Cavalry* *Infantry*

Prussian ____ *Cavalry* *Infantry*     French ____ *Cavalry* *Infantry*

British Miles.

Ransbeek

C    Ohain    C    St. Lambert

D

E

*Jeonice*    D

D    *Laine R.*

*A*   C     *le Guilot*

E

*la Haye*    D

*Frischermont*

*Smor Halte*   E     Couture

B   G

F

G   F

G    Aywiers

Planchenoit

REFERENCE.

A.A.A. *British Position on the Morning of the 18th.*

B.B.B. *French Do. ............... Do.*

C.C.C. *March of Prince Blucher thro' Ohain to form a junction with the British.*

D.D.D. *Advance of Genl. Bulow's Corps from St. Lambert to occupy their Covered Position*

E.E.E. *Advance and Charge of Genl. Ziethen's Corps towards the Close of the Battle.*

F.F.F. *Attack of the Prussians on the Enemy's Right Flank.*

G.G.G. *Movement of the Enemy's Reserves to oppose the Prussians.*

# A CLOSE RUN THING

## ALLAN MALLINSON

**BANTAM BOOKS**

LONDON · NEW YORK · TORONTO · SYDNEY · AUCKLAND

**A CLOSE RUN THING**
**A BANTAM BOOK : 0 553 50713 3**

Originally published in Great Britain by Bantam Press,
a division of Transworld Publishers

PRINTING HISTORY
Bantam Press edition published 1999
Bantam Books edition published 2000

9 10

Set in Times New Roman by
Phoenix Typesetting, Ilkley, West Yorkshire.

Bantam Books are published by Transworld Publishers,
61–63 Uxbridge Road, London W5 5SA,
a division of The Random House Group Ltd,
in Australia by Random House Australia (Pty) Ltd,
20 Alfred Street, Milsons Point, Sydney, NSW 2061, Australia,
in New Zealand by Random House New Zealand Ltd,
18 Poland Road, Glenfield, Auckland 10, New Zealand
and in South Africa by Random House (Pty) Ltd,
Endulini, 5a Jubilee Road, Parktown 2193, South Africa.

Printed and bound in Great Britain by
Clays Ltd, St Ives plc.

# AUTHOR'S NOTE

---

This is not just the story of an officer in the Duke of Wellington's army: it is the story of a regiment – that peculiarly British institution which John Keegan, the most percipient historian and observer of all things military, has described as 'an accidental act of genius'. Every regiment was – still is – different, and revelled in that difference. The difference was not just in the people but in the regiment's history and traditions – the received notions of how things should be done, the *esprit*, the spirit.

The 6th Light Dragoons are a fictitious regiment, but the events in which they take part are historical fact. The major characters outside the regiment are real figures of history. Occasional liberties have been taken – General Slade did not go to Ireland in 1814, for instance – but not in any way that changes the historical plausibility of the story.

The army of 1814 was singular. It had endured five years of campaigning in the Peninsula, and it had gone from success to success, until the duke was able to remark, famously, that it 'could go anywhere and do anything'. Sir Charles Oman, one of the two greatest historians of the campaign (the other being Sir William Napier), made also this interesting observation: 'A very appreciable number of men were of a religious turn – a thing I imagine to have been most unusual in the army of the eighteenth century.' (*Wellington's Army, 1809–1814*.)

The army was not, of course, without its faults. Neither was the duke. One of the most controversial matters was the purchase of commissions, the system by which officers of

the cavalry and the infantry bought their promotion, a system
that the duke strenuously upheld long after the war. This is a
complex issue, however, and not one to be taken at face value.
I know of no better (or more entertaining) explanation of it
than that in Volume One of the Marquess of Anglesey's
*History of the British Cavalry 1816–1919*, which, incidentally,
is also the most readable authority on horse-soldiering in the
early nineteenth century.

Readers who wish to know more about the organization
and equipment of the army at this time should consult the
detailed reference works by Mr Philip Haythornthwaite: they
have no equal. I am indebted, too, to Major (retd) John
Oldfield, sometime curator of the Small Arms Museum at the
School of Infantry, Warminster. The museum is an unrivalled
collection of both weapons and knowledge, and (though the
fact is little known) is open to visitors, by appointment. My
wife, whom I met in a stable, has been an unfailing aid in
finding the right words to describe the horses and their world:
she has kept me from the worst metaphorical falls.

Any Englishman writing even a little about Ireland
needs an Irish interlocutor of exceptional patience. I have
been immensely fortunate in the friendship and support of
Brigadier-General (retd) Pat Hogan, late of the Irish Defence
Forces and president of the Irish Military History Society. But
he can in no way be held responsible for anything that smacks
of *perfide Albion.*

I owe a very great deal indeed to Mr Patrick O'Brian –
directly and indirectly. His Aubrey/Maturin stories enthralled
me for so many years that I began to fret for anything
remotely comparable for the cavalry of that period, until
eventually I found the resolve to attempt, myself, to do something about it. He has been most generous in giving me advice
and encouragement.

I must acknowledge perhaps my greatest debt, however, to
Paula Levey (Mrs Piers Fletcher) – soldier's daughter,
soldier's sister, and wife of a former soldier, who, as editor of
the early manuscript, knew exactly what was what, and never
flinched from telling me.

To

*The Light Dragoons*

(formerly the 13th/18th and the 15th/19th Hussars)

In whose history, character and personalities I have
found much inspiration for this story.

# A CLOSE RUN THING

'Oh! pity the condition of man, gracious God! and save us from such a system of malevolence, in which all our old and venerated prejudices are to be done away, and by which we are taught to consider war as the natural state of man, and peace but as a dangerous and difficult extremity. Sir, this temper must be corrected. It is a diabolical spirit and would lead to interminable war . . . At what time did we ever profit by obstinately persevering in war?'

Charles James Fox, to the House of Commons,
3 February 1800

# 1814

Britain had persevered in war with revolutionary France, with but one short break, since 1793. The Royal Navy, at Aboukir in 1798 and Trafalgar in 1805, had confined Bonaparte to Europe; British money had financed the allies when they were ready to come forward; and a British army in the Iberian peninsula had, from 1809, maintained a front which had drained French resources and given hope to other Europeans. By the beginning of 1814, Bonaparte could defend only France. Russian, Prussian and Austrian armies were closing in from the east, while the British, already in the Pyrenees, stood ready to invade from the south-west.

## PART ONE

# PRIDE AND PREJUDICE

---

'But if you cannot make peace with Buonaparte in
the winter, we must run at him in the spring.'

The Marquess (later the Duke) of Wellington to the Cabinet,
10 January 1814

# CHAPTER ONE
# IN THE HEAT OF BATTLE

_____

*The Convent of St Mary of Magdala,*
*Toulouse, 12 April 1814*

'It is a very singular thing indeed, Mr Hervey, for a cornet to be placed in arrest upon the field of battle.'

Joseph Edmonds was deploying all his considerable facility with words in order to convey the gravity of the matter at hand.

'Tell me, if you please, precisely and dispassionately, the circumstances by which this was brought about.'

Cornet Hervey stood rigidly to attention before the major's desk, his left hand clasping the sword scabbard to his side, his right hand clenched with the thumb pointing downwards along the double yellow stripe of his overalls. His eyes were set front, and filling the limited arc of their fixed gaze were two symbols which, while if not to his mind entirely contradictory, in their juxtaposition seemed somehow incongruous. For on the wall behind the desk was a large wooden cross with a painted figure of the crucified Christ. Next to it – perhaps even leaning against it – was the regimental guidon, a piece of red silk on a beechwood stave, its richly embroidered battle honours still resplendent despite the staining and fading. The irony, that he had been raised in a household whose world was shaped by the first symbol, and had then elected to throw himself wholeheartedly behind the second, was not lost on him even at this exigent moment. He had little imagined such a convergence, however, nor its place – a nunnery hastily and rudely requisitioned for the purposes of the military. He drew in a deep breath, his stomach feeling tighter than ever it had done when he had been awaiting combat, and began the recollection of the events which had brought him now before his commanding officer.

'Sir, yesterday forenoon I was in command of the flank picket, as you had placed me, one quarter of a league to the west of our lines of attack upon this city . . .'

The fateful encounter with authority had begun spectacularly. Edmonds had not expected any affair on the left flank. Not that that was why he had entrusted the picket to Hervey: he had long been of the conviction that the worst that could happen in battle usually did (and as a consequence he had never been wrong-footed – at least, that is, in the field), and Hervey and his standing patrol were a trusty yet economical insurance.

Hervey had disposed his command, a half-troop (by the Sixth's depleted muster scarcely two dozen men), in the dead ground to the rear of a shallow ridge running obliquely to the army's front. They were dismounted and standing easy. Posted as vidette a furlong to their front, with a view into the valley beyond the ridge, was his picket serjeant. And it was the sudden animation in that sentinel that alerted Hervey now.

'Mount!' he called, and his troopers began tightening girths before springing back into their saddles. Without an order the contact man – the picket corporal – galloped off to Serjeant Armstrong, who had by now worked his way in cover along the ridge and further to the flank.

Five minutes passed before the corporal returned, with intelligence that thrilled through the ranks: 'Sir, there is a horse battery, six guns, approaching.'

'And supports?' pressed Hervey.

'None observed, sir.'

'None? No supports? That is not possible!'

'Serjeant Armstrong says there are none within the mile as he can see, sir.'

Hervey could scarce believe it. But, supports or no, it would still be David and Goliath if the guns came into action before they could close with them. He hesitated not another second and took the patrol in a brisk hand-gallop towards Armstrong. As they broached the ridge he held them up and edged forward with just his covering-corporal to where Serjeant Armstrong was crouching in the saddle to observe over the bracken.

'They've halted, sir, just this minute,' said the serjeant in his melodious Tyneside.

'Why ever do you suppose they have stopped *there*?' asked Hervey, peering through his telescope.

'Can't make it out at all,' Armstrong replied.

They both watched the battery, halted in the valley two full furlongs away, eager to know in which direction it would next move. Armstrong thought it must turn about; Hervey was sure it would wheel left and run parallel to the ridge. Suddenly both their predictions were confounded: the French began dismounting to unlimber the guns.

Hervey's reaction was instinctive: 'Draw swords! *Charge!*' he cried, ramming the telescope into its saddle holster and digging his spurs into his mare's flanks.

His troopers took off after him as eager as greyhounds springing a hare, but Hervey would not check his pace for the sake of dressing: he was a dozen lengths clear of the front rank by the time they were half-way to the battery, only his covering-corporal within challenging distance. The French, who had seen them the instant they crested the ridge, were now frantically ramming charges down the barrels of the eight-pounders, the limbers racing back whence they had come. At a hundred yards Hervey stretched his sword-arm fully to the engage and fixed on the narrow gap between the centre guns. Not one had managed to load with canister by the time the troopers fell on them. In panic two guns were fired with charges only, adding smoke to the confusion but nothing more injurious than the deafening reports. Had the gunners taken up side-arms instead, they might have inflicted some damage, but it was too late now. Hervey slashed at the battery commander as the Frenchman belatedly reached for his pistol, and the officer fell from his horse screaming, his arm all but severed at the shoulder. Hervey galloped on to the limbers, which were making heavy weather of crossing a half-sunken track (the guns were no immediate threat now and could wait – the limbers and teams would not). They showed no sign of yielding as Hervey made for the lead team, and he glanced behind to see who was with him. More than a dozen, and he could see Serjeant Armstrong still at the guns. It would do.

If only the drivers had yielded. Then they could have been made prisoner, or even set free. But no, they tried to run. In panic, or in duty to the teams? There was no time to care, even had there been time to think. Hervey pointed rather than cut at the lead driver, using his forward momentum to take the blade halfway to the hilt in the Frenchman's side. He followed through as if at sword drill in camp, effortlessly recovering the sabre to set about the wheeler-drivers in the same fashion. Behind him it was the same, his dragoons doing swift execution. And then they cut the traces to set loose the teams, and began driving them back towards the British lines.

Still the fight was not gone from the battery, and small-arms fire (albeit ragged) began at the guns. Hervey galloped at once to the relief of Serjeant Armstrong and his half-dozen prize-takers, but the firing was ended by the time he came up. 'Start spiking, then, Serjeant Armstrong,' he called, 'and fire the limbers.'

'Ay, sir,' Armstrong replied grimly. 'Jesus, but some of these bastards were a time dying!'

Hervey sheathed his sabre and leaned forward in the saddle to adjust the breastplate which had somehow twisted. In that instant a bombardier sprang from beneath one of the guns and thrust a spontoon in his thigh. Hervey's covering-corporal leaped from his horse and launched so ferocious an assault that the Frenchman had no time to parry the downward swordstroke. It cleaved his skull in two, and blood bubbled like a spring for a full minute where the body lay twitching. Armstrong rushed to support Hervey in the saddle.

'Leave go,' he said sharply, angry with himself for the lapse of alertness that was costing so much pain to body and pride.

Corporal Collins spluttered an apology.

'Don't be a fool, man,' snapped Hervey, gripping the gash hard. 'I'm not a greenhead. For heaven's sake, Serjeant Armstrong, let's get these guns spiked and then back to our post before worse arrives.'

A second later Hervey and his arresting officer would have galloped into each other. Hervey had crested the rise, however, just in time to evade the collision. Reining hard right, he cursed as his mare crumpled then struggled to regain her footing, the air bursting from her lungs as they fought to keep their balance, her nostrils flaring wide and blowing blood into his eyes. And although searing pain from the gash made it difficult for him to keep his right leg pressed on the girth, with blood spreading its sticky warmth the length of it, neither this nor the damned fool galloping about *his* corner of the battlefield was going to dull the exhilaration of success. He had led the charge to the French guns, judging the moment to perfection so that his dragoons had caught the battery at its most vulnerable – unlimbered but not yet in action. Had he charged too soon, the French would have been off; a fraction too late and his little command might have been swept away in a hail of grapeshot. The surprise and terror in the faces of the gunners, the frenzied cutting, thrusting and slashing, the hammering of nails into touch-holes, then the dash back to their picket post, expecting French *lanciers* to appear at any second to spear them like dogs – it had been the stuff of a cornet's dream.

In truth it had been an affair, and a prize, *beyond* his dreams, a prize which by rights ought never to have been in the offing: for a whole troop of horse artillery to come into action on a flank without cavalry supports was abominable to any professional. Half a dozen eight-pounders disabled, three score and more horses captured or driven towards the British lines, and as many gunners now lying with their lifeblood draining into their native soil – barely a dozen Frenchmen had escaped to seek the protection of their errant lancers. Somewhere, Hervey knew, there was a *lancier* officer who ought to be cashiered – or shot – for that dereliction of duty. But he at least knew that he had done *his*, and he had been scarcely able to bear the wait before he would make his report to Edmonds, afterwards to bask in the praise with which the major was as a rule so sparing.

To have collided with the mounted interloper would have denied him that satisfaction for sure. At such a speed a broken neck, and death, was the likely outcome. Or perhaps – and what many would have counted worse – it might have meant invaliding to the Chelsea hospital and a lifetime of milk pobs spooned haphazardly by some old soldier. Either fate would have been a terrible irony after escaping the French, and he could only wonder at how often he had had cause to be grateful for his little mare's cat-like agility: more than nine times, certainly, she had saved him from disaster.

Shortening the rein and completing his circle, he looked about angrily for the man who had nearly ridden him down. Anger then turned to astonishment as he recognized him to be one of Slade's aides-de-camp, and he wondered what in heaven's name *he* was doing on this flank. Then two staff dragoons galloped on to the ridge as Hervey's own men caught him up. But his own anger was nothing to that which he was about to face.

'What the devil do you mean, sir, by abandoning your post?' bellowed the ADC as he bore down from the opposite direction, having himself circled right, though nothing like as tightly as Hervey and his mare had managed.

Cornet Hervey was aghast. Blood from the gash in his thigh, where the French bombardier had thrust the spontoon, was soaking the entire leg of his canvas overalls. From this alone, even to the most purblind, it must have been clear that something had been happening. But Slade's staff could be as obtuse as their general.

'What in God's name are you talking about, Regan? We did

no such thing!' he protested, sliding painfully from the saddle to loosen the girth.

'Then tell me how lancers have been able to loot the general's own baggage!'

By now Hervey's covering-serjeant had joined him, still in a frenzy from the slaughter they had just dealt the hapless battery. He seized the ADC's reins: 'Look, mister, what d'ye think—?' But the staff dragoons reached for their sabres.

'As you were, Armstrong! Go and settle the patrol!' snapped Hervey.

The ADC was now beyond mere anger, and his voice rose in shrill rage. 'Mr Hervey, you have disobeyed orders and that insubordinate serjeant is proof of your unfitness for this command!'

Hervey's groom had brought up a second charger, and he now remounted, though not with the easy vault he would ordinarily have taken. Instead he was helped up awkwardly, grimacing as more pain shot the length of his leg. It hardly made for a conciliatory response.

'Regan, you are a confounded ass! We've just spiked six guns, for pity's sake; we have seen no lancers!'

Lieutenant Regan's voice lowered menacingly. 'Then, how, pray, did they get to General Slade's baggage?'

'How in hell's name do I know? I am responsible for this flank, not for the whole battlefield!'

The contempt was unequivocal, and Hervey might have anticipated its consequences had he not been so entirely exasperated by the lieutenant's seemingly wilful ignorance of the affair with the enemy battery.

'You are a damned impudent officer as well as a disobedient one; you will hand me your sword this instant!'

Hervey's jaw fell. 'In the middle of a battle? Have you taken leave of your senses?'

The contrast between the red jackets of the ADC and staff dragoons and the blue of Hervey's regiment seemed to be intensifying the confrontation. Serjeant Armstrong spat and let out a string of oaths, but so thick was his Tyneside accent that Lieutenant Regan was not sure what he had heard. The staff dragoons recognized the tone well enough, though, and drew their sabres. Hervey shot an angry look at Armstrong, but it was another voice that was to quell what had by now become little short of a brawl, a voice infinitely more measured than Hervey was capable of at that moment.

'Go to your post, Serjeant Armstrong,' it commanded, in mellow tones of Suffolk. And then, with admirably contrived understatement: 'Mr Hervey, sir, is there some difficulty?'

Hervey's composure began returning. The voice had often steadied him – steadied many of them – and more so now for its being unexpected.

'Serjeant Strange, I am in arrest. General Slade appears to think we abandoned our post. Have you come with orders?'

'No, sir,' replied the troop serjeant, in a manner so matter-of-fact they could have been at a review, 'only with a report of guns moving in the direction of your picket.'

'Well, they do not move any longer,' said Hervey with a sharp edge. 'Look, Serjeant Strange, you had better take command. I will tell you briefly of the circumstances and then you must send someone to report to Major Edmonds.'

Serjeant Strange listened impassively as Hervey gave a hasty account of the disabling of the battery.

'I trust Mr Regan here will have that wound attended to properly and with all dispatch, sir?' was all that Strange said in reply, turning to the ADC.

Of course he would, said the lieutenant testily. 'I do not need to be reminded of *my* business, thank you, Serjeant!'

Serjeant Strange saluted, reined about and trotted over to the patrol, leaving Hervey feeling not a little awkward at his own intemperance compared with this non-commissioned officer's bearing.

Matthew Hervey was not invariably quick-tempered. Twenty-three years old, six years with the cavalry, most of it on active service, he still retained a surprising belief in humanity. But the proverbial wrath of the patient man could from time to time overwhelm his cautious instincts, a risky proclivity for an officer who valued his prospects: anyone who thought that survival in this war depended merely on fighting the enemy was naïve in the extreme. Jealousy, snobbery, intrigue and patronage were the preoccupations of men of ambition in the Marquess of Wellington's army; and Hervey and others like him, decent officers with little but their ability to recommend them, were increasingly resentful of Wellington's indifference to it all. Indeed, many believed he actively connived at it. But they remained wholly powerless to effect any change whatever; and, besides, they each had a stake in the system, however small, so long as their commissions were obtained by purchase and held their value.

Lieutenant Regan's dislike of Hervey, inasmuch as it could be rationally analysed, stemmed from just these preoccupations. Intensely jealous of the distinction which his campaign service might bring – though few would suppose that he envied the service itself – he regarded Hervey's lack of means with open distaste. Six years' service and still a cornet. *He*, Regan, had purchased *his* lieutenancy even before his regiment had seen him at a field day! And if he had known Hervey to be distantly related to the earls of Bristol he would doubtless have dismissed the connection with a sneer at the Whig propensities of that family. Whatever ecclesiastical influence the Herveys may have had (and, in truth, they had none, for Bishop Hervey of Derry had been dead these past ten years), they were wholly without influence in the military. It had not been long before someone in Regan's family had managed to get *him* appointed to a general's staff. And what a general – John Slade, 'Black Jack' as he was known throughout the Peninsular army, as incompetent an officer as was ever placed in command of a brigade of cavalry, and a coward, too, by common consent. But, if Hervey had only qualified contempt for the system which could put an officer like Regan where he was, his contempt for the man himself was absolute. As he unbuckled his sword-belt and handed him his sabre he saw the utter triumph on the ADC's face, and he knew that there was not the slightest thing he could do about it.

Serjeant Strange chose to send the news to Edmonds with Hervey's covering-corporal, for he could not trust Serjeant

Armstrong to deliver a coherent report in the circumstances, let alone a detached one. And he knew that the combination of Edmonds's temper and Armstrong's was the very last thing that was needed now. Corporal Collins's big gelding had once been the proud possession of the commanding officer of a regiment of French hussars, but the corporal had cut him down in a brilliant little affair at Campo Mayor three years before. Even a French aristocrat's charger could rarely outpace a good British troop horse, but this gelding was an exception and the corporal covered the three-quarters of a mile or so, to where the rest of the 6th Light Dragoons were drawn up, in a fast straight line.

It would not have taken a practised eye to discern that the Sixth had been on campaign for several seasons. For though they stood in perfect order of three squadrons in line, numbered from the left, they were in double rank only, the regiment's strength having fallen to two troops in each squadron. The troops were still able to front the regulation sixty men, however (less the half-troop of Hervey's patrol from Number 1 Squadron), and twenty or so dragoons stood with the farriers as supernumeraries to the rear. The horses were a mixed bag, Irish mainly and beginning to regain the semblance of sleekness as their winter coats grew out. Some were of real quality: those which the regiment's colonel had purchased when they had been in England, and for which he had reached deep into his own pockets. Since arriving in the Peninsula, however, remounts had been found under collective arrangements, and from divers sources, and some were barely up to weight. It was the lament of every cavalry mess that England must indeed be in peril to have run short of troop horses. The same in its way could have been remarked of the dragoons themselves: without doubt, many of the troopers would never have got the better of a recruiting serjeant's pride in peacetime. As for their clothing, an untutored observer might have concluded that a hatmaker had reached some advantageous arrangement with the quartermasters, for every shako seemed as new compared with the rest of the uniform, which was faded and patched to a marked degree. In truth the shakos *were* new, of a pattern only recently authorized, and although they were nothing in appearance to compare with the older Tarleton helmets they stayed put in action and the oilskin covers kept them dry. At a distance of fifty yards the regiment was a fine sight: only closer inspection would reveal the signs of wear, as it would, too, that 'A' Troop's jackets were in distinctly better condition, their captain having used his own wealth to engage the services of Spanish tailors during winter quarters.

The Sixth were sitting easy on the same piece of ground they had occupied since first light that morning. Many of the troopers were leaning forward on the rolled cloaks over the saddle arches, and a good number were smoking clay pipes. Corporal Collins found Edmonds not in his appointed position to the front of the regiment but as a serrefile to the left of the first squadron, doubtless attempting, but vainly, to conceal his frustration with the regiment's enforced inactivity. Edmonds's bad humour was exacerbated, too, by the worst toothache he had ever known. He had already taken two size-able draughts of laudanum that morning, more than three times the quantity prescribed as efficacious by the regimental surgeon, and it would be many hours before he could expect to have the offending molar drawn by a tooth-operator. He certainly had no intention of risking the surgeon's pelican after that hamfisted fool had dislocated one poor trooper's jaw earlier in the week.

Scarcely had Corporal Collins begun his report but Edmonds began to rage. 'Damn it, all he had to do was sit on a hill and watch for a few Frenchmen fool enough to cross the canal! What in God's name . . . ?'

The major's facility with words extended also to those of the barrack room. Indeed, they frequently seemed his natural and preferred idiom.

'No, sir, wait, that's not all.'

Edmonds's notorious temper, and his present irritability, would have unnerved many an NCO, but Strange had picked his man well: the victor of the single combat with the French colonel would not be frighted by the major's anger. Besides, the cannier NCOs (and Collins was one of the canniest) knew what lay beneath it. The corporal did what he had done many times before, since the days when he had been a young dragoon in the then Captain Edmonds's troop: he affected blithe unawareness, and pressed his report with determination. The major listened to the account of the attack on the battery, and what followed, with mute but growing disbelief until another pang of excruciating pain made him explode again. 'Why, for mercy's sake, was he placed in arrest, then? What the devil is going on up there?'

Corporal Collins judged it beyond the responsibilities of his rank to comment, though he could for certain have given a perceptive enough appreciation. Instead he sat silent: opinions about the staff would have to wait for the canteen. The major, taking a strong but not altogether effective grip of his anger, and biting hard into a lint wad soaked in oil of cloves, summoned 'A' Troop's leader who, as one of the senior captains, was also the officer commanding Number 1 Squadron.

'Captain Lankester, I may presume that you heard our corporal-galloper, and it will be no shave, I'll warrant. A very pretty mess indeed! I wish you to send an officer at once to the flank picket to relieve Serjeant Strange.'

Another spasm jerked him as if a musket ball had struck his jaw. 'Corporal Collins, you stay here. Go and rejoin your troop!' he barked.

Joseph Edmonds reined about to face front again, and cursed audibly and even more foully than before. It was not the pain so much – he had endured worse under the surgeon's knife during his service – but the way that all before him seemed to be unravelling, like a loose horse-bandage. He had not the slightest control over matters, and seemingly no influence. He began wishing Lord George Irvine were back; that damned *tirailleur*'s bullet which had smashed the colonel's shoulder at Croix d'Orade three days earlier had been about the worst-timed shot of the campaign! He was relishing this acting command right enough, albeit without even a brevet promotion to lieutenant-colonel (as he might have expected), but he knew General Slade despised him – a conclusion it was not difficult to come by, although Slade seemed to despise everybody, especially if they showed the remotest chance of doing something that might reflect his own inadequacy.

'Laming will relieve Serjeant Strange, sir,' Lankester informed him after dispatching his lieutenant to the picket. He might as easily have resumed his place in front of his squadron, and with every propriety, for Edmonds had all but formally dismissed him; but Lankester had seen the storm cones hoisting and experience suggested that a weather eye would be prudent.

'Captain Lankester, do you suppose that damned stupid fellow has the remotest idea what he is about?'

'You refer to General Slade, sir?'

'Indeed I do, sir, though I cannot claim any novelty in that description, as you very well know. It was Lord Uxbridge's, and never has his opinion of Slade been more fully justified than during these several past months. What deuced ill-fortune has placed us in his brigade? And now it seems that his own staff are every bit as stupid as he!'

'I think he has never recovered from the affair at Maguilla.'

'I do not think that Wellington himself has recovered from Maguilla. The whole Maguilla business was absurd. A few of the Royals' squadrons become over-excited, press on too far for their own good and get a fraction cut up, and Wellington says that all his cavalry are fit for is drilling on Wimbledon Common! What a confounded insult! What a—' Yet another spasm contorted his face, and a string of expletives followed. 'And now Slade tries to curb all vigour in his subordinates, and hangs the arse at any price rather than risk another of Wellington's scoldings. The man's fit only for a depot squadron!'

'It has certainly made him cautious,' Lankester agreed, with a greater disposition towards discretion.

'Uxbridge at least would have been able to advocate a little more equanimity,' continued Edmonds. And then, casting aside all reserve, he opined that if the Earl of Uxbridge had remained the cavalry commander for this second expedition to the Peninsula, instead of Sir Stapleton Cotton, Wellington might by now have been prevailed upon to have Slade dismissed. He could but wonder, he declared with a sigh, at the complicated web of patronage that made Wellington drive his army so hard and yet at the same time ignore such monstrous inaptitude.

But he knew at least that it was a web, a web as unfathomable as that which was the Fates'. The strands might be barely discernible but they could hold a man like him fast; and, for all the twenty-five years which separated them, he and now Hervey were caught like worthless carrion while others who knew its secrets were able to traverse the delicate threads and go wherever they pleased. He had accepted it with remarkable forbearance during most of his service, but he had of late become of the mind that when skilfulness amounted to a disadvantage because of a superior's resentment, then the web was no longer merely recondite – it was corrupt. Why it had taken him so long to reach this conclusion, when he pondered on it, puzzled him, for a full five years earlier he had had a taste of Slade's ineptness. There, at Sahagun, he had deftly manoeuvred his own squadron while Black Jack, in action for the first time, had fiddle-faddled at the head of his brigade and almost let the French slip – and all this in front of Uxbridge too (who had never troubled to conceal his poor opinion of his subordinate). Edmonds's mere proximity ever afterwards could excite Slade's resentment, and that his subsequent advance to major had been by field promotion rather than by purchase (a manner of advancement that Slade had more than once in his hearing derided as fit only for officers from the ranks) had done nothing to assuage the general's envy and detestation. Jealousy and snobbery, patronage and intrigue – the web.

'By heaven,' Edmonds sighed, 'the French are nothing to fear compared with that blackguard.'

'It has always occurred to me as singular that adultery should be grounds for dismissal during times of war.'

Lankester's proposition did not immediately reveal its sense to Edmonds, who was all but lost in contemplation of his brigade commander. 'What? Slade – adultery?'

'No, Uxbridge!'

Edmonds shook his head with disbelief at his own slowness. 'Well, perhaps it was hardly the breaking of the seventh commandment but the manner.'

'Another commandment, you mean,' smiled Lankester. 'Thou shalt not elope with the Marquess of Wellington's sister-in-law?'

Edmonds could not but reflect the smile, the first he had been tempted to that day. 'Well, certainly not in a post-chaise from under the very nose of his younger brother!'

Lankester thought he perceived the storm cones to be lowering. 'It occurs to me that, if Nelson had been deprived of his command because of Lady Hamilton, the French fleet might still be at sea instead of under it at Cape Trafalgar – and we might yet be patrolling the Sussex coast.'

Edmonds nodded and frowned: Lankester had judged the storm's passing over-hastily. The major's bile rose again at this reference to the Royal Navy, whose utilitarian principles he had long held in admiration. 'I do not see why we must be foisted with knaves and imbeciles when the Admiralty are perfectly able to order their affairs in so eminently business-like a fashion,' he snorted.

'Or does the Navy have its patronage, too,' countered Lankester, 'less manifestly connected with birth perhaps, but patronage none the less?'

'All I know is that if Nelson had been an officer under Slade's command he would not have risen beyond a troop!' rasped Edmonds, deciding that it was time he took up his position in front of the regiment, and pressing his charger forward with sudden urgency.

Major Joseph Edmonds, his left eye almost closed by the pain in his jaw, peered into the distance as the infantry pressed their assault across the Languedoc Canal towards the outer defences of Toulouse, the first city they had reached since coming down from their winter quarters in the Pyrenees. He might rant against the likes of Slade, but the object of his profoundest disapproval – the conduct of the campaign itself – he kept privy. With a concealed passion he utterly disputed the need to fight Soult here, especially since rumours had been circulating for days that Bonaparte was finished, dead even. The French had been deserting in droves: many had given themselves up to the Sixth's own patrols. And, so far as he was able to make out, Bonaparte's more general situation was no more felicitous. In the east the Continental allies – Austria, Prussia, Russia and Sweden – were making ever better progress towards Paris. A month ago Wellington had occupied Bordeaux, but to what end? Surely now there was no more need than to invest, with the merest token force, any garrison which stood in their path. Paris was the cornerstone of Bonaparte's edifice; there was little purpose, therefore, in trifling with outworks. Edmonds began to wonder whether anyone had any notion of strategy other than fighting the enemy wherever and whenever he stood, as if every last French musketeer must be slaughtered, or put into a prison hulk, before victory might be claimed. Was there no campaigning art? Were they to continue breaking windows with guineas? Edmonds knew his history and despaired that the commander-in-chief seemed not to share his perception of the wars of antiquity, of Caesar and Hannibal. Why was Wellington so Fabian a general? Quintus Fabius Maximus – *Cunctator* ('the Delayer') – reviled in life for his caution and then lauded for it in his later years: Rome would never have been defeated at Cannae with such a general, the Senate had mourned. But why so many officers, Wellington included, took Fabius Maximus as their paradigm rather than Hannibal was quite beyond him. No wound in the dozen or more during his service had cut him so deeply as the rebuff he had received two winters before when he had submitted a stratagem worthy, he felt sure, of the grace of Baal himself, to manoeuvre the French out of Spain. It had been returned with a peremptory note that the commander-in-chief did not wish to distract his field officers from their first duty of attending to their commands. Afterwards he had brooded, and contemplated selling out, but in the end he had turned once more to his trusty volume of Seneca and, taking deep draughts from the treatise on 'The Steadfastness of Wise Men', he had redoubled his stoic efforts in the place that Fortune had appointed him.

If the final victory were, by rumour and his own reckoning, so close, however, then he knew these low spirits made little sense. Was it that he considered himself to blame for Hervey's arrest? He had given him command of a flank picket, and it was by rights a lieutenant's command; but, then, Hervey had seen more service than many of the lieutenants. Why in any case repine over the fate of an insignificant cornet when a sou's worth of powder and shot might carry off his young head at an instant? The adjutant had cautioned him more than once that, if he were to take responsibility so personally for every last man in the Sixth, dyspepsy would soon overcome him. But the warning had had no effect.

He wondered what Lord George Irvine would do if he were here. He had not the inkling of an idea, however, for Lord George understood the complexities, and possibilities, of the web in a way he never could. But, be whatever that may, he knew well enough that, behind him, the Sixth were restive, for they had been posted thus for four hours without a move. Pain shot through his jaw again, catching him off guard. 'Christ!' he exploded. 'Dismount!'

His trumpeter, with no cautionary word of command to alert him, blew the call hastily, cracking the first 'Es' badly and earning a blistering rebuke. There could in any event have been no more calculated an invitation to bring down Slade's wrath upon the Sixth than this order. The brigade commander's belief that cavalry should remain mounted ready for immediate action kept his regiments in the saddle for hours on end, and to no purpose. Edmonds considered Slade's notion of immediate action to be positively risible in view of his chronic indecisiveness. Sore backs were the bane of the cavalry, and, whether Slade liked it or not, he was damned if he was going to sit there a moment longer for no good reason.

Yet he was not without his doubts, too. He had to admit

that the French were fighting with a tenacity he had not seen since Badajoz. Yesterday, Easter of all days, Soult had left three thousand dead and dying on the field before retiring behind the canal and the Garonne. And now, after another day's fighting, it looked as if that fox of a marshal was going to contest every street in this lovely city. Edmonds was beginning to concede the likelihood of a Fabian march on Paris after all.

These were self-indulgent thoughts, however. One consideration above all pressed to the fore (besides, that is, the ever receding prospect of seeing a tooth-operator): how was he to secure Hervey's release? Come what may, there were bound to be charges: Slade would be eager to take the opportunity to humiliate the Sixth. The only chance lay in having a general court martial convened instead of one of the cosy field courts where the only concern was to uphold the dignity and authority of the commander – usually, and in this instance, the very officer to have initiated the charges. With Slade it was more a matter of *shoring up* that dignity and authority, he admitted with distaste. But a proper court, not one packed with toadies, would take the affair with the battery as mitigation. Damn it all, he almost exclaimed aloud, they ought to regard it as justification!

But, pressing though Matthew Hervey's arrest might be, there was at that moment even more immediate business at hand. All Edmonds's instincts told him that this was turning into a scrimmage of a battle. A pall of smoke was rising over the city, and he began to wonder whether Slade would stay all afternoon watching, making them mere onlookers to another of Wellington's infantry battles, with the commander-in-chief's admonitions afterwards to add insult to injury. Any cavalryman with a sure *coup d'œil* would now on his own initiative order a steady encircling movement to the north-west to occupy the prominent high ground in anticipation of the artillery. Lord George Irvine had such an eye; so did Lankester and the other squadron leaders; so did a good many of the troop officers – Hervey included. Edmonds was equally sure that Slade did not and never would in a hundred years.

The trouble with Wellington, fumed Edmonds (though he would readily admit of his many soldierly virtues), was that he wanted – *insisted* on – order in his battles. Yet was not the battlefield the very apotheosis of chaos? And was it not the side that could impose the greater chaos that carried the day in battle? And was it not that arm – the cavalry – the arm for which Wellington had least regard, that could create such chaos?

Edmonds sighed. By his estimation they could afford only five more minutes standing like this before the opportunity to take the ground unchallenged might be gone. If no orders came within that time, he knew he would not be able to contain his frustration and that he would go to Slade to suggest the manoeuvre, knowing full well how unwelcome that would be. And, indeed, after five more minutes of fidgeting and stamping by the troop horses, and increasingly tart commentary by the troopers, Edmonds had had enough. Sighing deeply, and cursing some more under his breath, he remounted and called again for his senior captain.

Lankester trotted up on his big bay thoroughbred and saluted.

'You are to assume command. You are to prepare to occupy yonder hill with the white church,' began the major, pointing to a small chapel a mile away. 'That bridge midway will have no more than a few videttes, likely as not. I shall now alert the brigadier to my intentions. However, on no account save for the immediate security of your command are you or any part of the regiment to quit this ground until I return.'

Edmonds did not have to elaborate on the manoeuvre or its purpose. Indeed, he would have been dismayed to think that Lankester had not anticipated it. The captain simply saluted to acknowledge the orders, and a half-smile indicated that he recognized the tone well enough. Edmonds had reverted to the formal and precise manner which prudence suggested was necessary when in the field with General Slade. It added, too, a distinct charm to the Sixth's campaign journal, written up assiduously at the end of each day by the adjutant, who scribbled every word faithfully in his pocket-book to that purpose. But principally, and at Edmonds's insistence, the scribbling was less a matter of historical detail than a record to be used in evidence – not *against* an officer, but *by* one if events did not prove propitious: he wanted no subordinate to be in a position of disadvantage. It was needless in this instance, for the notion that Lankester would plead superior orders in mitigation if events went ill would have been entirely repugnant to that officer.

The gallop to the knoll on which Slade and his staff had posted themselves, half a mile distant, steeled Edmonds to the exchange to come, but as he neared the top he saw General Cotton galloping towards them from the opposite direction, waving his hat and hallooing wildly. Hervey was lying on the ground nearby with Slade's physician hunched over him, but it was the cavalry commander's dramatic approach that gripped Edmonds's attention. Cotton began shouting from fifty yards distant. 'Slade, the French are giving way! Soult's pulling back into the city: there's no fight left in 'em!'

Sir Stapleton Cotton, lieutenant-general, sixth baronet of Combermere, and Uxbridge's successor – there was little doubt that his birth had recommended him to Wellington, but there was such a close physical similarity between the two men that Edmonds could not but ponder on the tendency of commanders to select subordinates in their own image. There were the same dark curls, the long face, the hooked nose, and hardly a year between them, too. What was Wellington now, forty-four? forty-five? Four years younger than Edmonds himself – it was enough to test the resolve of a saint. Admittedly he liked Cotton well enough. The man had done his share of fighting in the Peninsula, and before that, too, and he had been sound enough on the retreat to Corunna – but he was no Uxbridge. Edmonds knew that, in the business of war, he was Cotton's equal. What, then, had ordered their respective military estates? Just twenty thousand pounds for a baronetcy a couple of centuries earlier when King James had wanted money for his Irish army, he supposed, and one or two judicious marriages thereafter no doubt. Well, so be it: *his* father had been a professional soldier who had died in the

American war while Edmonds was still a child, leaving nothing but the value of his commission with which his widow could buy an annuity. And he himself had chosen to marry a soldier's daughter without a penny, either. A stoical smile almost overcame him, but another stab in his jaw made him grimace instead. What he was to hear next, however, as General Cotton pulled up sharply, almost cannoning into the brigade commander, would certainly tempt the smile back, albeit a wry one.

'The commander-in-chief desires his cavalry to stand fast for the time being but wishes you to send, if you please, a troop to occupy the high ground north-west of the city. It is his intention to send guns there directly.' Cotton was pointing to the same high ground that Edmonds knew Captain Lankester to be contemplating at that very moment.

A look of contentment settled on the major, for at a stroke these orders relieved him of the necessity of risking the altercation with his brigadier.

'Edmonds!' Cotton exclaimed when at length he noticed him, and in a manner uncommonly genial. 'A very good day to you! That was a smart little action on the flank. One of Lord Wellington's observing-officers was concealed nearby and witnessed the whole affair. It seems the French were intent on harassing our flank but were discouraged into thinking we held there stronger than we did! Who was commanding the picket?'

Every nerve and sinew in him tensed at this promising development: 'Cornet Hervey, General.'

'Well, Cornet Hervey did us deuced fine service. That battery would have wrought a pretty destruction had it come into action. I shall meet him in due course, I trust?'

The fortunes of war could still take Edmonds by surprise in spite of his long years in the king's service. An observing-officer, gone to ground on his way back from behind the enemy's lines no doubt – by heavens, this was opportune, a most *capital* turn of events! But he knew there was a distance still to run, and he avoided meeting Slade's eye, hoping to give him time to choose a line of withdrawal. Slade had indeed been studiously ignoring him, failing to acknowledge his presence even; but years of intriguing had told Black Jack when to withdraw, and he now seized the opportunity which Edmonds's rare composure offered.

'Cornet Hervey was hurt slightly in the action, Sir Stapleton; my own physician is attending to him over there now' – indicating the tree under which the Edinburgh medical man, in his incongruous black Melton coat, was fussing with bandages and salving oil. Did Slade know of the battery action after all, wondered Edmonds, or was he just quick to sense a tight corner? Likely as not he would never know.

Cotton trotted over to Hervey who struggled to his feet despite the physician's remonstrations.

'Mr Hervey, I am glad we meet. You did well today. How is that leg?'

'Thank you, sir; it is very well enough. The surgeon here says it will not keep me out of the saddle.'

'I said that it *may* not,' corrected the Edinburgh man, with barely concealed indignation at being called a surgeon.

'Then, indeed, it *will* not,' insisted Hervey.

'Good man, good man!' said Cotton approvingly. 'But I doubt you will need to be in the saddle for much longer. The French are done for – and I mean not for today only: our agents are reporting that the end cannot be far off.'

After a few more words of solicitude and encouragement, and some further intercourse with Slade out of earshot of the others, the commander of Wellington's cavalry spurred his horse back in the direction whence he had come, leaving Slade to give the orders which Edmonds had anticipated a full half-hour before.

'Shall I take Cornet Hervey back with me, then, General?' he ventured.

'Yes, yes, he is obviously fit for duty,' replied Slade dismissively, without reference to the arrest.

Private Johnson, Hervey's groom, whose own lowly *coup d'œil* was every bit a match nevertheless for this delicate moment, had already brought up the black gelding. An uncomfortable, if localized, silence followed as Hervey limped across to where Lieutenant Regan stood, like a small dark cloud, in mute brooding. Without a word he stooped to pick up his sword, which lay, as in some allegory of dishonour, at Regan's feet. The ADC said not a word, either: none was necessary, for his look said everything, none of it pleasant.

As they left the knoll Edmonds was careful to do so at a trot, though all his instincts, and not least the horses', were to gallop like fury. 'I am sorry, sir, that—' tried Hervey when they had put some ground between themselves and the brigade commander.

'God preserve us, boy!' snapped Edmonds, leaving Hervey to wonder from what precisely. Little purpose would have been served by his asking, however; for Edmonds had scant idea, either, only a sense of the need for divine providence. It had been the narrowest of escapes, and he did not doubt that the last of it was yet to be heard.

Hervey was by no means entirely comfortable back in the saddle for, expertly though his leg had been bandaged, it was not the place to be resting it. But this was nothing to how he was to feel when they reached the regiment. Corporal Collins's dispatch had evidently been relayed through the ranks for there was loud cheering as they approached, and though he might well bask in that approval – for he had certainly had none from Edmonds – so loud and triumphant was the clamour that it must surely have carried across to Slade's knoll. He sensed as well as Edmonds that it would only fuel the general's resentment and make worse the eventual retribution. But the cornet's horizon was the next hill and the next minute, and the discomfort would soon pass. Edmonds could not afford to set his sights so close, however: too much in his service told of the hundred and one ways Slade's vindictiveness might be visited on them. Their best hope lay in this war's coming to the rapid end which Sir Stapleton Cotton had predicted, though there was little enough sign of that. Nor was there any sign of the activity which he presumed might be consequent on that assessment. If the French were on the point of collapse, then it was the function of the cavalry to hurry them along. Now was surely the time to throw caution to the wind and launch them all at Soult's lines of communication, was it not? What in heaven's name was there to lose? he wondered.

'Mr Barrow!' he roared.

The adjutant closed up from where he had posted himself, three horse-lengths behind, next to the guidon and Edmonds's trumpeter. The Sixth still carried the colonel's guidon in the field – many regiments had abandoned the practice – though the squadron guidons had been left in England. When any movement was to be executed, the adjutant took up his position with the other serrefile officers to the rear, but he otherwise liked to keep close to Edmonds so that he could heed his orders at first hand.

'I wish you to have the following prepared for my signature at the first opportunity. Do you have your pocket-book?'

'Sir!'

'Very well. To Lieutenant-Colonel Lord Fitzroy Somerset, Military Secretary, Headquarters, etc., etc. Sir, I have the honour— No, wait – begin again. It is my humble duty to submit with regret my resignation, to be effective at your Lordship's pleasure.' Edmonds paused. Barrow looked up with no more expression of surprise than if he had been taking orders for bivouac. Edmonds cleared his throat and continued. 'In so doing, I place upon record my— No – begin again. I thereby protest at the want of ardour in the employment of the cavalry and' – he paused once more – 'the tergiversation in the conduct of the campaign.'

Barrow raised an eyebrow, not certain that he would be able to find anyone capable of spelling this latter complaint, nor even of explaining its meaning. 'Is that all, sir?'

'That is all, thank you, Barrow.'

The adjutant raised both eyebrows and then resumed his place with the guidon, knowing it to be unlikely that the draft would ever be called for (it was the third that Edmonds had dictated that year alone).

For another three hours the Sixth stood fast, Edmonds with every expression of serenity conceivable, and more, certainly, than anyone could have imagined. But as evening drew on he became less composed, and by dusk he was as thoroughly agitated as he had been that morning. The temporary remitting of the toothache in the afternoon past, he was sorely vexed now by the general inertia. '*Fabius Cunctator*!' he spat.

Barrow and the trumpeter looked at each other, startled. Neither of them had quite heard every syllable but it sounded the vilest of curses. And it just might have been provoked by the sudden appearance of the brigade major (though in truth Edmonds had not seen him), who the adjutant now noticed was trotting across the regiment's front. He sighed as he took out his pocket-book and closed up to Edmonds again, sensing more trouble.

'Ah, Heroys, with orders for the night perhaps,' began the major, with more than a trace of irony. 'Tell me, are they to be as strenuous as those of the day?' But he gave the BM no time for reply, thoroughly warming to his opportunity: 'Let me guess. A brigade steeplechase perhaps? Or a foxhunt? Maybe even a levee, or a masque – yes, I have it, a masque! Now, which might it be? *Comus*, perhaps; that would seem apt: "What chance, good Lady, hath bereft you thus? Dim darkness, and this leafy labyrinth!"'

'Very droll, Edmonds. You are perfectly well aware that thrift in deploying one's assets is a sound precept in war.'

'That's a piss-fire answer!'

'Edmonds, some days you try my patience, and then again others you quite exhaust it!' replied the brigade major with a resigned smile: he had long years of acquaintance with Edmonds's vituperation. 'I have instructions for a comfortable billet, no less.'

The particulars took Edmonds by surprise: 'A convent!' he exclaimed. 'And where will the nuns be?'

'You need worry not,' replied Heroys. 'They are all in the hospitals with the *blessés*, and probably a good many of our own wounded, too. Never have I seen so many. But you will need to make haste: it will be pitch-dark before the hour's out. Come, I will guide you down myself.'

'Lead us not into bloody temptation!' sighed Edmonds as they began the descent into the city.

41

*   *   *

Hervey had lost more blood than he had supposed. After all but fainting in the saddle on the way down, Serjeant Armstrong and Private Johnson half-carried him to one of the nuns' cells in spite of his protests that first he must see to the horses. 'Heaven help us,' sighed Armstrong aloud. 'These gentlemen-officers and their duty!' But neither he nor Johnson had the time to argue, and Hervey, for sure, had not the energy. Leaving him with a lantern, they slammed the door closed, and he lay down on the narrow bed without even unfastening his sword-belt. With the comparative comfort of a straw-filled palliasse beneath him, the first in three months, he fell asleep at once.

The chapel and cellars had been locked before the sisters had left for the hospitals; nevertheless Serjeant Armstrong reappeared half an hour later with arms full of bottles. One crashed to the stone floor as he pushed the cell door open, and Hervey woke with a start.

'Bordoo, sir – the best. Not like that rot-gut in Spain. Shall we drink to the troop?'

They had drunk together before, not frequently but often enough for Armstrong's invitation to be unremarkable. The circumstances had never been quite so intimate, however; and, while Hervey might in the ordinary course of events have welcomed the opportunity of informality with his covering-serjeant, he was uneasy about allowing any intimacy at this time, for there was the business with the ADC to address. Without doubt many an officer, perhaps even the majority, would have chosen to disregard Armstrong's momentary loss of control since it had been directed at so reviled a man as Regan. Especially might they have been so inclined if the offender were so warmly and genuinely solicitous of their comfort as was Armstrong now. But Hervey could not. He held the simple, if at times uncomfortable, conviction that no case of indiscipline should go at least unremarked, for not to have held so encouraged, in his judgement, a lack of constancy which made for confusion during alarms. Not that this was to advocate a regime of punishment for each and every transgression. Indeed, Hervey's zeal was tempered by the enlightened attitude which characterized the Sixth, where not a man had been flogged in a decade, but there were other concerns now than simply that of good order and military discipline. He raised himself unsteadily on an elbow.

'Serjeant Armstrong, what in the name of heaven did you think you were doing today? Those dragoons from the Staff Corps were within an ace of arresting you!'

'I'd 'ave tipped 'em both a settler if they'd tried!'

'Well, that *would* have decided matters! And how do you suppose you would manage on a trooper's pay?'

'I'd at least have my pride.'

Hervey sighed. 'Serjeant Armstrong, I don't seem to be making my meaning clear, do I? Has Serjeant Strange said anything?'

'Oh ay, Strange has had at me right enough. But he didn't have to say a thing. I've known 'Arry Strange for nigh on ten years.'

'Geordie Armstrong, just listen to me for a minute. That you are a fighter is beyond doubt – one of the best. The whole regiment knows it – and most of the army, too, I shouldn't wonder. But that temper!'

'The pot calls the kettle black-arse!'

Hervey sighed again. 'Serjeant Armstrong, if I encouraged you by my own—' But he was not allowed to finish.

'With respect, Mr Hervey sir,' which was no warranty that any would be manifest, 'you just look out for General Slade, and I'll look to me own devices: I'm too small a fish for them staff to concern themselves over.' And he grinned.

Hervey could but hope that it might be thus. So much for his withering rebuke! But there was, at least, no good reason any longer why he should not take wine with his serjeant and, albeit without much sense of celebration, that is what he did – a copious quantity, in measures which Armstrong referred to as medicinal. And the Bordeaux was to have its medicinal effect, for Hervey slept until late the following morning.

\*　　\*　　\*

43

The silence first told him it was no ordinary reveille. And then the height of the sun, whose rays streamed into his cell through the window high above his head – he had not lain in bed with the sun so high, nor for that matter with the sun *up*, for as long as he could remember. Reveille preceded dawn: that was the invariable rule of field discipline, even in quarters. There they might only feed and water the horses, but in the field they stood to, saddled, ready for any alarm which first light might bring. Wellington may have cursed his cavalry, and compared them unfavourably with the hussars of the King's German Legion, but the Sixth would allow him no cause for complaint over that routine at least.

Hervey lay motionless, still drowsy though conscious of a dull ache in his leg, but he had no great inclination to discover for himself why he was not on parade. Lowly cornet though he might be, he was confident that the regiment would not have moved on without him, and he was sure that no sleep could be so deep as to shut out the sound of a battle. For once he might let events take their course. In any case, all was silence now, and a curious scent of rosewater, mixed with that of the wine spilled the night before, began to have an uncommonly quiescent effect. Soon he was succumbing to a faintly illicit relishing of the missed exertions of the pre-dawn, labours of which few outside the ranks of a horsed regiment could have any conception. An infantryman merely had to turn out of his bivouac and stand to his arms, but both before and after a trooper's stand to there was a deal of toiling with mount and equipment, dawn and dusk, day in, day out.

But the dull throb in his supine leg was increasing, and he forced himself up in order to restore the circulation. There were choice curses at the stiffness as he hobbled round the cell, his sword-scabbard clanking on the flagstones, and the noise was evidently enough to alert his groom who appeared after ten minutes of this clattering and cursing.

'Good mornin, Mr 'Ervey sir. I 'eard thee moving and thought tha could be doing with some breakfast.'

Hervey shook his head in mock despair. He was Private Johnson's third officer in a year, though they had now been together for ten months. The others had complained of excessive cheeriness and an impenetrable Sheffield dialect, but Hervey found his ingenuity as a groom more than made up for these alleged shortcomings. Comprehension, he had told them, was ultimately a matter of determination: could they not recognize a black diamond?

Johnson brought in a canteen of tea, some boiled fowl and a loaf of grey bread. 'An' there's some brandy 'ere an' all, sir,' – holding up a silver cup which looked to have been intended originally for a less secular purpose.

'Private Johnson, it is as ever a pleasure to see you of a morning, but unusual in its being so late,' he replied with a bemused smile.

'Tha means why didn't I wake thee afore?'

'Just so, Johnson.'

'Well, Johnny Crapaud's quit t'town, and Cap'n Lankester said tha were on t'sick list. And when tha was awake t'surgeon said that tha were t'ave thee bandages changed.'

Though Hervey had counted on his not being abandoned, he knew it was the greatest good fortune to have received his wound not a day earlier, if the notion of fortune *and* a wound were in any way appropriate. Had the regiment moved on after the battle, he would have been left in some makeshift hospital on a pile of filthy straw, struck off strength and already becoming but a memory: the needs of the fit and the necessities of the campaign did not often admit of retrospection. But to remain on strength, local-sick, to be tended by the regimental surgeon who would be answerable to Edmonds, was a different prospect; for, however much Edmonds might curse the surgeon as a cast-off from a parish poorhouse, he would perforce be more diligent than many to be found in a so-called army hospital.

Not that this nunnery was anything like as comfortable as some they had seen in Spain, where they resembled more the houses of grandees than of religious orders. The Convent of St Mary of Magdala had a peculiar austerity, a chill which did not come from the weather, for it was seasonally warm and dry outside. Hervey's sick-quarters were no cell in the purely figurative sense, for they had every appearance of the clink's lodgings. The walls were white and in poor repair. A crucifix above his bed was their one adornment. The bed was the only piece of furniture except for a prie-dieu with three books. As Johnson arranged the breakfast in a niche of the thick wall, Hervey picked up each book in turn. The Latin bible, strangely perhaps for a son of the cloth, was the first he had ever opened, and he felt a mild revulsion at seeing the scriptures rendered thus – the Englishman's revulsion at the martyrdom of Tyndale and others for the vernacular. The second volume was in Spanish, *El Via de Perfección*, and he puzzled for a time whether this was 'The Way *to*' or 'The Way *of* Perfection', for his Spanish was still rough. But he understood enough to learn that it was the testimony of St Teresa, the mystic from Avila about whom he knew little, and *that* only because his father had once made a study of the works of St John of the Cross. If he had felt uneasy at the Vulgate, however, the third volume might have thoroughly revolted him, for in the common consciousness of Hervey and his kind the very word *Jesuit* proclaimed every perfidy imaginable, and this volume was the work of St Ignatius of Loyola, no less.

But the title intrigued rather than repelled him – *Exercitia Spiritualia Sancti*. The coupling seemed somehow discrepant: he had studied books on exercises for light cavalry, manuals on sword exercises and pistol exercises, signalling exercises even, but *spiritual* exercises – an altogether arresting notion. He sat down and began to leaf through its pages while at the same time struggling to wrest the stringy meat of the fowl's leg from its bone.

Meanwhile, Private Johnson had slipped from the cell without his noticing. By the time he reappeared only bones remained of the fowl, and Hervey was wholly engrossed in *The Spiritual Exercises.* Johnson was grinning broadly but unseen, for Hervey did not immediately lift his head.

'Mr Evans says this sister will change thee bandages now, sir!' announced his groom at length.

In his struggle with the complex Latin constructions of St Ignatius' epilogue, Hervey did not catch this communication from the surgeon. Nor did Johnson wait for any acknowledgement: he was out of the door with the speed of one of the ferrets which travelled in his valise and supplemented the rations with rabbits. He had no intention of being the butt of Hervey's protests when he tumbled to.

Hervey looked up absently and was all but transfixed by the image of other-worldliness. A white-habited nun, head bowed, holding strips of cloth and a bowl of steaming water, stood framed in the arched doorway like a phantom, albeit of a distinctly celestial kind. As she stepped into the cell, and light from the window fell on her, he saw that her overmantle was more blood-stained than white, though the habit beneath was brown like those of the nuns in Spain. Her face, what little of it was revealed by the wimple, was also smeared with blood and looked excessively drawn, though it was not old. In other circumstances it might have been described as prettyish, but a haunted look made any such worldly adjective inappropriate. It was certainly unlike those of the Spanish sisters, some of whose more sensual features had been decidedly tempting.

Suddenly he recollected himself and sprang up, though pain stabbed his thigh as he did so, adding to his discomposure.

'I am sorry, Sister, but I was not expecting—' he began in French. 'I really think it better if the surgeon attends to this.'

'Sir, the surgeon has been working throughout the night,' she replied, in the measured voice of the Languedoc, by contrast with Hervey's more guttural Alsace, and with evident distaste. 'There are many soldiers – private soldiers – French and English, yet to be attended.'

Her tone stung him. In his confusion he had conveyed something wholly other than what he had meant. 'I am sorry; I did not mean to . . .' he stuttered; and then, sensing that any explanation would be pointless, he tried to dismiss her: 'The dressing is perfectly well, Sister. In the circumstances I think you should return to the wounded.'

'I think we must both do as we are bidden, sir,' she replied firmly, putting the bowl on the floor and beginning to tear a piece of cloth into bandages with considerable violence.

Hervey could not have been more dismayed. Though the

idea of being ministered to by a nun was by no means alien, since he had seen them, and women of rank, in hospitals in the Peninsula, *this* nun made him uneasy. To begin with, there was her spectral appearance. And, though the Marquess of Wellington may have issued instructions that the army was to enter France not as conquerors but as liberators, it seemed prudent first to be certain that this was how the French themselves regarded them. How he was to dispense with her ministration, however, was entirely beyond him; and at length, after it became apparent that no amount of protest would weaken her resolve, and with more chagrin than he could lately remember, he gave up, sat down and removed his blood-stained overalls. He need not have been concerned, for pain soon proved a great distractor: he suspected that this sister might be more devout than most, but she could scarcely have been less tender, cutting the dressing off briskly, and none too gently wiping away the caked blood.

'It is clean, but some of the sutures are broken. I do not think the wound will putrefy, but I think they must be replaced.'

Hervey bit his lip and nodded, and she re-bandaged his leg without speaking. Her eyes were reddened, and he surmised that she had had no sleep for three, maybe four days, for that had been the duration of the fighting. And, though the armies may have had sleep, those tending the wounded could not have found their work slackening during that time. He would have asked her of the *blessés*, but her manner seemed not to invite it; and he suspected, too, that she was a woman of few words, perhaps ordinarily under a vow of silence. Instead he thanked her as she left, but she made no reply, glancing only at the *Spiritual Exercises* lying next to him and then bowing slightly. Hervey noticed for the first time that her feet were bare, and thought of the broken glass which, in stepping over, she must have taken to be evidence of his carousing.

The rest of his day promised little, and for a while he limped around the convent's grounds to try to keep the leg from stiffening, though he might have wished for a less congested place to do so. The courtyard had become a forum for what seemed like every staff officer in the army, as it emerged that the Marquess of Wellington had also made it his advanced headquarters for the formal surrender of the city. The place had, indeed, more the air of Bedlam than of a convent, or even than of a cavalry billet. Had he suspected that in the midst of this seeming babble there might be the commander-in-chief he would have taken pains to make himself scarce; but nothing suggested such a distinction, and he almost literally stumbled on him around the east corner of the cloisters. Sir Stapleton Cotton, one of several generals in the assemblage, spied him before he could turn away.

'Cornet Hervey! How are you, my boy? Come hither!'

He tried hard not to limp as he crossed the yard, wanting no sympathy.

'Lord Wellington, this is Cornet Hervey of the Sixth. It was he who saw off the sortie on our left yesterday.'

The commander-in-chief nodded without smiling. 'Smart work, boy, smart work,' he said simply.

It was very probably the first time he had said anything complimentary to anyone in the cavalry for months, certainly to anyone in the Sixth. For all the regimental ambivalence towards Wellington, however, Hervey could not but feel a warm glow in those sparse words of praise. There were some in the cavalry, and Hervey would count himself among them, who would own that his strictures were all too frequently justi-fied. If a regiment could not be relied on to rally after a charge – the marquess's principal and recurring lament – then to what purpose was it in the field? Hervey knew full well that there was many an officer, though mercifully few in the Sixth now, who derided outpost work and the like and considered mere celerity of movement to be the criterion of efficiency. And it seemed that all were to be judged in Wellington's eyes by their meagre accomplishments. But for a cornet to air such deprecating views risked regimental oblivion, as he had once discovered when venturing the opinion that the cavalry's horsemastership was deficient – only that Edmonds had somewhat unexpectedly agreed with him. Wellington's chiding for Maguilla and Vitoria had been a different matter,

49

however. The affair at Maguilla had been misconstrued because Slade had not had the courage to tell him that his intelligence was faulty. As for Vitoria, with its rapaciousness and letting slip Marshal Jourdan and much of his army, no-one could but denounce it; but to single out the cavalry when all they had done was steal a march on the infantry in the pillaging seemed not a little peevish. The day had been hot and long in its coming, and there had been wine in riverfuls. Hervey had detested the orgy of relief as heartily as any, but such was the mood of the army. Nor had Wellington himself fared ill from it, for the Eighteenth had taken the marshal's baton, and Wellington had sent it to the prince regent. 'You have sent me the baton of a marshal of France,' wrote the prince in reply, 'and I send you that of an English one in return.'

But for the present Hervey was content simply to bask in that economical praise 'smart work'. Then, as suddenly as he had found himself in that grand assemblage, a trumpeter of the escort sounded 'Markers'. The courtyard ceased to be a forum and became instead a parade square as volleys of shouted commands echoed from the high walls and signalled the time for Field-Marshal the Marquess of Wellington to ride in triumph into the city.

Captain Lankester was in his cell when Hervey found him, writing letters to the next of kin of the dozen dragoons from 'A' Troop who had died in the previous fortnight. How the orderly room would discover who and where the troopers' kin were, and how many of them would be able to read the letters for themselves, was another matter, but that would not deter him. Hervey stood at the open door watching him – Captain Sir Edward Lankester, baronet, the senior troop and squadron leader, with a good-sized estate in Hertfordshire and a handsome income: he could have delegated this task to anyone and spent his time arranging comfortable quarters for himself in the city, and few outside the Sixth would have thought a deal of it. But he had not, and scarcely would he have contemplated it, for it was as much his own as it was the Sixth's way. Lankester could give him no news, however, save that Edmonds wished to see him the instant the surgeon warranted him sound.

'Why does the major wish to see me? Is it on account of General Slade?'

There was more than a note of foreboding in the question, but Lankester did not seem minded to allay it, even if he had had the power to do so. 'I have not the shadow of an idea, since he has evidently elected not to confide in me – and, you may be sure, with every good reason.' Hervey made no reply. Lankester dipped his pen in the silver ink-bottle of his exquisitely fitted writing-case and signed another letter with painstaking care: an illegible hand was to him as abhorrent as rust on a sabre. 'My advice is that you present yourself before him at once,' he added at length, and without looking up, for there were three more letters to write (the month had taken an unusually high toll) and his cornet's troubles were trifling by comparison.

Hervey supposed well enough what the reason for Edmonds's summons must be. But, God willing, he would endure no more than a rebuke. Even that, however, would be disagreeable in the extreme: some of the NCOs might take refuge in the knowledge of Edmonds's soft heart, but his tongue could scourge an officer as surely as the lash scourged a defaulter. Hervey's release from arrest had also been irregular – of that he was only too aware – and Edmonds's imprecation 'God preserve us, boy!' rang in his ears still. A mere rebuke seemed improbable.

Hervey's grip on the sword-scabbard had become clammy, even inside his glove, and his right hand was clenched so tight that his fingernails dug into the palm. The crucifix and the guidon had blurred as one, his eyes stinging with the effort of not blinking. Edmonds had addressed him with pronounced formality: 'It is a very singular thing indeed, Mr Hervey, for a cornet to be placed in arrest upon the field of battle.' He had asked for an explanation of the circumstances, 'precisely and dispassionately', and Hervey had in some measure done his bidding. He had at least given as wholly indifferent an account as anyone might. It was, perhaps, a more exact report than Edmonds had required, but Hervey had been at pains to elaborate on Serjeant Armstrong's conduct in the affair with the battery, which he had deemed to be of the highest order. As he finished, he glanced down for the first time, as if to reinforce his closing cadence. He saw at once, and he had not done so before, perhaps not surprisingly in view of his trepidation, that Edmonds's face was no longer swollen. So trivial was the observation in the circumstances that it discomfited him still further. The fact was not without its significance, however, for the tooth-operator had cleanly drawn the abscessed molar that morning, and the pain had at last given way to a soreness which the laudanum, in prodigious quantities since, was able to ease. The opiate was undeniably an element in the unexpected warmth with which the major now addressed him.

'My dear boy,' he began, rising from his chair and indicating another to him. Major Joseph Edmonds always took inordinate trouble to guard against any sign of favour towards Hervey, though heaven only knew how difficult he found that. Sometimes he concealed his regard so well that he appeared abrupt and unsympathetic, and it would have been the profoundest wonder to Hervey to discover in what affection, admiration even, the major held him. Lankester may have been the regimental paragon, and Edmonds would have been loudest in his praise, but something in the captain's Corinthian accomplishment put Edmonds not wholly at ease in his company. In Hervey he saw something of himself as a young cornet, but – and this was the distinction – he saw in him, too, a quality, not easily defined, which might with care and good fortune secure his advancement beyond mere field rank. 'My dear boy,' he repeated, 'everything you have told me accords perfectly with all that I have heard from several different quarters. The matter is entirely closed.'

Hervey's relief was palpable. That relief in itself was sufficient balm in his troubled circumstances, but Edmonds's next pronouncement was in the nature of a miracle-cure.

'I have, no less, a letter of appreciation from the commander-in-chief,' the major continued, his words now betraying just the faintest trace of the opium's solvent. 'The field marshal seems to be making a particular effort to praise his cavalry for a change, doubtless because there has been no riot since Vitoria. But then again, everyone will ascribe this new and godly discipline to an increase in flogging,' he declared sardonically, for he himself loathed the practice intensely, and he considered the Sixth's discipline to be the stronger for its absence. Clearing his throat he began to read the formal commendation: ' "His Excellency the Commander-in-Chief is pleased to express his appreciation of the valuable service performed yesterday by the 6th Light Dragoons under the immediate command of Major Edmonds" – no doubt they had to delve hard to discover my name,' he added caustically, ' ". . . the soldierlike conduct . . . the constancy of duty . . . the celerity and gallantry of execution . . . The Commander-in-Chief will commend these observations to the Horse Guards in the highest possible terms of approbation . . ." '

Edmonds placed the letter on the table. 'But the honour is all yours, my boy, and you may be assured that I shall convey that fact in my reply, though I must confide that my recommendation will hardly count for much. But Sir Stapleton Cotton, too, wants you to have some preferment. There will be a lieutenant's vacancy soon when Rawlings goes to the Tenth and, while you are not the next in seniority, there would be no objection in the circumstances to the lieutenancy's being yours if you can find the money.'

Praise had been one thing, but Hervey was taken wholly aback by the offer of seniority. He had been superseded so many times by others with greater means that he had reconciled himself to a long wait. By his rapid reckoning he could own to six hundred pounds – just – but he would need twelve hundred for the lieutenancy, and his cornetcy would bring, say, eight hundred and fifty. It would be tight, especially with new regimentals to buy, but if he could purchase lieutenant's rank it would mean that in twelve months he would be eligible for a captaincy, and a troop, though how he would be able then to find the additional two thousand pounds when his father was a mere country parson, with no other patron but the diocese to the living, and a modest enough living at that, was quite beyond him for the present.

'Well, then, Mr Hervey? How say you? Is it "yes" or are we to put up the lieutenancy for auction in Craig's Court?'

Hervey accepted with alacrity, and left the orderly room in higher spirits than he had known in many a month. But as he did so a voice hailed him from across the courtyard, a voice which only another from the Black Country could find appealing, and which, for a cornet, invariably portended something bothersome. Lieutenant and Adjutant Ezra Barrow's eighteen years in the ranks of the 1st Dragoons had made him long on soldierly wisdom but short on ceremony – the 'inelegant extract' as he was known by the dandier officers.

'Mr Hervey, you look sound to me; you can be picket officer. Stables now, if you please.'

In God's name, Hervey recoiled, how those Birmingham vowels grated! He wondered how anyone could deride Johnson's when Barrow's sounded so witless.

'Oh, and congratulations on the lieutenancy. I reckon your troop'll pass the plate round if yer father can't pass his: they're all sitting high in the stirrups – there's a deal of Vitoria gold in them 'aversacks!'

Hervey smiled thinly. That Barrow of all people should taunt him for his lack of means irritated beyond measure. It was bad enough with the likes of Rawlings sneering, good-natured though it might have been. He had a perfectly adequate allowance – adequate, that is, for campaign service: he did not suppose it would amount to much in Brighton or Dublin. Perhaps Barrow did not think much of the clergy or their younger sons? Queer fellow – efficient, certainly, but no boon companion. He supposed Lord George Irvine must have known what he was doing when he brought Barrow in from the Royals, though Hervey could hardly believe that there were not others as congenial as they were capable.

'Thank you, Barrow. Decent of you to say so,' he replied with as much courtesy as he could summon: he would have preferred the company of his mess, and its table, to this sudden imposition of picket duty.

As he entered the cloisters, where standing stalls for the three hundred or so troop horses had been improvised, just within the letter of Wellington's ordinance that churches should not be taken for stabling, there was an audible groan. Every dragoon knew that Hervey on picket meant twice as long an inspection, but if the respect were grudging it was real none the less. 'This hay is poor, Sarn't-Major,' he began, though he might have said the same at any stables parade since the summer before.

'As bad as I've seen, sir. We're damping it down but I hope the quartermasters come back with better soon or they'll all be coughing on it.'

It was C Troop's man on duty, a long-limbed Salopian whose father had been the Wynnstay's huntsman for twenty years, and with the best hands in the serjeants' mess.

'And what is the ration of hard feed today?'

'A half-stone of corn, sir; and good crushed barley it is, too. They had two pounds with chop first thing, then the same again at midday.'

'Better than it has been but still not enough.'

'About half what they need. We would not be hunting on this at home now.'

Hervey's eye was next drawn to a sorrowful-looking chestnut tied up in a dark corner, away from the others, with its head down almost to the floor.

'What is wrong with him?' he asked the farrier close by.

'Moon blindness, sir. I'm to shoot 'im as soon as I've taken 'is shoes off.'

'Moon blindness?' he replied.

'Sir; it's a disease of—'

'Well, I know what it's a disease of, Corporal, but there has not been a single case since I have been in the regiment.'

'Tell the truth, sir, I 'aven't seen a case, either.'

'And nor have I,' added the troop serjeant-major, whose fourteen years as a dragoon settled the question of its incidence.

'This is the veterinary officer's judgement?' asked Hervey, though it was unlikely that it could have been any other's.

'Ay, sir,' replied the farrier. 'He saw 'im after first parade and then again after watering this afternoon.'

Hervey stepped closer and reached out slowly to the gelding's head, but the horse made no move. He crouched down and saw that the left eye was closed, with swelling around it and a heavy discharge.

'Careful, sir,' called the farrier, 'he's terrible shy about the head.'

'How does his eye look?' Hervey asked.

'Tell the truth again, sir, I 'aven't seen it. It's been closed all day. I'll fetch his trooper.'

Private Clamp was a young man, eighteen or so, recently joined from the depot squadron. He wore his stable-clothes with the mark of the recruit and he looked unhappy.

'Clamp, have any of your troop officers seen this horse?'

'No, sir, not today. They're all on outpicket.'

'How long have you had him?'

'Since I came, sir, just after Christmas,' he answered, sounding even more unhappy.

'Clamp, there is no need to look quite so troubled: I am not about to have you arrested.'

Clamp's eyes began to go misty.

'God help us,' sighed the serjeant-major.

'It's not that, sir,' continued the trooper, his soft Devon voice in a quaver, 'I 'ave two 'orses to do, an' they're both chestnuts, an' the other one were bad like this when I got 'ere, and if he goes like this one, too . . . well . . .'

'That's enough, Clamp, and stand properly to attention there!' snapped the serjeant-major, though with just enough sympathy in his voice to stay the boy's rambling without precipitating tears.

Hervey's brow furrowed at the thought that there might be

a second case. 'I don't understand it at all, Sarn't-Major. Moon blindness – Specific Ophthalmia – it's so rare that none of us has seen it before, and now there sounds as if there might be two horses in the same troop! Clamp, the other chestnut – he has been well enough since Christmas?'

'Sir!'

'And did anything cause that sickness that you know of?'

'He'd had a bang on the 'ead from something, but I can't remember what.'

'Had he indeed! And this one, number . . .' Hervey stooped to find the regimental number on the off-fore hoof (the Sixth had lately adopted this practice instead of the approved method of cutting the number into the coat). 'J77 – did he have any knocks about the head?'

'He 'ad a thorn in 'is eye a week ago, sir.'

Hervey made a thoughtful *umm* sound. 'Fetch a candle, Clamp!'

'What are you thinking, Mr Hervey?' asked the serjeant-major.

'I'm thinking that I should like to see the eye for myself. Would you hold up his head for me?'

'His eye will be way back in its socket by the time you prise it open.'

'That's why I'm not going to force it. Hold the candle up close, Clamp!' He placed his hand carefully on the gelding's brow and gently extended his thumb so that it rested on the margin of the upper lid.

'What exactly are you doing, then?'

'There's a muscle just above the eyelid, the retractor muscle,' he replied. 'If you press gently but firmly on it, it ceases to act with any strength and the lid can be lifted quite easily.'

Hervey pressed for almost a minute and then drew up the lid slowly, using his other hand to pull down the lower lid. The gelding stood quite calm and still.

'Well, I'll be damned!' muttered the serjeant-major.

'An old trooper taught me that: Daniel Coates – he was with the Sixteenth in America. He taught me to ride, use a sword and a pistol, and everything about handling a troop – and all before I was twelve! I should think there is very little that Daniel Coates does not know,' said Hervey absently.

'Do you see anything?' the serjeant-major pressed, even more intrigued.

'Take a look at the pupil for yourself, Sarn't-Major. What do *you* see?'

'The middle's very blue.'

'What else?'

'Nothing that I can tell, sir. It's very watery of course.'

'The pupil – is it diminished?'

'No, I would not say it was.'

'Just so, Sarn't-Major!' And with that Hervey let the eye close. 'We must summon the veterinary officer.'

'I'm afraid he's been bedded down, sir – fever again.'

'The poor devil's riddled with it. He ought to give up. Well, Sarn't-Major, this horse is not to be shot. He needs some damp muslin over his eyes and then turning out in a day or so. He has Common Ophthalmia, not Specific. The symptoms are all but identical, except that with moon blindness the pupil is invariably diminished. Clamp, what is the other chestnut's number?'

'J78, sir. Him and 77 was bought as a pair in England.'

'Umm,' went Hervey again. 'Order feeding-off, then, Sarn't-Major.'

And now at last he could go and see his own chargers, stabled in a tithe barn on clean straw, the first they had seen in months. Inevitably they were chewing it.

'It's all right, sir,' chirped Johnson, 'it's wheat straw.'

Hervey's little mare whickered in recognition while continuing to chew her bed, but she looked badly run up.

'Is there no hay anywhere?' he asked, pulling her ears.

'Not yet, sir, nothing decent; quartermasters are still out progging.'

Jessye was by common consent the handiest charger in the Sixth, although when Hervey had first joined for duty she had been derided as a covert-hack, fit only to take a blade to a meet but not to follow hounds. Barely an inch over fifteen hands, yet she had the sturdiness and intelligence of her dam, a Welsh cob which for twenty years had carried his father round his parish, and the speed and endurance of her sire, a thoroughbred whose bloodlines went directly back to the Godolphin Arab. She had struggled out of the womb on Hervey's fourteenth birthday, the day he left the vicarage for Shrewsbury School, a birthday present of such apt timing that his understanding of natural history was unusual for some years to come. He alone had schooled her, though she had taught him almost as much as he had imparted to her, and he always counted it an act of providence that an outbreak of farcy prior to sailing had kept her behind in England during the first campaign: the thought that he would have had to shoot her on the beach at Corunna with all the others filled him still with a peculiar dread.

'"An horse is a vain thing for safety; neither shall he deliver any by his great strength."'

'Eh?' challenged his groom.

'Not my words, Johnson – the Psalmist's.'

'Well he must have been fuzzed!'

'I mean that it is written in the Psalms,' Hervey explained with a smile of mild dismay. 'Thirty-three, I think' – as if Johnson might somehow wish to look up the reference for himself.

'They don't say owt about 'orses that makes much sense.'

Hervey gave up. 'Her coat stares, Johnson. We must find her some blankets and make a mash – she'll have colic before midnight, I'll be bound. Wheat straw or not, tie her up for the time being.'

A shrewd observer would next have noted a subtle change in Hervey's manner. With Jessye he was easy and familiar; with his second charger he was perceptibly distant, respectful rather than affectionate.

'Nero looks fine enough,' he said.

'Oh ay, sir, 'e's all right; that cut's nothin'.'

Nero had been bred to look fine. A full hand and a half higher than Jessye, he had come to Hervey from the king's stallion depot outside Hanover via an ensign in the

Footguards. Lieutenant d'Arcey Jessope had been officer of the guard one day when His Majesty, in one of his periodic derangements, and conceiving himself to be in the Herren-hausen rather than at Windsor, had become convinced that Jessope, in his scarlet, was one of his Hanoverians. The king had taken him at once to the royal stables and presented him with the first animal that His Majesty considered appropriate for an officer of his *Leibgarde*. Jessope had thereby become the owner of a mount which, though magnificent, he sub-sequently found unmanageable. He would always ascribe this to late gelding, not wholly convincingly, whenever the subject arose, and he had been relieved to pass him on to Hervey for a song after the battle at Salamanca, a generous token of gratitude for his rescue half-dead from the mêlée. As Jessope himself had remarked laconically from his hospital bed, with an arm almost severed by a sabre slash he had little hope of being able to manage a 'rig'.

*Jessope.* Hervey smiled at the thought of him, and wondered what recovery he was making since his return to England, and when indeed he might see him again. Doubtless he was being fêted at this very instant by the ladies of St James's. He smiled again as he recalled Jessope's description of Nero: 'unmanageable'. Yet in one sense it was exact enough, for in the hands of any but those which had been trained in the classical method he was wholly unresponsive, positively wilful. In *Hochschule* hands his manners were impeccable. He could cover ground better even than Corporal Collins's gelding and had jumped four foot six, though he lacked Jessye's endurance. There had been times as a boy, in the riding-hall at Wilton House, when Hervey would gladly have quit his lessons with the Austrian *Reit-lehrer* and gone back to his simple hunting seat, but he had frequently thanked God that the option of doing so had never been his. No riding master had been able since to disabuse him of his conviction that to be master of both a classical and an English seat was a peerless asset.

Jessye was his concern that evening, however, and they managed eventually to rug her up with blankets from the chaplain's quarters – the priest had not been seen since their arrival – and make a mash of what seemed to be bran, which Johnson had discovered unattended somewhere. The quarter-masters came in with two waggon-loads of good hay soon afterwards and, though it meant turning out the troopers again to replace the dusty stuff in the lines, the work was done quickly and Hervey was able to have the orderly trumpeter sound the mess call by six o'clock. A jaunty little tune, it put a skip into his spirits, if not into his step, as he left:

> An officer's wife has puddings and pies,
> A serjeant's wife has skilleee . . .
> But a soldier's wife has nothing at all
> To fill her empty belleee . . . E, E, E

Thank heaven there were no soldiers' wives with them this time, nor any others for that matter. He knew their worth on campaign, for sure, but he knew their trouble, too; and the balance lay heavily, in his judgement, with the latter. In any event, all that might soon be behind them: no-one at the stables parade had said as much, but there had been a distinct air of anticipation, a sensing that the end of their long ordeal, this seemingly unending war with Bonaparte, was near.

But even these comparatively light duties were telling on him, and he was glad of the opportunity to get to his own mess. However, his hopes of any immediate rest were dashed as soon as he entered the noisy and smoke-filled refectory. Cries of 'The child Samuel!' greeted him, though he was at a loss to know why.

'First book of Samuel,' called Harding, the senior lieu-tenant, in mock despair. ' "And the child Samuel grew on, and was in favour both with the Lord, and also with men"!'

Hervey smiled as he tumbled to the reference. The intelli-gence of Lord Wellington's pleasure had, it seemed, reached the mess before him, though he hardly expected that he was in favour with the stable details after calling them out a second time. A press of officers formed to shake his hand, and the steward, trying manfully to find some ingress, was jostled this way and that before being able to proffer a silver tray on which there was a letter for him.

'It has been some time in reaching us, sir,' he said apologetically, though the delay was none of his making.

Hervey was pleased with the excuse to seek out a quiet corner, but as he did so the sight of the envelope at once discomfited him. Though he had never been given to too much introspection – nor, indeed, had there been any great opportunity for it during this campaign – there was something in the three short lines of the address which brought him up short, made him abruptly aware of just how much his life belonged to the Army. That would not ordinarily have discomposed him, for this *was* his life and he held no other to be more honourable, but the sudden notion that his soul might have been taken by the drum, too, disturbed him more. Perhaps it was the terseness of the address:

*Cornet M. P. Hervey,*
*6th Lt. Dgns.,*
*Spain*

Three lines – name, regiment, country – the very essence of his being in so short a space. And then another chill, a portent of the contents: he stared for some time before he could bring himself to open it, for the hand was unmistakable, though months had passed since any word from Wiltshire, and it was a hand conspicuously more restrained than he had seen before.

*Horningsham,*
*17 January 1814*

*Dearest Matthew,*

*I am afraid that this letter bears the saddest news. Our John has died in Oxford on this 12th instant. According to Mr Heywood, his vicar, this hard winter we are enduring was taking its toll most cruelly on his parish and he was much about the poorest parts trying to bring relief.*

*He became ill a fortnight ago and then succumbed to pneumonia.*

There were three more pages in his sister's round script, but he could not read on. Though his expression must have reflected the news, and little to his mind could have been worse, he was able nevertheless to slip the letter into his tunic and escape without giving away his anguish. In the quiet of his cell he sat with his head in his hands for what seemed an age. The irony, that surrounded by death, as he had been these past six years, it was death at a distance which was finally to pierce him, only added to his grief.

There was a knock at the door. 'Not now, Johnson!' he called. But it opened slowly, and there appeared, diffidently, the regiment's veterinary officer.

'Pardon my intruding so, Hervey, but I wished to have words concerning the chestnut in C Troop.' The voice was equally hesitant.

Hervey would have wished for this at another time but he sensed he had little choice but to yield. 'Well, yes, indeed, Selden. Come in, sit down,' he said, indicating a sedile which Johnson had acquired during the day.

'Hervey, the farrier-major has reported to me what transpired at evening stables.' He began coughing badly, his face in a feverish sweat. Hervey gave him a cup of water.

'You ought not to be out of your bed, Selden, for heaven's sake!'

'That I know; it's a damned potent attack this time, but I had to speak with you about my diagnosis. You examined the eye, I'm told?'

'Yes.'

'I could barely see it, I confess. What did the pupil look like?'

'Undiminished – a little dilated, if anything, I should say.'

The veterinary officer sighed. 'I should have got someone to look, but the eye was so far back in its socket . . .'

Hervey nodded.

'And I looked at my notebook and saw that the horse had

had a previous attack of ophthalmia. If there is recurrence, then it signals progressive blindness, and there is no recourse but to the bullet – as you very well know. Thus I made the presumption of the specific condition. I have only seen two cases before, both in the Indies, but I do not understand how there could be a recurrence of the simple.'

'I think you will find,' said Hervey quietly, 'that it was the other chestnut – J78 – that was the previous case. You have made the two as one.'

The veterinary officer's jaw fell. 'Then, I must go at once and offer my papers to the major,' he replied.

'There is no need for that,' insisted Hervey. 'You were in no condition to be attending to them in the first instance. Here, take this brandy.' And he poured a large measure from the bottle which Johnson had left by his bed. 'None of us, I dare say, is in the best of sorts.'

'But your judgement seems not to have been impaired by your own infirmity,' said Selden, gesturing towards Hervey's leg.

'That is as may be, but I dare say I would not be so attentive now,' he replied.

'How so?' asked Selden, at once puzzled but faintly encouraged by the reply.

'Oh, it does not matter,' said Hervey dismissively, realizing he had let on more than he intended.

Selden had another fit of coughing, which required more brandy to subdue, and he mopped his brow with a large, ochreous silk square which matched almost exactly his feverish complexion. 'Horse doctor that I may be, I am still able to recognize obvious symptoms of dispirits in humans.'

Hervey sighed, but in truth he was glad to share his ill news, which Selden received attentively. 'And your brother was, I would hazard, a fine sort of man, an active clergyman, no mere time-server,' said the veterinary officer when Hervey had finished.

'Of all the worthless creatures I have seen survive – no, *prosper* – these past six years, I cannot understand why a man so full of goodness as he should die.'

'A cruel and troubling paradox,' agreed Selden: '"The secret things belong unto the Lord our God: but those things which are revealed belong unto us."'

'Indeed, and John would quote Deuteronomy just so, but it all seems remote and . . . *conjectural* now.'

'I find it ever to be so, frankly. I confess that I cannot put any faith in the claims of the Church. What will you do? Are there any family obligations which now befall you?'

'I have just accepted a lieutenancy and I do not know if I am in any position to do so. I simply do not know what are my duties at home. I shall write, of course, and apply for furlough as soon as the war ceases – they seem to think it is imminent. Until then . . .'

'What other family do you have?' asked the veterinary officer, coughing again but warming to the intimacy he was rarely afforded in the mess as a whole.

'A sister, one year my senior – but I should of course first say my father and mother.'

'They are all well?' Selden interrupted.

'Yes, I believe them to be. My parents are no longer young but they are both active and have always enjoyed good health. They are the very best of people: I have always felt their absence more keenly than might be supposed. And my sister – Elizabeth – she has spirits to equal anyone. I own to having been in her thrall since childhood!'

'And, Hervey, is there any other in your affections?'

So direct a question, and from a quarter he would least have expected, took him aback, and his disinclination to make any reply was plain. Selden was a kindly and cultured man, unusually gentlemanly for a veterinary surgeon, yet he generally remained aloof. His periodic bouts of fever racked him dreadfully, but although he had completed eighteen years' service, and was entitled to retire on half-pay, he struggled on. He had been with the Sixth only since the start of the second campaign – and there was a whiff of sulphur in his history, said some – yet Hervey had always found him the most decent of company.

'Forgive me, Hervey, but I have watched you with advantage these past three years. You have an uncommon facility for soldiering, and yet no preferment has come your way, and never will as long as money determines things.' He began coughing again, so violently this time that Hervey thought he must choke. Another cup of brandy brought relief, however. 'You must go east. Take up with John Company. They would value your aptitude – you would have a regiment in no time.'

Hervey might have had a thousand objections but he chose simply to point out the circumstances of which he had just spoken: 'I cannot even begin to think such a thing when matters at home are so indeterminate.'

'Of course you cannot. But after you have settled these concerns . . . or is there perhaps someone else you must take account of?'

'Not at all!'

'Forgive me once more, but I had thought that young Laming's sister . . .'

Hervey blushed, and stammered slightly: 'I . . . that is, how could you possibly have thought that? It is a year – more – since she came to Portugal, and then for a month only!'

'Oh, I thought I saw something. Perhaps, then, it was more on her side? And the young Portuguese lady, what was her name . . . ? Delgado, was it not?'

Hervey was even more astonished, for Selden's observation these past three years had indeed been active. Frances Laming had enchanted him with her pretty smiles, but Isabella Delgado had positively tortured him with her dark beauty. 'No, Selden, there is no-one. I had once a passion for the girl with whom I shared a schoolroom, though since that was a full ten years ago, and I dared not own it to her, I hardly think it need be taken account of now!' But a smile overcame him at the thought.

A trumpet-call signalled that watch-setting was imminent, and Veterinary-Surgeon Selden took his leave, with much violent coughing, to allow Hervey to ready himself for that parade. It had been an extraordinary, if agreeable, meeting; but now that he was alone all his earlier disquiet returned, and with interest, for Selden had stirred up so much. The second call, however, began to reclaim him for the regulated world that was his daily existence, and as he fastened on his sword-belt he found once more that he could bury his uncertainties in the minutiae of his soldier's routine. He almost spoke it aloud – 'hitch up the scabbard, free the sabretache, set the shako square, draw on the gloves'. In the short term, at least, it never failed. So much so that, by the time he reached the picket, where he would take longer than any of the dragoons would have thought possible in determining their fitness for the night watch, his only thought was how sharp he would find their sabres.

# CHAPTER TWO
# CRUEL PUNISHMENT

*13 April, 4 a.m.*

'Boney's beat! Boney's beat!'

Hervey woke with a start and sprang from his bed, but he almost fainted with the first step, so nauseous was the pain, and he fell against the wall, retching. The candle flickered in the sudden disturbance of still air, and he had to grope for his sword-belt in the half-darkness. Outside his cell it was no brighter, for the lantern in the corridor had dimmed to little more than a glow, but he could just make out the figures of the orderly corporal and Trumpeter Pye approaching.

'It's over! Boney's habdicated.'

This time he heard the words – and was speechless.

'It's right enough, sir,' continued Corporal Taylor as other officers began appearing, likewise roused by the commotion. 'Boney's finished. I 'eard Major Edmonds telling the sarn't-major only ten minutes ago; but before that, even, a staff dragoon from headquarters was by and told me the intelligence had come from Paris last evening.'

The news, which they had awaited so keenly, and for so long, somehow lacked the inspiration that he presumed great news must have. It seemed unfitting that it should be hawked along the corridors of a cloistered billet by a corporal at this ungodliest of hours. He had imagined some ceremony or other would be attached to its heralding.

Next there appeared the adjutant, fully dressed, and at first Hervey supposed that this portended the ceremony he had anticipated, yet Barrow had so much an expression of the everyday that he again began to doubt the corporal's information.

'First parade at seven, details as usual, gentlemen,' announced the adjutant. 'Officers to assemble in the mess at eight. Sound reveille, Pye!'

Barrow was as ever spare with his words and did not wait for questions, marching briskly off towards the orderly room, spurs ringing on the flagstones. Hervey was angered. He was picket officer, and yet the adjutant had confided nothing to him. He may have been a mere cornet, but – *confound it* – Barrow would have been forthcoming enough if there had been an alarm.

When the echo of Trumpeter Pye's long reveille had died away – the first time the extended rather than the short call had been used since winter quarters – there came the gentler sound of a bell, and Hervey saw at the furthest end of the cloisters several nuns making for the chapel. The bell struck every second, and with so insistent a ring that he found his annoyance diminishing with each stroke. He wandered into the courtyard. It was too dark to make out the time by his watch, as dark as it had been at midnight when he had trudged the streets of the defeated city to do his rounds of the outlying picket. There had been no moon, and the streets had been as black as pitch, for the lamplighters had fled, and the occupants of the houses had shuttered and boarded their windows so that it was impossible to know whether they were lit inside or had been abandoned. How different it had been at Vitoria. There had been no question then of not knowing what lay behind the shutters, for they had all been prised off and the property sacked, Spanish property. Yet here, a French city, where the fighting had been immeasurably more bloody than at Vitoria, the provost-marshal's men were patrolling the streets as if it had been Westminster. The Marquess of Wellington had ordered that there was to be no looting, and no looting there was – on pain of death by an English musket. Not that Hervey disapproved of such an order. He loathed the larceny where it exceeded what might reasonably be counted as foraging, but he hated most the bestiality to which men would sink in the process. Never did he imagine, on entering the king's service, that one day it would be his duty to shoot a man wearing the same uniform – or, rather, the same king's uniform – as he had done after Badajoz. The vision of that Connaught private, crazed with drink, taking the ball from Hervey's pistol full in the chest yet still setting about him with murderous strength, would long remain. Yet the terror in the dying eyes of the young Spanish girl whom the man had violated, and the blood from her slashed throat, would more than mitigate any guilt, or even regret, that he might feel.

As the regiment woke to the call of the trumpet and began its familiar routine, he walked back to his cell, passing the chapel with its plain windows lit dimly from within. A frail chant, *Te Deum Laudamus*, drifted out, with an occasional whicker from the cloister stalls punctuating the plainsong. He found his cell a blaze of light compared with the gloom elsewhere, for each corner was filled with candles, and an oil lamp burned brightly on a small table, these meagre but useful camp-stores bearing witness to the ever-resourceful Johnson's nocturnal activities. Next to the lamp stood a steaming canteen of tea, and a clean pair of undress overalls lay on the bed.

'Baggage came in last night, sir,' explained his groom. 'I'll bring t'rest along presently – thought these'd be more comfortable. I'll take thee field overalls to mend now. I 'ear it's all over?'

But Hervey had to admit that he had no more information than the barrack room evidently had. 'Do you have my sketchbooks yet?' he asked.

'Ay, sir; they're with t'rest of thee things.'

There was no more news at first parade, either, only speculation – Bonaparte was dead, Bonaparte had escaped to America, Bonaparte was in a cage in the Tuileries. By the time the officers assembled in the refectory, at eight o'clock, there was at least unanimity that Bonaparte was finished. There were barely a dozen and a half officers on parade that morning, fewer than half the establishment with which they had begun the campaign. Hervey could picture the absent faces as clearly as if they were standing there: the colonel would, no doubt, return to duty in good time, but the two captains, Lennox and Twentyman, would never again hear reveille; nor would Martyn and Mayall, the lieutenants who had fallen at Salamanca; nor Cornets Wyllie and Lord Arthur Percival, killed at Badajoz; Cornet Bruce would never again see the wild flowers of whose names, both vulgar and botanical, he had such astonishing recall, for the explosion of the arsenal after Ciudad Rodrigo had scorched his eyes terribly. And there were others, more fortunate, who had been invalided home with wounds or sickness: they had filled the mess with laughter and companionship (and Hirsch with the uncommon beauty of his flute), and he would miss them even more now that peace brought a respite from the exertions of this campaign. The noise which the gallant and fortunate remnant made suggested double their number, however, and Cornet Laming had to struggle to make himself heard: 'D'ye see Edmonds, Hervey?'

Hervey looked to where Laming nodded and saw the major at the far end of the refectory, looking sombre. Barrow was speaking into his ear and appeared equally grave.

'Something's up,' said Laming. 'I heard after stables that the Fourteenth are for America.'

'I would not mind America. Why should that trouble us?' replied Hervey, momentarily forgetful of his own pressing need to return home.

'Because the regiment's worn out, that is why.'

'We might still have a march on Paris if Bonaparte's flight is but rumour,' he countered warily.

'That is another matter entirely. Look around: we have been campaigning longer than any corps in the army – we are at less than half-strength! Look at Edmonds, his nerves have frayed to nothing; he's had the blue devils for months! And there's scarcely a horse that I'd warrant through another winter out.'

But before Hervey could reply Barrow called them to order and Edmonds began speaking. 'Gentlemen, I have a dispatch from General Cotton. It reads as follows:

'"Lord Wellington has received intelligence of the abdication of the self-styled Emperor Napoleon Buonaparte and of his custody with the Royal Navy. There shall be an immediate armistice, for two months. Marshal Soult is to surrender his army of the south to the Commander-in-Chief directly. The Garonne is to be the line of demarcation and Toulouse will remain in our possession. The administration of the country is to be vested immediately in the appointed representatives of His Majesty King Lewis the Eighteenth, who are to be treated as our allies."'

'See how quickly will they make white cockades out of tricolours,' whispered Laming.

'Too cynical,' Hervey whispered back.

'"Si foret in terris . . . ,"' declaimed Laming airily.

'"Rideret Democritus." What has Horace to do with it?'

Laming nodded with faint surprise, and Hervey took the opportunity to tilt gently at the senior cornet's self-esteem.

'Laming, contrary to what might have been supposed at Eton, we were not barbarians at Shrewsbury.'

'Oh, a most apt riposte, I do acknowledge!' said Laming rather too loudly. Barrow glanced their way sharply, and then Edmonds continued.

'But there is to be no rest, gentlemen. Two divisions under Lord Hill are to proceed to America as soon as possible. The Fourteenth are to accompany them and a squadron of the Staff Corps; we shall be asked for nominations of men of the highest character, as usual, for the Corps. Meanwhile we shall remain in Toulouse until the acknowledgement of King Lewis is universal and the French army and marshals have taken oaths of allegiance.' The cadence seemed to indicate that this was an end to it, and a general hubbub began.

'Thank God it's only the Chambermaids for America, then,' said Laming. 'We can decamp to Paris and then be in Leicestershire for next season!'

'Venery and then venery!' quipped Hervey.

Laming frowned, but at least the Sixth's prizes at Vitoria had not landed them with so ungraceful a sobriquet as the

Fourteenth's: a silver chamberpot belonging to Bonaparte's brother had at the time seemed amusing booty to the 14th Light Dragoons.

'Gentlemen, *please*!' called Barrow, and silence quickly returned.

Edmonds paused. 'Gentlemen, this is, I believe, the end of what we were coming to think of as a never-ending war. You have done well – the regiment has done well, but I fear that this end may be but a beginning. We are not for Paris, however. We have been warned for England together with most of the rest of the cavalry, and I need not speak aloud my worst fears, for you are only too aware of the economies which this parliament will now seek. I pray that our seniority will afford us some security. And the Earl of Sussex will not let his regiment disband without protest – of that you may be assured. Meanwhile we must continue to conduct our affairs with the same fidelity, trusting that virtue is in itself, ultimately, a sufficient reward. That is all, gentlemen.' And, turning about, he left the room with not another word.

'A very pretty speech, I do declare,' said Cornet Laming. 'What say you, Murray?'

Their troop senior's brow furrowed angrily. 'So we're going to be paid off, are we? And what price d'ye think our commissions will fetch now, eh? It's all very well for the likes of you, Laming, but I paid twice over price and all my people's estates in the Americas have been lost,' he snapped, turning on his heel.

Hervey and Laming looked at each other blankly as Lieutenant Murray stalked away. Barrow had not left, however, and he now came up to them looking no less preoccupied than he had before Edmonds had spoken.

'The major wishes to see you directly, Hervey.'

'About what?' he replied. 'There is no more trouble surely?'

'Not in your case, not personally. Armstrong – bloody business, bloody, bloody business,' he replied, shaking his head.

The regimental serjeant-major was already talking with Edmonds when Barrow and Hervey entered the abbess's library, which was beginning to look like the orderly room in Canterbury, for the regiment's silver had arrived with the baggage train. The crucifix had been more reverently draped with a white sheet, and the guidon was unfurled so that the regiment's four battle-honours (though still to be officially authorized) were clearly arrayed: *Tournay*, where they had lost every third man while covering the infantry's hard-pressed retreat; *Willems*, where they had almost stuck fast in the Flanders mud; *Egmont-Op-Zee*, where they had galloped along the beach and dunes for six miles to cut off the French. He knew the battles well enough from accounts which lay in the regiment's reading-room. But that which he admired the greatest, that which he wished most to have been party to the honour, lay not in the Low Countries but in a place so distant that it could exist for him only at the extremity of his imagination: *Seringapatam*. There were still a few old hands in the ranks who remembered that day, though most had by now taken their prize-money to begin life out of uniform (those, that is, who had not drunk or whored it in the three years they remained in India after that affair). Edmonds was the only officer remaining who had been present. He would never speak of it, except of late to say that the sack of Vitoria was but revelry compared with that of Seringapatam.

The adjutant joined Edmonds and the RSM beside the guidon, but Hervey saluted and stood at attention in front of the major's writing-table – for a second time in as many days. The RSM's appearance was more than usually imposing, and Hervey felt his habitual unease when in his company. Mr Lincoln had been in the same action as the rest of the regiment two days before, but for all the world he looked now as if he were ready for a review on the parade ground at the Horse Guards, his Hessian boots gleaming like patent. He looked as fit as any rough-rider, only the grey of his half-mutton-chops giving any clue to his real age. Abandoned as an infant in the undercroft of Lincoln's Inn, raised subsequently on the charity of the benchers and given the customary surname for such foundlings, he had enlisted as a boy-trumpeter at the age of twelve, in the second year of the American revolt, and his attestation papers had long been conveniently lost. Hervey's gaze fell on the four silver-lace chevrons, surmounted by the crown, on his upper right arm. The effort, the years of duty, which they marked would awe any cornet, and he wondered what Lincoln must be making of his handling of the picket: perhaps the RSM thought it all that could be expected from someone whose rank rested solely on the deposit of £600 with the regimental agents.

'Mr Hervey, I will be brief,' began Edmonds as the three turned towards him, Lincoln saluting briskly. 'General Slade is pressing charges of gross insubordination against Serjeant Armstrong. He will allow me to deal summarily with the charges if I order him to be flogged, otherwise he will have Armstrong court-martialled and dismissed with disgrace. He knows the Sixth does not flog; I *will* not flog! It is the vilest thing – cruel punishment, corrosive of true discipline and morals. Yet Armstrong will be broken for ever if I do not. Was there anything more in mitigation that you have not already told me?'

Hervey glanced at RSM Lincoln, who remained impassive, doubtless thinking that if he, Hervey, had kept calm, then Armstrong might perhaps have kept his temper. 'Sir, Serjeant Armstrong was insubordinate, but he was my covering-serjeant and it surely might be taken to be mere excess of zeal. Lieutenant Regan was guilty of undermining my authority in front of the picket, and no doubt Serjeant Armstrong felt he should act in this respect.'

'I do not doubt that, Hervey, but insubordination is a military offence whereas Regan's conduct was ungallant, and that is not. Do not misunderstand, mind – Regan behaved like an ass by all accounts.'

Edmonds now looked across to Barrow, whereupon the adjutant began speaking in an uncommonly warm tone. 'There is but one chance, Hervey. You might petition for redress of grievance in respect of wrongful arrest. The prospect might cause the general to abandon the charges.'

Hervey did not hesitate. 'Then I will do so, of *course*. Will it work, sir?' he asked, looking at Edmonds.

'I think it very probably will. We do not know whether it was Slade himself who ordered the arrest or whether it was Regan who was overzealous. Even if it were Regan's doing, he has such connections that Slade would not want a squeeze. But the thing is this, Hervey: I am afraid that, whichever way it goes, you will be a marked man so far as Slade is concerned – as, indeed, will I, though that is a different matter.'

'So be it, sir!'

'And, if this stratagem is a success,' asked Edmonds, turning to Mr Lincoln, 'what should be done with Armstrong then, Sarn't-Major?'

'Well, sir,' began the RSM, 'you know it is my opinion that a senior rank should not be humiliated for a momentary lapse of good sense. There was to be no punishment before General Slade raised these charges. My mess would not be dismayed if we followed that same course now, and I tender my apologies that one of my mess should fail his officer as Armstrong has done. I have yet to speak to him in connection with this: he will not forget it when I do.'

No-one could doubt it.

'Very well, then, Mr Lincoln,' said Edmonds, 'a rebuke and nothing further. Mr Barrow, I suggest that you make the brigade major aware of Mr Hervey's intention to petition without delay. With any luck it may never come to a formal submission. That is all, gentlemen; but, Mr Hervey, stay a moment.'

When the others had left, Edmonds motioned him to sit in the chair by his writing-table and he himself sat on the edge, his earlier formality easing. 'Look Hervey, this is really a deuced tricky business. Slade is a vindictive man, and his reach is long. I do not even know whether approaching Sir Stapleton Cotton would be to any avail. In truth I wish Lord George were here now. We must get you out of Slade's reach. There is an appointment with the Staff Corps squadron for America, and after the affair of the French battery I feel sure that we could place it for you, for you are aware of General Cotton's opinion of your action. The last thing I want to do is see you leave the regiment, even temporarily, but I really do urge you to take this opportunity.'

Hervey said nothing, stunned by Edmonds's pessimism. At length he reached into his tunic. 'Sir,' he began, unfolding his sister's letter, 'I would have welcomed the prospect of America, but yesterday I received this from home. My brother has died. He was my elder, and I feel that I must at least return home to discover my father's circumstances and wishes. I am not sure now that I may accept the lieutenancy even.'

Edmonds nodded. 'Yes, I understand well enough,' he sighed. 'There comes a time in this whole wretched business of fighting when the spirit just yearns for something peaceful and decent – yes, and gentle even. And you are aware, as I indicated in the mess, that this news of our returning straight to England may well mean disbandment? Your investment might then be lost.'

'Yes, sir, though I would hazard all in that respect.'

'I am glad to hear it. Those loobies in Parliament will make unconscionable reductions in the Army. Mr Pitt's income tax will be repealed, and there'll be beggars in scarlet aplenty on the streets. That is what Cotton believes, too. I do not wish to talk about it with the regiment just yet. As long as you understand all the implications of not going to America – there might even be promotion with the Corps, whereas you might be thrown on to half-pay with a worthless cornetcy to sell if you stay. You are a courageous officer, brave, but . . .'

'Thank you sir,' he replied a little uncomfortably.

'Not just that,' continued the major. 'I mean that you have yet to acquire sufficient guile . . . but, then, so have I, for that matter. It might be a case of crabs for us both if Black Jack Slade has another turn. I will leave the question of the lieutenancy for a while, but I must have an answer on America tomorrow. That is all, Matthew.'

Captain Lankester's advice was at least unambiguous – and exactly as Hervey would have predicted. Lankester the Corinthian always squared up to difficulties, as he had done to ill-breaking balls on Upper Club at Eton, though always with a sobering realism. He hardly looked up from his journal, which he kept with the same diligence that he would his game-book in Hertfordshire, as Hervey recounted the America option. 'Petition and stay put!' he drawled. 'Slade has been the death of enough good men. Do you want to be shot like a blackcock by some half-breed in a racoon hat?'

Hervey laughed for the first time since the letter from home. He was pleased with the advice, for though he was perfectly happy to take his chance with an American militiaman, the option seemed too much like running. Edmonds's was without doubt the more prudent of the advice – he knew that full well – and it was all very fine for Sir Edward Lankester, with wealth and rank in his favour, to urge the devil-may-care course. But prudence in a cornet was a questionable attribute – like coyness in whores, Edmonds had once said. What would it profit him to evade this challenge to his self-respect, now, when other challenges would surely follow? He knew right enough that for him there was but one option.

As in some medieval scriptorium, Hervey sat in his cell making a fair copy of the draft petition which Barrow had given him. There was a knock at the door. 'Come in, Johnson,' he called absently. But Johnson never knocked, and Hervey looked up to find instead the same sister of the day before. Her habit was no longer bloodstained and her face not nearly so drawn. He might not have recognized her but for the ice-blue eyes which, now less sunken, were more piercing than before. She had cast her overmantle, and he was able to gain a more faithful impression of her figure, as pleasingly slender as any he had seen. Her bosom, too, suggested an aptness for fashion, unlike the Spanish nuns whose amplitude would have challenged the corsetier's art. Having had the broken sutures replaced by the surgeon only the afternoon before, he was perplexed at her being there – though much charmed. 'Yes, Sister, can I help?' he asked in French.

And she replied, to his evident astonishment, in English. 'Mr Hervey, I have heard that Lord Wellington has said that if King Louis were to be restored we would be treated as if liberated rather than conquered.' Not only did she convey her sense perfectly, with an admirable mastery of the subjunctive, but her aspirates, as alien to a Frenchwoman as they seemed to be to Johnson, were breathed consummately. And there was scarce a trace of accent, though she did not Anglicize the king's name as Cotton's dispatch had done – or, at least, the way in which Edmonds had read it. 'Mr Hervey, forgive me,' she continued. 'Yesterday you paid me the compliment of speaking in French, and I have not returned that compliment until now. Yesterday was . . . well, a most tiring day: I had not slept in—'

'Sister, there is no need,' he interrupted. 'I believe you thought me . . . indulgent, in so far as I appeared to demand the surgeon in person. That was furthest from my intention.'

'I do not doubt it for a moment, Mr Hervey. You are an honourable man, I think, one who might be trusted,' she replied softly.

'I hold myself to be so, Sister,' said Hervey thankfully. It was curious how he felt the need of this nun's approval.

'Sir, I wish to explain something to you and then I have a kindness to ask.'

'By all means, Sister,' he replied, intrigued by both the warmth of her tone and the notion that he might be of assistance to her.

'Mr Hervey, my name is Maria de Chantonnay. My people are from the Vendée. There was much suffering there after the rising for the king. You may know of General Turreau's *colonnes infernales*?'

'Yes, it was some time ago, but we all know of it.'

'My father lost his estates there, after the fighting. We have been under suspicion ever since. My family will learn of the fighting here in Toulouse and they may fear the worst for me . . .' Her voice trailed off.

Hervey nodded in sympathy but was at a loss to see where this might lead.

'Sir, your army will, I think, have couriers whom it can trust. I wish to commit a letter to my people to you.'

He was not even sure where the Vendée was. He said that he supposed it must be possible, although he could not immediately think how. When she rectified his ignorance of the French seaboard he was even more sceptical. 'I will, of course, do all I can, Sister. I cannot say whether your letter might be carried by courier, however. And I fear that it is quite impossible for me to carry it in person since I do not suppose the regiment will march further than Bordeaux for our passage to England. And the Vendée will scarcely be on the marching route to Paris for those regiments which are to furnish the garrison there. Why cannot you entrust it to French hands, Sister?'

'Mr Hervey, there would be a price on any letter addressed to the comte de Chantonnay. Where may I find one of my own countrymen to trust at this time?'

The appeal was irresistible. 'Sister Maria, I will do all I can,' he said at length, 'though what that is I am not in the least sure.'

Sister Maria de Chantonnay could now at last rest; for an Englishman, an English officer, had given his word, and she owned that there was no more she could ask for – nor, indeed, *need* ask for. 'Mr Hervey,' she resumed, her aspect and tone becoming once again solemn, 'when I came here yesterday you had in your hands St Ignatius Loyola's *Spiritual Exercises*— Oh, but please sit down and rest your leg.' (She seemed suddenly to notice the slight awkwardness with which he stood.) 'Did you read sufficient of it?'

What constituted sufficiency in her mind he was not sure, but he reckoned it would be a demanding measure. 'In a cursory fashion,' he replied truthfully but guardedly.

'St Ignatius was a remarkable man, Mr Hervey. You will know of him, I feel sure?'

'Nothing but that he was founder of the Jesuits,' said Hervey flatly.

'Yes, indeed, he was,' she replied with the suggestion of a frown.

'And the Jesuits were expelled from Spain and Portugal half a century ago for political intriguing, and from your own country, too, Sister, were they not?' he added.

'Yes,' she sighed, 'and His Holiness dissolved their order, it is true – though some there remained in Russia, I believe. But St Ignatius *himself*, Mr Hervey: do you know anything of the man and his faith?'

Hervey admitted that he did not and shifted uncomfortably in the sedile. His leg was beginning to ache and, with apologies, he began loosening the bindings of his overalls, grateful for the opportunity of distraction.

Sister Maria kneeled on the bare stone floor, sitting back on her heels, oblivious to any sign of his discomfort other than his leg. 'Like you, St Ignatius of Loyola was a soldier,' she pressed, 'the younger son of a Spanish nobleman. I think you, too, perhaps are such a son, Mr Hervey – of a nobleman I mean.'

'No,' smiled Hervey, 'not a nobleman. My father is a clergyman, a minister of the Church of England.'

'Then a gentleman certainly,' she replied, reflecting his smile. 'St Ignatius was from the Basque country: you must have passed close to Loyola when you crossed the Pyrenees, Mr Hervey?' (But the name meant nothing to him.) 'He was wounded during the siege of Pamplona in the war with France – about 1520, I think. He made a long convalescence and read much of the life of Christ and of the saints, and he determined to give his life wholly to God's service. He gathered others about him, and they bound themselves by vow to become missionaries among the Mussulmen of the Holy Land. But when war barred their way to the east they offered their services instead to His Holiness.'

Hervey wondered where this could be leading, but thought better of trying to interrupt her homily.

'It was then that they resolved upon founding a religious order, the Society of Jesus, with an additional vow of placing themselves entirely at His Holiness's disposal. St Ignatius brought his soldier's discipline to the order, you see, Mr Hervey.'

'But I do *not* see, I am afraid, Sister. I do not understand your purpose. It is not unusual to find oneself, as a soldier, with wounds.'

She paused, and then startled him with her candour. 'Do you pray, Mr Hervey?'

'Yes, of course,' he replied.

'And do you meditate?'

He recoiled at the intrusion. But then, so disarming was her voice and manner, and so innocent her directness, that instead he found himself welcoming her solicitude. He knew full well that every officer maintained a pose – a mask – in which the worst effects of war were immured. But this pose, however habitual, was not maintained without effort, and with this nun he perceived the mask to be unnecessary: indeed, he felt in its slipping a glow, a warmth – a release even.

'I *think*, Sister. About certain things I think much. But meditation would imply some system, would it not?'

'Yes, and *The Spiritual Exercises* are just that.'

He could not but permit a smile at the adroitness with which she had brought the colloquy full circle. He was out-manoeuvred. It was now obvious to him how she had managed to survive both the reign of terror and the repression since! He freely confessed that the *Exercises* had engaged him, such as he had found the time to read – and, indeed, within the limits of his Latin, which was of late unpractised.

But she was no less ready for this self-deprecation. 'St Ignatius, also, found he had insufficient Latin at first. He took to studying with the schoolboys of Barcelona, no less. If you wish, I will conduct you through the exercises.'

Hervey hesitated. 'I am not sure . . . that is . . . I . . .' And then, with a note of resolution: '*Thank* you, Sister; I accept, with gratitude.'

Sister Maria made a small bow and said she would return later to begin the catechism.

But now that the stiff formality between them had eased he felt it possible at last to ask of *her* certain matters. 'Sister, a moment if you will. My regiment has so abruptly intruded on the peace of this place that . . . well, I think what I am trying to say is that we have not seen the like of your order hitherto. You seem more' – he paused again, searching for a word that would convey his meaning without disparaging others he had seen – 'more . . . *austere.*'

'Mr Hervey, even the Benedictine orders have fallen on hard times in France since the Revolution. The Church is mistrusted, and much of its earthly wealth is gone. We have been left alone here, I believe, because Toulouse was not a place of importance in the wars, but also because we are Carmelites. We pose no threat.'

That answered in large part the second question he would have asked, but he was still unsure of the nature of her order. 'I know of the *name* "Carmelite", Sister,' he continued, 'but nothing of your origins or rule.'

'Our roots are in Palestine, Mr Hervey, among the hermits of Mount Carmel. When the Holy Land was overrun by the Turks they moved west and began living in community, but always poor and solitary communities. Perhaps when you were in Spain you saw, or heard of, the city of Avila – near Madrid, I think?'

He knew where the city was but had not been there.

'Well, if you had been there you would have seen the place where our greatest saint, Teresa, lived – a little time after St Ignatius. She wrote a new rule for our order, and it is that which we follow here in Toulouse. She lived by the simplest of precepts.'

He nodded and made as if to ask a further question, but she instead raised a hand. 'Forgive me, Mr Hervey, but I must go now: there are duties for me as there are with you.'

He rose and made a bow after the fashion of the King's Germans. She smiled, and there was warmth in her eyes.


'Mr 'Ervey sir,' – how Johnson's attitude to aspirates stood in sharp contrast to Sister Maria's – 'adjutant wants to know straight away if tha wants t'go t'Staff Corps.'

Hervey sat up and rubbed his eyes. 'What time is it?'

'About seven o'clock. Tha's slept all night. Why didn't tha tell me about America?' he added in a distinctly resentful tone. 'Last thing I want to do's roust off there.'

'Because I heard only yesterday,' Hervey replied. 'In any case, I am not going. And why must you be so damnably crabby?'

Johnson chose to ignore the question (it was not difficult to see, sometimes, why Rawlings and Boyse had dispensed with his services, thought Hervey). 'Well, thank God for that, Mr 'Ervey, but wouldn't it 'ave meant promotion?'

'Private Johnson, may we revert to the usual practice of officer and groom in this regiment?' he replied with a wearied sigh.

'Suit thi'sen, Mr 'Ervey sir – I'll wait till I'm spoken to!'

The adjutant seemed less surprised than Johnson on hearing Hervey's decision. Edmonds would be disappointed, he said, but he really did not think the major had expected him to take the American option anyway. 'We'll just 'ave to sweat things out for a day or so until we hear about the petition,' was his verdict.

Edmonds had calculated that it would be three days, perhaps four, before they would know if the ruse had worked. It would take Slade a day fully to comprehend the options; it would take him another to come to terms with the indignity of the compromise, and it would be the third day before his brigade major would press him for an answer (if they did not forward it within three days, they would be in default of Advocate-General Larpent's standing orders for redresses, and to be in default of Larpent's instructions was to invite the wrath of Wellington himself). Sure enough, just before evening stables three days later, Heroys, the brigade major, himself arrived at the convent to offer the reciprocal arrangement that Edmonds had predicted. And Heroys knew full well whose stratagem it was: 'Oh, and by the by,' he added casually, with a smile that might just have been described as conspiratorial, 'I was surprised not to see young Hervey's name put forward for the Corps. You have heard, incidentally, that General Slade is being recalled to England?'

No, he had not! The most capital news it was, too, and Edmonds had no qualms about saying so. But Heroys's next news was not.

'The brigade is to commence the march for embarkation in five days' time,' he began. That in itself was not bad news; but they were not, as everyone had expected, to sail from Bordeaux, where shallow-draught claret-boats, which made excellent horse-transports, would be able to get right up from the mouth of the Gironde.

'Boulogne!' exclaimed Edmonds when Heroys revealed the port at which they would embark. 'For heaven's sake, man: that must be all of eight hundred miles!'

'Nearly nine,' replied Heroys, matter-of-fact.

'What in God's name is Slade thinking of?'

'Not his doing.'

'Cotton?'

'I should not think he was even asked.'

'But has he protested? Damn it, I'll go and see Wellington myself!'

'I think that would be foolhardy even by your standards, Edmonds. You have not exactly endeared yourself to Slade. I know I said that he has been recalled, but stick your neck out any further and . . . well, let us just say that in the present scheme of things I counsel extreme caution. Even Sir Hussey Vivian is having a hard time of things with Wellington.'

Edmonds accepted Heroys's advice with reluctance and had set about readying the Sixth for the long march north. Lankester forbade Hervey to take part in any active duty in the hope that his leg might thereby stand the journey. Instead he arranged for him to receive each morning a pile of French documents – of which there seemed no end in the *préfecture* – to scrutinize for anything of intelligence value. But they proved to be of a mundane nature, with nothing of military interest. His work was made less tedious, however, by the assistance of Sister Maria de Chantonnay whose Ignatian catechism had to be conducted in snatches while they sifted through endless titles and land deeds confiscated over the previous two decades. Come the third day she had, by degrees, revealed the circumstances of her life before entering the convent. Her fine English she had learned from her nurse, the daughter of Lancastrian recusants, who had lived with them in the Vendée. Hervey's own French, he told her, had been acquired in the same fashion, for his governess had been of an old Jansenist family from Alsace, and she had taught him German, too, although it was not quite so fluent perhaps as his French. At this Sister Maria laughed, and mocked his Alsatian accent: 'But you would almost certainly pass for a Frenchman if ever it suited you, Mr Hervey.'

'An unlikely requirement now, I think, Sister.'

And she agreed. 'I think so. I surely pray that there will be no more fighting between our countries. And what of you, then, Mr Hervey – what are your intentions?'

Only three days before, he had rounded on Johnson for wanting to know his business, yet now he was content to tell all to this nun – about his family, about his joining the Sixth and his hopes for promotion, and how these were suddenly in doubt with the news of his brother's death.

'It seems very strange to me, Mr Hervey, that a man must pay for his position in the Army. Any man with aptitude in France may become an officer: it does not turn on a question of money.'

'No, sister, it *is* strange, and I for one would not long defend it, but it is supposed that it has its merits – besides, that is, making the Army a good deal cheaper for Parliament.'

'What might be these merits, Mr Hervey?' she asked sceptically.

'Well, I think if you knew of the dread in which any return to the late Commonwealth is still held in our country you would own that by having officers with so tangible a stake in the system there was less chance of their throwing in with some dictator.'

'You are suggesting that such a system in France might have stayed a republic?'

'France is not England, Sister, but such a notion is not infeasible.'

'Is this notion not at heart dishonourable, though? Is it money *only* which commands loyalty in England? Would not an oath suffice?'

'Sometimes the best of men are subverted by evil ones who are able to confuse them as to where their duty lies.'

'That is well said, Mr Hervey,' and she laughed.

He liked her laugh. He admired her mind and her soul, but her laugh made both accessible. 'Sister, do you suppose there might be anything in these documents of the slightest import to matters of state?' he asked, reflecting the smile.

'Not especially,' she replied. 'In fact, not at all, I should say.' Her look turning to one of conspiracy.

'Then I believe we might permit ourselves some respite. Would you like to take a turn about the horse lines?'

'Indeed, I should,' she replied, still smiling.


Never, perhaps, had Sister Maria de Chantonnay expected the cloisters of the Convent of St Mary of Magdala to throng with so great a number of men, let alone horses. As she and Hervey made their way through the lines they had to step this way and that around piles of hay and soiled straw, and buckets of water (for the watering call had sounded ten minutes before, and the troopers were working in relays from the well in the courtyard). Stopping here and there when Hervey thought there was some point of interest with a particular animal, they were paid no more attention than if they had been at a fair. C Troop were evidently to furnish some escort, for a dozen troopers were in the throes of saddling up under the supervision of the troop corporal.

'This seems a most elaborate routine, Mr Hervey,' said Sister Maria, watching a trooper folding saddle blankets.

'Yes, the saddles are different from any you will have seen, most likely. The necessity is to keep all the rider's weight, and that of his equipment, well clear of the spine – as, indeed, it ought to be with any saddle. But we cannot afford the luxury of measuring a saddle to individual horses, so each is built up to suit. Look' – he picked up a crude wooden saddle-frame – 'the saddle itself is composed simply of two arches joined by pieces of wood called side-boards. This is then placed over as many blankets on the horse's back as is required by its particular conformation.' Sister Maria nodded. 'How many does this one take?' he asked the nearest trooper.

'This un's broad-backed, sir – needs six,' replied the man.

'If the saddle isn't set up right, then the horse will have a sore back within the hour,' added Hervey. 'And that is the gravest source of our trouble – that and poor feed.'

'But', said Sister Maria, looking puzzled, 'you cannot possibly sit in such a saddle? It seems so . . . crude.'

Hervey smiled. 'No, Sister, a sheepskin goes over the top of it, secured by a surcingle. We officers have a shabracque, too, for reviews – you will know of shabracques?'

'Oh, yes, as had the warhorses of the knights – but not very practical, I should suppose?'

'No, which is why we no longer take them on campaign. But see also, the holstered pistols have to be strapped to the front arch of the saddle, along with the rolled cloak, and the carbine boot strapped to the offside, and the sword to the nearside. It is something of an art,' he added.

'So it indeed seems, Mr Hervey,' she replied, 'but tell me, you have spoken before of troops and squadrons in the same breath, as if they were one. How is this so?'

'No, they are not one, Sister, though I understand your confusion,' he began. 'A troop may number up to a hundred or so and is commanded by a captain. Usually there are six such troops in each regiment. When there is a royal review both the colonel and the lieutenant-colonel, and the major, too, would each take command of a squadron. The squadron would comprise two troops, and each squadron would carry a guidon. But on campaign it is the lieutenant-colonel who commands, and the senior captains each command a squadron, with command of their own troop devolving impermanently to their senior lieutenant. It sounds perhaps a little complicated but it works well.'

'Oh, evidently so,' she smiled, as the dragoon they were watching finished saddling. 'You fit the head-harness last?' she added with a note of surprise.

'Because it gives time for the animal to adjust to the girth, which can then be tightened before mounting. The breastplate must, of course, be fitted at the same time as the saddle, then the crupper and last the bridle. This is the new 1812 pattern,' he said, holding up a practical-looking piece of harness. 'Much better than that we had before, but it can still be the devil of a job to fit in the dark, especially with cold fingers. This rosette here on the crossed face-pieces must be set dead between the eyes, and just below the bridge, or the orderly corporal will round on a man once daylight reveals otherwise!'

'It is a handsome bridle, Mr Hervey, for sure. But what is this chain across the top?'

He gave a faint smile of satisfaction. 'That is an additional device which we ourselves – in the Sixth I mean – have made. A sabre-cut through the headpiece would mean the bridle falls away and the rider would lose control of his mount. The chain prevents that.'

She turned and looked at him intently, and then spoke more softly than hitherto. 'You are proud of your regiment, not just of your army, are you not, Mr Hervey?'

He seemed surprised. 'Oh *yes*, it is *everything*!'


Their parting, a week later, was a curious affair. In the days that had followed their visit to the cloister stalls Hervey had looked forward to subsequent meetings with increasing anticipation. The routine each day had been the same. She would first dress his wound (removing the sutures when the time came). Then followed several hours of sifting papers, and then a half-hour's catechism (but of no great earnestness). In the afternoon they would walk together – further each day as his leg regained its strength. So that, as the time came for

Boulogne, there had formed between them a considerable bond, a respect, an affection.

Only once had he felt any desire to stay her enquiries. One afternoon, as they walked in the orchard, she had asked him if there were anyone waiting for him at home, to which he had replied that in war a soldier must have no such ties. It was a conviction not unheard of in France, she countered, adding, however, that the denial of any part of God's creation was innately sinful.

Already he had been able to tell her that he could deliver the letter to her father in person since the Sixth were to march to Boulogne through the Vendée, and her evident pleasure brought a smile to his lips. So, when they met on the morning that the regiment was to leave, her apparent resumption of the formality of their earlier meetings surprised him, and he felt awkward with what he now intended. He had had one of the armourers fit a shako plate to a piece of ebony to make a paperweight, its cross-pattée seeming especially appropriate. 'To remember the regiment by, Sister,' he explained uneasily as he gave it her. 'It is the Garter cross, from our country's most honoured order, with the regiment's numerals in the centre.'

' "*Honi soit qui mal y pense*," ' she said thoughtfully, yet with a smile.

'Just so,' he managed to croak.

'I was happy that we were able to read St Ignatius together, Mr Hervey,' she began, 'but there was so little time to begin the discipline of his way. You will not, I think, have time or occasion much to ponder directly on these hours, but there will come a time . . .' She paused, as if to assess whether or not she might complete the prophecy. 'There is a desire in you, a spiritual desire, as there is in all of us, and I have composed this vade-mecum for you,' she continued gently, pulling from her pocket the diminutive volume. 'It will tell you how St Ignatius himself might speak to you.'

Hervey took the primer without a word and opened it. Sister Maria's handwriting, a compact, almost medieval script, filled its pages, the effort it represented apparent in an instant. He did what he could to find the right words, but he knew that he failed. 'I hope we may meet again, Sister,' he added, and this perhaps said what his more formal civilities failed to.

'And I, too,' she replied, 'though is it not ironic that our meeting was in war, and peace makes its prolongation impossible, or its repeating unlikely?'

Hervey smiled, awkwardly, and was about to hold out his hand when, on an impulse, it seemed, she reached into her pocket again to retrieve a gold signet ring with a blue silk handkerchief knotted to it.

'Sir, I have one more kindness to beg. This ring is the de Chantonnay seal. It has been with me for safe keeping these past five years. The title papers of my father's estates were taken by the revolutionaries, and if he is to recover his inheritance he will need the seal now that the war is ended. Please take it to him, but please on no account place it in anyone's hands but his. On *no* account. Better it goes back to England with you than risk its loss.'

Time was running out for their farewell. The ring begged certain questions (and he would have wished to address them), but it was no hardship to carry a ring as well as the letter. 'So be it, Sister – I shall do as you bid. We must hope that I find your father home: he will have a long journey to Wiltshire otherwise.'

'We must risk that at least,' she replied with an empty expression. And then at last she smiled – not the wide, sparkling smile of their earlier hours together, but warm enough.

He reached out his hand, fully this time, and she took it. 'Goodbye, Sister. And thank you.'

'God bless you and go with you, Mr Hervey.' She rose on her bare toes and kissed his cheek. 'And, please, the ring – you must keep it safe and give it into no-one's hand but my father's.'

# CHAPTER THREE
# THE DIVIDEND OF PEACE

---

*St George's Day*

Since the raising of the regiment, on 23 April 1760 (to consolidate the triumph of the gallant, and late, General Wolfe over the French on the Heights of Abraham), every man of the 6th Light Dragoons had worn a red rose in his head-dress on St George's Day. Even during the worst of the recent campaigns the Sixth had maintained the tradition, and that morning bud-roses were distributed at muster, as was the custom, by the commanding officer. But at ten o'clock, after watering parade, the major broke with tradition (and thereby instituted a new and cherished custom), for, as the regiment mustered one last time at the Convent of St Mary of Magdala, Edmonds dismounted at the appearance of the elderly abbess and with great gallantry presented her with his rose. And by the time the Sixth had reached the city's north gate a remarkable number of roses had been plucked from shakos and handed to women of the town – so many, in fact, that Edmonds began to wonder in what state of discipline his regiment had truly been during its ostensible period of interior economy those several past weeks.

Hervey's rose did not remain in his shako beyond the convent's courtyard, for as his troop formed threes and wheeled into column he saw Sister Maria at an open window near the arched entrance. Breaking ranks and trotting over, he stood at full stretch in the stirrups and presented her with the deep-red bloom whose petals were no longer primly clasped. And she in turn presented him with a smile equally open, and a sign of benediction.

'I cannot say that *I* am sorry to be leaving this place,' said Laming as Hervey rejoined his file. 'None of this sisterhood ever looked like praying with their knees upward.'

Hervey sighed. His fellow cornet held the vow of chastity in scant regard after Spain. Laming's own rose was gone by the time their troop had left the elegant square outside the convent, and in truth he had need of three more before they were clear of the city walls. And as they left this place, whose welcome had been as warm as it had been surprising, their minds turned once more to those who were unable to join that final march. The bones of 150 dragoons, and more, lay in pits, or whitening on bare hillsides between Corunna and Toulouse, for it had been four years since the regiment had left Southampton, and of the 600 or so who had landed in the Peninsula that day in May 1810 almost half had been killed, or wounded, or else evacuated home sick – broken men with scant likelihood of entire recovery. Some of these invalids might by now have acquired a skill with which a cripple could eke out a living. Others might have become in-pensioners at one of the veterans' establishments. Many more would be reduced to begging in the streets, desperate to avoid the workhouse. Some would, without doubt, have found themselves back in the jails whence they had been all but impressed, or to avoid which they had elected to enlist – 'paying with the drum'. The horses had fared even worse. There were scarcely four score of the original 600 (and a dozen more of these would fail to finish this march): 'You would have thought that someone in the Treasury might have been discomposed,' said Hervey. 'What economy is it to deny us a new saddle at forty shillings, only to have us replace the wretched animal itself a month later at thirty pounds when its back is done?'

'My dear Hervey, you and I know that our boast as a nation of horsemasters amounts to little more than that a few studgrooms know their business,' Laming replied, taking Hervey aback by the unusual candour of his opinion.

If it had been left to Edmonds, then further loss might at

least have been avoided, but the decision to march to the Channel ports had, in his view, been the final testimony that no-one cared in the least measure for man or beast now that Bonaparte had been brought down, and his anger had been profound and brooding as a consequence. Had it not been for Barrow, so rumour in the squadrons held, Edmonds would have knocked down the staff captain in Wellington's headquarters (which he had visited in spite of Heroys's advice to the contrary) when that officer loftily dismissed him with the explanation that they were marching to Boulogne to spare the horses the distress of the passage through the Bay of Biscay. But why they should now be taking so indirect a route, avoiding the towns and adding more than fifty leagues to the journey, was wholly beyond him, and not even the most languorous staff officer could advance a plausible reason. The sullenness of the country people was in marked contrast to what they had become accustomed to in Spain, and indeed Toulouse, but they hardly constituted a threat. Rests and bivouacs – and these were few enough – were solitary affairs indeed. Only in the Vendée was there any respite. The wretched condition of the towns and villages in the other *départements* had brought the regiment hateful glowers. Or that at least was the interpretation placed upon them: appre- hensiveness might equally have been the reason, for if the Grande Armée had so fearful a reputation for rapaciousness in its own country, then why should the British be expected to be any better? Once or twice the Sixth had the opportunity to demonstrate their good faith when, outpacing the commissary waggons, they had to find their own forage, and in doing so astounded the corn merchants by exchanging properly receipted promissory notes rather than merely making off with the feed. But as to how the population truly regarded them the Sixth were at a loss. The wretched condition of the people was in part the result of the Royal Navy's complete and utter blockade of the Continent, but Bonaparte's war taxes had made greater ravages. It was not the British who had ordered the *levée en masse*, putting every man, woman and child, sick or healthy, to war-work intermittently for the past twenty years. The people might have complained about the infamous *gabelle* and the sundry other extortions of the *ancien régime*, but what had revolution profited the peasantry if the evidence now were anything to judge by?

In the Vendée, at least, it appeared that this was understood. There, things looked even more wretched at times, but royalist colours flew from the public buildings and from a good many private houses, and the regiment was made welcome. The brigade was permitted a four-day billet, and the Sixth quartered themselves in the little town of Clisson, near Nantes. And in Clisson they were presented with evidence for the first time that they might indeed be liberators rather than conquerors, for while there was much work for the troopers, and even more for the farriers, the officers found the hospitality of the *noblesse* most generous.

Nor was it a hospitality born of plenitude, for there had been an intermittent reign of terror since the uprising. The château to which the officers had been invited on the second evening had little remaining of the fine paintings and furnishings that had once filled it. Its master and his *châtelaine*, the former of whose three brothers, and their two sons, had died by the guillotine or the firing squad during the past two decades, had dug up their plate that very morning, the first time it had seen daylight during that same period. But the red wine of the Loire valley had filled the elegant silver decanters of the unearthed service, and these in turn had kept the officers' glasses full throughout the night until the adjutant, at Edmonds's bidding, had called the party away to its unsteady attendance at morning stables.

Hervey had missed this entertainment, however. He had ridden some thirty miles eastward, to the Château de Chantonnay, in a fruitless attempt to deliver Sister Maria's letter and ring into her father's hand, learning as he arrived that the family had left for Paris the day before. He was glad at least that he would not have occasion to describe to her what he found, for the house was a veritable ruin. From the one man who did not run away on seeing him, a crabbed old gardener from the former estate, he learned that the family had been living in what had been the stables after the house had been requisitioned and turned into a button-making factory. Sister Maria de Chantonnay's injunction had been uncompromising, however: the ring was to be given to no-one but her father in person, so all that Hervey was able to do was hand her letter to the *vieillard*, whom he hoped was a faithful enough remnant of the household. The ring would go with him to England after all.

That four-day billet was indeed a labour: 'I've fair pissed me tallow dawn to dusk since we stopped 'ere, Mr 'Ervey,' complained Johnson on the last morning. The farriers had re-shod every horse, and the dandy brushes had been hard at work removing the vestiges of winter coats. There had been green fodder to cut – there was no commissary provision on the march – and saddlery and harness had been stripped down, cleaned and mended. But there had been opportunities, too, for diversion; and when the regiment left on the fifth day it was amidst more emotion, even, than at Toulouse. Indeed, the final muster bore so little resemblance to a military parade, so numerous and pressing were the onlookers, with buttons, rings, notes and promises being tearfully exchanged, that the exasperation of the adjutant and Mr Lincoln was plain to behold. Edmonds himself was so alarmed at the suspension of good order and military discipline that once under way he trotted the regiment hard for four hours on and off to put bite back into them.

The country through which they passed subsequently was never as pretty, and in no degree as friendly, as the Vendée. They were jeered and spat at in Le Mans, and stones were thrown at them in Rouen, although the flats of a few troopers' swords exacted swift retribution. The flats, mind, for the British trooper could possess an uncommon magnanimity. Prussians, Austrians, Russians – all seemed to perceive it their duty to avenge their national dishonour, a dishonour which thereby became a personal quest for vengeance, and a vengeance which might therefore be exacted indiscriminately. Beyond the immediate right to quench his prodigious thirst the *British* trooper cared not overmuch for loot, unless it could buy more drink. Wanton destruction and rape sometimes followed from too much of it, but terror and pillage were not instruments of war or conditions of service, and, though it was of little consolation, those of the fair sex who were taken in such moments were not ravished with method, the Sabine way. It was true enough that Britain had never been invaded by Bonaparte, but the ranks of the Sixth (and the Sixth were in this respect not untypical) were scarcely made up of idealists. They were not inspired by royalist fervour in the way that so many French were inspired by revolutionary fervour. There were upright and loyal subjects of King George in the ranks: there were as many, probably more, who were the flotsam and jetsam of the realm, the sweepings of the alehouses and the streets, and occasionally of the prisons. But they were under authority; and under that authority, these men, these very dregs of the country, comported themselves with no little chivalry. They did not habitually put to the sword prisoners of war and civilians caught in a siege. And they were more likely to share a scarce canteen of water with a wounded enemy than do him further harm. Authority could make of them tolerably fine fellows: Hervey could not conceive of a life without them.

At Boulogne the regiment had two further days' rest while the commissary officers arranged their loading in three transports, all merchantmen. One was a particularly filthy Kent coaler in which Edmonds flatly refused to embark men or horses until a working party from the town gaol had scrubbed its holds. 'Damn it, man!' he had thundered to the startled embarkation officer, 'we had better to take us off at Corunna, even!' And the regiment had smiled. They liked to hear the major's ranting occasionally. It seemed to reassure them that at bottom there was nothing to worry about; for if the major raved, then it must be because things might be changed thereby, and if things might be changed then the situation could not be so bad. Few would have allowed the thought that such explosions might mask Edmonds's growing sense of powerlessness in what he perceived to be the regiment's imminent betrayal.

On the second morning there was no sign of rage. Despite his efforts at cheeriness, however, there was an edge to him which revealed that his better spirits were indeed an effort. And everyone knew why, for the news that orders for their eventual destination had arrived with the tide had spread even quicker than would orders for pay parade.

'Canterbury, my boys,' he told the assembled regiment as breezily as he could at muster, 'though to what purpose I am yet unaware. The Fourth are for the depot, too, and they have no inkling why, either.'

Gloom then settled on the squadrons, the like of which Hervey had not seen since being ordered to abandon all but their side-arms before wading out to the ships in Corunna bay. For the depot, surely, could mean no other but that they were to disband forthwith. Fane, the new brigadier, visited the lines soon afterwards but he knew no more of the purpose, nor could he see any more sense in what they presumed to be the purpose, than anyone in the Sixth.

'I wish the marquess were here, or even Sir Stapleton Cotton,' he said. 'For sure *they* would have been told more. I think it wicked that men – men with families about whom they have heard nothing in years – and officers with affairs overdue for attendance, should be treated in so ill-considered a fashion.' They were fine enough sentiments but of little help, concluded the cornets at mess that evening, and the gloom remained as the Sixth began embarking just before noon the following day.

There were few in the regiment with any expertise in embarking horses. Only those who had been there at Southampton, four years earlier, had even seen it done. But the march to Boulogne did at least have one advantage: it meant that they could embark direct from the wharf rather than by lighter – a perilous enough adventure at the best of times. Nevertheless, the operation went as smoothly as Edmonds could have wished. The horses were first led by the collar-rein (saddles and bridles off) to the side of the transports, and here their dragoons placed a sling made of sacking around each. Johnson was one of the first to protest that it must end in disaster for any of the bloods, but the slings were securer than they perhaps looked, reaching from the withers to the flanks and with breastplate and breeching also of sacking to prevent the horse from slipping out. Then, under the watchful eye of the quartermasters, the dragoons fastened two strong pieces of wood on the top of the sling to stretch it out, in the centre of which a hole had been made to put the tackle hook through. At the given signal a team of convicts from the local prison hoisted the sling aloft and the horse disappeared into the ship's hold. Embarking was laborious work, by any account, but it kept minds from the ill news of the morning.

It went on until a little before six, when at last they were able to set sail on the ebb tide. And whatever fate might await them in Canterbury, the gloom was by degrees overtaken by the growing anticipation of returning home. As the three transports, led by a frigate, passed the harbour mole, the regiment's spirits lifted visibly with the fresh offshore breeze which filled out the sails and began to throw spray into the faces of those on the weather rail. And they were, too, the first regiment to get away.

Hervey watched the frigate take up station a quarter-league to windward, her hands deftly altering sail, the line of her single gundeck in the black hull, a brilliant yellow band broken by the black hatches of the gunports – *Nelson-style* – betokening a defiant confidence. A frigate was a world apart: she sailed independently of the line; she passed both land and fleets, ghost-like, on secret missions, a lonely but independent command which, Hervey reflected, was exercised by men no older than him. That he must lodge that six hundred pounds soon with the regimental agents, before any more talk of disbandments curtailed the vacancies, was never more certain in his mind. And then somehow he must find two thousand pounds more for the captaincy. But *two thousand pounds* – he almost laughed out loud at the sum! And, in any case, did he not first have to discover his father's wishes?

Turning towards the larboard side to see how the other transports were faring, he saw Edmonds standing at the rail. There was a more distant look to him than Hervey had yet seen, and it would have been easy – prudent even – to let him alone. But if companionship in the Sixth were to mean anything, then this was not the moment to let differences of rank intrude. Nevertheless Hervey approached him cautiously. 'Good evening, sir. Do you know, I have calculated that we have marched almost three thousand leagues since landing in Portugal.'

Edmonds at first made no reply save for several slow nods of the head. When at length he did speak, the reply took him aback. 'Matthew, those three thousand leagues have been added to your life; they have been taken away from mine.'

It was a reply so far removed from his image of Edmonds, an image shared in large measure by the whole regiment, that he could scarcely begin to conceive of its cause. Ill-tempered and violently suspicious of authority though Edmonds might be, he was first, foremost and for ever a soldier. In their six years of campaigning in the Peninsula, before and after Corunna, no matter how appalling the conditions or how desperate the situation, Edmonds had shown no emotion beyond explosive but short-lived anger – or, indeed, simple kindness. Did he now really abhor those years?

'What will you do when we reach England, sir?' Hervey asked, searching for a different tack on which he might lift the major's spirits, though he could hardly have chosen a worse one.

'Once I have settled the regiment in Canterbury and discovered what in God's name those lickspittles in the Horse Guards are intending – and I have no doubt that a grateful Parliament are at this very moment exacting their dividend from the peace which so many good men have bought with their lives – well, once I know what our great nation plans for us, I shall write a dispatch for the colonel and Lord George, hand over to Captain Lankester as fast as I decently can, and go and see Margaret and my girls,' he replied, his tone increasingly defiant. And then, turning and walking towards his deck cabin, he added, 'If they're still alive.'

Hervey might at that moment have begun a long (but utterly futile) brooding on this unaccountable change in Edmonds's humour, had it not been for the appearance of Serjeant Strange on deck. The admirable Strange, ever formal and correct, was still as much an enigma to Hervey as the day they met when the regiment sailed for Portugal on the first campaign. Strange had left Southwold, and its fishing fleet, the year after the guillotine had been set up in Paris, to enlist in the Sixth, who were encamped nearby at Ipswich. He was the best swordsman and shot in the regiment, even better than RSM Lincoln, and he had passed out of the riding school quicker than anyone in the riding-master's memory (until Hervey's own skill had both impressed and dismayed the RM in equal measure). These accomplishments would in them-selves have been sufficient to hold in awe both officers and other ranks, but in addition Strange held a curious authority because no-one, but *no-one*, had ever heard him swear – not an obscenity, nor even a faintly indecent remark, not an oath, nor the mildest profanity even. He was a temperance Methodist, though he would preach at no-one. He kept his own company and permitted no-one to become close. No-one, that is, but Serjeant Armstrong – Armstrong, the hard-drinking, frequently foul-mouthed ex-miner. Armstrong was no Methodist: he was not even baptized. What they saw in each other had long been a matter for speculation in the officers' mess. The simple attraction of opposite natures seemed an inadequate explanation. There were some who said that the reason for their enlistment might reveal a cause. But neither man seemed the sort to be afraid of the deep mine or the deep sea, nor the sort to run from some domestic sorrow. Besides, Strange was married, was he not? Hervey thought meanly of himself for not knowing more about both of them, though Strange would not have volunteered the smallest piece of intelligence, he felt sure. In any case, Hervey would always recall his first troop-leader's advice: *Do not get too close – sending them to their deaths will be all the harder.* A humane,

101

if cynical, doctrine, it had been sound enough counsel for a young cornet in his greenness. Perhaps that advice was as good now as it had been, but Hervey could no longer bring himself to believe so.

'Good evening, Mr Hervey sir,' Strange said quietly, and with a relaxed salute. 'The major looked thoughtful.'

'Yes, he was thinking of home.'

'Major Edmonds was my lieutenant when I joined, sir. He and his lady taught me to write.'

This was possibly the first time that Hervey had exchanged any talk with Strange that was not strictly related to duty – certainly the first time he could recall – and even after six years' campaigning he did not feel at his ease doing so. While many a dragoon liked the attention of the officers, Strange seemed to have no need of their company. Or, that is, as little need of theirs as any other's. And soon, despite his initial discomfort, Hervey could not but feel a warm glow at this initiation of intimacy.

'What will you do when we get to Canterbury, Serjeant Strange?'

'I have not seen my wife for nigh on six years, either,' he answered without a trace of emotion, 'nor my father or mother.'

It was the same mellow Suffolk again, curiously soothing, reassuring. Hervey probed gently. 'What will you do if the regiment disbands?'

'I have two years to a pension,' he replied resolutely. 'I reckon they would pay me off fairly, but I would have liked my own troop, and then to be a quartermaster if Colonel Irvine wanted me.'

Hervey would ordinarily have shared Strange's trust that Parliament would treat fairly with them, but Edmonds's cynicism these past weeks had begun to erode that confidence. He wondered how many other good men would be lost to the king's service in this way – indeed, whether he himself would be placed on half-pay – and he shuddered at the thought in the cool evening breeze. The intimacy was fleeting, however, for Serjeant Strange suddenly stepped back, as if the act of so doing were necessary to break that intimacy, and took his leave formally saying he had to be about his duty below. Hervey thought of staying on deck awhile but instead he, too, went below, to the cabin he was to share with three other cornets. There was a half-hearted attempt to carouse, with wine they had brought aboard, but they were all more tired than they had cared to admit. In less than an hour they were happy to turn in, and Hervey slept tolerably well as the ship gently pitched and rolled in the Channel's swell.

He was awakened at dawn by cheering from the upper deck and straightaway went up to see the cause. The bows and fore-rails were packed with troopers peering towards the land three miles distant, the chalk-white cliffs reflecting the first streaks of daylight. Though few of these men, if any, had ever seen those cliffs before, they were an image of England as powerful as the standard of St George itself. Within the hour the transports were reefing sail in Dover's outer harbour and the towing-boats were approaching to take them in to berth on the morning tide. The frigate had left them moments before, firing one of its eighteen-pounders in farewell and breaking out what seemed like every yard of remaining sail so as to take her in a fast turn back towards France – *so* fast that she heeled over at a breathtaking angle with the wind, exaggerating her speed still further. 'Who is she?' Hervey asked one of the transport's crew.

'*Nisus*, mister,' replied the hand, with evident respect for the name.

'*Nisus*, was she not the frigate that—'

'Ay,' said the man before he could finish. 'It was 'er an' *Euryalus* that shadowed them French durin' the night before Trafalgar and signalled the rest of the fleet to follow. Blue light ev'ry hour if standing to the southward or the Straits; three quick guns ev'ry hour if headin' westward!'

'You sound as though you might have been there?'

'Was *I*, sir,' he replied with passion, and with the same vowels as Armstrong. 'I watched them lights all night from the nest o' *Royal Sovereign* – one of Admiral Collingwood's "Tars of the Tyne", I were. If Cap'n Blackwood's an' yon frigate 'ad lost them French, it would've been different next day.' And then he chuckled and held up the stump of his right arm: 'This would've been a mite longer for a start!'

How Bonaparte had thought he might defeat a navy with men like this, or an army of men like those now crowding the fore-rail, Hervey could only marvel. The Corsican had, it seemed to him, failed to heed his own dictum that the fighting spirit of a man was worth three times the weapons he bore. And Bonaparte had paid the price for underestimating that spirit in *these* men, for sure.

# CHAPTER FOUR
# 'THE COMMANDER-IN-CHIEF DIRECTS . . .'

---

*Dover, Sunday, 12 June*

Before the transports were berthed a torrential downpour had begun, making disembarkation of both horses and men more than usually hazardous. And in the middle of this operation Edmonds found himself confronted by an envoy from the institution he reviled only fractionally less than Parliament. Even above the noise of the rain and the occasional peal of thunder his voice could be heard haranguing the unfortunate messenger from the Horse Guards.

'Cork! Immediately? What in God's name . . . ?'

And then another peal of thunder, deafening this time, making it impossible for the onlookers to catch the precise terms in which Edmonds was expressing his opinion of the Horse Guards' administration. The messenger, a young Coldstream ensign, stood rigid in blank astonishment.

Joseph Edmonds's inclinations mattered not the slightest, however. The orders were explicit: 'The Commander-in-Chief directs that a regiment of light dragoons be dispatched with all urgency . . .' So the first to land were to be re-embarked as soon as was expedient, and were to sail for Cork – tomorrow possibly, or the day after, just as soon as transports could be found. Why Cork? he asked. Was there yet more trouble there? To which the ensign replied that, from what he read in *The Times* and *The Daily Courant*, there was trouble periodically everywhere.

By prodigious efforts, and not a little cursing of innkeepers and proprietors of livery stables (for even in this busiest of ports the Sabbath seemed to be kept with remarkable fastidiousness), Edmonds and the quartermasters managed to get covered standing, and on straw, for all the horses, and billets for the dragoons. Hervey found himself on picket once more, and it was well past midnight by the time he finished his rounds, so scattered about the town was the regiment. The officers' lodgings were in a decent enough hotel; and there, a little before one o'clock, he found Edmonds sitting at a writing-table in the drawing room, quite alone.

'Hervey, come over here,' he said without looking up. 'Take some of this Madeira and sit down. I have an assignment for you.'

Though he was happy to be sharing Edmonds's company again – and by this time the major seemed truly to have regained his usual robust spirits – Hervey would in truth have preferred his bed, for there were only three hours to his next rounds.

'These dispatches enumerate our losses and the action required for amendment to our current parlous condition, as well as sundry recommendations in respect of those officers who remain. You are to convey them to Lord George Irvine and to the colonel. To their London houses, that is: I cannot vouch that they will be there, but the dispatches can best be forwarded thence without delay. I want you then to take the leave that is owing to you and deal with that outstanding family business. I want no second thoughts in the future about taking the lieutenancy.'

The comfortable chair, the warm fire, the Madeira and Edmonds's confidential manner – Hervey might have nodded, but the mention of home was too much, and thoughts of family rushed in on him as water through a sluice-gate.

'Matthew, do you hear?' said Edmonds when at length he saw that he did not have his attention.

Hervey blinked and looked surprised. 'Sir! I—'

'For heaven's sake man, try and keep with me,' he drawled. And then, with a smile: 'You might have missed the most felicitous part: I want you to wait, at home, for the colonel to be in touch in respect of the matters I have laid before him. It might be a month or so, but that is no matter – I'm sure Wiltshire must have some charms to amuse you, though I cannot think of any myself. And we will see you in Ireland, *perhaps*, before autumn is out.'

Hervey detected no more in Edmonds's '*perhaps*' than a passing reference to the delay he might expect in the colonel's expediting (or otherwise) the major's recommendations; he acknowledged the instructions with a simple bow of the head and a smile.

'Oh, and while you are about things in London you may go and lodge the purchase money with the regimental agents,' added Edmonds in a tone which indicated that he wanted no reply, only compliance.

The inrush of home thoughts would have made sleep impossible. Besides, Edmonds seemed in no haste to dismiss him, and now that the major's spirits were truly restored it became once more a pleasure to tarry in his soldierly company – and it emerged that the restoration of those spirits was the result of two separate items of intelligence. The first, though Hervey would have made no wager that Edmonds would have given it that priority, was that all his family were well: a remount corporal from the Canterbury depot had arrived earlier that evening with several letters from Margaret Edmonds, written over a period of six months, marked 'to await return'. With a prescience as to the course of the campaign which many in the Horse Guards might have envied, she had concluded that once the army had entered the Pyrenees the mails would be erratic. Better, therefore, to consign them to the one establishment that years of following the drum told her she could rely on – the regiment's own depot. Edmonds admired her logic yet despaired of her want of perceptivity, however, for surely the most favourable course would have been to send him the letters direct, and insure against her concerns by sending duplicates to Canterbury? In any case, it mattered not now: she was in good health. As were his daughters, who must surely during his absence have passed from childhood – and charmingly, he trusted.

The second piece of intelligence surprised him, but bore him equal relief: there would be no immediate disbandments in the cavalry. 'I had forgotten about the damned Irish, God bless 'em!' he laughed, pouring Hervey and himself yet another glass of Madeira. 'And the magistrates here, too, are terrified of rick-burners and machine-breakers. There are, it seems, formed bands intent on disturbing the peace. God bless 'em, too! Parliament seems to have come to its senses, though when they'll ever see real sense and establish a proper constabulary I could not begin to suppose. So the returning heroes will have to keep order – which means we shall not be heroes for long! Still, it's an ill wind . . .'

An ill wind indeed, thought Hervey, for he had no love for the idea of being a mounted constable, even in Ireland. He no longer, if he had truly ever, expected to be treated as a hero, but here was surely the quickest way to universal opprobrium. Yet there were felicities at that moment which displaced such concerns. Home thoughts again ran freely, for he had not seen the parsonage in Horningsham these past four years, and his last visit, in the wake of the evacuation from Corunna, had been fleeting. At first the thoughts were as a swirling flood, but then they began to order themselves, and soon, with perfect clarity, he perceived in what fashion this return must be. To his father he must give account of his means and intentions, and hope that these might be congruent with what the changed circumstances demanded. To his mother he must needs be all that a mother expects, and be wholly tolerant of her incomprehension. And his sister? He longed simply that he and she might be what they once were to each other.

Johnson was the first to feel the effects of Hervey's wakefulness when at four-thirty he received a shake from the picket and an order to report to the Marine hotel. Here there followed a half-hour of instructions, and a good deal of what might have passed for discourse, before Hervey felt confident he could leave his horses for the first time in his groom's care. Barrow would for sure have counted Johnson's part in that dialogue as verging on the mutinous; but, then, Barrow would not have apprehended the reason for the groom's disquiet – and nor did Hervey: 'Look, Johnson, I grant you that there is every right to be discouraged that you, too, are not to go home, but how can I trust Jessye to anyone else after all this time?'

Johnson looked bemused. 'Mr 'Ervey, there's nowt for me in Sheffield – tha knows 'ave no fam'ly.' Johnson always bore his workhouse origins with a perverse pride.

'Then why are you so vexed with the notion of going to Cork?' asked Hervey, with a look of equal astonishment.

'Because without thee there I'll get the poke, an' be back in t'ranks quick as lightning!'

Hervey assured him that this need not be the case, that he would speak with the adjutant. 'But you might try to help yourself by being less . . . less *obstinate*.'

'Obstinate? *Me?*' began his groom, but Hervey rapidly deflected the challenge.

'You will at least be glad that we are not to disband.'

'Bloody 'ell, ay, sir. It'd be t'pit or t'foundries fer me otherwise.'

And the coalpits or the steelworks, Hervey knew full well, would mean in all probability an earlier grave than would service with the Sixth now. 'You might have found employment as a footman,' he tried light-heartedly. 'There are some fine houses thereabouts, are there not?'

Johnson looked genuinely affronted. 'I'll be thy doggy, but I'll be damned if I'll be a bloody fart-catcher!'

The Angel inn, where Cornet Hervey hoped to find a seat on a London-bound coach, was crowded and noisy. And he had to endure it for two days since every seat was reserved by government messengers and officials, many in-bound from the Continent. Those that were not were taken by men of commerce already returning from hurried transactions in France (for Europe had been closed to trade for over ten years by the Royal Navy's blockade, and the merchants and financiers of the City of London were anxious to stake early claims to the dividends of this sudden peace). Cornet Hervey did not take to these officials and commercial people who bustled about the Angel. He neither expected nor wanted attention as an officer returning from the war, but the insouciance which many of the travellers displayed, not to say the insolence with which they treated the Angel's servants, landlord and potboys alike, angered him.

'Forgot'n already the likes o' you made their trade poss'ble, sir,' said the landlord after one particularly self-satisfied consol-dealer had outbid Hervey for a seat in a fly-coach.

He could not but agree. But, then, he told himself, perhaps he had forgotten, too, that it was England's commerce that had financed her war, and her allies', too, and that he could not sniff at it too much now. Nevertheless, it was not until the third morning that he managed to get a seat inside on the *Dolphin* stage, whence he was glad to see the back of these men of affairs.

The *Dolphin* was a big and painfully slow coach. Its team comprised four strong Suffolks, and their short legs, with so low a point of draught, gave immense pulling power. But the big chestnuts were ill-matched for trotting, so much of the journey was at a walking pace. It meant, however, that the gentle green countryside of Kent could soon begin to ease the frustration with which he had set out. Indeed, the country seemed to him prettier even than in his recollections, and full of labouring men and women who showed no sign of the starvation or terror which blighted those of Spain and France. It was not long before he was minded of the equal, perhaps even greater, tranquillity of Wiltshire, and of his corner of the Great Plain of Salisbury. There he had known nothing but peace and happiness, and his thoughts now meandered, like the gentle chalk stream in which he had cast many a boyhood line, from one pleasurable recollection to another: his first pony, his rides on the Plain with Daniel Coates, his sister's nimble fingers at the keyboard, his mother's fussing as they made ready for Shrewsbury each term, his father's long yet absorbing sermons, his brother's—

The sudden recollection was disturbing, painful even. For Hervey knew he would never again – not in this world, at least – feel the strength that came of John's peace of mind.

And then, as it were, the stream's sudden turbulence ended, and he saw a girl of about twelve, the same as he, in fine silks, with ribbons in her hair. She teased him and teased him, until he put his pony at an elm that lay uprooted in front of a large house, clearing it – just – but losing his hat, which the girl then ran with into the great house, beyond his reach.

He was jolted out of his reveries by a particularly large pothole into which both nearside wheels fell in succession. He looked about him, but none of his fellow passengers stirred, so he resumed his study of the tranquillity beyond the window. Here and there, however, even England's garden bore the signs of the violence of which Edmonds had spoken. There were the charred remains of a barn which had fallen to the torches of the rick-burners. At a crossroads there was a lonely gallows with the stiffened corpse of a footpad hanging from its hoist, though here at least the body was without the marks of torture. At one halt near Faversham, an inn surrounded by hop fields, Hervey heard how a steam engine (he knew of steam engines but had never seen one) had recently been installed at the manor farm to drive the new threshing machines from Norfolk, and how, less than a month later, a band swearing allegiance to 'General Ludd' had destroyed both engine and machinery. The Maidstone Yeomanry had been called out but arrived long after the wreckers had gone. It was too frequently the case, said a fellow passenger, a Lancashire cotton man who feared for his own looms, declaring it quite beyond him why the magistrates were not able to keep order with so many yeomanry, militia and fencibles embodied or at call. Hervey had never held high in his estimation either yeomanry or magistrates: it seemed to him that their interests were too often more than decently entangled, and brutality too often a substitute for foresight and efficiency. But he had been away for some time, he reminded himself, and he did not wish to provoke this choleric weaver with views that would no doubt be taken as – at best – feckless.

The *Dolphin* stopped overnight in both Canterbury and Chatham, and arrived at eleven on the third morning at the Swan tavern in Southwark. The Swan, which was the *Dolphin*'s terminus, was no different from the half-dozen other inns by which they had staged from Dover, set as it was in the leafy Kentish environs of the Thames. But a keen eye could detect in the quickened pace of its servants, and that of the people of the street, proximity to a great city. And for the first time Hervey was to *see* a great city; for, in his reckoning, Lisbon could not answer to that description. He could scarcely bear the wait while his lodgings were arranged and a chaise summoned to take him across the river.

He had not imagined how the greatness would be manifest, however. He caught his breath at the sight of the Thames at Blackfriars, its wide, sweeping curve more majestic than anything he had seen in the Peninsula or in France, and he gazed in awe at the noble dome of St Paul's as they trotted up Ludgate Hill. But it was in the streets that his senses were all but overwhelmed, for the press of people and carriages, especially in the Strand, was immense. And, above the hubbub and noise of hoofs and wheels, vendors cried their wares, assisted by trumpet or bell, in a continual cacophony: 'Buy my *floun . . . ders*!' 'Sixpence a pound fair *cher . . . ries*!' '*Crab, crab*, any *crab*!' 'Buy a dish of great *ee . . . ls*!' 'Hot baked *war . . . dens*!'

His progress was slow, and twice he had his driver stop to buy cold ginger beer, and once to buy a muffin, so that it was almost four o'clock before he reached the premises of Mr Gieve in Piccadilly, the tailor who kept the sealed patterns for the uniforms of the 6th Light Dragoons. But he needed less than an hour there, for his letter had arrived ten days before and his new regimentals were ready for fitting. He was pleased at having been able to steal a march on the legions of officers whose own uniforms, too, had been worn to rags, and who would doubtless soon be descending on their tailors to amend their pulled-down appearance (as well as the many officers who had received brevets and field promotions who would be wanting to make the appropriate embellishments).

'They look very fine, sir,' said the little round cutter who attended him, adjusting his equally round spectacles as he made deft marks with a chalk on tunic and overalls. 'We will only require a day or so to adjust them, sir. May we now fit the levee dress?'

Hervey noted with satisfaction how the pelisse hung from the left shoulder, examining its fall with particular attention between two standing looking-glasses. 'Yes, they *are* fine. Let us to the levee dress, then.'

The Sixth's levee dress consisted of a tunic of the same pattern as the other regimentals but of finer cloth – a dark blue coatee with gold epaulettes, a high collar and bib-front in buff, the regiment's facing colour. With it were worn white cotton breeches rather than the heavier buckskin for review order, and tasselled patent-leather knee (or Hessian) boots.

'You may of course wear court shoes instead of the boots, sir, when not a strictly military occasion,' prompted the genial cutter.

Hervey added a pair to his order but made the economy of specifying pinchbeck for the buckles rather than anything grander: he had gold enough from the Peninsula but he did not care to see it on his feet.

'Finally, sir, we must fit your court overalls.'

Hervey was generous in his praise of the stitching of the gold lace on these: 'Upon my word, the stripes are most beautifully executed. And the court hat?'

The cocked hat with its white ostrich feathers, worn perfectly fore-and-aft in the Sixth, was to his mind an unnecessary extravagance since he could not conceive of any occasion for its use, unlike the overalls which were also worn as undress in the evening. Nevertheless, the hat was tried and it, too, was a sound fit.

'You did not specify a pelisse coat in your instructions, sir. May I enquire if that is still your intention?'

Hervey swallowed awkwardly. His pelisse coat had been lost at Corunna, and the compensation paid for the loss of private property had not been sufficient to replace everything: he had chosen to forgo a coat, extravagantly frogged and braided, hoping that one might be acquired on campaign at a reduced price. But there had been no such opportunity. The pelisse coat was an indulgence, a conceit, for nothing in regulations prescribed it. However, now that they would be returning to the ways of peace he knew that without one he would be bound to take endless rib-bending from the dandies. Besides, it was a very *handsome* conceit. 'How much would a coat be?'

'Twelve guineas, sir.' And a coat was added to the order. 'To where do you wish these severally to be consigned, sir?'

Hervey had not considered this and, after a moment or two reviewing the options, he decided on Horningsham.

'Very good, sir. And may I on behalf of Mr Gieve be so bold as to say how gratified we are to see the first of our officers home, and safely.'

Very prettily put, thought Hervey – and genuine enough, he reckoned. 'I am very much obliged to you, Mr Rippingale, and I hope to have occasion to visit you oftener in future.'

His next appointment was with the regimental agents, Messrs Greenwood, Cox & Hammersly of Craig's Court. Here his reception was courteous enough but stiff, without any of the warmth of his tailor's, and he soon formed the impression that to them he was no more than an inventory item, and a not especially valued one at that. For, although he would have, as a lieutenant, a book-value of twelve hundred pounds, lieutenants, even of light cavalry, would soon be the proverbial ten-a-penny, and the extra profits from officers paying over price would all but disappear. He was dealt with throughout by a clerk (and not over-civilly), none of the partners emerging to take notice, though at least one, he was sure, had walked through the chambers.

'"Every man thinks meanly of himself for never having been to sea nor having been a soldier."'

'I beg your pardon, sir?' said the clerk in some confusion.

'Nothing; it is nothing,' replied Hervey, sighing to himself how optimistic had been Dr Johnson's view. First the officials and bond-dealers at Dover, and now a clerk in an army agent's. Was England tiring already of her soldiers? 'Damned quill-drivers!' he muttered as he left.

The Earl of Sussex was not at home when Hervey called the following morning. In June he habitually left the Albany for his seat in Oxfordshire. The earl had been colonel of the Sixth since before Bonaparte had crowned himself emperor, and had always exercised a distant but proprietorial interest in his regiment. Unusually, Hervey had never been presented, for his gazetting to the regiment had been on the recommendation of the Marquess of Bath, which the earl could not but have found acceptable enough. His absence meant that Hervey would remain ignorant of the contents of Edmonds's dispatch. He had hoped to discover something, at least, of the nature of the instructions which he was to await in Wiltshire. He now hoped, therefore, that Lord George Irvine might be able to throw some light on matters instead. However, Lord George was not at home, either, his butler announcing with great solemnity that his master was convalescing at Brighton.

The dispatches would have both gratified and appalled him had he but known their contents. Edmonds had been especially pleased to compose them. He had been able to report the momentous end of the war and the honourable part the Sixth had played in the final battle. He had written of the continuing difficulties with Slade. He had been able to commend many of the officers for their distinguished service. He had in particular made one quite explicit recommendation:

that Cornet, soon to be Lieutenant, Matthew Hervey be appointed to the staff at the Horse Guards in order to prepare him for the high rank for which he was sure he was fitted. And two sides of manuscript urged the earl to use all his influence with the Duke of York to arrange it.

The third call that morning was more successful. In a large first-floor apartment in Queen Anne's Gate, overlooking St James's Park, he found Lieutenant d'Arcey Jessope in the brilliant scarlet of the 2nd Foot Guards. Jessope was ready for his caller; indeed, he had been awaiting him keenly since the arrival of his note the evening before. Two servants in startling canary livery brought in coffee, tea and chocolate, together with sundry sweet delicacies which Jessope recommended effusively: 'I know the most exquisite Neapolitan confectioner whom the late Sir William Hamilton brought home after his consulship there: he is an excellent fellow, a veritable genius with sugar and spices!'

Hervey smiled as he took, in addition to his coffee, the glass of Madeira proffered by a third footman. It was all so typical a Foot Guards display, he knew, but a generous one none the less.

'My dear *dear* friend, tell me how you are!' began Jessope as the footmen left the room. 'I have so much to thank you for I could not begin to honour you properly.'

'There is not the slightest need,' replied Hervey, a little bemused. 'And I am very well. What is more the point, Jessope, how are *you*?'

'I am capitally well, and especially so for seeing you: I was becoming affeard that I never would!'

'I swore that I would visit the moment I could,' said Hervey, now distinctly puzzled.

'I meant that I was not certain that I would see you again in this life!'

'Why, Jessope! the worst of your injuries were over when I left you in Spain. Has there been some complication?'

'*No!*' he said with a look of dismay. 'I meant that I was fearful for *you*! You seemed to have such utter disregard for the French that I felt sure it would end in disaster.'

'On the contrary, I assure you!' replied Hervey. 'I had very careful regard of the French! No, the worst that happened to me was a spontoon thrust into my leg at Toulouse – though I confess it bled and hurt like the very Devil! *So*, you are now recovered and, it seems by your appearance, returned to the active list?'

'Yes, indeed – recovered *and* at duty,' Jessope replied emphatically. 'And, of course, I owe that to you.'

'I do wish you would desist from that line. We shook hands in the field hospital at Salamanca, and that should be that. You must not keep making that I did anything exceptional.'

'Of course not!' Jessope smiled. 'Anyone would have fought his way into that throng of frog cut-throats to rescue a man he'd never met!'

'To what duty have you returned?' asked Hervey, ignoring Jessope's persistence.

'I am aide-de-camp to the adjutant-general at the Horse Guards.'

Hervey nodded. 'And this brings promotion?'

'Yes,' said Jessope, 'I am lieutenant and captain as of April.'

Hervey smiled again. The Guards and their system of double rank!

'And, you know, Hervey, I have not been idle,' he continued. 'I have arranged for you to exchange into the Second Guards here.'

Hervey laughed, a good-humoured laugh. *Rus in urbe*, he mused. 'My dear Jessope, I thank you for your kindness but I have not the slightest intention of leaving the Sixth, not for promotion *or* position!'

And on this, to both Jessope's surprise and very great disappointment, Hervey proved unshakeable. All the way through the park, as they walked to White's Club in St James's, Lieutenant and Captain d'Arcey Jessope extolled the virtues of service with the Guards, but Hervey was entirely unmoved. Only on the very steps of White's did Jessope give up, whereupon he applied himself instead to the pleasure of luncheon with his saviour-friend, a celebration at which the wine-coolers were employed to capacity in chilling champagne for the dozen or so habitués keen to make the acquaintance of the ADC's gallant companion.

Hervey stayed three days at Queen Anne's Gate. It had not been his original intention to remain in London so long, but it did at least allow him a final fitting for his new regimentals and to see something of the society which so enthralled Jessope and his fellow officers. He enjoyed it more than he expected. Jessope's circle was gay, frivolous, but wholly restorative of the spirits. The two of them dined together at White's on the evening before Hervey left for Wiltshire, and with the port Jessope produced a velvet-covered case which he passed across the table to him. Inside was a gold Westerman hunter with an inscription on the cover:

*M.H.*
*from d'A.J.*
*Salamanca*

'I wanted it to say so much more, but I could not find the words.'
'My dear Jessope, it says everything,' replied Hervey.

# CHAPTER FIVE
## OLD SOLDIERS

---

*The City, 22 June*

The Saracen's Head in Skinner Street, Snow Hill, incorporated the office of the Universal Coach and Wagon Company, and at three o'clock each morning the inn was all scurry and noise as mailbags and passengers arrived for their early departures to the West Country, and with them a cloud of hawkers with provisions for the journey. Here and there, preferring the shadows to the light of the oil lamps, lurked a shifty character on the lookout for pickings, honest or otherwise, and a doxy or two on the catch for one last customer before tripping home to sleep. And into this bustle came Hervey and Jessope, who, after White's and Drury Lane, had suppered with two Italian actresses whose acquaintance Jessope had evidently made some time before. The balloon coach for Salisbury was due to leave on the half-hour and would wait for no-one, however. The Universal, licensed to carry mail, prided itself on punctuality and speed, and at 6 miles per hour its coaches were some of the fastest in England, if not yet quite up to the speed of the Bristol Mails. The last of the bags, brought by gig from the General Letter Office in St Martin's-le-Grand, were thrown into the boot by the postboys at twenty-eight minutes past three, urged on by the driver with watch in hand (for he would have to answer with his pay for any delay), and Hervey, bidding Jessope a final farewell, took the remaining place inside.

As the carillon of St Paul's struck the half-hour, the *Swiftsure* pulled out of the inn yard and up the sleeping street towards the great cathedral. By four the team was trotting over Southwark Bridge and Hervey was beginning to doze. He had paid two and a half guineas for an inside seat and the carriage of two chests, and he was now counting it worth while, for he did not expect to be able to get a coach on to Warminster until the following morning. At a quarter past eight they halted at the Talbot inn in Ripley, where bowls of hot water, towels and then a breakfast of kidneys and steak, rashers and poached eggs, buttered toast and muffins, coffee, tea and small beer revived the *Swiftsure*'s passengers. Hervey kept his own company at table awhile before leaving the fug of the Talbot's low, dark, wainscoted room to watch the team being changed. Old and new were quality horses which looked as though they would serve equally well under the saddle, able to trot with rare velocity on the newly macadamized turnpike – horses to admire.

'I'll warrant ye didn't see *their* like in Spain often, sir,' said the guard.

Hervey looked up quizzically, and the big, open-faced man smiled from his seat next to the driver's. 'No, indeed,' replied Hervey. 'And I am to presume, therefore, that you have knowledge of that country.'

The second guard's 'yard of tin' emitted a shrill recall to the other passengers, drowning the first guard's reply, and Hervey would have asked him to repeat it had he not observed that one of the outside fares was an elderly woman, a farmer's wife perhaps, for she had the stamp of the country. With difficulty at first – she thought he wished for some payment – he gave up his seat inside to her and climbed to the coach roof.

'A gentleman indeed, sir,' said the guard, offering his flask.

'I thank you,' said Hervey, taking a full draw on it. 'This is uncommon smooth brandy. I fear I did not catch your last against the long horn, though.'

'I said, sir, that a part of me remained yet in Spain.'

'It holds that sway with many, I believe,' agreed Hervey.

'Bless you, sir,' smiled the guard, 'for it is my sally only.'

And he tapped his left shin with the butt of his fowling piece – wood on wood.

Hervey did not return the smile, wide though it was. 'Then I am sorry for you. Was this the French's work?'

'Ay, sir – Albura, a musket ball point-blank,' the guard replied, still smiling.

'Then the musket's aim was most curious if you were anywhere but astride a horse!'

'That is right sagacious, sir. I were astride one of the Third DG's.'

'Indeed?'

'And with three stripes up.'

'Well, serjeant, I am glad at least to see you in employ.'

'Thank you, sir. And yourself – you are an admirer of horse-flesh, a professional eye, one of General Cotton's, too, perhaps? And captain, I would suppose!'

'Cornet,' replied Hervey as cheerily as he could. 'That's an arsenal worthy of a heavy,' he added quickly, nodding to the collection of firearms about the guard.

'The fowling piece and pistols are right enough for the close country, but when we get on the heath a long-range shot or two from a carbine will see off a pad,' he explained.

'And the sword?' queried Hervey.

He smiled. 'I've 'ad it since I joined the Third.'

'And that curious item by your feet – it has the look of the Paget, and yet . . . ?'

'It is that, sir. Haven't you seen one with a folding butt before?' replied the guard, passing it to him. 'The Sixteenth had all theirs so in America. They were handier for foot work and they're better balanced on the pouch-belt swivel. Can't think why the rest of the cavalry never adopted it.'

'Like as not because it bore General Tarleton's stamp, I shouldn't wonder,' suggested Hervey (that is what Daniel Coates would have thought: with the fall of the general had gone many of the innovations of that ill-fated campaign). 'You know, I should very much like to own one of these. An officer cannot carry a carbine in a saddle bucket – it would not do – but I reckon I could stow this in something little bigger than a pistol holster over the saddle arch.'

'That's easy enough, sir. For three pounds you may have a folding-butt Paget within the week, for as well as guard on this here coach I am serjeant-armourer with the Wiltshire Yeomanry, and carbines are simply enough purchased. The butt I shall adapt myself.'

'Very well, then, Serjeant . . . ?'

'Smeaton, sir, William Smeaton.'

'Very well, Serjeant Smeaton, it is agreed. Shall you have it sent to me in Horningsham? It is near Warminster.'

'No, sir, I shall bring it myself, for I have dealings with the Warminster Troop this very week.'

And then, business concluded, Hervey was content to listen to Serjeant Smeaton's recollections of the war, to his commentary on the sights, greater and lesser, along the road, and to his general observations on the state of the country as would a returning regular find it. When they set down that evening at the Red Lion in Salisbury, in the shadow of the great cathedral, Armourer-Serjeant William Smeaton shook his hand as an old friend. 'That Warminster Troop, mind,' he warned, scratching his head and smiling still more, 'they're not as you and me, as reg'lars, would know things – not as things would be in the Third or the Sixth.'

Hervey caught his meaning well enough: 'I'm obliged, Armourer-Serjeant!' And he smiled, too.

No stage ran through the night to Warminster, and the hire of a coach of any sort would rob him (so he reckoned) of a preposterous sum. Instead, he took the early post the next morning to the old wool town thirty miles along the Bath road. Warminster's rooftops looked comfortingly familiar when first he saw them as the post crested the final rise and ran along the turnpike under the south-western scarp of the great plain, its ancient hillforts standing silent picket. And the press of people at the sheep fair filling the high street was as he had always remembered it. Or perhaps not quite as he remembered it, for the driver of the gig which then took him on to Horningsham said that the fairs were double the size and twice as frequent as before the war. Everywhere, indeed, there was the look of prosperity.

His letter had preceded him by two days, although at what time he would arrive, or even which day, it had not been possible to say. So when the gig pulled up to the vicarage his reception was as clamorous as if he had been wholly un-expected, the family all but tumbling from the door. His father's only reserve (though little enough) was occasioned by advancing years; his mother showed none whatever; and his sister was almost as unrestrained. He had thought so long of this moment that in the event he found himself un-accountably composed, and made apology for being so. It was of no moment, his father insisted: it was but the manner of the soldier. His mother ascribed it to the long journey; but Elizabeth thought otherwise, fearful that she had, to all intents, lost a second brother (though she had forborne to say so in the weeks before his keenly anticipated home-coming).

But Elizabeth seized her brother's arm resolutely, none the less. 'Come, Matthew; there are others who wish to see you.' And she took him inside to the servants' hall.

Francis, their ancient footman, now bore a pronounced stoop, but cook was as large and merry as ever he remem-bered. 'Master Matthew, do they not feed you in the Army any more? I've seen more meat on a tuppenny cony!' she exclaimed, hugging and pinching him.

'Mrs Pomeroy, a week of your puddings will right all, have no fear!'

A kitchen maid giggled in the corner. 'Not to be so silly, Hannah,' said Mrs Pomeroy with some primness. 'This is Hannah, Master Matthew, Abel Towle's young'n.'

Abel Towle, gardener-cum-groom, who could not speak one full sentence without cursing, albeit of the mildest sort within the family's hearing, bade his welcome when Hervey and his sister went to the stable. Towle and Ruth, his elder daughter, completed the vicarage's modest establishment.

Next they took a turn about the garden, Elizabeth pointing out keenly the additions since his last brief visit home all of five years before. They embraced from time to time, but it was too soon for them to speak of anything of consequence. Hervey stopped by some of the new cold frames and looked at her sheepishly. 'You will think me strange, Elizabeth, but is there still the big leaden tub? I have never looked forward to a soak in it as these past weeks!'

'Indeed, there is the leaden bath! And Ruth and Hannah shall fill it at once. And while they do so you must go to the orchard and see the old chestnut tree of which you were so fond. You will still see Longleat from its branches, I'll warrant!'

So long was he in his bath that a giggling Hannah was sent to discover if he were awake. In truth, the anticipation of soaking in that big leaden tub had sustained him throughout the march north from Toulouse; and the happy memories were now too vivid to dismiss willingly, for he knew that once downstairs he must confront the grief for his brother that was being so bravely, and privately, borne by his family. At length he went down to his father's study; and there, for the first time, they met as men of equal consequence, the accident of his brother's death having removed, so to speak, the enfolding wall which his father and mother had long ago built. They talked of the pain, the waste, the memory. And, after tears, some smiles and even a little laughter, the vicar of Horningsham poured his son a large glass of sherry and fixed him with the same piercing gaze he had known as a child. 'Matthew,' he said firmly, 'John's death must be of no moment to you beyond that which is one brother to another. The obligations that are placed upon you are no greater than were his, and John was making his own way in the world.'

'It is perhaps too early for me truly to know my feelings, Father,' replied Hervey with an appreciative smile, 'but I should not want to leave my profession if there were no necessity.'

'I am glad of it, and glad, too, that you speak of the Army

in such terms: I think it, indeed, an honourable profession. At least, that is, a profession in which honourable men may serve.'

'Just so, Father, but it is difficult not to feel the shadow of John's worthier calling.'

'And in that you reveal still your simplesse,' said the vicar of Horningsham, shaking his head. 'John's was not a higher calling but a different one.'

There was a knock at the door, and Hervey's mother entered with Elizabeth. And there followed a conversation of the utmost warmth and intimacy concerning John's virtues as a son, brother and human being. Of his qualities as a priest, said his father at length, they knew a little, but more would be forthcoming that evening when they would receive a visitor who had known John in that calling.

Dinner was late – past two – and the fast before the next day's patronal feast of St John the Baptist was prematurely, but formally, abandoned at the grace. Hereafter began Hervey's own inquisition. Campaigning was what his mother expected to hear of, and she would allow no other conversation. But his was, necessarily, an incomplete account, and perhaps a somewhat sentimental one thereby, for without the carnage and bestiality it could only be thus, and any essay by him into those horrors would have been repugnant in that company. It was, however, pleasing to a mother swelled with pride, and a father wishing some consolation for another son's death. But the Reverend Thomas Hervey's spirit was stronger than the flesh: he stayed with the account until Salamanca and then succumbed to the comfortable feeling induced by the safe return of his remaining son and the celebratory claret, an Haut-Brion of pre-war vintage (the blockade's having prevented, in any case, newer being obtained).

Elizabeth stayed longer with the account but absented herself, regretfully, as Dover was reached in order to be about her weekly business in Warminster's workhouse. Hervey walked with her to the stables where Towle had the ageing barouche ready.

'Matthew, I have seen enough of distress these past five years in the town to know – well, perhaps to have a presentiment at least – of the miseries of war. You were all consideration itself at dinner but you must remain patient with us,' she said, 'and especially so this evening with Mr Keble, who was a dear friend of John's at Oxford. Mr Keble himself is a dear man and, by all accounts, an exceptional one – John was always speaking of him. He was a scholar at only fifteen, and a fellow of John's college before he was twenty. He has fine degrees in divinity and mathematics, and has won prizes for poetry. He is to be made deacon next year and was to have joined John's parish as second curate. Father already thinks of him as if he were our John, so like him is he. And, I confess, also do I.'

Hervey smiled at once. 'I am *delighted* to hear it,' he replied, and with such emphatic stress on the participle that Elizabeth looked at him askance. There was no time, however (and it was perhaps as well), for her to enquire why his delight should be so pronounced, and she left him instead to his fancy that one day she and Edward Lankester would meet, and that she might thereby become wife to that noblest of soldiers. No man could hope more for his sister, and Elizabeth, he felt sure, would in the event share that opinion.

'What of religious observance in the Army, Mr Hervey?' John Keble asked as they began supper that evening, a collation which included the vicar of Horningsham's favourite neat's tongue in aspic, and Mrs Pomeroy's revered frigize of chicken and rabbit.

'Well,' began Hervey, startled somewhat (he would rather, even, have faced questions about the commissary system, for, bad as that was, he considered the commissaries marginally more effective than the chaplains), 'it is better than when I first joined,' he suggested, hoping that this might be enough. It was a vain hope.

'Indeed? How is it now, then?' Keble continued.

'In truth, Mr Keble, it is not at all good. It varies greatly from regiment to regiment depending on the colonel, but also on the chaplain – we now have one to each brigade. This is the Marquess – or the Duke, rather, as he has been elevated since Bonaparte's defeat – this is the Duke of Wellington's doing. Prior to this campaign we had no chaplains – well, very few. They are not on the whole of the quality you will see at Oxford, though.'

'And it will be no housling ministry, I warrant. Do they celebrate the Holy Communion with any regularity and frequency?'

Elizabeth looked anxiously at her brother, who understood her meaning at once.

'As a rule, no,' he replied patiently, though he might easily have omitted the qualification and simply answered with the negative.

John Keble shook his head.

'They do preach and pray with the wounded,' he added in a half-hearted plea in mitigation.

'And Methodists?' Keble continued. 'I have heard that they make converts.'

Hervey's father huffed loudly. 'Mr Keble, to my shame, we have here in Horningsham the oldest dissenting chapel in England!'

'It is nonsense to speak so, Father,' smiled Elizabeth. 'You and the minister get on like houses on fire!'

'Indeed, we do,' replied the old man chuckling, 'though only when we avoid any mention of religion. On the whole it is better that way with men of God! But I would sooner spend an evening in the company of the old Jesuit from Wardour. *He* does not quote scripture at me the while, and we may have gentlemanly conversation about such matters of doctrine that are unknowable, and which therefore we may discourse upon without acrimony.'

'And with good claret,' chuckled Mrs Hervey.

'This latter is very sage, sir,' John Keble acknowledged; and then, with a smile so full that his face was wholly transformed, added 'as is yours, ma'am.'

'They are not my words, however, Mr Keble,' sighed the Reverend Thomas Hervey, 'but dear Archbishop Laud's.'

'God rest his soul,' said Keble before turning back to Hervey to press his point. 'But, as to these Methodists, I would think that the meeting of soldiers in their cantonments to sing psalms, or to hear a sermon read by one of their comrades, is in the abstract perfectly innocent; indeed, it is laudable, but I think it might become otherwise.'

'And I think that is precisely what the duke believes, too,' agreed Hervey, surprised by Keble's evident grasp of the requirements of good order and military discipline, 'but I wonder why the established church makes no greater impression.'

Keble was quick to answer, though with more sadness in his tone than enthusiasm. 'The Church has, I believe, in many quarters turned its back on its true origins. The best men do their duty faithfully but without fervour; the worst . . . well, let us say they are free from the tumults of conscience.'

'But what of the Claphamites, Mr Keble?' Elizabeth interjected. 'They do their duty with fervour and confront their consciences squarely, do they not? And see what good deeds they do!'

'Oh, a worthy movement, Miss Hervey, but fired by Protestant fervour.'

'And is that to be denounced, then?' she challenged, with some perturbation.

'By no means, Miss Hervey,' he replied, seemingly stung by her rebuke, 'but the Church of England was not conceived in Protestantism: it is Catholic and reformed. Is that not what we affirm in the creed?'

Elizabeth looked to the head of the table. 'Father, what is your opinion in this?'

The vicar of Horningsham spoke with unusual animation. 'Mr Keble is wholly accurate upon this point, my dear. You must read the Thirty-Nine Articles as an affirmation of the doctrine of the Fathers of the Church, not as a Protestant tract – which latter is all that people seem to do today. As you read they will be a revelation to you! Lancelot Andrewes and the other Caroline divines were wholly lucid on this matter – poor Laud went to the scaffold because of it. We have drifted into Protestantism. It needs younger men of integrity and energy, however, to recall the Church to its proper destiny!'

'And I believe your elder son to have been one of these, Mr Hervey,' John Keble replied in a tone approaching ardour. 'You should have heard his sermons at Oriel and seen his ministry in the hovels of Cowley. He was worthy indeed of taking up Andrewes's torch.'

But Hervey's mother had become likewise agitated: 'Then are we to throw vipers at the Methodists again, Mr Keble?'

John Keble looked at her with polite but evident incomprehension.

'Mr Keble,' Elizabeth interjected sheepishly, 'some years ago a Methodist was preaching outdoors in Warminster and a townsman threw an adder at him.'

'"O generation of vipers, who hath warned you to flee from the wrath to come?"' Keble replied, hoping that the gospel after whom her younger son had been named might deflect them.

'Just so, Mr Keble,' said Mrs Hervey, equally opaquely. 'And now, Matthew, turning to lighter matters, will you be going to see the marquess tomorrow?'

'Well, Mother,' he began hesitantly, 'perhaps not tomorrow; but, yes, I shall pay my respects.'

'I think if you knew whom you might also see at Longleat you would not long delay,' she added with a smile.

'Oh, Mother!' sighed Elizabeth. 'Do you have no artfulness?'

Hervey looked bemused, and all the more so for Elizabeth's prim reprimand.

'Henrietta Lindsay is come back to Longleat, Matthew; that is all,' his sister explained.

Hervey felt his gut twist, and he fought hard not to show it. 'Well, that is agreeable, Mother. No, you are quite right, it is *very* agreeable to hear. I have not seen Henrietta Lindsay in years. I expect she is quite grown now.' He looked at Elizabeth, who looked down at her plate, and he searched for some way by which to change the subject. 'But I thought that first I should go to see Daniel Coates!'

'Coates!' exclaimed the vicar of Horningsham, suddenly come back to consciousness. 'The only man with any idea at all how to deal with those rick-burners!'

'And how is that, Father?' asked Elizabeth kindly, laying her hand on his forearm. But her father had slipped peacefully back into upright yet profound sleep.

Daniel Coates – *rick-burners*? What was the connection? wondered Hervey. Coates was not a violent man – at least, he had not been when last Hervey had seen him before leaving for Spain. Had the unrest at home taken its toll of yeoman fortitude? But Coates was a tenant sheepfarmer: why might he be troubled by rick-burners?

'Daniel is a churchwarden now, and a magistrate,' revealed his mother. 'At Upton Scudamore. Your father holds the benefice *in commendam*.'

Daniel Coates a churchwarden and a magistrate! Hervey could only wonder at the change in the country these past few years. Daniel Coates – old soldier, his childhood hero, a poor tenant farmer who had once been shepherd on the Longleat estate: it had been he who had taught him to ride cavalry-fashion, to shoot straight and use a sword so well that on joining the Sixth he had been dismissed riding school and skill-at-arms quicker than anyone could remember. Hervey could not present himself unannounced to Henrietta Lindsay, but he most certainly could to Daniel Coates! And in Coates was, perhaps, his best chance of gaining a reliable secular opinion of what the country had become while he had been away; in John Keble he knew he had such a mentor in the clerical view. 'Mr Keble,' he said, with sudden resolution, 'may we take a turn about the garden? I should be obliged for your opinion on this country to which I return, it would seem, as something of a stranger.'

# CHAPTER SIX
# THE YEOMEN OF WILTSHIRE

*Salisbury Plain, Midsummer Day*

His father's cob knew the way to Upton Scudamore well enough, and the pace at which the vicar of Horningsham liked to cover the five or so miles of rutted lanes which crossed the vale, skirted the prehistoric mystery that was Cley Hill, and connected the handsome estate village with the rougher settlement by the great west scarp of Salisbury Plain. Daniel Coates's farm lay on the edge of the downs, virtually under the scarp. When he had taken the tenancy fifteen years earlier it had been nothing but a few dilapidated buildings and three acres of poor pasture, with a hundred or so more of common land on the Westbury side. He had rebuilt it stone by stone, brick by brick – Hervey had carried many of them himself. There was nothing poor-looking about the place now, however.

Coates received him with an easy combination of deference and familiarity, but 'Master Hervey', and soon thereafter simply 'Matthew', was subjected to a veritable cannonade of questions, a bombardment lasting a full half-hour without respite. Finally, Coates seemed to become aware of his insensibility and was then much abashed: 'My dear Matthew, how could I 'ave been so inhospitable – your glass is empty, and you have not spoken except for to speak back,' he said, reaching for a jug of purl.

'Dan, I have so keenly imagined this time for many months, but I want more than anything to ride on the downs again, as we have done together since I was on the leading-rein. There I promise I shall answer every enquiry you have a care to make!'

'And so shall it be, Matthew; so shall it be!' Coates replied with the broadest of smiles, and he summoned his housemaid to take word to the stables.

Hervey had never known a groom before at Drove Farm: when first he had gone to Spain there had not been so much as a labourer, and certainly no housemaid. Now as they went into the stableyard there was a smart-looking fellow holding a fine pair of bay hunters. Prosperity indeed, thought Hervey. But their discourse did not immediately resume on leaving the yard, for Daniel Coates took Hervey at his word and waited until they had reached the downs before pressing him once more to the details of his campaigning. So with scarcely an exchange they rode out along the empty expanse of Warminster Bottom, past Dirtley Wood and up the steep scarp of the great plain on to Knapp Down, both men happy to let the memories stir in silence.

To Hervey's mind the plain had no rival for both bleakness *and* beauty. In winter, with a strong, cutting north-east wind, and sleet, hail or heavy rain driven in sheets over the lonely plateau, the scene, broken here and there by a few clumps of dripping trees or a misty barrow, was dismal – desolate even. He had been as cold here – more so even – as on the retreat to Corunna. But in fine weather (and that midsummer morning was as fine as they came) the air was as pure as in the Pyrenees and the sun, high and directly ahead, as warm as in Gascony. The turf was soft and yielding (it had cushioned many a fall in his youth), and the whole face of the down was carpeted with flowers whose names he was surprised to be able to recall: harebells, centaury, dark blue campanula, scabias, milkworts, orchids and meadowsweet. And where there were no flowers there was broom and furze.

Still they rode on without speaking until, cresting the rise of Summer Down, Hervey saw, and heard, the source of Daniel Coates's wealth: sheep – many, many more than he could ever remember, so many that for the best part of a mile it was scarcely possible to see the carpet of turf and flowers. 'Yes, they're all mine,' said Coates, guessing his thoughts. 'Every bale of wool these past five years has gone to clothe His Majesty's troops. The war has upped demand beyond anything I could've imagined. The flock's grown a hundred-fold, and I've five shepherds tending 'em. I've been sole agister on these downs for three summers now. I'm a rich man, Matthew!'

Hervey nodded: he could find no words adequate for his admiration.

'But I doubt demand'll remain high now that regiments and ships are being paid off. I shall sell 'em all before winter.'

This last was perhaps the true measure of Coates's acumen: energy and good fortune alone might promote wealth but, it seemed to Hervey, real judgement was needed to know when to sell out. But Coates did not want to speak of business. 'I see the Army hasn't given you a taste for the straight leg, then, Matthew?' he smiled approvingly, nodding to the hunting length of Hervey's stirrups.

'No, Dan, it has not. I cannot abide it. All through Spain we bumped along. The King's Germans didn't: they ride at half our length and always rise to the trot, and their horses are the better for it. Ours seemed to have no end of sore backs.'

It gave Coates no pleasure to hear it, but he could take satisfaction in Hervey's opinion: it had been one of the hard lessons of America, lessons of which he had spoken endlessly when they had ridden out together. 'Yes, I always said I learned more about campaigning from the colonists than from our own officers: they had little idea other than how to drill. How in heaven's name can you lean out with a straight leg?'

'I reckon I had the advantage of an extra half-sword riding at hunting length – all the difference when cutting at an infantryman trying to use his bayonet. There's an ensign in the Coldstream who would be dead but for that reach.'

'Ay, I saw that time and again. But the reach has no purpose unless the sword is sharp.'

Hervey sighed. 'We put straw in our scabbards as best we

could, and it stopped the rattling, too, but that steel sorely blunted the blades. The Germans had wooden scabbards and had not half the trouble.'

Daniel Coates's interest in each and every detail seemed limitless. They crossed Summer Down with the old soldier apparently oblivious to the vastness of his flock, which calmly parted for them as they trotted through, and they descended the east slopes, into the dry valley where, legend had it, King Alfred hid his army before Edington. Yet scarcely did Coates seem to notice their progress. Only when they climbed on to Chapperton Down, where the Imber shepherds grazed their flocks (though on this morning the Imber sheep were the other side of the valley), did he return to the present. 'Come on!' he called suddenly, urging his bay into a canter, 'keep with me till Wadman's Coppice an' then it's flat out to Brounker's Well. D'ye remember the gallop, Matthew?'

That he did! Though he would have preferred to be on Jessye now, for that fast and sure-footed little mare was made for just such a run on the plain. But this gelding felt handy, too, and soon revealed a turn of speed, pulling the whole mile and more to the ancient coppice and making Hervey work hard to check him. Letting him have his head for the last half-mile into the dry valley beyond, they reached Brounker's Well a dozen lengths clear. As he pulled up and turned south for the Imber road, Hervey laughed and called to Coates: 'By heavens, you're spending some of your wealth on horseflesh, Dan!'

'What else is worth it, Matthew? Not a woman in a thousand, that's for sure!' he called back.

They both laughed even louder.

'The gelding is yours, Matthew!'

'What? Dan . . . I can't *possibly* . . .' Hervey spluttered, but his protests were unlikely to make any impression.

'I've more to be grateful to your family for than ever I could repay – not even with a *troop's* worth of horses. Without your father I would have trudged on down that lane where he found me coughing up my lungs thirty years ago and more. It was 'im that found me employ on the estate, and it was 'im that lent me the money for the first year's rent on Drove Farm fifteen years back. The horse is yours for as long as you wants 'im. Take 'im – at least until you go to Ireland. And by then you won't want to leave him anyway. He's a home-coming present, Matthew – why should I not give you a homecoming present?'

Interest to pay or not, he was sure that such a gift was more than he could accept, and he might have continued protesting but for the sudden appearance of a score or more horsemen on the Imber road.

'Warminster Troop. Come on and see 'em,' said Coates, spurring into a canter again.

Though the troop had been raised before he had left for Spain, this was Hervey's first encounter with them. Their appearance was, in one respect at least, impressive, for the blue dolmans and Tarleton helmets looked almost new. But the troopers themselves did not have the stamp of men under habitual discipline, hardened by service in which a bed was the infrequent alternative to a straw billet or a muddy bivouac. Indeed, in some respects they had a faintly theatrical appear-ance, for the Tarleton had been out of regular service for two years at least. But, although the Tarleton had been disliked for field service (it was almost as cumbersome as the hussars' mirleton), he considered it still a very handsome head-dress.

'Good morning, Coates,' called their lieutenant.

'Good morning, Mr Styles,' replied Daniel Coates, raising his hat to the guidon. Hervey blanched at the man's lofty manner, and looked with disdain at the pallid face and fleshy thighs of this leader of yeomen, but he raised his hat to the guidon nevertheless. Styles, however, assumed that both salutes were his and waved his hand airily in acknowledge-ment.

'And who, indeed, was that?' asked Hervey when the troop had passed.

'Mr Hugo Styles, son and heir of Sir George Styles of Leighton Park at Westbury,' replied Coates, 'and a right Johnny Raw!'

'I do not know of a Sir George Styles,' said Hervey, puzzled.

'No, you would not. He bought Leighton Park three years ago, and a baronetcy a year or so before that. He owns most of the mills in Devizes.'

'Not a man at home much in the saddle, I should say.'

'I dare say not,' sighed Coates. 'He fancies himself very much the gentleman, though, and disports himself as a blade hereabouts.'

'Then I am doubly certain that I shall not call on him.' A supercilious yeomanry officer was, by all accounts, nothing unusual, and hardly something to be troubled by: it did not appear to trouble Coates. But, simmered Hervey to himself, that Daniel Coates, JP and sometime trumpeter to General Tarleton, should not receive the commonest of courtesies from someone wearing the king's uniform was detestable. 'Dan, that milksop hailed you as if you were Dick-in-the-green!'

'Not to worrit, Matthew. You'll be looking to a troop yourself next,' said Coates, seeing his anger and wishing to divert him.

'Hah! And where would *I* find two thousand pounds, Dan?'

Coates whistled. 'Is that what it takes nowadays, Matthew?'

'In *addition* Dan, in *addition*. *Three* thousand is the price.'

'Well, I'll be . . . You should go to India!'

'You are the second to tell me that,' replied Hervey, with a smile at last, 'but I have no desire to leave the Sixth. They are the very finest of fellows.'

Hervey had expected a dinner of mutton at Drove Farm – a joint perhaps, or a pudding even – but not venison.

'Shot by me on Summer Down this last week,' said Coates with evident pride as Hervey remarked on its tenderness. 'And when dinner is finished I'll show you the means by which I dropped her.'

That morning's ride had given them both prodigious appetites, and it was not until a custard of some size had come

136

and gone that Coates revealed the means by which he had taken the venison, fetching from the hall an ordinary-looking carbine. 'It's not what it seems, though – well, not what you might think,' he explained.

'Rifled?' suggested Hervey.

'Ay, that, too,' said Coates, delving into a leather bag and pulling out a cartridge that looked longer than usual. 'This here is powder *and* bullet, and it's fired by an initiator in the base – I mean a cap which gives off an igniting spark when this pin here strikes it,' he continued, pointing to the firing pin. 'The pin's held in this block,' he continued, 'and is struck by a cocking hammer – see?'

Hervey did see, and quickly enough: 'A breech-loader? I had heard there were such but never saw one before.'

'The breech-loader is nothing new – we had 'em in America!' Coates laughed. 'They had their problems – they were slow, for a start – but instead of trying to improve them the Ordnance gave up! You see, you can lie down, behind cover, and load one of these easy enough. You can't very well with a muzzle-loader.'

'But I have never heard of this initiator,' said Hervey, still puzzled.

'*That* is the most significant part – more so merely than breech-loading. The piece is called a percussion lock. Come, see.'

They went to the paddock beyond the stables where Coates handed him both carbine and cartridge-bag. 'Try it first and then I shall tell you the story of how I came by it,' he said, lifting the hinged firing mechanism at the point where stock and butt met, and placing a cartridge in the breech for him. 'You pull back the hammer – it locks itself back, *see*? There's a safety catch here, too – and then the trigger releases the hammer just like a flintlock. No exterior spark – nothing. And the cartridges are waterproof, too, made of goldbeaters' skin.'

'Of *what*?'

'Well, not strict as: goldbeaters' skin is from ox gizzards. These are sheepgut; I make 'em myself.'

Hervey tried the carbine, firing at a tree a hundred yards

distant and watching with satisfaction as pieces of bark flew off with some velocity. Coates even dropped several cartridges into a bucket of water, and these fired instantly, too. It took only a fraction of the time to reload that it would a loose charge, and the accuracy compared well with the Baker service rifle.

'Dan, such a weapon – it is astounding. Tell me how you came of it.'

'From a minister of the Kirk, would you believe!'

'What?'

'The Reverend Alexander Forsyth, doctor of divinity no less, the minister in Margaret's village near Glasgow. He made it in his own workshop! And you know what, Matthew? He took it to the Board of Ordnance, and they said they had no use for it! No use! *Bonaparte* had use for it right enough – offered him twenty thousand pounds for the secret. But he would not sell it, so the Ordnance have promised him a pension for keeping silent! He now has a shop in London – sporting-guns and the like.'

'*Yes*, Forsyth's in Piccadilly – I saw it only days ago! So this is from London?'

'No, he has no permit to sell them yet. This I made myself after he'd shown me the principle!'

'Dan, at every river in Spain it was the same – the Devil's own job just to keep powder and fire-locks dry. Then we would have to prove the carbines although we were meant to be scouting: you risked either giving yourself away or a misfire when you least needed it. I've seen every carbine in a troop flash in the pan so.'

'Well, the carbine is yours, Matthew – I have a pair. There's no reason why *you* should not have dry powder at least. Though, now that Bonaparte is done for, His Majesty's Ordnance will no doubt consider it timely to make it a general issue!'


The next morning, before seven, Hervey drove with his mother into Warminster for the Saturday fair, where she bought turbot and lobster fresh-caught from Weymouth. On settling for the fish, as had been her routine for as many years as he could remember, she took a letter for her sister in Hereford to the letter office in the high street, and afterwards they drove home, returning to the vicarage before nine. Each way she spoke of little but Henrietta Lindsay – how fine a lady she was grown, what society she kept, how distinguished a peer was her guardian, the marquess, and on what close terms Henrietta and Elizabeth had remained. She urged him to pay her a call at Longleat that day, and lamented that she had not the servants to ask her to dine with them at the vicarage. What thoughts Hervey entertained in that direction he now sought hard to conceal; for, much that he might look forward keenly to meeting once again the sparkling child whose schoolroom in Longleat House he had once shared, he knew that both the years and the society in which she moved must place a distance between them. *No*, he insisted politely, and to his mother's consternation, he would wait a little while more before calling. Instead, when they had breakfasted, he took out his new bay, intending to put the gelding through its paces in Longleat Park.

The yeomanry were being put through their paces in the park also. Hervey saw them from some distance as he rode towards the deer enclosure, and first impressions of their manoeuvring were of handiness. He knew well enough the difficulties with which the volunteers were beset – largely the want of anyone to train them, since all the regulars had been sent to the Indies or Spain, or to Ireland or the coast at the supposed invasion-points. He halted fifty yards or so from them as they drew up in double rank on the edge of a piece of open ground which evidently served as their drill field.

'Telling off, by files, *number*!' began the troop serjeant-major. The words of command were somewhat eccentric, not strictly the Dundas manual, but effective none the less. But then the serjeant-major began telling off by sub-divisions, and after that by quarter-ranks. The process seemed interminable, and to what end Hervey could scarcely imagine: had they been militia there might have been some benefit in numbering aloud (for many a militiaman would not have been able to count beyond a dozen), but there hardly seemed the need in the solid citizens of the yeomanry.

Beyond the troop was a vocal gathering – several carriages and half a dozen blades astride quality horses, the kind of group that assembled anywhere the military paraded. And, if these yeomen troopers had not the edge in drilling that the regulars had, they were a diverting enough sight to any who would admire a fine uniform. Indeed, Hervey began to wonder at whose expense they had been clothed: the fur-crested Tarleton would have cost double, perhaps treble, the new shako. Whoever had paid was also of an independent mind, he concluded, for the plume was still in what he presumed must be the yeomanry's facing colour – blue – rather than the national white over red to which other corps had changed a decade before. He could not but admire the skirted, tailless blue dolman jackets, slightly longer than the new-pattern coat which his own regiment wore. And he noted with approval that the jackets were worn with just a sword-belt and snake-fastening instead of with the barrelled girdle which used to be popular: this way their belts would be kept tight even if the effect were not as eye-catching. But it was clear that in white breeches and boots these men were not meant for serious field service, for overalls were what anyone who spent whole days in the saddle would choose.

His eye moved to the drill ground, where two parallel rails, set on posts about four feet high and painted white, ran for fifty yards down the middle of the open area, and to which the troop was drawn up at a right-angle. The rails were about three feet apart and, at intervals of ten yards, and three feet from the rails on both sides, there were posts about the height of a man, on each of which was fixed a sheaf of straw. It was much like any cavalry skill-at-arms field, but the rails gave it more the look of the medieval tiltyard. By Hervey's reckoning, two troopers would gallop towards each other, safely separated by the rails, and in a backhand cut would slice the sheaves. Indeed, he would soon have a demonstration, for the first pair were trotting out to their starting positions – two corporals, the chevrons on their sleeves larger even than a regular's.

They began their approach at a trot, and he judged that they would go forward to canter at the start of the rails and then gallop a couple of lengths before the posts. To his astonishment, however, they maintained the trot throughout, and – worse – they simply held out their swords to cut at the sheaves with forehand swipes. Even at that modest pace, however, it should have been possible to cut them, but the swords were so blunt that they knocked all but one off the posts. The corporals seemed pleased with their demonstration nevertheless, as did their officer, the same pallid lieutenant of the Imber road. Hervey groaned. There then followed a ponderous half-hour while the thirty or so troopers went through these same evolutions. Why he stayed was uncertain. Perhaps he hoped for some redeeming feature of drill before the parade was over; but there was not, and he was puzzled why. If it were too much to expect these volunteers to learn to cut at the gallop (and he would be the first to acknowledge the skill in that manoeuvre), surely it were better then to point with the sword and quicken the pace? But, without anyone of experience to drill them, how might such a practical solution be advanced?

'Good morning, my fine fellow; so you are taken by the sight of regimentals, eh?'

Wrapped in his thoughts, Hervey had not noticed the lieutenant ride up to him.

'Well, you look as though you could be made to sit well and be useful with a sword. Want to try your hand on the gallops?'

Hervey could but stare at the lieutenant's leg, stretched in regulation fashion, the very tip of the toe, only, in the stirrup, and it took the greatest effort to suppress his smile at the word *gallops*. A less appropriate one he would have found difficult to imagine, and, in the face of such delusion, laughter was tempting in the extreme. 'I thank you, no,' he managed instead.

'Oh, now, *come*: there is nothing to be afraid of. My men will applaud your efforts, be what may.'

Had this milksop assailed him with any kindness, then he might have hesitated, but the lofty treatment of Daniel Coates on the Imber road the day before sealed it. Now was the time for Lieutenant Hugo Styles, the slightly too corpulent leader of men, to learn a little humility. 'Very well, then,' Hervey conceded.

Oh, to have Jessye, or Nero, or even a troop horse! But he knew this little gelding, though green, had a turn of speed, and he guessed that with a strong leg he would not shy at another horse bearing down. He wished he were wearing a shorter coat, not his father's long grey one; but this, too, was beyond amendment, and he contented himself instead by shortening his stirrups two holes. One initiative he might take, however, was to find a sharp enough sword. He declined the first one offered and rode over instead to the only yeoman whose sabre had cut cleanly. Styles eyed him quizzically. The lieutenant of yeomanry may even have begun to have second thoughts as he himself rode to the other end of the gallop, two hundred yards distant. But there he drew his sword with an exaggerated flourish, and his chestnut thoroughbred, an entire, began prancing and snorting. The serjeant-major gave the signal, and Styles plunged forward, containing the charger in a steady canter only with difficulty.

Hervey was not without his difficulties, too, as his young horse began bucking, but he managed to get him back into his hands and thence to a goodish canter – and then gallop – and closed with the posts before Styles had even reached the check rails. But instead of running down the *outside* of his posts he went *between* them and the rails. Ignoring his own sheaves, and leaning far out of the saddle and stretching over the parallel rails, he sliced each of Styles's cleanly with economical backhand cuts. At the end of the rails he turned the gelding on its quarters and, with Styles shouting after him incomprehensibly, galloped back down the line on the outside of the posts, slicing each of his own sheaves equally cleanly with neat backhand cuts to the nearside.

The troop's acclamation was immediate but just as quickly silenced by Styles's rage: 'What the *deuce* d'ye think yer playing at! Who the deuce d'ye think ye are!'

Hervey, who made no reply, had not noticed one of the open carriages drive up to them, and nor had Styles, whose language was rapidly becoming that of the proverbial trooper. Its occupant, a young woman of obvious fashion, with dark tresses and large eyes the colour of the yeomanry's mid-blue facings, knew exactly who Styles's recruit was.

'Hugo, this is Cornet Matthew Hervey of the Sixth Light Dragoons, just back from France,' she said with some solemnity, but with the suggestion of a smile, too. 'Have you not met?'

Hervey was taken aback, though he did not at first see the full import of that recognition. Poor Styles, he thought – not only distressed (humiliated was perhaps too strong a word) in front of his troop, but in front of a lady with whom evidently he had some connection. He could hardly take satisfaction in that.

Styles struggled visibly to bring his rage under control as he turned and saluted the carriage. 'Good morning, Lady Henrietta,' he spluttered, and, turning to Hervey, he bowed slightly: 'Pleased to make your acquaintance, sir.' But it carried no conviction.

Hervey was at once mortified by the discovery of who occupied the carriage. Much though he had contemplated the manner of his re-acquaintance with Henrietta Lindsay, he could never have imagined this. She would, he felt sure, think his display showy and vulgar, and would be angered by the discomposing of Styles. He raised his hat but could find no words, not even a commonplace greeting. He might not, indeed, have recognized her at any casual meeting, but a second or so's study of her eyes left him in no doubt. His stomach heaved and his head swam.

But how had she recognized him?

'Have you not read of Mr Hervey in the *Miscellany*?' she asked Styles with what seemed mock surprise.

'I have not seen the *Miscellany* yet,' Styles replied coolly.

'Why, indeed, it is printed this very morning, and up with the latest news. Here, let me read you a little.

'"Matthew Hervey, Esquire, the only son of the Reverend Thomas Hervey, Vicar of Horningsham, has lately returned from the French war in which he has been nobly serving as a cornet in His Majesty's 6th Light Dragoons. Mr Hervey accompanied his corps to Spain soon after the commencement of Lord Wellington's campaign and has seen much fighting in the four years thence. It is understood that this gallant officer will remain in the district upon furlough for some two months before returning to the Dragoons who are to be garrisoned in Ireland."'

Styles glowered, and Hervey shifted uneasily in the saddle.

'And what do you think of our yeomanry's appearance, Mr Hervey?' she added.

'Very fine, very fine indeed, madam,' he replied. If she had chosen the word *appearance* in order to restore the wretched Styles's self-esteem (and she had a look that said she might), then he did not wish to risk any discourtesy by a critical remark. In any case, his reply was honest enough if by *appearance* she meant only their fine uniforms.

'And do you not agree with Miss Austen that there is nothing finer than the volunteers in their regimentals?'

'I do not know Miss Austen, ma'am,' replied Hervey, puzzled.

'You do not know of Jane Austen?' Her incredulity again had the ring of mock surprise. 'Miss Austen is our foremost authoress,' she explained, holding up a small volume. '*Pride and Prejudice*, Mr Hervey, published only recently. It tells of how the militia win the hearts of the ladies when they come into the district.'

Hervey confessed that neither had he heard of the title.

'Upon my word, Mr Hervey! You are not so conceited a regular as to disdain the affairs of the volunteers?' she chided.

'No, madam,' he stammered back, 'not at all. I—'

'Then, *do* permit me to read some,' she interrupted. 'Miss Austen is *so* keen an observer of human nature. *Here*, I have it.' She leafed through several pages until a little smile of triumph overcame her. 'I must first tell you, Mr Hervey, that the book's heroines are five sisters of singular intellect and sensibility, but all are enraptured by the presence of the militia officers – just as our own yeomanry steal the hearts of all they meet. *Now*, here is what she writes: "They could talk of nothing but officers; and Mr Bingley's large fortune" – Mr Bingley is a coarse-bred sort, Mr Hervey, much given to show' (she smiled, but her continuing irony eluded him – how was he to know Bingley's true character? – and he presumed this to be some sort of rebuke) – ' "Mr Bingley's large fortune, the mention of which gave animation to their mother, was worthless in their eyes when opposed to the regimentals of an ensign." '

Hervey felt the deep water into which he had stumbled about to close over him. Here again was the mocking child of the schoolroom, of the fallen tree and the captured hat. The message was as clear as it might be: she indeed thought little of his show, and the yeomanry were as close as she chose to come to the profession of soldiering. 'Forgive me, madam,' he said, shaking his head, 'but I must be away. It was a pleasure to make your acquaintance.'

Even as he spoke he thought the words absurd, but he was angry that she had enabled Styles, this pompous ass of an ornamental officer, to reinflate himself. But, more, he had made her re-acquaintance in such a manner as to appear both brash and artless. As he trotted away he knew they would be laughing, and great was his relief when, out of sight beyond the trees, he could spur into a gallop.

He stayed a long time in the stable rubbing the gelding down, cleaning saddlery, filling hay-racks – anything, in fact, which might distract his thoughts from the encounter in the park. It was a full hour before he felt ready to go inside. 'Matthew,' began his sister the moment he did, and with the air of someone about to impart good news, 'we are to dine with Lord Bath this evening.'

'*Oh!*' he replied – groaned almost – as he thought what must come next.

'Matthew, I am astounded! Do you not wish to see the marquess after so long away?'

'Yes . . . of course . . . I . . .' he stammered.

'But do you not realize that Henrietta Lindsay will be there also? And there is to be *another* officer, too – well, from the yeomanry, that is.'

Hervey groaned even louder. 'Elizabeth, I must needs recount the events of the morning: they are not propitious.'

No, not at all propitious, for it occurred to him that Henrietta Lindsay must have known in the park of this invitation, and she had played him as a cat's-paw.

Elizabeth spent much time contemplating her journal the following morning. She had much to write that was merely narrative – though dinner at Longleat was never occasion for a commonplace entry. She had first to describe the evening – the food, the music, the cards (there was no dancing), and such conversation as was of a routine nature. This much was straightforward, although she spent longer than she anticipated recalling the details of the elegant table laid before them: the Moroccan quails fattened in Normandy, ortolans from the Loire, truffles and champagne – all to be had easily, if at prodigious expense, now that the Royal Navy's blockade was lifted. And she had to record, too, how they had dined *à la Russe* (no doubt at Henrietta's insistence), with each course served by footmen in white gloves, to the ladies first, rather than the older fashion of laying all the dishes before them on the table.

Her principal difficulty, however, lay in first comprehending, and then finding the appropriate words to describe, the sentiments and purposes of the three (as she put it) *dramatis personae.* Henrietta gave her most cause for perplexity, for her demeanour throughout the evening suggested some 'understanding' with Styles, although she had never confided anything of the sort. And Elizabeth began to doubt whether, indeed, she might claim any particular fellowship with her in light of this. Styles himself, she observed, had carried about him a sort of proprietorial air which at times verged on the possessive. It was evident, too, that this was exacerbated – perhaps deliberately encouraged even – by the attention that Henrietta showed to Matthew. Though, curiously, it seemed to her that Styles was more discomfited by adulation of Hervey as a soldier than by what Henrietta's notice might truly portend.

Of her brother, Elizabeth was in a state of mild despair. She had hoped that his service might have wrought something more masterful in him, yet last night he had been as ever. During dinner itself he had seemed at ease enough: there were occasions when he might even have been said to be expressive. Yet when coffee was served, and with it a renewal of Henrietta's childhood teasing, he had relapsed into silence, whence nothing could tempt him for the remainder of the evening.

At length she sighed, aloud and deep. She picked up her pen and wrote with a noticeably firmer hand than the plainer narrative had demanded: 'I have ever held to Dryden's avowal that none but the brave deserves the fair. And I cannot doubt that Matthew is brave, for he was ever so. Yet deserts are never wholly just, and I pray that his heart will not be faint.'

CHAPTER SEVEN

# WHEN PRIDE COMETH

*Horningsham, The Feast Day of St Mary Magdalen,*
*22 July*

'O come, let us sing unto the Lord: let us heartily rejoice in the strength of our salvation,' began the vicar of Horningsham.

'Let us come before his presence with thanksgiving: and show ourselves glad in him with Psalms,' came Hervey's strong, clear response, in contrast to the frailer versicle. And so throughout the *Venite.*

The Reverend Thomas Hervey opened the smaller bible used for the daily offices and announced the first lesson while, opposite, Matthew and Elizabeth Hervey sat alone in the choir stall. 'Here beginneth the eleventh chapter of the Book of Proverbs: "A false balance is abomination to the Lord: but a just weight is his delight. When pride cometh, then cometh shame: but with the lowly is wisdom. The integrity of the upright shall guide them: but the perverseness of transgressors shall destroy them . . ."'

As a boy Hervey had regularly attended the daily offices with his father, for whom it was the command of the Book of Common Prayer that they be said publicly: 'And the Curate that ministereth in every Parish-Church or Chapel, being at home, and not being otherwise reasonably hindered, shall say the same in the Parish-Church or Chapel where he ministereth, and shall cause a Bell to be tolled thereunto a convenient time before he begin, that the people may come to hear God's Word, and to pray with him.' Since John's going away to Oxford, and Matthew's to the war, Elizabeth had filled the antiphonal void (for the vicar of Horningsham could afford neither curate nor clerk), though Thomas Hervey had never been entirely at ease with a woman in his chancel. There was little doubting the old man's pleasure in having once again a son at Morning Prayer.

Afterwards, however, as they walked to the vicarage, the sun warm on their backs even at that early hour, he seemed to be at some pains to show his esteem for Elizabeth's succour during those long years: 'I think it a pity that, when the prayer book supplanted the breviary, St Mary Magdalen's became no longer a holy day,' he began, 'for it was she to whom the risen Lord first appeared and gave a message for the brethren.'

Elizabeth saw at once his meaning: 'And it was she who remained at the cross.'

The vicar of Horningsham nodded.

'Could it be that her former sins stood against her still?' wondered Hervey, somehow of the mind that Cranmer had been, perhaps, less forgiving than some.

'Oh, I think not. She was a true penitent. Yet there are those in the Eastern churches, as I believe, who hold that it was not the Magdalen who was the sinner but a third woman.'

'How so, Father? I have not heard this,' asked Elizabeth.

'Oh, my poor scholarship is insufficient, I am afraid. That must be a question for Mr Keble,' he replied.

'*Dear* Mr Keble,' sighed Elizabeth. 'I hope he will stay with us again, do not you, Matthew?'

Hervey agreed, for there was in John Keble's certain faith much that gave comfort – as there had been with Sister Maria.

The thought of Sister Maria was especially apt that day, for it was the convent's patronal festival. He felt uneasy still about his promise to her, though he was at a loss to know what more he could do as things stood: while he had been in London he had taken a letter to the French consul-general for the comte de Chantonnay; but there had been no word from France, and it looked as though the ring he carried constantly would go with him to Ireland when the time came.

*     *     *

149

When breakfast was ended Elizabeth took her journal to the garden. Hervey went with her, taking the April-quarterly edition of the *Edinburgh Review* which d'Arcey Jessope had sent him that very week, with the first article marked for his attention, a lengthy piece on 'The State and Prospects of Europe'. 'Do you hear this?' he began after some moments perusing it. ' "The first and predominant feeling which rises on contemplating the scenes that have just burst on our view, is that of deep-felt gratitude, and unbounded delight, – for the liberation of so many oppressed nations, – for the cessation of bloodshed and fear and misery over the fairest portions of the civilized world, – and for the enchanting prospect of long peace and measureless improvement, which seems at last to be opening on the suffering kingdoms of Europe." ' He sighed. 'A long peace and measureless improvement – that is a happy prospect is it not?'

'A *truly* happy prospect,' she replied. 'But though improvement is contingent upon peace, certainly, it does not of itself follow. Do you suppose that *our* parliament shall embrace improvement as vigorously as they did war?'

'Not for one moment,' he smiled, 'but they will pursue the dividends of peace, and some of these might as a consequence promote improvement.'

'So you are not for *Reform*, Matthew? The marquess is, I believe, though Sir George Styles is not.'

'Am I not so obvious a radical, then?' he laughed. 'I care not one jot how Styles – father or son – stand on *Reform*!'

'When pride cometh, then cometh shame!' she chided.

'You were attentive during the lesson, sister.'

'I am ever thus, I assure you! But the marquess – he has a right judgement in such things, think you not?'

'I confess an admiration for the marquess,' he conceded.

'And for his ward surely?' she teased.

'My dear Elizabeth, we were speaking of matters of substance.'

'And is not admiration a matter of substance?'

'Only if the admiration is substantial!'

He was pleased with his response, but she was too quick.

'Then you must now answer for the extent of your admiration rather than for its mere existence!'

Hervey sighed again, but he was not entirely without the skill for a riposte. 'I confess to more admiration for Henrietta Lindsay than she for me, yet that need not amount to a very great deal.'

Elizabeth thought it prudent to make no reply, and instead she carefully recorded her brother's assessment in her journal.

'Tell me, Elizabeth,' he began after several minutes' silence, 'you and Henrietta are close, yet . . .' His words trailed off.

'Oh, Matthew, do not scruple to speak of the truth. You mean that Henrietta is rich, or at least comparatively so, and moves in the best of society. And she is uncommonly pretty, and has graces, and . . . *refinement.* Whereas I—'

'No! I did not mean it so,' he interrupted.

'What did you mean so, then?'

'What I mean is that it is unjust to speak of those qualities as if the very opposite were the case with you, for it is *not* – well, not those which are qualities of the person for sure!'

'You are ever sweet, Matthew! And yet, though there are differences between Henrietta and me, we are, I think, *confidantes*, or as near as may be so called. And have been so these many years, since the schoolroom with its childish intimacies. But, for my part, Henrietta's love of society is sufficient for the both of us, for I truly do not think I have the inclination for it, as well as not having the means. And for Henrietta's part – you must ask her, for she will freely confess to a fascination for the parish and poorhouse but only at a remove, only in my telling. She is the same person whom we knew in the schoolroom, but her circumstances permit her no true purpose in life: I can have no envy for her position. Yet I *know* there is something deeper which may inspire her. You have been here a full month: you must have some sense of this yourself?'

'But I have seen so little of her, and then only without any intimacy in the least part. She is as distant as first she was in the park. I am to school her mare again today, but it will be the same.'

'There is no reason, I think, why it should be. You have much that is of mutual interest: she admires greatly your facility with horses.' Elizabeth could not bring herself to be more direct.

'But she is so well versed in the works of the literary men – and women – of the moment that at times we may as well speak a different tongue. It would seem that all England has been busy with the pen these past five years.'

'Matthew, they are, as you say, of the *moment.*'

'Well said,' he laughed – it was time to be done with that concern. 'So tell me, Elizabeth, what have *you* seen of the saddle of late?'

'Next to nothing, I confess. It is three seasons since I saw hounds.'

'Then, at least I may remedy that. You must visit me in Ireland as soon as I am settled there: the word is that there is no finer country outside the shires.'

'Shall I find a husband, too?' she smiled.

'Only if you are able to choose between the many who will propose!'

'You are ever loyal and gallant, brother!' she laughed. 'I fear that it will be your undoing!'



He did not return until almost four, having spent two hours first longeing then attempting some of the simpler evolutions with Henrietta's new mare. Afterwards she had asked him to take some refreshment at the house, but since Hugo Styles had latterly attached himself he had declined, though he was now regretting his pique.

'The family is in the garden with a caller, Master Matthew,' said Francis as Hervey strode into the cool darkness of the hall.

Taking tea at four was (to Hervey's mind) a conceit lately come to Horningsham, an import from neighbouring Bath. Whose choice this was he had not been troubled to discover, but he would have hazarded the opinion that his mother had succumbed to the influence of Longleat House (though he would have been wrong, for Longleat held to the older custom, and it was Elizabeth who had urged the practice on the household, having read of it in one of Miss Austen's novels). The scene in the garden of that comfortable parsonage was not one of *perfect* fashion, however, for the sight of a china teacup and saucer in a hand that Hervey had only ever seen holding either sabre or bottle was so incongruous as to be positively bizarre. The caller sprang up, deftly transferring cup and saucer from right hand to left, and knuckled his forehead, though bareheaded, as was the custom in the Sixth. 'Good afternoon, Mr Hervey sir!'

'Serjeant Armstrong! What in heaven's name—? Forgive me, Father,' he reddened, checking his mild profanity. 'What could possibly bring you *here*?'

'Matthew,' began his mother before Armstrong could manage a word, 'the serjeant has been given leave but has chosen to come to see *you*! And he has told us so much about you and the war: I cannot think why you did not tell us yourself!'

'Oh, Mother!' laughed Elizabeth, 'we women are not to hear of such things! We should swoon, should we not?'

Armstrong was smiling. He looked as untroubled as if tea in a country parsonage were his everyday habit. So many times in Spain and Portugal Hervey had seen, or heard of, this rough-and-ready serjeant fighting with the fury of a wildcat, and yet he now seemed equally capable of charming the gentlest of souls that were his mother and father, and likewise engaging the most discriminating of mortals that was his sister. 'Sit down, Serjeant Armstrong,' he said with a wry smile as he took a chair himself. 'What *really* brings you here? You have orders for me, I'll warrant.'

By now the family had acquired a sufficient ear for Armstrong's Tyneside vowels and idiom (as alien as anything that had been heard in the village), and were able, just, to discern that he had been sent from Dover to the depot in Canterbury to collect a draft, and that, just before he was to leave for Ireland with them, the recruits were sent instead to the Nineteenth in Canada. The depot's commander had granted him leave (no doubt a less troublesome option, thought Hervey, than having him with time on his hands in Canterbury), and Armstrong had decided to make his way to Cork via Horningsham.

Hervey could not but feel it a flattering, if unusual, choice of route. 'So you are not carrying orders from the regiment?'

'No, sir. Are you expecting any?'

'Major Edmonds instructed me to remain here until such arrived.'

There followed much pleasant but inconsequential conversation, during which the serjeant was able to recount other instances of his cornet's capability (and, indeed, occasions, too, of less distinction), though Hervey himself was lost in contemplation of the continuing absence of orders. Suddenly, however, Armstrong's turn of story sounded alarm – the affair of the Alcalde of Mayorga's daughter and the barrel of sardines. 'How *much* leave is owing to you, Serjeant Armstrong?' he asked abruptly, anxious that the subject be changed.

Armstrong was quick to the signal: 'More than I'm ever likely to be permitted to take, sir!'

'Well, I have an idea,' he began. 'I have another month's leave, perhaps more. Major Edmonds said that I was to stay until receiving orders from him or direct from Lord Sussex. I think that *you* should stay here, too – we can arrange lodgings hereabouts – and drill into our yeomanry troop some practical elements of the profession.'

At this Elizabeth frowned. 'Do you think that Hugo Styles would welcome that?' she asked doubtfully.

Hervey looked faintly surprised. 'He is not so great a fool as to decline it, surely?'

'I was thinking less of the strictly military side, Matthew. Might he not consider it further rivalry?'

But her brother did not catch her meaning. 'That business in the park is long past,' he replied.

Elizabeth raised her eyebrows and sighed to herself. Armstrong sensed at once what her brother had failed to,

154

though he could not know the precise details. She, equally sensible of his position, hastened to make some explanation: 'You must forgive me, Serjeant; I did not intend trespassing on military questions. I am merely anxious to avoid any unnecessary ill-feeling in the district: the yeomanry are so intimate a part of our life at present.'

'No offence, Miss 'Ervey, none at all. These yeomen are proud men: regulars have to step lightly with 'em. To call 'em cat-shooters is horrible cruel.'

This was uncommon diplomacy, thought Hervey: it would have done even Serjeant Strange credit. Nevertheless he was pleased when his father's repeating half-hunter came to his aid, striking the half-hour so as to make the Reverend Thomas Hervey spring up with singular speed muttering something about Evening Prayer. Hervey's mother felt a need to speak to cook, and Elizabeth said she would go with her father to church.

And so, alone in the garden, Hervey and Armstrong sat for some time without speaking, the late-afternoon birdsong supplanting their earlier talk. Both found themselves listening to it intently, even. From the tops of the elms around the house and the yews in the churchyard, and from deep inside the beech hedges, there came a ceaseless chorus of blackbirds and finches which would soften between midday and this hour, and then resume until only a last, solitary thrush remained in the gathering dusk, deposed in turn by the eerier night sounds. Out in the vale rooks chattered and cawed continually. Over the cornfields the sky was full of wood-pigeons with their buzzing and queer calls; and even up on the downs, where there were no hedges and precious few trees, the larks were so numerous that there was continuous song from one end of the plain to the other. How little birdsong there had seemed in Spain and France by comparison.

'By God, Mr Hervey sir, this is grand,' said Armstrong at length.

'Grand? Yes,' replied Hervey, 'but you should see Longleat House to know what is grand in the . . . *grand* sense.'

'And that's a grand family you've got, too.'

Hervey smiled. 'You have never spoken of *your* people, Serjeant Armstrong.'

'Never seemed any point,' he replied with a half-shrug.

'How so?'

'Because they're all dead, sir.'

Hervey was disconcerted: this was something he surely ought to have known. 'Serjeant Armstrong, I . . . I am truly sorry to learn that . . .'

'Well, that's why I enlisted – had to start again.'

'Start again? What do you mean?'

'Well, you remember that tar on the transport from France, the one that 'ad been at Trafalgar?'

'Yes,' he replied, intrigued by the association.

'Well, how many of 'is mates d'ye think were killed in that battle?'

'Four hundred or thereabouts, was it not?'

'Ay, nearer four hundred and fifty, and nearly three times that many knocked about bad. Now, Lord Nelson 'ad twenty-seven ships o' the line: that makes seventeen killed on each, as near as makes no odds.'

Hervey wondered how this surprising grasp of naval statistics connected with the circumstances of Armstrong's family. But he forbore to hurry him: Armstrong had a way with stories.

'And every man at Trafalgar is an 'ero, and every one of them four hundred and fifty is a dead 'ero. But no-one 'as ever heard of the men and bairns killed that same day in 'Ebburn colliery – thirty-five of 'em, two of Nelson's ships' worth of dead 'eroes, and as many cripples. And the dead all sent to their Maker in a split second's explosion of firedamp – my father and 'is father, and my two brothers. I was the youngest and should've been there with 'em except I'd been 'urt in a roof-fall a day afore.'

Hervey was all but overcome, not just by the horror of the accident but by his knowing so little of things. From time to time news reached Horningsham of accidents in the coal-mines nearby in Somerset, but the details were always sparse. 'But I never knew that men could be killed in such numbers,' he said at length, his brow furrowing in disbelief.

'And *bairns*, and their *mothers* and *sisters* an' all sometimes,' added Armstrong emphatically, though more in resignation than in bitterness. Bitterness was reserved for what followed. 'And you know what, Mr 'Ervey? That explosion made two dozen widows and a hundred orphans in 'Ebburn village, an' all thrown on the parish with no extra from the coal owners. My mother died in three months in a damp and lousy poorhouse.'

The birdsong swelled as Hervey sank once more into silence. Armstrong sat impassively, disinclined to tempt him from his thoughts. At length Hervey confronted his shame. 'Serjeant Armstrong, I am truly humbled to admit of my ignorance of all this, and I cannot conceive of how I have never read of these things in the newspapers if they are so frequent.'

'That one at 'Ebburn was small by comparison! And you know why you don't hear of 'em? Because the papers are forbidden to report 'em, that's why.'

They remained a full hour talking, though much subdued. And they spoke of matters of which, only a short time before, Hervey would never have dreamed. That they were able to do so said much perhaps about mutual respect, but equally, it seemed to him afterwards, about the Sixth and its discipline, a discipline of which martinets like Slade could never have any comprehension. *Slade* – even at this time the ghastly remembrance could intrude!

Serjeant Armstrong's temporary assignment with the Warminster Troop proved not nearly so quarrelsome as many had anticipated. He was in any event unlikely to have failed to win the esteem of the yeomen troopers themselves, for any demands he would make on them would surely derive from experience rather than solely from the drill book. In a remarkably short time he was able to improve both their horsemanship and their sword-skills. He had been particularly careful, however, in his dealings with the troop serjeant-major, a foreman on the Marquess of Bath's estate, and had shown him the deference that he would his own in the Sixth – probably more. And with Hugo Styles he was so correct in his compliments, and so leading in his instruction, that the lieutenant's standing in the eyes of the troop must have been considerably enhanced thereby.

They drilled on a Wednesday and a Saturday, and occasionally on a Sunday. Styles attended every muster, for his fortune was sufficiently mature not to require his presence elsewhere, and Henrietta Lindsay accompanied him. Hervey, who, at the outset at least, felt a duty of supervision lest his serjeant be placed in any position of disadvantage, was an equally punctilious spectator. At first he would stand aloof in some position of observation and watch the drill intently, until, by invitation or some other contrivance, he would find himself in the company of Henrietta and Styles. The latter tolerated his presence always with the very least civility that their status as gentlemen and officers compelled. Hervey's disdain of Styles grew by degrees to detestation, for he could find in him no redeeming feature. His dress, speech and manner were contrived to an absurdly exaggerated extent. There were those in the Sixth, Hervey knew, who would certainly excel him in each, but they would give no offence in the doing. Styles was a man of considerable means, it was said, but there were some in the Sixth who were richer and yet would excite no such animosity. All these would-be candidates for equal disdain had the very quality, and in large measure, that Styles wholly lacked: generosity of spirit. And, what was perhaps more, they had shared the privations of a campaign. Hervey concluded that Styles was a man profoundly unsuited for anything but the most ornamental of commands. What a great good fortune it had been that the yeomanry had never been required to repel Bonaparte's troops! One thing only puzzled Hervey: what it was that Henrietta found so agreeable in Styles.

Henrietta herself was always entirely civil at these meetings, but nothing more (or so it seemed to him). As the weeks passed, however, Hervey showed less attention to the evolutions on the drill ground and greater address at joining the other two observers, and so obvious was that address that the lieutenant's duty of civility was placed under a greater strain than he was sometimes capable of bearing. But when Hervey found himself in Henrietta's sole company, as when, for instance, Styles took command of the troop for some manoeuvre or other, she spent so much time asking whether he did not admire this or other about the lieutenant and his yeomen that he became wholly cast down.

Then, on St Bartholomew's Eve, a fast day which the vicarage at Horningsham kept strictly, Hervey's long-expected letter arrived.

'You look puzzled, brother. It is not ill news surely?' asked Elizabeth, sipping her unsweetened tea with no great relish.

'It is from my major. I am to rejoin the regiment in Cork within ten days,' he replied.

'But you were expecting these orders, were you not?'

'I was, but there is something more. It seems that Major Edmonds – he is acting as officer commanding since the lieutenant-colonel was wounded in France – it seems that he had asked the colonel to secure me an appointment at the Horse Guards, but that this had not proved expedient.'

'But that is surely a most agreeable compliment, is it not, Matthew?' she asked, further puzzled by his want of enthusiasm.

'Perhaps so, but the major said nothing of this to me, and it astounds me that he should think I might welcome such a preferment. It is almost as if he wished positively to see me away from the regiment.' He knew, or at least confided, that this latter could not be so. Curiously, however, he sensed that, if the choice had been his now, then it might indeed have been for London rather than for Cork. For, much as the Sixth meant to him, at that moment the thought of quitting Horningsham for so distant a station as Cork, without resolving his feelings for Henrietta Lindsay, filled him with profound gloom. Had he now been with the regiment he would have been able to do what he had always done when troubled: he would have thrown himself at once into an excess of duties, not emerging until he was quite sure that his feelings were, like some difficult remount, in hand. But he was not with the regiment, and the feelings were not, in truth, an unwelcome intrusion. Elizabeth sensed all this better than he might have supposed, but again she said nothing.

'I think I shall ride out on the plain a while,' he said suddenly, almost jumping from his chair. 'Shall you come with me?'

She declined, however, judging the invitation to be but politeness. 'But call, do, on Daniel Coates, Matthew. He is ever wise in all matters,' she urged.

He went to the stables, saddled Coates's bay and within the hour he was on the downs, walking along the scarp with its distant views of Somerset, the Bristol road, and beyond, he supposed, to Cork. In some way or other he had imagined the ride might clear his mind, or steel him perhaps to what he must do. But the purpose was unaccomplished, for as he turned back at Wadman's Coppice all he had succeeded in doing was to identify, by a process not unlike the appraisal of some military problem, two equally impaired options. First, he might proceed to Cork and put Henrietta Lindsay from his mind. The flaw in this, it was soon apparent, was that he did not possess the initiative in matters of the mind. Alternatively, he might make his still-indistinct feelings known and leave for Cork with some understanding between them. Here, however, the flaw seemed even greater, for he was near-certain that his feelings must be wholly unreciprocated – or else he might be deemed unsuitable by the marquess who, though no longer strictly her guardian since she had come of age, was unquestionably a man whose blessing must be sought. But in truth the real impediment was an incapacity to press himself with Henrietta, especially in light of her attachment, however imprecise, with Styles.

For a while he contemplated returning via Drove Farm, where he hoped Daniel Coates's wisdom might extend to matters of this kind. But their talk had always been of the soldier's art and of horses, and there was no reason to suppose that a facility with these might apply equally to his newer concern. Daniel Coates had, indeed, expressed himself only once on the subject: of soldiers marrying he had opined it 'a cruel thing to make a camp-follower of a decent maid'. So instead Hervey made straight for Horningsham by descending the near-vertical sides of Arn Hill (it gave him cause to make much of the young gelding for his balance), and thence through Norridge Wood, the furthest place he and Henrietta had ventured on their childhood rambles together. (He could picture, with surprising recall, her old nurse huffing and puffing, and protesting at the distance they had brought her from Longleat.)

As he neared the edge of the estate he saw the yeomanry again, leaving the park, and they looked more than usually purposeful. He had not known they were to have a drill day and was surprised to see Styles at the head of them. 'Haven't time to dawdle with you, Hervey. There's work to be done,' he called loftily as they broke into a trot.

Armstrong rode up with a resigned look. 'Afternoon, Mr 'Ervey sir. They're off to sabre some poor noddleheads hereabouts.'

'What?'

'Seems there's a gang intent on breaking up machinery at Hindon and the justices have called out the yeomanry. Mr Styles asked me to go with 'em but I said I'd rather not if he didn't mind. An' d'you know what he said? "Damn you for a Luddite yerself, Serjeant – or don't the regulars have the stomach for it?"'

'Ass!' rasped Hervey.

'Well, yer cannee get sense out'r haddock on a Saturday night,' pronounced Armstrong in his broadest Tyneside. 'An' yer wastin' yer time the rest o' the week an' all! Come on, sir, don't worry about it. Come on back to me lodgings and we'll toast the regiment.'

'No, Serjeant Armstrong – tempted as I am. Orders for Cork have arrived: you and I are to be there in a week or so, and there is much to be done. And, besides, today is a fast day,' he added with a smile.

Armstrong looked appalled. 'Well, I for one will go and

drink to our return to the regiment!' he said, striking his boot with his whip. 'Oh, an' by the way, Miss Lindsay has been looking for you, and proper keen to see you she appeared to be.'

Hervey was at once quickened by this report, though he tried to look otherwise. 'Very well, then, Serjeant, I am for home: I will see you at the Bell some time tomorrow or the day after when arrangements for Cork are made.' And he turned the bay sharply back in the direction of the village, putting him into a fast trot.

He did not expect to encounter Henrietta so soon, but as he rounded a corner a half-mile on, he found her walking her hack, alone, in the same direction. His bay's hoofs on the hard-baked road gave away his approach, and she turned. 'Mr Hervey!' she called, 'I was on my way to ask Elizabeth and you to come with me to the great henge tomorrow. Shall you?' she asked, in a manner altogether warmer than ever he had observed at the drill ground.

'With the greatest of pleasure, ma'am. I have not seen the henge since we shared the schoolroom. I cannot speak for Elizabeth, of course, but I am sure—'

'I am going that way,' she replied. 'I will ride with you and save you the trouble of sending word. Tell me, do you cherish those schoolroom days?'

He sighed to himself. She was the model of self-possession, more captivating than ever. Her riding habit was the same blue as the Sixth's uniform, its finely cut bodice accentuating her slender waist, and the full skirt, reaching almost to the ground, was all elegance. Her black silk hat was oiled to a high gloss, her dark tresses were pulled back, and her blue eyes shone. 'I might wish we were there still.'

Even as they rode to the village, however, his doubts began returning. Why had she chosen now to reveal a warmth hitherto concealed? It was not as if she had known he was about to leave. And when she had said 'Poor Hugo will be away at Hindon for several days, I fear', it seemed both invitation and caution. But was he under some obligation to Styles in the lieutenant's absence in aid of the civil power? So many questions of propriety did the circumstances pose that instead he fell into silent confusion.

When, an hour or so later, Henrietta had left the vicarage with his sister's acceptance of the invitation to the henge, he resolved to end his dilemma. 'Elizabeth, I must speak with you about . . . that is, I should welcome your opinion as to . . .' But he was again unable to summon the words.

Hervey was relieved that there was a fourth occupant of Henrietta's barouche, and especially pleased with who the occupant was (the early return of Styles would have been more than he could have borne). The evening before, John Keble had called on his way to Oxford from Lyme Regis where he had been taking the sea air and writing poetry. At first Hervey had thought that the object of his calling might have been Elizabeth, for whom the poet seemed to have formed a strong regard at his first visit (and Hervey had begun increasingly to think that this would be a wholesome match). But John Keble had no other object but to deliver letters of introduction to several clerics beneficed in the neighbourhood of Cork and Dublin, a gesture of kindness for which Hervey made fulsome show of gratitude. And when Elizabeth had asked him to join them for the excursion to the henge Hervey, too, pressed him to accept, word being sent to Longleat that, with Henrietta's leave, a man of letters would accompany them in the morning.

An hour or so before their barouche departed, another coach, not so grand but also bearing the Bath arms, left Longleat for the same destination. It conveyed the elaborate luncheon and the attendants who were to serve it – and Serjeant Armstrong. He had learned of the excursion from one of the Longleat lady's maids, whose coolness towards him hitherto had had a most beguiling effect, and he had offered his services as guard, ingeniously citing the trouble at Hindon to gain a favourable response (forfeiting, thereby, a soldier's farewell from one of the kitchen maids at his lodgings).

If Armstrong's conversation in the first barouche was of an unusually respectable nature, however (sensible as he was of the lady's maid's disposition), that in the principal carriage was positively high-minded, for John Keble's presence, mannered yet warm though he was, seemed not at first to admit of gaiety. Elizabeth was troubled by the disturbances at Hindon, it seemed, fearing that they might spread to the malcontents on Warminster Common. John Keble believed the situation to be a paradigm for the general condition of the realm, and spoke with some passion, and evident knowledge, of poverty in the cities, and also in Ireland. 'You will do well there, Mr Hervey, to keep clear of the disputes between the owners and their tenants, for it is very bitter, much worse than here, more bitter than you can possibly imagine, fuelled as it is by religious bigotry.'

Hervey nodded.

'An unhappy place indeed, Mr Keble,' agreed Elizabeth.

'As unhappy as ever a country could be, I believe, Miss Hervey, and the scars are deep. There is a saying there: "Old sins cast long shadows".'

'Whose are the greater sins there, Mr Keble?' asked her brother. 'Is it possible to discern? For I have read of perfidy on all sides.'

'It is without doubt a confused and confusing story, I am the first to admit. Neither am I the best to tell it. Indeed, I know it very imperfectly. You must call on Canon Verey in Cork as soon as you are able, and he will tell you fairly. He is of the same mind as those in the Church of which we spoke when last we dined together. He is leading his congregation back to proper observance and will do great things.'

But Henrietta would have done with politics. 'I do not like only talk of trouble, especially now we learn that Mr Hervey is to go away so very soon. Mr Keble, you have been composing poetry at Lyme, have you not? May we hear some?'

John Keble blushed. 'Lady Henrietta, you are most flattering. I should in ordinary have been honoured to read some, but that which I have been composing recently is of a religious nature and, because of the sentiments you express, not, I think, what you have in mind. I do, however, have some Shelley with me.'

'*Shelley*, Mr Keble! You do surprise me,' she replied with a smile which conveyed nothing but approval nevertheless.

Hervey looked mystified: 'Shelley, ma'am?'

But Henrietta did not catch his meaning in the inflection (he neither knew of Shelley nor had the slightest idea why Henrietta might be surprised that Keble should carry his poetry), or else she did not reveal it. 'Yes, Mr Hervey, I am quite astonished!'

'You mean, I think,' ventured John Keble, 'that Shelley is a notorious atheist?'

'*That*, Mr Keble, is the very *least* of his transgressions, is it not?' she challenged, and with an even greater smile.

Elizabeth now resolved on some evading action to spare John Keble's blushes. 'I think, Mr Keble, that we are alluding to Mr Shelley's elopement with Miss Westbrook, and she barely sixteen.'

But, before John Keble could respond, Henrietta positively shrieked with horror. 'My dear! That is *nothing*. He has eloped once more, this very month – and to Switzerland, it seems – leaving poor sweet Harriet and two children! And his new paramour is but sixteen, too! *Really*, Mr Keble, how these Romantics have a strong attachment to innocence!'

Elizabeth was dumbfounded at her failure to avert the moment. John Keble sat in open astonishment as Hervey tried manfully to suppress the laughter which threatened to convulse him.

'Mr Hervey,' said Henrietta, seeing his condition and deciding he was not to be spared, 'do *you* approve of Mr Shelley?'

'I must confess, ma'am, that I do not know of either Shelley or his poetry.'

This was in truth scarcely a confession of towering ignorance, for during all the time that Shelley's star had been rising Hervey had been on campaign. Conversation touching on such things was not uncommon in the regiment by any means, but six years was a long time. In the course of the next half-hour, though, the extent of his nescience was truly to disturb him: Byron, Wordsworth, and so many others, were all unfamiliar names. Had he been in some profound sleep? Milton, Dryden, Pope – these he had learned at Shrewsbury, yet not once were they spoken of. Not even Coleridge whom he had of his own volition read copiously. Southey they praised with something bordering on reverence – Elizabeth dazzled them by her discourse on *The Curse of Kehama* – yet when Hervey had become a soldier Robert Southey was known only as a hothead whose Jacobin sympathies were attracting the attention of the authorities. How might he now have become a high Tory and poet laureate? And then John Keble read some (unpublished) sonnets by a surgeon's apprentice whose work he predicted would yet surpass even Southey's. The war, it seemed to Hervey, had touched little beyond the battlefield.

But in the midst of this feast of letters Henrietta gave Hervey perhaps the surest sign of her regard: 'Matthew, will you tell us something of the countryside of Spain? I believe it can be called magnificent, can it not?'

It was not merely that she had said 'Matthew' (she had not called him by his name since his return), it was her evident sensibility in so changing the course of their conversation. He responded keenly, describing the landscape of the Peninsula as best he could, though he found his words less than adequate after so much poetry, and each time he appeared to be nearing a conclusion Henrietta would smile encouragingly, prompting him to reminisce yet more. When he recounted the aftermath of the battle at Toulouse, John Keble pressed him to details of the nunnery, which he then recalled in more precise terms.

'I conclude from your description of their dress and rule that your Sister Maria is a discalced Carmelite,' said Keble at length.

Henrietta giggled. 'That sounds faintly disreputable!'

John Keble smiled: he was getting the measure of her. 'No, Lady Henrietta; the Carmelites are a very ancient order which trace their origins to the desert fathers on Mount Carmel. *Discalced* simply means that the order goes barefoot. It is part of their austere regimen.'

'Do not you remember,' smiled Elizabeth, '*calceus* – a shoe?'

'Of course. How could one forget those days in the school-room! How I admired Matthew for the way he could decline a noun!'

Hervey shifted in his seat, unsure whether her remark portended a return to mocking. But he did not have to trouble with a reply, for the appearance of the great henge itself, a half-mile distant, brought instead little cries of awe and appreci-ation from Henrietta. And the object of that appreciation was not only the henge, for here, on the eastern extremity of the plain, as empty as it must have been in the earliest times but for sheep grazing unattended, the resplendence of Longleat House had been transported to the middle of the ancient stone circle. Silver stood on damask tablecloths, wine lay chilling in huge coolers, and gilded chairs were arranged by a round table. Two footmen, conceding nothing to the heat of the day, neither wig nor livery, attended close by.

'Have you seen the stones before, Mr Keble?' asked Henrietta as they got down from the carriage, feigning not to be overly distracted by the Longleat extravagance.

'Only once, ma'am, but I have read much of them.'

'They were erected by the Romans were they not?'

'No, I do not think so,' he replied. 'That is what Mr Inigo Jones concluded because he did not believe any people of antiquity in these islands other than the Romans could have carried out such a task. He was an architect of the classical school, and it is therefore not surprising that that was what he conceived it to be. He made a very fine drawing showing how the stone circle might have looked as a classical building. But it is very circumstantial – indeed, almost wholly conjectural, I would say.'

'What of the theory that it was a place of coronation for the Danish kings?' suggested Hervey.

'It is remarkable that whoever has treated of this monument

has bestowed on it whatever class of antiquity he was particularly fond of.'

'That is a very shrewd judgement,' he replied.

'Oh, not my words, Mr Hervey – Horace Walpole's. No, of all theories I think the Danish is the least convincing. There is sufficient literary evidence to suggest it is much earlier.'

'Then, what do you think *is* the explanation of the stones, sir?' Hervey pressed.

'Well, I consider that Mr Aubrey's study is the most scholarly. He suggests that the henge is a religious site of the Ancient Britons and their priesthood, the Druids.'

'Ritual sacrifices?' said Hervey.

'I fear so.'

But for sheep beyond the cursus, and the footmen, the four were quite alone. Sitting in the middle of the stone circle after their luncheon, even with so much Longleat finery, it was not difficult perhaps to imagine these Druids, especially since John Keble seemed to know so much about their religion, its rites and ritual. Elizabeth and Henrietta wished to view the circle from one of the tumuli, leaving Hervey and Keble to the Druids and a last glass of Madeira. When they were gone, John Keble interrupted his own speculation on the nature of primeval belief to ask Hervey so direct a question that the latter was all but stunned. 'Mr Hervey,' he began, fixing him with a benignant expression that belied his junior years, 'you are, I perceive, much troubled by your affections for Lady Henrietta. Are you uncertain of them, by some chance?'

Hervey made not a sound.

'Permit me, my friend, but is it – as I suspect – that you are not able sufficiently to discern what is love and what is merely admiration? Do not misunderstand me, mind, for there is infinitely much that a man might admire in Lady Henrietta – and love might follow as a consequence. Yet, it seems to me, after so many brutal years in Spain one might be inclined to be enamoured of something merely because it stands in such contrast to the brutish.'

Hervey smiled thinly. 'You have said "merely" twice, sir; I wish it were indeed thus!'

John Keble smiled, too, but warmly.

'Holy, fair, and wise is she;
The heaven such grace did lend her,
That she might admirèd be.'

Hervey threw his head back, smiling broadly:

'Is she kind as she is fair?
For beauty lives with kindness.
Love doth to her eyes repair,
To help him of his blindness . . .'

'Bravo, Mr Hervey! We are two gentlemen indeed, if not actually of Verona. But permit me to make one more observation on the matter of searching for perfection – and a profound one, I trust. At the beginning of the gospel which bears your name, the apostle sees fit to place the genealogy of our Saviour, and in it are the names of four women: Tamar, Rahab, Ruth and Uriah's wife, Bathsheba.' Hervey studied him intently as John Keble's expression turned to one of even greater warmth. 'Tamar's sins we both know of, as indeed we do Rahab's; Ruth was an alien, and Bathsheba was both adulteress and conniver to murder. Yet these women are of our Lord's family. I commit this to your reflection, Mr Hervey.'

Never before had Hervey considered the passage in more than the driest genealogical terms, but before he was able to reflect, or even to make some interim acknowledgement to this man whose charity now seemed as great as his incisiveness, the contemplative peace of the stone circle was broken by the return of his sister and Henrietta.

'Mr Keble,' began Elizabeth 'my companion is tired of the sun. Would you hold my parasol while I sketch the stones?'

John Keble agreed readily.

After they were gone, and after an even longer silence,

Henrietta asked: 'Is it not perfectly horrid to imagine human sacrifice in this very place?'

'It is; *horrid*,' Hervey agreed, somewhat abstractedly.

'But, if there were sacrifices, there must surely have been weddings here, too!' she added brightly. 'Do you not think it a perfectly wonderful idea to be wedded in such a place, the stones draped with mistletoe perhaps?'

Hervey was startled. 'I . . . I had not thought of it,' was all he could manage by reply.

'*What?* Had not thought of marriage, or not of such a thing in this place? Surely you do not lack heart?'

The mocking again – why *did* she taunt him so? He said what first came into his head (and cursed himself as he did so): 'Are you thinking of such a place for marriage with Mr Styles?'

'Matthew,' she began quietly, 'how could you possibly have supposed that I should wish to marry Hugo Styles?'

He struggled for some explanation. 'Well, I . . . that is,' he stammered. 'That day in the park when you read from your novel – you seemed to be suggesting—'

'Suggesting what?' she continued softly.

'You seemed to be suggesting that a yeomanry officer was irresistible – something about regimentals, and the ladies of the district or whatever. I took it to mean that you referred in particular to Styles. He has a very handsome income at least, has he not?'

'Matthew,' she said with a smile, taking no apparent offence at his actuarial recommendation, 'have you since read *Pride and Prejudice*?'

'No, I—'

'Well, go and do so!' she laughed. 'At least, read that passage carefully when they are all at Meryton, the one I read aloud that day – chapter six or seven, I think it is!'

*More* riddles. Why? How was he to discover her meaning? Was it merely that a spoiled existence was to be relieved by dallying? Or was this sumptuousness around them another kind of riddle, a sign of the gulf between them perhaps? However close their childhood in that schoolroom, and however close Henrietta's friendship with Elizabeth, perhaps that gulf were so wide as to be a chasm, unbridgeable. It was a wretched, hopeless conclusion, and he lapsed into unhappy silence.

As if then, at some unheard trumpet-call, Serjeant Armstrong, who had so far dutifully stood aloof (indeed, unseen – on the instructions of the lady's maid), now appeared from between two of the sarsens. And never had Hervey been so pleased by his appearing, for it reminded him of the promise of their return to the regiment, and the promise of— What? Relief from the necessity of confronting these other . . . . *intrusions*?

Henrietta seemed equally delighted. 'Serjeant!' she called, 'come here and give us your opinion.'

*In God's name*, thought Hervey, was he now to be humiliated by having his serjeant drawn into this? He made to protest, but—

'Serjeant, we have been discussing these stones. Could they have had some military purpose, do you think?' asked Henrietta.

Relief coursed through him.

'I couldn't honestly say, miss,' began Armstrong, 'but a circle's a powerful defensive position, for sure.'

'Could you imagine that the circle was used for sacrificing maidens to pagan gods?' she asked, smiling coyly.

And, with the sure *coup d'œil* that had so evidently deserted Hervey, Armstrong smiled, too, pausing only for an instant: 'Not if they were as bonny as you, miss!'

Hervey was dumbstruck as Henrietta shrieked with laughter.

Three days later Elizabeth made the shortest entry in her journal in many months:

August 28th, St Augustine's Day
Today Matthew and his serjeant left for Ireland, and
the house is once again silent. Matthew is grown to

manhood yet somehow there is an innocence about him which, though endearing, is cause enough for concern. His serjeant is a fine man, however, and devoted to him, and I think no ill should become him while he has such a man to serve with. Of any expectation that we had of Matthew and Henrietta we must no longer speak, for he showed not a moment's feeling for her, or, rather, no ability to convey any feeling if feeling there were – though hers for him was plain to see.

# CHAPTER EIGHT
# THE LESSON OF HISTORY

---

*The Cove of Cork, 3 September*

'Have you *ever* seen the like of it?' thrilled Hervey, so taken by the prospect of Cork's great sheltered bay as to be oblivious to all else. 'Anything so . . . *inspiring* as those headlands, and the sheer *size* of the anchorage?'

Serjeant Armstrong leaned over the weather rail and retched loudly again. 'For God's sake, Mr 'Ervey, never 'ave I known ought like this crossing. Even Biscay after Corunna was no match for it. I've been throwing up me accounts 'alf the night.' And he leaned over the side again and retched even louder.

Strong south-westerlies had made St George's Channel no place for a soldier in whom the gentlest of swells invariably induced nausea. The Bristol merchantman which regularly plied this route – no longer in convoy now peace was returned – had hove to for a night in Carmarthen Bay rather than risk entering the channel with St Gowan's Head on a lee shore. However, by this, their fourth morning, the winds had backed and moderated to no more than a fresh breeze which now took them effortlessly into the great harbour at Cork. Three men-o'-war – a first-rate and two frigates – lay at anchor under the sentinel of the gun batteries on the headlands, in scale no more than daisies on the lawn at Horningsham. And the land itself, distant though it still was, looked as green as legend had it.

'Do you know what day it is, Serjeant Armstrong?'

'If you said Judgement Day, I'd believe you,' he replied, still clutching the rail for all he was worth, though there was but the merest swell now.

'It is the anniversary of the battle of Worcester.'

'Is that right, sir?' Armstrong sighed. 'And what might that 'ave been about?'

'The Civil War – you must surely know of the battle of Worcester? After Worcester the king was a fugitive, and his officers, too. I was thinking of Captain Thomas Hervey: he came here, to Cork, after the battle.'

'And what then?'

'He lived peaceably in Dublin, so I understand, until the plague carried him off. He had been a cavalryman, with Prince Rupert.'

'That's right cheering, Mr Hervey,' said Armstrong, a little colour at last returning to his face.

Hervey continued to peer at the distant hills through the small telescope he had purchased from a French artillery officer captured at Salamanca. 'Did you have any family in that war, Serjeant Armstrong?' he asked, seeming not to notice, still, Armstrong's indifference to conversation.

'I 'ave no more idea than Adam,' he replied. 'I 'eard tell my grandfather was a collier, but further back than 'im I 'aven't a notion. My father's younger brother were a tar, died of fever in the Indies – that's all the service I know of.'

Hervey closed his telescope and looked at his serjeant standing squarely and very much the better for the sheltered waters of the Cove. 'I beg your pardon: I did not mean any show by it. It seemed uncommon chance that we should be sailing into Cork on this day, that is all.'

'No offence taken, as usual, sir.'

'I wonder how living in barracks shall suit us,' Hervey continued, but changing tack.

'A novelty sure enough. It might suit the Guards and Marines, but I think I should prefer the old way,' Armstrong replied with a shrug.

'Doubtless the Horse Guards would, too,' agreed Hervey, 'but billeting in Ireland is an altogether different matter. It is one thing to discompose a few English farmers and innkeepers, quite another to foist troops on a sullen population. No, there have been barracks here, and fortified too, since Cromwell. We shall have to take their measure.'

So large was the anchorage that it took a full hour to see them berthed, and it was a further hour before they reached the Royal Barracks. Armstrong was first to remark on their size, larger, as they were, than even the Guards' in St James's. Built not ten years before, there was space for over one hundred and fifty officers and two thousand men. On this day they were half-empty, however, only a small rear-party from the Sixth occupying the cavalry quarters. The rest of the regiment, explained the quartermaster in charge of rear details, had sailed to Dublin a fortnight earlier for a review. It was no use Hervey's trying to join them, he insisted, since they were expected back within the week.

Hervey might have been glad of some breakfast, but the regiment's mess was closed, and although he could have messed with the Fusiliers, the other occupants of the barracks, he felt disinclined to be too sociable at such an hour. Instead he went to the stables to see Coates's bay brought in from the harbour by one of the ostlers. Armstrong had already been collared for duty by the rear-details serjeant-major.

''Ey up, sir!' called a voice from the hayloft as he entered the otherwise deserted stables. Johnson clambered down the ladder to cast an eye over the new charger. 'He looks a good 'un, but tha won't be able to call 'im Brandywine, he said, looking at the nameplate on the headstall.

'Why not?'

'Because t'adjutant's just bought one an' called 'im that. Tha should know 'e were at t'battle o' Brandywine 'imself!'

Hervey sighed. Johnson had brought him rudely back to the trying niceties of regimental life. 'Very well, then – *you* choose.'

Johnson did not hesitate. ''*Arkaway*.'

'You reckon he may be a Derby runner?' laughed Hervey. 'Well, why not? Harkaway it is, then. What is the news otherwise?'

Johnson was always abreast of the news, be it from the

orderly room or from the canteen. 'Quartermaster Hill has died of an ague,' he began.

'Oh,' said Hervey, 'I am right sorry – a good man and an honest quartermaster.'

'Ay, t'canteen raised a fair sum for 'is widow. There's a new vetinry an' all.'

'How so? Has Mr Selden retired at last?'

'No – 'e was caught in fleegranty,' replied Johnson breezily, as he got to work with the curry-comb.

Hervey looked more than a little surprised, but easily the master of Johnson's pronunciation. 'What, with a woman from the town?'

'No,' replied the groom as he continued brushing. 'With that blackie in the band.'

'Great heavens!' said Hervey, abashed, 'I had no idea that—'

'And who do ye think the general is in these parts?' added Johnson before Hervey could elaborate on the extent of his surprise.

'I have no idea.'

'General Slade!'

'Oh!' he groaned, before checking himself in front of a subordinate – and then quite forgetting himself. 'Oh, that is very ill news indeed.'

They talked for an hour or more. But only when Hervey said that he must go to find lodgings in the city did Johnson remember that there were rooms ready for him in the mess – he had a key, and there was an invitation to dinner waiting there, too.

'From whom?'

'Som'dy from t'cathedral,' Johnson replied with a shrug.

And Canon Verey's invitation to dine the instant he arrived in Cork was curiously insistent: Hervey would have found it hard to ignore even had he other duties to attend to. Johnson was therefore dispatched with a note announcing his officer's arrival and intention to join him for dinner at six that evening, an hour that seemed a reasonable compromise between the older and newer fashions, in the absence of information as to which prevailed in Cork.


The canonry was a more modest establishment than Hervey had expected. It was a fine enough house, in a new terrace in Dean's Yard, but small by comparison with one in an English close. Canon Verey himself was a tall, spare and somewhat austere-looking man in his fifties, a Hebrew scholar and a bachelor. Hervey knew of the scholarship from John Keble but guessed his celibacy within minutes of entering the house, for its walls were lined with books in an entirely haphazard manner and lacked any sign of a feminine hand, either present or past.

There were two other guests. One was about the same age as the canon, though shorter, bald, a little round, with a ready smile and a Dublin accent – which Hervey recognized from having heard so much of it in the Peninsular army. This Dublin man was the chapter clerk, a Trinity College attorney called Nugent. The second guest was altogether less genial. Perhaps a little younger, small-framed and with a full head of black hair, he gave Hervey a searching look as they shook hands. 'Dr O'Begley, here, is my physician, when he is not at his infirmary,' Canon Verey explained.

Proceedings before dinner were uncommonly brisk. They drank but one glass of sherry apiece (giving, thereby, the lie to Hervey's notion that Ireland would put even his own mess to the test), and then dinner was announced by the same maid who had answered the door. This same girl then served them dinner itself, which began with a cold, but palatable, soup of shellfish and potato. Scarcely had Hervey lifted his spoon, however, but that Dr Verey began the serious business of the evening: 'Mr Keble writes that you are a *thinking* soldier, Mr Hervey.'

'I hope I am that, sir, but it is nothing remarkable.'

'A thinking soldier nothing remarkable, Mr Hervey?'

enquired Dr O'Begley, with the faint suggestion of a challenge in his tone.

'I saw many in the Peninsula,' said Hervey cautiously.

'Then, *that* is where they have all been!' replied the physician drily.

'You must not mind Dr O'Begley,' said Nugent with a smile. 'He has nothing against soldiers as such, just English ones! And, indeed, they do not even have to be soldiers!'

'Mr Hervey,' continued Canon Verey, feigning not to notice the exchanges, 'my purpose in inviting you here is to explain something of the complexities of this country. You are a junior officer, of that I am aware, but even *one* officer who understands something of the country will be a beginning; and it may be that you will be minded to pass on some of that understanding to your fellow officers. *I* have little enough opportunity to do so. Indeed, I would not in the ordinary course of events have made your acquaintance, other than after morning prayer on a Sunday perhaps. The garrison keeps itself very much to itself, except for the hunting field. Mr Keble's introduction is therefore most felicitous.'

Hervey felt disinclined to take offence. He had somehow expected to be preached at this evening, and Dr Verey's manner, though grave, fell well short of being sanctimonious. In any case, the notion of discovering something of the country other than the received prejudices of the Ascendancy engaged him not a little. But therein lay an assumption surely. For was not Dr Verey the apotheosis of that Ascendancy, the sub-dean of a cathedral of its alien church? Might this evening not be, in spite of John Keble's best intentions, no more than a protracted sermon to its greater glory? He sighed inwardly, resigned to the ordeal. But to what purpose might these other strange birds be present?

'Even after so many years in this country I have an incomplete understanding,' Dr Verey explained. 'Nugent here is a formidable historian, a Trinity College man. O'Begley is, too – or, rather, he is a formidable historian but not a Trinity College man.'

'No, indeed I am *not* a Trinity College man, Mr Hervey,'

began the doctor testily, 'though that is neither by my own choice nor through any insufficiency of learning, merely by chance of religion.'

'Chance of *persuasion*, Doctor – we are all of one religion surely.'

'Persuasion it is, then, Canon,' he replied briskly.

'Indeed, I would go further and say that we are all of one faith.'

'Canon, this is not the night for divinity, if you please.' O'Begley was becoming impatient, and Dr Verey bowed. 'The Penal Laws, Mr Hervey,' he continued. 'They are ameliorated but not gone – as ye surely know – and they were a damned sight more severe in my youth. It was America or France to study my medicine: a Catholic was denied such learning here. And when came I home, for mercy's sake, I might not, under penalty of said laws, own a horse worth more than five pounds! Can you credit *that*, Mr Hervey? Catholics were not allowed to own a horse worth more than five pounds! You are a cavalryman; that ought to amuse you!'

Hervey tried to imagine the military necessity of such a limitation, but could not conceive of any that might be represented to the doctor with any credibility. 'We had Catholic officers in the army in Spain,' he tried.

'Any senior ones?' rasped O'Begley.

Justification of the Penal Laws was the least of his concerns, however, for it suddenly occurred to him that Canon Verey might be no more a loyal instrument of the Ascendancy than was his irascible guest. And if the sub-dean of Cork were some kind of latter-day non-juror, then it might be less an evening of tedium and rather more of sedition.

He need not have worried. Canon Verey followed Dr O'Begley's intemperance with an uncontentious chronology of the Norman and earlier English settlements, most of which was, in any case, vaguely familiar from his Shrewsbury days. But then came Cromwell to the story, and Nugent and O'Begley began to relate, alternately, what Hervey had never before heard referred to as 'the War of the Two Kings'. The canon's method, as well as his purpose, was now clear: O'Begley was to be the champion of the Catholic explication, and Nugent of the other. Yet he guessed, from the ease at which these three men were in each other's company, that there would at some stage of the evening be a reconciliation of opposing views, a denouement to which he might therefore look forward keenly, though he would listen intently meanwhile to the unfolding of the history.

A large salmon, which Dr Verey was proud to reveal he had himself netted the day before on the Kenmare, came and went during the recounting of the War of the Two Kings, as did some fine hock. By the time the narrative reached the battle of the Boyne – the only occasion on which, it seemed, the two kings actually confronted each other in the field – the chapter clerk and the physician had thoroughly warmed to their subject.

Hervey had begun a tally of the grievances as soon as it had become apparent that such listings were to be made. O'Begley's list included the Ulster plantation, Cromwell's sack of Drogheda and Wexford, the forcible transportations to Connacht, and the martyrdom of Oliver Plunket. Nugent's was equally compelling, the 1641 massacre in Ulster, and Tyrconnel's confiscations of 1687, seemingly every bit as bloody and incomprehensible. But, in respect of the crucial question of where loyalties lay *now*, Hervey had received no answer nor yet could he suppose there might be one in the face of this welter of contradictory evidence.

A mutton pudding had also come and gone, and some good burgundy. Candles had been lit, then new ones brought in, and the maid had been dismissed for the night. The house martins had long since gone to their nests in the eaves, and only owls and bats made any intrusion on the conversation. Canon Verey now raised the question of loyalty which remained. 'The question *is*: was Ireland loyal during the late war with France?' he insisted.

He did not address it directly to the doctor, however. Rather he offered it as might a don to his seminar. Again, Hervey thought it had the ring of well-rehearsed disputation, for O'Begley did not immediately respond, leaving Nugent to speak to it first.

'Have you heard of Wolfe Tone and the Society of United Irishmen, Mr Hervey?'

'Imperfectly,' was his prudent and honest reply.

'Well, permit me to remind you . . .'

And Hervey was indeed reminded – and at length – of the strange, convoluted history of that nationalist rebellion. But the account was ultimately more perplexing than enlightening. Such, it seemed, was the canon's intention; for, as if this were indeed a Trinity College tutorial, he now embarked on a summing-up which, if not exactly the denouement Hervey had been anticipating, in its way began to explain why these three men might share – more or less amicably – a table. 'You see, Mr Hervey, it is wholly illusive to regard the troubles here as unbridled religious animosity. To begin with, the label "Catholic" is as misleading as is "Protestant". *Which* Catholics, ask yourself always – the Normans, the Old English, the later recusants or the native Celts? Nor would you expect me to own that *my* church is Protestant – at least, that is, it is not akin to those dissenters who take it upon themselves to claim that mantle. No, the troubles here are at heart a conflict between an often weak and corrupt land-owning class and a peasantry in, for the most part, abject poverty. Indeed, it is almost a tyranny. The guilt of the landlords' co-religionists is largely by association only. I am tarred with the same brush as the worst rackrenter simply because my faith is the same as his, although I am ashamed that he should pretend to the same, for, indeed, my church was conceived in Catholicism – but that is another matter. And O'Begley here is likewise suspected by the Ascendancy because he shares the declaratory faith of the most murderous Whiteboy, though he, too, would be appalled to share the altar rail with such a wretch. Understand this, Mr Hervey, and you may begin to serve the king wisely – God bless him.'

So scholarly and humane a summary deserved – to Hervey's mind – a respectful silence by return, but he felt a greater need to make some acknowledgement, to express some appreciation of the erudition. Prompt and unqualified endorsement he thought wanting in aptness, however, so there was indeed a respectful silence while the three worthy historians sipped their port, eyes elsewhere but on him. 'One more thing, Dr Verey,' he enquired, after several sips of his own. 'This "rack-renting" – what is it precisely?'

The canon looked at the doctor, who began by shaking his head. 'Put very simply, Mr Hervey, it is the greed of the landlords – absentees often enough – in stretching the rents to the utmost value of the land. The tenant has no margin therefore either to improve his smallholding or to insure for a year when crops fail. The tenancies are for the most part on short leases, too, and when they expire the landlord jacks up the rent again, knowing the wretched tenant will agree to anything to avoid eviction.'

'The problem is not always directly with the landlord,' added Nugent, aspiring less than enthusiastically to some balance. 'Those not resident rely on agents, many of whom are short-termers and downright unscrupulous. Some of the tenancies are in truth sub-lettings, too, the middlemen taking the marginal yield.'

There was another moment's pause, and then Dr Verey made a minor prophecy. 'You will come across its worst effects soon enough, Mr Hervey: families by the roadside evicted without a thought for their well-being, either physical or spiritual. And there is no Speenhamland system here: they will starve without the private charity of their neighbours – who will be in no condition to assist them – or that of their church, which has nothing. They will not seek or accept ours for the most part, either. Your own namesake, Lord Hervey, bishop of Derry – a distant relative, I understand – was assiduous in arguing the Catholics' case, and indeed used much of his own wealth to improve their condition. He is fondly remembered still in those parts, but even he was able to effect only the most modest relief.'

'A *very* distant relative,' confirmed Hervey.

And finally Dr O'Begley added his advice – and with just a suggestion of warmth, it seemed to Hervey. 'You must read a novel called *Castle Rackrent*. You may know of it? It is full of truth. Indeed, it should be, since it recounts the events on the neighbouring estates to the author's father in County Longford at the turn of the century: Miss Maria Edgeworth is the author – a quite remarkable work for so young a lady. She has written more lately, and still it is the same.'

'I now seem to have a veritable *list* of lady novelists,' replied Hervey ruefully as they rose to begin their leave-taking.

Pulling the oil-lamp at his bedside closer in order to begin reading *Castle Rackrent*, which Dr Verey had pressed on him as he had left that same evening, Hervey felt a sense of purpose that had been wanting since Toulouse, a deficiency made worse by the confusion of feelings that was his attachment for Henrietta Lindsay. He desired keenly to understand this place, a country he was already beginning to think might be as alien as Spain or France. But another book had been pressed on him, too (on leaving Horningsham), and he had made a promise to read it sooner rather than later. He put down Miss Edgeworth's novel and picked up Miss Austen's instead, trying to remember which passage Henrietta had urged on him – something about Meryton, chapter six or seven? He opened the red-leather volume and began to read, though with little enthusiasm. It seemed full of talk of getting a rich husband (and Styles was certainly *that*), and a good deal of London, of St James's (where he had observed as much that was vacuous as fine), and of superior society and the like, but nothing that suggested any explanation of her remarks at the henge. He began chapter seven, now yawning and struggling hard to keep his eyes from closing: he had had little enough sleep during the crossing, and Miss Austen's was not a voice that commanded them to remain open.

And then he saw it. *There*, at the bottom of the first page, veritably *leaping* from the page! 'They could talk of nothing but officers; and Mr Bingley's large fortune, the mention of which gave animation to their mother, was worthless in their eyes when opposed to the regimentals of an ensign.' He cursed himself for not having looked up the passage before. It was no riddle. Why had he not seen beyond the here-and-now when first he had heard those words? If Henrietta Lindsay were not apt to regard Styles as an *officer* – and, indeed, how *could* she? (it was plain to him now) – then the passage made perfect sense. True, the militia were no more or less soldiers than the yeomanry; but if she likened this Bingley and his large fortune to Styles and *his* large fortune, then the approving reference to an *ensign* (for she must be wholly sensible of the difference in name only from *cornet*?) must surely mean . . .

He sprang out of bed and took the lamp to the table where Johnson had laid his writing-case. Now was the time for resolute action. His earlier uncertainty, his vacillating, his downright incapability (the very contrary to what was, in his understanding, the essence of the cavalry spirit) – all this must be a thing of the past. He must make up ground. He had heard, as it were, hounds speak, or the sound of the guns: as both a sporting man and a soldier he knew he must gallop at once towards that music.

# CHAPTER NINE
# BEYOND THE PALE

*4 September*

At 6 a.m. a drummer began to beat reveille in the Fusiliers'
lines, echoing around the barrack squares so as to wake even
Hervey in the next-door quarters. He stretched his arms
wearily in the chair where he had spent half the night, his
greatcloak falling from his shoulders to reveal one of the
cotton shirts he had brought from the Peninsula. Around him
on the floor lay crumpled sheets of writing paper, testament
to his hard cross-country ride to rejoin hounds or to reach the
field of battle. In front of him, on the desk, lay one sheet three-
quarters filled by his careful handwriting. Only two clean
sheets lay in reserve. When he had begun his bold dash, in the
early hours, he had written freely, expressively, with some
passion even. But when he had read that first draft he had been
unhappy with its presumption and had taken a new sheet.
Each subsequent draft had lost a little more in candour until,
shortly before dawn, he had settled for something not unlike
a dispatch from the Duke of Wellington's headquarters. He
had omitted any exegesis of *Pride and Prejudice* and had
instead contented himself with inviting Henrietta to come and
hunt with him and his brother officers. Picking up the pen, as
the drummer finished with a long roll and emphatic tap, he
signed the letter *your humble servant.*

An hour later he was in the stables telling Johnson he
would take out Harkaway. 'But a hunting saddle, not the
Hungarian,' he insisted, 'and no shabracque, just a sheepskin.'

'*Right*, sir,' said Johnson in a resigned but reproving tone. 'If t'adjutant were 'ere, though, there'd be words.'

'Look, the horse has never seen an army saddle; I want to stretch his legs after the crossing and I have not the time to start fitting one now. The RM would understand, even if the adjutant would not.'

But the riding master would not be able to save Johnson's skin. 'Why does tha 'ave t'ride in uniform, though?'

'Because I think the adjutant would want me to, that is why,' replied Hervey, tiring already of his groom's primness in matters of saddlery.

Johnson was quick to recognize the hopeless circularity of the argument and shuffled off to the harness room, muttering.

'And just a snaffle – no curb,' Hervey called after him. But if he thought it prudent to ride out in uniform (and it was not merely the adjutant's expectations which had decided it) he had at least resolved that it would be undress. That way he showed himself to be a soldier yet without the appearance of being on official business. This had been the practice in the Peninsula, and was, for the most part, a modest guarantee of being able to ride unmolested by the provost-marshal's patrols. But he would go armed nevertheless. After Johnson had saddled up the bay, therefore, Hervey fastened his double pistol holsters on to the saddle arch. It was not easy with a hunting saddle, but he managed by improvising straps through the D-rings meant for the breastplate. He then unhitched his sword and sabre-tache from his sword-belt and mounted with his customary vault. Johnson let go the bridle and then waved him off. Hervey sighed to himself. Three months in barracks had seen no conspicuous amendment in his groom's bearing; an ostler might wave off a postboy, but Johnson was meant to be a trooper. There seemed little to be gained by reminding him of that, however, and formality was left instead to the fusilier sentry at the gate who presented arms briskly, though quite unnecessarily since a butt salute was all a lieutenant was entitled to.

The map he had studied earlier that morning suggested a route to the south of the River Lee, along the road due west which, in a day's hard riding, would take him to the Atlantic.

Then there would be nothing beyond but America, with whom the nation was still at war. But this was to be a morning's ride only, a preliminary reconnaissance in order to gain some feel for the country. He thought he might go as far as Macroom, eight leagues or so distant, and if Harkaway were supple enough perhaps a little beyond to catch a glimpse of the mountains dividing County Cork from Kerry. Then, crossing the Lee, he would return to Cork city along its north bank.

It was a fine morning. It had been fine for weeks (Johnson had told him), and the stubble fields were witness to this soon after leaving the city. The road was not unduly busy but, even so, no-one gave him so much as a second look. That came as no surprise: there had been a large garrison in Cork for centuries, and it could not have been unusual to see individual officers riding out. He hoped, however, that soon his appearance might be rather less familiar, for he wanted to see the Ireland of which they had spoken the night before rather than what seemed to be just an outpost of the Pale.

It was a disappointment therefore when, after several miles of what he supposed was a road which would soon bring him to 'real Ireland', he came across a troop of artillery in the road, trotting towards him at ease as if on morning exercise. He saluted their captain, who acknowledged it as if such a meeting were an everyday occurrence. Puzzled as to where they were going, or where they had come from – for there was no artillery in the city, as he believed, he trotted on another mile or so until reaching Ballincollig. According to his map it was a small town of no significance; but, curiously, there was an artillery picket on the road at the town limit. The gunners saluted him, but the bombardier in charge said nothing, allowing him to pass unremarked. Half a mile beyond, however, he was to discover the reason for the picket; gunpowder mills of colossal proportions, and barracks next door for an entire artillery brigade. Little wonder the map made no reference to them, he supposed, for here was a part of the nation's great war machine which was better kept privy since it lay within such easy reach of a hostile landing. Cork was home and victualling station to the Irish squadron of the

Channel fleet, he knew well enough, but *this* . . . He wanted no tour of the mills, however, nor to dine with the artillery, both of them gracious enough invitations offered the instant the picket officer saw him. He wanted simply to get on.

'That I would not advise – not alone, that is,' said the picket officer. 'A mile or so west of here and it can be as wild as Cantabria; I surmise that you will know my meaning well enough.'

Hervey was encouraged, much to the artilleryman's dismay.

'Believe me, we had a courier ambushed not five miles from here last week.'

He had no intention of abandoning his reconnaissance, however. 'I thank you for your warning, sir, and I will prime my flintlocks. I must see something of the country, though, untamed as it is.' But he wished he had his folding carbine, and as he took his leave he resolved to have the saddler enlarge one of the holsters at the first opportunity.

Harkaway, it was soon apparent, was incapable of a fifty-mile march that day, especially in the unexpected heat of that early-autumn morning. A couple of miles further, therefore, Hervey turned south into the gentle hills which formed a watershed between the Lee and the River Bandon, and reconciled himself to a pleasant country hack rather than the more purposeful reconnaissance he had intended. In the event, however, he could not have achieved his purpose more subtly or economically. Had he pressed on towards Macroom, and beyond, he would have seen the English influence gradually diminishing until, had his gelding possessed the stamina, in the Derrynasaggart Mountains he would have found the meanest hovels – every bit as mean as the worst he had seen in the Peninsula. And they would have been as popular imagination supposed them, with turf roofs, filled with peat-smoke, in a remote and hostile landscape beyond the frontiers of the civilized Pale. Instead he entered a less elemental landscape (though he felt it distinctly alien nevertheless) within a few miles of Ballincollig – and thus within but a dozen miles of

Cork. What he first noticed here, in countryside which otherwise looked no more remarkable than east Somerset, was the absence of church towers. From a hill anywhere in England, especially from the parts he knew so well, it would be possible to see several towers or spires. But not here. There was, indeed, a curious flatness to the landscape despite the gentle hills. Canon Verey's history lesson ought perhaps to have alerted him to it, but the physical consequences of academic history were not always easy to foresee.

He rode through several settlements – *village* hardly seemed an appropriate word for them – and, although there were some decent stone buildings, the majority were rougher, consisting of timber-framed daub or unshaped stones. Some, especially those lying outside the settlements, were rougher still, no better than he would have seen further west. There were remarkably few people about, too, and none working in the fields that he could see, unlike the busy acres of Wiltshire. He freely greeted those he did come across – touching his cap to the women – but the most he received in reply was an expressionless nod.

At about midday, six miles or so south and west of Ballincollig according to his uncommonly accurate map, he came upon the ruins of a religious house, a small monastery perhaps, standing isolated amid ungrazed pasture. The map told him the place was Kilcrea but nothing more. The heat was now beginning to tell on Harkaway, and so he dismounted and let him drink at a stream nearby. There was not a soul to be seen, reinforcing the impression of isolation. Yet it did not look to him like a Cistercian house; for, although the setting was characteristic of that pastoral and reclusive order, the ruins themselves lacked the grandeur of Cistercian buildings. These had the look of a much later, and smaller, establishment. What was more, and in contrast again with all he had seen in England, the building was as a whole intact, the walls high and unbroken. In England a monastic house would have been given, or sold, to some favourite by Henry VIII at the time of the dissolution and converted into a dwelling-house, or else its stone would long since have been carried away for other building. But these

189

remains seemed almost to have been preserved, cherished even. He was uncertain of his history. Were the monasteries dissolved here as in England at the Reformation? Somehow these ruins had the stamp of Cromwell's work – a more malign destruction, perhaps, a spoiling rather than a dismantling.

He pulled up Harkaway's head from the water. The stream was cold, even on so warm a day, and he risked the colic. He led him closer to the ruins, loosening the girth and then unfastening the snaffle at the cheek-piece so that the gelding could eat some of the lush grass. Through the arched west entrance he could see that there were many gravestones within the walls – new ones, not the occasional ancient tomb of some medieval knight as in an English church. He took a picket peg, drove it into the ground and then tied Harkaway's halter rope to it, leaving himself free to explore inside the walls.

The silence was broken only by the call of rooks in a distant coppice and by the faintest whistling of the light breeze through the broken lancets above the arch. It was not difficult to imagine why this must have been – was *still* – a favoured place for the dead. Many of the stones were worn and their inscriptions indecipherable, although they were better sheltered from the elements than in most graveyards. Those which *were* decipherable were in English: he had thought some at least would be in Gaelic. Were the Gaelic-speaking poor not buried with headstones? Or perhaps the stonemason's art was too refined for the language? Was this a place reserved only for Catholics of substance?

He sat by one headstone whose inscription was too recent to have undergone any weathering.

*Here lyeth the body of Tim McCarthy*
*of Balineadig who depd this life*
*June 19th 1797 aged 73yr also*
*Anorah his wife died Nov 2 1780 AGd*
*46 years also Tim their son June 4th*
*1797 Aged 26yr.*
*God Rest their Souls in Peace*
*Amen*

What, he wondered, had connected those two deaths in the same month of the same year? Had Tim McCarthy, his wife having pre-deceased him, died of sorrow at losing his son? Had some contagion been responsible? Or was it more sinister? Could they have been killed in skirmishes with the militia? *Surely* not the old man.

But curiosity as to how they had come to die was only part of what intrigued him about the stone. More engaging was the simple diminutive 'Tim'. He felt sure he would not have seen its like in an English churchyard: even if Tim had been the life-long familiar, in death he would have been Timothy. The warmth in that cherished rendering 'Tim McCarthy', and the union in death with his spouse, brought to mind Genesis: 'There was Abraham buried, and Sarah his wife.' Here was a special place. These McCarthys were not simply of the past but of a country he did not know. He felt so at peace that he might have lain down in the sun and been put to sleep by the distant cawing of the rooks and the gentle whistle of the wind, had he not thought better of leaving Harkaway to gorge on the rich green grass. Instead he left repose within the walls to the departed, and put an end to his bay's feasting. As he re-fastened the bit, tightened the girth and then remounted, he resolved to return soon. And next time he would be in no hurry to leave the walls which had once enclosed so many devout men, and which now provided shelter for the last remains of so many beloved fathers, mothers, children.

Half a mile on down the road – though *track* might have been a more apt description – he crested a small hill to see a plume of black smoke rising over a settlement a few hundred yards ahead. It would have been nothing unusual, perhaps, except that even at this distance he could hear shouting. His first instinct was to gallop there, for it was his duty to go to the aid of authority in a disturbance, and that was what he surmised to be the cause of the shouting. But he did not know the country or its ways and so he decided on a more circumspect approach. He checked that his flintlocks were still properly primed and then put Harkaway into a steady canter across the

191

heath, rather than spurring him to a gallop down the road, and made a wide half-circle left towards a clump of trees just short of the settlement. From here he would be able to observe unseen, and if necessary approach the settlement on foot using the cover of the gorse which dotted the heath. He had just tied his gelding to a tree and taken his telescope from its holster when out of the village burst, like Phoebus, a horse hitched to a blazing waggon. At first Hervey thought this to be a consequence of the tumult; but then, as more and more villagers rushed from the settlement shouting, he realized that this alone was the cause of the disturbance. Straightaway he untied the reins, sprang into the saddle and wheeled round to give chase.

A bolting horse, terrified by blazing hay which stays with him no matter how fast he gallops, has a prodigious turn of speed and endurance, even taking account of his cobby make and the load he pulls, and it was all that Hervey could do to press an already tired Harkaway into a gallop fast enough to begin making ground. It was three hundred, perhaps even four hundred yards before he was able to close with the deranged animal, but his difficulties had only thus begun as Harkaway himself began shying at the blazing hay. Hervey used all the leg he could to press his gelding closer to the other horse, and even drew his sword to lay behind the girth, yet it was only after several attempts to lean out (during one of which they almost fell as Harkaway missed his footing) that he was at last able to seize hold of the bridle. With all his weight now braced in the stirrups he heaved on it for all he was worth, but still he could not get the cob to pull up. In desperation he was about to leap on to the runaway's back to try to clap his hands over its eyes (something he had known to bring even an artillery team to a halt) when he saw the river ahead, and the ford with its entry and exit cut into steep banks.

Hervey would never know whether he steered them into the ford or whether that was the way the runaway had determined on, but they plunged in and he now dropped his reins to pull on the cob's bridle with both hands, trusting to his legs alone to turn Harkaway sharply up against the bank downstream of the exit – a bold gamble on a well-schooled horse, let alone a green one. As he had further gambled, the bank was too steep to jump – though the runaway attempted to, rearing between the shafts as burning hay fell around. But all forward movement had now ceased and Hervey sprang from the saddle in order to separate cob from cart. Holding on desperately to its reins, he used his sword to slice through the straps which held the yoke in place. As he cut through the last one he let the reins go and the still-terrified animal lunged from the shafts, leaped the bank and bolted again. Hervey cursed furiously, and, though he had burned his hands, he vaulted back into the saddle (his bay having stood quite still throughout not ten yards away drinking from the stream) and took off again after the runaway. For a common horse it would give a blood a good run over this distance, he rued, and it took him another half-mile to catch it and bring it to a halt.

They trotted back to the village in a lather, each exhausted. They gave the waggon a wide berth, for all its timbers were now fiercely ablaze, and were met at the edge of the settlement by the crowd of villagers who had alerted him to the distress and who had then watched his dramatic intervention. They were barefooted and looked pulled down. But, more than that, they were silent and unsmiling.

One old man, though how old it was difficult to tell, in thick tweed trousers and rough flannel shirt, stepped forward to take what was left of the runaway's reins. 'Buíochas le Dia! Go raibh míle maith agat, a nasail!'

The words meant nothing to Hervey, but the sense was clear enough. He had little idea how much the villagers had seen, but the return of the horse was probably cause enough for gratitude, whether or not its value was less than O'Begley's five pounds. As he dismounted, those nearest stepped back, the reason for which he could not judge – mere apprehensiveness he suspected. His overalls were thoroughly soaked and his face was black, but it was the backs of his hands, beginning to blister, that were the object of the older man's attention.

'Are ye by yerself, sor?'

For a moment he hesitated, wondering whether to draw his sword.

'I mean, sor, them hands – they'll be needing seeing to.'

An old woman, black shawl over her head in spite of the heat of the afternoon, stepped forward and took hold of one of them, examining the burns.

'Tar liomsa nóimead,' she said, beckoning him through the crowd, which parted to let her lead him and Harkaway towards one of the turf-roofed cottages. She motioned him to enter, and he had but an instant to decide whether or not to risk handing over Harkaway, pistols and all, to the boy who had followed them. It was, said his instincts, a moment for trust.

The old man came in after him. 'Fíor cinn fáilte,' he said quietly with a bow of the head, indicating a chair near a window which, with the door, was the sole source of light for the room.

'My father says you are welcome.'

Hervey looked round to see a much younger woman – little more than a girl – standing in the doorway. Her hair was copper-red and as thick as a blackthorn bush. Even in the poor light he could see that her looks and complexion would have been the envy of many a fashionable in St James's.

'Caithlin, where is the balsam?'

'In the stone jar beside the yeast, Mother. I'll get it,' replied the girl. Turning to Hervey she smiled. 'You see, we speak English perfectly well. It is by choice that we speak Gaeilge, though.'

The old woman relinquished the task to her daughter and sat down in a chair near the smoking fire to stir a pot simmering away gently. Hervey now felt it time to say something – anything – for here seemed the very opportunity he had been seeking.

'I am Lieutenant Hervey of the Sixth Light Dragoons, in Cork,' he offered.

'And I am Michael O'Mahoney, sor, and right grateful for saving my horse. This is my wife Brigid and my daughter Caithlin.'

Caithlin O'Mahoney, now crouching at Hervey's side and smoothing the balsam on his hands, looked up and smiled again. Hers were the only native smiles he had seen since leaving Cork, but such smiles they were – warm, open, full and free, in such contrast to the sullenness of the rest of the village. They did more to soothe the pain in his hands than the balsam. He almost sighed with the ease, but suddenly the dim light by which she worked failed and he turned to see two men filling the doorway as completely as if the door itself had been closed. He braced himself ready to spring up with his sabre. Only when the two moved into the cottage and the light from the window fell on them did he see that they were unarmed – young men in their twenties and with the same thick copper-red hair as Caithlin O'Mahoney. She seemed unperturbed by the scowls on their faces, her own smile scarcely diminished.

'Fineen, Conor,' the old woman began roughly, 'say welcome to this officer. He has saved Finbarre, and burned himself in the bargain.'

They muttered a passable greeting, the scowls remaining but re-directed at their sister.

'These are my sons, sor,' explained the old man, 'two of them anyway.'

'Good day,' Hervey said. 'I am sorry I cannot offer my hand, as you can see.'

Neither son responded, leaving the cottage instead without a word.

'Forgive the boys' manners, sor,' said the old man, discomposed by their exit.

'Sure they're mad with themselves that it had to be an outsider who came to your aid, Father – and an Englishman at that. Everything that happens passes them by. I wonder they don't go to America as they're always vowing to.'

'We are at war with America, miss,' Hervey had said before realizing that 'we' might not have been the word the O'Mahoneys would have used.

The old man sighed. 'Will the English fight everybody, then? Ireland is a peaceable enough place: there's no cause for fighting,' he said, handing a cup to Hervey now that Caithlin

O'Mahoney had finished with the balsam. 'Sláinte!' he said, raising his own.

'Sláinte!' replied Hervey – the word was familiar enough from many nights in the Peninsula with Highlanders. He took a sip and knew immediately what it was. The old man winked, and Hervey laughed.

The regiment had returned from Dublin a week later, and after one night in Cork the squadrons had dispersed to their outstations, one troop each at Mallow, Bandon, Tallow and Gort, and three in Limerick, plus smaller detachments in places like Skibbereen, leaving one troop and headquarters in Cork itself. The best part of Munster was thereby covered by light, mobile reinforcements able to support the garrisons of infantry in the major towns, though what threat the native Irish were, from his perception of their condition at Kilcrea, Hervey could scarcely imagine. His own troop remained in Cork, but his initial disappointment at not being sent further west all but disappeared when, some weeks later, Captain Lankester took three months' home leave, giving him temporary command. 'I hear you have been riding the countryside,' Lankester had said to him when handing over. And to Hervey's reply his troop leader had fixed his gaze and added accusingly: 'I hope you have not started developing romantic notions about this place. It will be so much the harder when you have to draw your sword. Stay detached, Mr Hervey.'

Lankester was, by Hervey's own reckoning, the most humane of officers, and such an injunction might have given him cause for thought; but, since he would admit not the slightest fanciful attachment to the country, there was, to his mind, no cause. It was true that he had been back to the ruins at Kilcrea. He had learned that it was an old Franciscan house – Father O'Gavan, the priest whom he had met on his second visit to the village, had taken him there one afternoon. Hervey had been to Kilcrea village several times, in fact, and he had begun to learn something of both the language and the people. He had come to know the O'Mahoney sons not as *Fineen* and

*Conor* but as *Finghin* and *Conchobhar*, and not as O'Mahoney but *O Mathghamhan*. Was this not all useful intelligence (if not of direct then at least of indirect value to the authorities)? Caithlin was a good teacher and had already given him a rudimentary understanding of the language. He learned, too, that the brothers were married, with smallholdings of their own in Kilcrea, tenants in their own right. Too young to have been with Tone's United Irishmen, Hervey had little doubt that they would have been if given the chance. Neither of them could read or write, unlike their sister, and though they tolerated his presence whenever he came to the village they would not welcome him. Caithlin's father, on the other hand, had grown positively to relish his visits, and he and Hervey had drunk many cups of poteen together, preceded always by the wink. But Lankester had nothing to concern himself about, Hervey had assured him.

Lord George Irvine, now quite recovered from his wound, had remained the while in Dublin where he filled – in a temporary capacity, it was understood – the appointment of commander-in-chief's military secretary. Command of the regiment had once more devolved on Joseph Edmonds, who had elected to leave his wife and daughters in Norwich (the speculation in the mess was that gentlemanly lodgings in Cork were beyond his means). By convention, as commanding officer, he ought to have quitted his rooms in the mess and taken even the smallest bachelor establishment in the city. At first he had shown some interest in the apartments being constructed in the old fort at Huggartsland, amid the market gardens on the western edge of the city, but instead he had remained in the barracks, to the increasing discomfort of the few other officers with whom he shared the mess.

Hervey enjoyed his company there more than most, but soon he, too, had reason for disappointment that Edmonds had not set up a family establishment in the city, though this was less to do with the major's irascibility and more because he had received a reply from Henrietta and his sister to say that they were accepting his invitation to visit. Where, therefore, would he accommodate them – at least, without a hefty bill? Lady George was in Dublin with her husband, so there was no other regimental lady with whom his guests might stay. But then by a following post came another letter from Longleat to say that she and Elizabeth would stay at Lismore, the home of the Cavendish family. Lismore was over thirty miles away, but since there was a troop at Tallow nearby he thought it a good enough plan – not that he knew the Cavendishes in the least, except by reputation. November could be an inhospitable month, Michael O'Mahoney had told him, but it could also provide the best hunting, and he concluded that it would be good that they should have such comfortable lodgings – and in so advantageous a place from which to follow hounds.

The last of the summer was soon gone, and the first cold mornings of autumn brought mists over the city and the countryside. The fields were now empty of crops as well as of labourers, the late wheat and barley having been cut and the potatoes on the smallholdings dug. Through such a mist one morning Hervey rode over to Kilcrea for another of Father O'Gavan's discourses on the history of monastic Ireland. He expected that Caithlin would also be there, as she had been hitherto. She seemed to have more appetite for learning than the whole of the village, the result, no doubt, of the priest's faithful instruction (despite there being no obvious purpose to which it might ever be put). Hervey had even found his Greek, which was better than the priest's, being for once sought after. He had come to know the byways well and could find his way to Kilcrea without passing through any settlement larger than a dozen dwellings. That morning, with the mist shrouding everything, he reached there without seeing a soul. The village itself seemed deserted except for another mounted figure in the main street, a rare enough sight. A second man then joined the other, his horse in a lather. As Hervey got closer he saw, and heard, that they were angry.

'Good morning, Captain,' said the younger of the two, though twice Hervey's age at least, a solid-looking man riding an equally solid iron-grey. He wore a green coat and top hat, which he lifted. The other man had the look of a bare-knuckle fighter, and remained silent.

'Good morning, gentlemen,' replied Hervey, touching the peak of his forage cap, 'but I am a lieutenant not captain,' he added cautiously, for there was something about these two.

'What brings you here, Lieutenant?' the man asked cheerily enough.

'Visiting friends,' he replied.

The man's eyes narrowed.

'Then, you must be well out of your way. Shall we point you back to the high road?'

'No, thank you. This is Kilcrea, is it not?'

At that moment Caithlin O'Mahoney emerged from a cottage with Father O'Gavan. She smiled, the same warm smile that greeted him each time he came.

'Ah, Lieutenant, now I see your purpose here right enough. You find the Cork ladies less obliging,' leered the younger man.

'But ye'll find it hard to crack her pipkin with the priest forever around!' laughed the older one.

Caithlin looked away. Father O'Gavan's face went red with anger, and Hervey's sabre flashed from its scabbard, the point reaching the man's throat in an instant.

'For God's sake, man, take that sword away,' he gasped, the colour draining from his florid face with the speed that Hervey's sabre had reached it. His accomplice's horse nearly threw its rider in the commotion, giving him a convenient pretext not to intervene.

'You will apologize to this lady for that slur, and to the father here for saying as much in front of him.'

The apologies came at once, though the man almost choked on the words. Hervey shouldered his sabre, and the two galloped out of the village with the vilest threats and curses.

'I do not like violence, Mr Hervey, but heaven knows it is a fine tool in good hands,' said the priest.

Caithlin looked him full in the eye. 'I thank you, sir; he and his like consider they have rights over any village girl.'

'You have come on a sad day, to say the very least,' added the priest. 'Mother O'Long in there' – indicating the cottage from which they had just emerged – 'hasn't but a few hours for this world, and those two have been serving eviction notices on the village – and this a village of English tenants, too! The man you berated was the agent – Fitzgerald.'

Hervey dismounted. '*English* tenants? I do not understand, Father.'

'Oh, it is an expression we have. It means the tenants pay their rents on the day they are due – as they do in England, do they not? On some estates there are arrears and duty work and Lord knows what else besides. But this is a regular English village, and the agent has no right to serve notice in that way.'

'In which case, Father, why does the landlord want to evict?'

'You would have to go to London to ask him that, I think,' said Caithlin with a rare note of resentment. 'His agent – the man you all but sabred,' she continued, though with less edge, 'has had the notion for years that this valley would be more profitable if the cottages were cleared and sheep run over it.'

'Sheep?' replied Hervey incredulously. 'But there are farmers in England selling their sheep for all they are worth, anticipating that wool prices will fall now that peace has come. Clearing this valley for sheep is no economy whatever.'

'I'm sure it's no better in God's eyes, either, Mr Hervey,' added Father O'Gavan, 'but the landlord seems set on "improvement" and that is that. When the tenancies run out there is nothing in law to stop him.'

'How long is your father's tenancy, Caithlin?' Hervey asked.

'Twelve months, the same as everyone else's here. It expires in the new year.'

*It will be so much the harder when you have to draw your sword. Stay detached . . .* All the way back to Cork, Lankester's words troubled him. He had drawn his sword sooner than he had imagined, and against an agent of the Ascendancy rather than a malcontent. It might have been well if Lankester had been at hand when he reached the barracks, but he was not, and Edmonds's was instead a counsel of equivocation. The major echoed the captain's warning, but in terms which expressed little but contempt for the likes of the Kilcrea agent. And, more, he appeared to encourage Hervey to maintain his links with the O'Mahoneys: they needed early intelligence of unrest. And so it was that, in the early hours of the following morning, having lain awake since turning in after watch-setting, there occurred to Hervey a prudent alternative to strife at Kilcrea. He would write to the landlord in England, stating baldly his doubts as to the agent's integrity, the dubious economy of running sheep, and the benefits, as they had been explained by Dr O'Begley, of bigger smallholdings on longer tenancy agreements.

The letter took him a full two hours to compose, and he sent it the next morning without reference to Edmonds. Nor, indeed, to anyone: soldier he might be, but that did not, in his estimation, preclude his expressing a view on matters other than soldiering. Indeed, had not that been Dr Verey's premiss, that the need for military aid to the civil power might be obviated by a better understanding of the country?

A month passed without his venturing south or west of the city, for the Tallow troop was hard-pressed mounting smuggler-patrols around Youghal, and Hervey's troop had been sent to assist them. It had been a relief in one respect; for, having sent the letter, there was little that would be served by his presence in Kilcrea. It had been a profitable relief, too, for the troop had won a Revenue bounty for apprehending, alive, six Bretons and taking their luggerful of Calvados, though one or two casks had been unaccountably written off in the process. But, if there had been nothing to be directly served by his visiting Kilcrea, he found himself nevertheless strangely fretful for want of the company of both Father O'Gavan and Caithlin, and the books which he had asked John Keble to send for her – a lexicon, Chapman's Homer and a Greek New

Testament – lay unopened in his room in Cork's barracks.

With the arrival at Youghal of additional Excise men, the troop returned to Cork on the eve of the anniversary of Trafalgar in the expectation of celebrating that providential victory the next day, but Edmonds warned them instead to be ready at six the following morning to ride to Ballinhassig to assist the Bench in serving writs.

'In heaven's name, sir,' Hervey protested, 'writs on whom? And why the whole troop?'

'Because a troop is what the justices have requested, and since the chairman of the bench of magistrates hereabouts is on close acquaintance with General Slade, so he informs me, I see no reason to demur. Stand down whom you please, but not fewer than fifty men to Ballinhassig.'

'Whom are the writs to be served on?'

'I do not know and I do not care. And nor should you. With luck they will be served on idle beggars who'd sooner shoot as look at you. In all probability, though, they'll be served on decent God-fearing souls who are in some evil rent-trap; but there is nothing that you or I can do about it, and it will be as well that you start out there tomorrow morning thinking thus! This is not the time for walking Spanish, Matthew!'

Later that evening Hervey sat alone in his room. There was no certainty that the evictions would touch on any at Kilcrea: indeed (as he understood it), Kilcrea was under the jurisdiction of Ballincollig. But the possibility was enough to disquiet him, and there was not a soul in whom he might confide his misgivings. Edmonds had said his piece, there was not another officer of the Sixth within forty miles, and even Canon Verey was away in Dublin. He might with advantage have engaged the wisdom of Serjeant Strange, but his principles would not permit him to unburden himself on the very man in whom he would have to place so much trust the next day. And as for Armstrong . . . But at least he might engage himself in some purposeful activity. So, in the absence of any troop officers, he passed his instructions direct to Strange (again acting as troop serjeant-major): 'Muster in marching order at five forty-five, then,' were his last words at evening stables before retiring to his rooms to write to Horningsham and to Oxford.

By the time he began putting pen to paper, his uncertainties had become a ghastly premonition. If not Kilcrea, then it would be *somewhere* – somewhere that conscience and duty would confront each other. Or, rather, duty would confront duty, for which might be the truer duty – to the civil power, or to simple justice? (He knew well enough that justice was not always the same as the law.) How might he neatly render unto Caesar?

To John Keble he wrote his thoughts, freely and without reserve. To Elizabeth he penned but a précis of the difficulties – in the abstract – which the military faced in aid of the civil power. And to Henrietta he wrote of the country and the people, a letter which, to his mind, would tell nothing of his turmoil, though to a reader of her percipience the intensity of his prose could tell nothing other.

When at length he finished the letters, near to midnight, he found that, though his limbs were weary, his mind raced, and the notion of retiring to bed was impossible. And so he took *Castle Rackrent* from his writing-desk, where it had lain unopened since he had brought it from Canon Verey's, and turned to its preface. He began reading with no great enthusiasm, hoping merely for some distraction from his concerns for the morrow, but in this respect it was a lamentable choice. 'To those who are totally unacquainted with Ireland, the following Memoirs will perhaps be scarcely intelligible, or probably they may appear perfectly incredible,' he read, and he wondered how acquainted with Ireland he had a right to claim. 'When Ireland loses her identity by a union with Great Britain, she will look back with a smile of good-humoured complacency on . . . her former existence.' He read it a second time, scarcely believing what he had read the first. But that was indeed what it said. Now, Miss Edgeworth, he would be the first to own, possessed an immeasurably greater acquaintance with the country than did he, but 'good-humoured complacency'? In the circumstances it seemed a most singular proposition. He put down the book with a sigh: perhaps it was to be, as the author warned, scarcely intelligible.

He turned instead to Sister Maria's vade-mecum. It, too, had lain at his bedside scarcely opened, the very sight of it a daily challenge to his conscience. The hand, its upright strokes and perfect loops a credit to any medieval scriptorium, reminded him at once of the few days' peace of mind he had found in her company at the Magdalen convent. 'Choose a passage of a devotional nature and read it before retiring. Select not more than three elements within it on which to meditate. On waking, recall the subject and, after short preparatory prayers – perhaps including an act of contrition – compose thyself by three "preludes" for the body of the meditation.' He could not but admire the economy of her English. 'Prelude One: recall the elements; Two: compose in thy mind's eye the place, with thine own self a part of it; Third: pray for grace.' He grew drowsy. Of the body of meditation itself he could read no more, and, turning out the oil-lamp, he closed his eyes and prayed for sleep. Yet, as if St Ignatius spoke to him direct through the pages of Sister Maria's book, he could only ponder on Miss Edgeworth's proposition, and whether it might indeed be flawed – fatally flawed.

## CHAPTER TEN
# IN AID OF THE CIVIL POWER

---

*Trafalgar Day*

It was raining hard as fifty men of 'A' Troop in their dark blue cloaks, oilskin covers over shakos and carbine locks bound with cloth, formed up in the chill darkness. The horses were restless. They would put up with most things but they did not like rain. In the dim glow of the oil-lamps around the parade square they could be seen backing and fidgeting, bringing curses for their hapless riders from NCOs trying to keep the three ranks straight. Private Johnson had brought Nero to the front of the officers' mess, and Hervey had mounted as the barracks clock struck the three-quarter hour. Within the minute he was exchanging salutes with Serjeant Strange on the square. It was no morning for excessive formalities: 'Subdivisions, to the left turn,' he ordered immediately, then 'Walk-march!' And without further ceremony, except for the orderly trumpeter sounding them out, they marched from the Royal Barracks south and west to Ballinhassig.

It took little but an hour to cover the six miles, and throughout Hervey said not a word, instead turning over and over in his mind *Castle Rackrent*'s proposition: 'Ireland . . . will look back with a smile of good-humoured complacency.' He wished profoundly that he had studied Sister Maria's vade mecum with more application, for he sorely felt the need of its method in weighing this notion. He knew he had to do whatever he judged right. That, indeed, was ever the duty of an officer. But where would right be this morning, and how might he know? With the law? The magistrate would, he supposed, be a reliable enough guide in matters of statute. With expediency? Again, the magistrate, as representative of the civil power – of government – might be expected to be the best judge of that. Would it be with justice? In this, however, there could be no higher judge than conscience. There was no counsel but his own, and he could confide now only in more prayer for strength and the wisdom to do his duty. Trafalgar Day – Nelson himself must have prayed at this very hour nine years before.

It was still raining when the troop made its rendezvous with the chairman of the Bench who was sheltering in a mean little inn near the edge of town. It was not many minutes before Hervey learned the worst: that they were to serve immediate eviction warrants on two dozen of Sir Dearnley Lambert's tenants in Kilcrea. The magistrate, a nervous man in his fifties whose shape suggested he had never known the want of four square meals a day, would give no indication as to how he intended to proceed with the evictions. All he would say was that they must first meet the agent and his 'crowbar brigade'.

As they trotted north up the rutted and uneven road to Kilcrea, with the first streaks of daylight to help them, Hervey learned the reason for the Ballinhassig magistrate's jurisdiction. Sir Dearnley Lambert's estates extended both north and south of that town and were treated therefore as an entity. This, he considered, was a faintly reassuring punctilio: he had at first assumed that it must be because the agent found the Ballinhassig justices more compliant than those from Ballincollig. However, when eventually they made the rendezvous with the agent, Hervey became uneasy again, for though Fitzgerald must have recognized him he made no sign of it, speaking instead, and pointedly so, only to the magistrate. It was proper enough in one respect, for only the magistrate had the power to summon the assistance of the military, and if the agent's aloofness were uncivil, then so be it (Hervey had hoped never even to see the man again). But it did not bode well.

Twenty yards away, in a huddle under the trees, trying to

shelter from the rain which still beat down in the grey dawn, was a gang of some two dozen men with crowbars and sledge-hammers. Just beyond them was a curious-looking waggon, with all manner of pulleys and levers, yoked to two sturdy draught-horses.

'What do you think is the purpose of that contraption, Serjeant Strange?'

'I'm no engineer, sir, but pound to a penny it's not for construction.'

'I was afraid so,' he sighed.

Father O'Gavan appeared, striding towards them in a great black cloak, his broad-brimmed hat taking a lashing from the sheets of rain. The crowbar brigade shuffled uncomfortably as he passed, and those with hats removed them. So much for Catholic fellowship, thought Hervey. The magistrate raised his hat, too, though perfunctorily, and Hervey saluted, but the agent sat impassively astride his big grey.

'Good morning, Mr Gould. What will your intentions be this day?' asked the priest.

'Good morning, Father O'Gavan. Twenty-two tenants have been served notice to quit by Sir Dearnley's agent and they have failed to comply. I have immediate eviction warrants, and they will be evicted forthwith. Peaceably, I hope, but forcibly if necessary.'

'Now, Mr Gould, you know very well they have nowhere to go. The landlord has forbidden any of his other tenants to take them in. Will you have them sleep and starve in the ditches?'

The magistrate looked about awkwardly, but not the agent, who was eager to begin his business. 'Your advice would have been better directed to the tenants before now, Father O'Gavan,' said Fitzgerald defiantly. 'They've had ample warning to quit the estate.'

'Mr Hervey,' began the priest, 'if these evictions are to proceed, then we must at all costs avoid bloodshed. I hope your men will show restraint?'

'Do you *know* this officer, Father?' asked the magistrate with some surprise.

'Indeed I do: he is a good friend of the village.'

Gould looked uneasy again as Hervey began to speak. 'Father, my men will show every restraint, but I am obliged by law, as you know, to assist the magistrate if called on to do so.'

'I am afraid that all have barricaded themselves in their cottages, Mr Gould,' explained Father O'Gavan. 'I have tried already to tell them that such resistance is futile, but I have to say that, with nowhere else to go, they believe they have no option but to resist the evictions.'

'Come *on*, come *on*, Gould! Let's be about it!' snapped Fitzgerald.

'Very well,' stammered the magistrate, 'let's be about it. Mr Hervey, please dispose your men so as to protect the agent and his men as they do their duty.'

Hervey would have liked to debate the notion of duty with him, but instead he began disposing the troop as the magistrate had requested. The first cottage to receive the crowbar brigade's attention was easy prey. A violent assault on the boarded window and barred door gained them rapid entry, followed by the ejection of the occupants, a man and his wife no older than Hervey, and their five children. The eldest, a girl of about eight, clutched a crucifix in the way that Horningsham girls clutched their dolls. As they stood hunched in the downpour, with as desolate a look as ever Hervey had seen, the man mouthed some plea or other to the agent, whereupon one of the foremen stepped forward and struck him on the back of the neck with his blackthorn, felling him head-down in the mud. Hervey's blood rose at once: he spurred Nero forward, drew his sabre and sent the foreman sprawling with the flat of it before anyone could say a word. How close the man had come to feeling its edge he would never know.

'You're too damned quick to draw that sword, mister! It's an abuse of government property,' the agent bellowed.

'I should have been as happy to use my bare fists but I would have done him more harm – and the sword is my own,' Hervey rasped. And, turning to the magistrate, he issued his own warning: 'Mr Gould, I am obliged to follow your instructions but I will not stand by and witness an assault.'

'I think the officer may be correct in law, Mr Fitzgerald: that was an unwise thing for your man to do,' replied the magistrate hesitantly.

Hervey meanwhile had dismounted and, followed by Strange and Armstrong, began to help the evicted man to his feet. The rest of the family were crying and shaking, Hervey took off his cloak and put it round the three younger children, and Strange's and Armstrong's cloaks covered the remaining two and their mother.

'In God's name will yer look at that!' exclaimed the agent, with so much contempt that Magistrate Gould shifted awkwardly in the saddle again, and he defiantly beckoned forward the wheeled contraption.

Its purpose was quickly revealed, and its work did not take long. Two hooks on the ends of ropes were thrown on to the roof, a man clambered up and fixed each to a coign stone, the ropes were tensioned by the pulleys and then, in three strides of the draught-horses, the upper walls were pulled in and the roof collapsed. The crowbar brigade set to work and within a quarter of an hour the cottage was no more.

The troop watched in silence, only Armstrong giving voice to his feelings: 'This's no way to treat a dog. Not even the coal-owners stooped to this.'

'Hold your peace, Serjeant Armstrong,' said Strange.

Mellow Suffolk again: Hervey would need every ounce of composure before the day was out.

The next cottage proved an altogether more stubborn proposition. Hervey knew well enough that it was Fineen O'Mahoney's, and that he would not walk out meekly as the others had.

The door and window were firmly barricaded, and the crowbar men could make no impression. 'Put the hooks on the roof, then; if they won't come out, we'll carry 'em out!' the agent called to his foreman.

'Don't be a fool, man,' shouted Hervey. 'There's a family in there, for pity's sake.'

'Then he's the reckless one for not coming out!' snapped Fitzgerald. 'Get them hooks on!'

Even above the noise of the rain and the crowbar men's hubbub Fineen O'Mahoney's voice could be heard shouting in a manner at once both pleading and defiant: 'I've a sick wife and mo pháistí in here, and a sister. For mercy's sake leave us!'

A *sister* – O'Mahoney had but one. Hervey's stomach tightened. That Caithlin was there put paid to his hope that the O'Mahoneys might be brought out without a fight, for he had intended bringing her from her father's cottage to try to persuade her brother to quit. And, while the eviction of the first family had been hard enough to bear, they were at least strangers to him: Caithlin's presence changed everything. 'Mr Gould, it cannot be lawful to pull a roof down on the heads of a family,' he shouted.

Fitzgerald glowered at the magistrate, who dithered. It was the due process of law, he replied. 'But go easy with the roof,' he called to the agent – as if the idea were even practicable.

'*No!*' shouted Hervey. 'You will not touch that roof!'


'Tell me, Mr Hervey, what then happened as a consequence of your altercation with the agent?'

Matthew Hervey's sodden uniform clung to him tighter by the minute. The big fire in Major Edmonds's office had begun to dry the front of his overalls (so long had he been standing at attention recounting the events at Kilcrea), and he struggled hard not to shiver lest it gave his commanding officer the wrong impression. 'I told Serjeant Armstrong to escort the crowbar brigade clear of the village, sir, and Serjeant Strange to dispose the remainder of the troop to prevent their return.'

'And what did the magistrate then say?'

'He kept ordering me to desist; but I repeated, several times, that I would not be a party to injuring women and children, whatever his orders were – sir.'

'Were those lawful orders, do you consider?'

'With respect, sir, I am not a lawyer.'

'No, Mr Hervey, indeed you are not. And if you cannot be sure that they were unlawful orders you had no business disobeying them.'

'I could not be sure that they *were* lawful, sir, and in that case I should have thought it reckless to conform, especially since there was no threat to life in disobeying – whereas just the contrary was true.'

'That is veritably a moot point. It does not pass muster with me, and I doubt it would in court. Are you sure that your friendship with these people did not cloud your judgement?'

'I do not believe so, sir. It would have mattered not to me *who* was inside that cottage.'

Joseph Edmonds sighed and then swore to himself. 'Mr Hervey, why are we stationed here in Cork?'

Hervey continued to look directly ahead. 'In aid of the civil power, sir.'

'Just so. And on what duty – in the general sense – were you engaged this morning?'

'Aid to the civil power, sir.'

'So, Mr Hervey, by your own admission you have failed to do your particular duty and, in that failure, you have set yourself not only against military authority but against the civil as well.'

Hervey assumed the judgement to be rhetorical.

'Answer me, Mr Hervey!' barked Edmonds.

'Sir, that is as Mr Gould and Mr Fitzgerald would see it.'

Edmonds sighed again. 'In heaven's name, Mr Hervey, I doubt you will find *anyone* who sees it any differently. This is not Merrie England; we are beyond the Pale – the arse-end of the realm. Who do you suppose is in the slightest degree interested in the niceties of conscience when there's rebellion lurking in every hedgerow?'

Hervey remained silent.

Edmonds picked up several sheets of paper on his desk and held them out towards him. 'Do you know what this represents?' he demanded. 'Never have I seen a deposition from a magistrate written so fast: it is a declaration of intent, an example to be made – exemplary punishment and all that!'

Hervey shivered, and was angry that he did so.

'Do you have anything more to say at this juncture?' asked Edmonds, shaking his head.

'No, sir,' replied Hervey calmly.

'Very well,' said the major, now equally composed, 'you will hand your sword to the adjutant forthwith and retire to your quarters on parole, and there I suggest you render your entire account in writing.'

Hervey unfastened the two belt-loops from the D-rings on his scabbard and held out his sabre. The adjutant took it and acknowledged with a brisk bow, and then Hervey turned smartly to his right, saluted and left the orderly room.

'Events have a strange habit of repeating themselves,' said the adjutant when the door was closed.

Edmonds's brow furrowed. 'You and I should have done the same. At least, I hope we should. Besides all else, the surest way to provoke trouble here is to become embroiled in the dirty business of absentee landlords. However, the law as it stands is unequivocal. I shall forward a report to General Slade, but I do not suppose that the great man will have gained one ounce in sagacity since his translation here. I very much fear that this will make the incident at Toulouse seem a tea-fight.'

That night Hervey wrote one letter, to Oxford. 'My dear Keble,' it began, and, after confirmation of the concerns of his letter of the night before, and of the events since: 'I fear that I am finished. But I believe I have done my duty to these people – and, indeed, to the king, for they are his loyal enough subjects if chance they be given. The law which should equally be their defender seems only to be the instrument of driving them to rebellion . . .'

# CHAPTER ELEVEN
# A NOBLE PEER

---

*County Waterford, 4 November*

Lismore Castle, set high on a crag over the River Blackwater, had nothing of the elegance of Longleat, but that was not its original purpose. William Cavendish, the same age as Hervey and recently succeeded to the dukedom of Devonshire, had spent most of the crossing from Bristol explaining just this to Henrietta and Elizabeth, together with his plans for embellishing the castle now that peace had come to Europe and circumstances in Ireland were more settled. An ancestor by marriage (Richard Boyle, first earl of Cork) had built Lismore in the seventeenth century to withstand attack. And while, the duke explained, the earl had laid out some fine gardens, with yew hedges and topiary, and woodland trails of rhododendrons, it was not yet a place of gentlemanly leisure.

A steam barge, a novelty to both women, had brought them up the Blackwater from Youghal (to where a brig had ferried them from the Cove of Cork), and a carriage had taken them the remaining half-mile to the castle. Here they had expected to find Matthew Hervey, but instead they found letters addressed in his hand. That to the duke was formal and brief, explaining that military duty had detained him and that he thought it unlikely that he would be able to accept the invitation to stay at Lismore. Those for Elizabeth and Henrietta were longer and, except in a few intimate details, each said the same. Both women felt the contents needed to be brought to the duke's attention immediately.

'William,' began Henrietta in perfect calmness but with an edge he had not seen in her before, 'Matthew is in arrest. You may read the details for yourself but it seems that he has refused to obey the instructions of a magistrate and is to face a court martial by that odious man General Slade.'

'Let me first read of the exact circumstances,' said the duke sceptically. 'But why do you describe this general as odious – do you know him?'

'Not other than by reputation, but Matthew has told me of the animosity that there was between the two of them in France, and I enquired of someone who is acquainted with the Horse Guards, and they affirm that the general is not thought well of in London.'

'So they send him to Ireland,' he smiled.

'Duke, I believe this is very serious,' Elizabeth interrupted. 'In France, Matthew was placed in arrest by this general, who believed he had abandoned his post – which of course he had not. Matthew was later congratulated for his conduct by Lord Wellington, and this caused bad feeling on General Slade's part. There was also some trouble over a serjeant whom Matthew stood up for against the same general. I fear that, whatever the rights or wrongs of the case, this general will be seeking retribution for the earlier affront.'

'Forgive me, Miss Hervey, but does your brother have an habitual difficulty with authority? He seems to have had a remarkable share of tribulation for so junior an officer!'

Henrietta motioned Elizabeth to say nothing. 'William, he is a very fine officer – everyone will tell you so. But he is no "yes man", and when he believes something to be wrong he will say so. I want you to go to Cork today and do all you can to have him released from custody.'

'Today! But we are only just arrived—'

'Yes, today, now!' insisted Henrietta. 'And I shall come with you!'

'And I,' said Elizabeth.

And nothing that William Devonshire said could persuade either woman that accompanying him would do no good. Only the most explicit threat that he would refuse to leave until the morning finally induced them to relent, and against all his better judgement he left Lismore for Cork, a journey by road of some fifty miles, before noon was out.

The arrival in Ireland of a descendant of Richard Boyle, even so distant a one, was already cause for remark in Cork. The two centuries that had passed since his ancestor had landed in these parts, almost penniless, to become within an uncommonly short time one of the richest men in the realm, had done little to dull the reputation of the first earl. And, whether the reputation were admired or reviled, William Devonshire now sought to use it.

'Well, Duke,' began Edmonds, who knew nothing of the Boyle connection but enough about the Cavendishes, 'I can assure you that we are not being idle in the matter. He is being advised by a local attorney in whom he – we – have great confidence: a Mr Nugent, who is also the chapter clerk here and an acquaintance of his. I will not hesitate to bring a man from Dublin, though – or London – if necessary. Do you wish to meet them? They are conferring at this moment here in the mess. Mr Hervey is confined to the barracks themselves, you understand.'

The duke did indeed wish to meet them. And when he had heard what the attorney had to say he was not entirely discouraged. 'Well, your Grace,' Nugent had begun, 'the law is not quite so precise in these matters as many seem to believe – and I include Magistrate Gould and General Slade in that category. It is without question the absolute duty of an officer summoned by a magistrate to do all in his power to prevent a breach of the peace, or to restore it. The means by which he disposes his forces is, however, his business and his alone. He can neither be ordered to do something which in his judgement is militarily unsound, nor for that matter can he relinquish his duty in this respect to the magistrate – whatever indemnities he is promised. He is answerable for that judgement, in respect of any breach of the civil law, to the civil courts, but in respect of his military judgement he is answerable only before an appropriate military authority. Do I make myself clear, your Grace?'

'Indeed, perfectly clear, Mr Nugent, but as I understand it there was no difference with the magistrate over military matters. It was rather more fundamental, was it not?'

'So it might seem. I wanted, however, to lay out the relative positions of the civil and military with respect to this frequently misunderstood point.'

'You have also, if I may say so, Mr Nugent, laid out a remarkable knowledge of the law relating to these matters for someone whose work is with ecclesiastical business,' said the duke approvingly.

'That is because, sir, I have studied the history of this country from a legal aspect. You would be surprised by how many grounds for appeal there are in an average parish hereabouts.'

'We will not pursue that,' replied the duke with a further smile.

'So let us return to the question at hand. You will recall that I said the military have a duty in the maintenance of the peace. This does not extend, however, to enforcing the law as such except where not to do so would lead to a breach of the peace. So Mr Hervey's troop at Kilcrea were not there to *assist* with the evictions but to prevent attack on the agent and his men proceeding about their lawful business.'

'But any magistrate knows that,' began the duke, 'and Hervey, here, refused even to allow them to go about their business.'

'Not so. The first tenants were evicted without incident,' insisted Nugent, 'except that one of the crowbar men struck the tenant for no reason.'

'And Mr Hervey struck the man in return,' countered the duke.

'That, I believe, would be most unlikely to result in charges against the officer – a blow for a blow is what it amounts to. And, indeed, it could be argued that the action was anticipatory, there being good reason to suppose that the assault might continue. No, the significance of the foreman's assault is its indication of a predisposition to violence on the part of the agent's men, a factor of which Mr Hervey would take account in forming his judgement. In all, it seems to me that the evidence would suggest that Mr Hervey was at the outset perfectly prepared to carry out his duty in respect of the evictions. Indeed, the evidence of the parish priest would corroborate this – Mr Hervey said as much to him.'

'Then how will you account for his subsequent obstruction of the eviction process?' asked the duke doubtfully.

'The agent gave an unlawful instruction to his men to collapse the second cottage on the heads of the occupants. The agent himself was thus about to precipitate a breach of the peace, even perhaps an unlawful killing. His men were already shown to be violent, and the magistrate took no steps to restrain them. As I said, Mr Hervey had an absolute duty to act at that moment, in the same way that he would have had a duty to ignore an unlawful order from the magistrate. It is the very devil of a position for an officer to be in, your Grace – damned if he does, and damned if he does not!'

Silence followed as William Devonshire contemplated the import of what the attorney had said. 'There is therefore only one question, Mr Nugent,' he suggested eventually. 'This is clearly your interpretation of the law – will it be that of others? Will it come to trial?'

The attorney raised his eyebrows and sighed. 'Your Grace, that question is of the essence. The fact is that in the case of military aid to the civil power there has been much confusion. You are too young to remember the Gordon riots. I was in London at the time. The riots could have been nipped in the bud if everyone had not laboured under the misapprehension that, in law, the Riot Act had to have been read, and therefore the riot to have begun, before the magistrates could call upon the military. After the riots there was a great deal of legal argument but, alas, there were few firm rulings. The best interpretation, ironically – though, alas, it has no force of law – was that given by the Archbishop of York in the House of Lords. Here it is,' declared Nugent with a flourish, holding open a large bound volume. 'It will form the centrepiece of my submission. The archbishop declares that "a fatal error prevailed among the military that they could not in any case act without the orders of a civil magistrate which is the case when a great mob has assembled but has not yet proceeded to acts of violence. But when they have begun to commit felonies any subject, and the military among the rest, is justified in Common Law in using all methods to prevent illegal acts."'

'That seems clear enough,' replied the duke. 'Who will make the ruling in this case?'

'It would be argued in front of a judge advocate at a court martial – the facts themselves are not in any material dispute. The judgment would turn on whether or not collapsing a roof with the occupants inside amounted to an illegal act.'

'Good heavens, man! We've hanged people in England this year for doing less than that – Luddites and the like. They get up great steel hawsers round the chimneys and bring them crashing through the roof. How in God's name is it any different here?'

'Your Grace, it happens here every *day*. A few months ago it was done in front of the Bishop of Meath himself. His protests at the time, and subsequently, came to nothing.'

William Devonshire, not yet versed in these disparities within the Union, was unsettled by the revelation, and a steely resolve came to him in that instant. Cornet Hervey, he now knew, had not only in his judgement acted honourably – indeed, in the only way a gentleman could – he had acted within the bounds of justice, and if the Law here could not admit of that, then he would ensure the case came before the highest court of appeal in the Union. Meanwhile he could at least use all his good offices to have Hervey released from arrest. He thanked everyone for their forbearance, declined, with much regret, the invitation to dine and stay the night, and instead, though it was already dark, began the journey back to Lismore.

Elizabeth and Henrietta had retired long before his return in the early hours, so it was breakfast before he could recount what had passed in Cork.

'Then Elizabeth and I may go and see him, at least?' said Henrietta as he finished.

That much was reasonable, he agreed, but he counselled

patience. 'I have already sent an express to General Slade asking for Cornet Hervey to be released into open arrest, for which I have agreed to stand surety if that be necessary. I do not think the general will find it expedient to deny the request. As to whether charges will be pressed – that is another matter entirely.'

Between them, the officers of the 6th Light Dragoons subscribed to four hunts, five if Mr Croker's scratch-pack at Ballingard in Limerick were counted. The Muskerry hounds had hunted the fox in County Cork for the best part of a century, and the home troop enjoyed their bank and wall country on Wednesdays and Saturdays. When that hunt met as far west as Macroom, however, the officers would instead join those of the Bandon troop to the south and ride out with the Carberry. Sometimes hounds would run right down to Bantry Bay where the field would then overnight riotously in the town, or the military followers might ride on to Skibbereen and billet themselves on the outstation there. The Mallow troop subscribed to the oldest pack, the Duhallow, whose southernmost meets were also accessible to the home troop. Hervey preferred their country to the Carberry's since there was less plough. But the hunt he loved best was the Scarteen: Mr Thaddeus Ryan's black and tan hounds hunted both fox and stag over the finest bank-and-ditch country imaginable, and so good was the scent that hounds ran faster here than anywhere in Ireland.

Before his altercation with the Ballinhassig magistrate had brought an abrupt end to his hunting, Hervey had managed no less than thirty days out, over half of them with the Scarteen. And on his release into open arrest (Slade having found the Duke of Devonshire's appeal more than compelling) his spirits were once again restored – at least outwardly – by some of the longest and fastest points he had ever known, and in the company of the two women for whom his admiration and affection knew no equal. Beyond what was necessary, however, the three had no conversation on the matter of his arrest, for if the outcome of the due process of military law were favourable, then there would be time enough to talk of it, and with the necessary dispassion. But if the outcome were *un*favourable, then it were better that he had at least some happy memories of carefree sport and good company to sustain him in the darker times to come. Throughout these weeks he enjoyed the generous and civilized hospitality of Lismore, or of the duke's hunting box in Tipperary, but not the company of the duke himself; for, on the pretext of business in connection with his estates, the duke was working assiduously towards Hervey's thorough acquittal. Indeed, his acquittal was to the duke an utmost imperative.

By the end of November, Hervey and Henrietta had spent the greater part of every week in each other's company, only the occasional field day or picket duty requiring his presence in Cork. Yet Elizabeth would confide to her journal that their association seemed no further advanced in those precious weeks than it had been on their parting at Horningsham. Hervey, had he kept a journal, would have confided the same: in general company Henrietta was easy, full of laughter and game, but each time there was any opportunity for intimacy she became perceptibly distant – distant enough, in any event, to daunt any affirmation of his true feeling. It was not that his heart had faltered, but the arrest had sapped at his surety, as a worm in an oak, and he supposed Henrietta's certainty to be likewise diminished. With each day he felt the initiative slipping yet further away, and he could conceive of no stratagem by which to recover it.

Then one morning, as the Black and Tans were drawing covert in some of their best country, near the southern end of the Golden Vale, Henrietta took him by surprise. 'Matthew, this is heaven, but I hear tell that the Muskerry are not to be missed. May we have a day with them, perhaps when next they hunt west of Cork?'

'We may, of course,' he replied, 'but it is poor hunting compared with this.'

'In truth,' she returned, 'I would see the country in which you made so gallant a stand with the magistrate. Believe me, Matthew, a woman might admire such courage.'

And Hervey had been nothing but encouraged by this apparent resolution of doubt on Henrietta's part, taking no note of the conditional in her assertion of admiration.

The arrangements were made easily enough, and the following week he, Elizabeth and Henrietta were to be found with the sky-blue collar of Mr Samuel Hawkes, the Muskerry's master, drawing the south bank of the River Lee from the meet at the artillery barracks in Ballincollig. By midday they were near Kilcrea, as Henrietta hoped they would be, and when Hervey disclosed this fact she asked if they might see the village. They left the field – and Elizabeth – and rode to the little settlement which he had not seen since the day of his arrest over a month before.

Peat smoke rose from the holes in the thatch-roofs and from the chimneys of the more substantial cottages, but there was not a soul to be seen. Scarcely had they turned into the single muddy street, however, than the occupants of the dismal dwellings began to emerge, and as Hervey passed each door he returned their greetings in the same tongue. But, wary though the greetings were, and ignorant of the tongue that Henrietta was, there was no doubting their benevolence. One face at least bore him a smile, however, and he could not but reflect it. As he reached the cottage where first he had begun his precipitous friendships, he sprang from the saddle to hold out his hand to Caithlin O'Mahoney, but she dismissed his formality and instead put both hands firmly on his shoulders to kiss him on each cheek.

Scarce a dozen words (of Irish) passed between them before Hervey turned to Henrietta, yet in the space of those seconds of vocal intimacy Henrietta's doubts seemed confirmed: all her instincts were to turn her horse for Cork. Only pride kept her hands still.

The fine cloth and colours of his uniform had thrown the village and its people into drab contrast, and his black coat for once made him almost a part of that scene, but the golden-yellow velvet of Henrietta's riding habit was in stark contrariety. Caithlin knew that the cash-crops of the entire village would not in one year be enough to buy such clothes. And, for certain, all that there was inside their cottage, into which Henrietta now stepped at her invitation (and with perfect graciousness), would buy neither scent nor gloves for such a lady. Caithlin was at ease, however, for if she had no need of such a habit, or scent or gloves, then the want of them was no deprivation. Whether such a costume would make her as desirable as Henrietta was a question which might later stir her, but it was one to which Hervey at least had never given the slightest consideration (unlikely that it may have seemed to Henrietta). Or, to be precise, he had never until that moment: Caithlin's copper-red hair and dark eyes were not without their effect after so many weeks.

The meanest of the Longleat tenants was better-housed and better-dressed than the O'Mahoneys, and Henrietta's self-possession was not so great that she did not notice. There was, in consequence, some warming towards this girl to whom, to her mind, Hervey had lost his reason (though she would be the first to own that he did not himself know it). And Caithlin for her part placed not a foot awry in the perilous mire that passed for conversation. Time and again she faithfully led their talk back from exclusively mutual matters, though Hervey blithely pressed question after question on her. But there was not any mention of arrest or the action he faced – though all the village knew of it.

'How have the regiment's patrols been behaving?' he asked at length with a smile.

'Oh, we're right thankful for them always, sor,' Michael O'Mahoney interjected. 'And pleasing it is always to see that Serjeant Armstrong.'

'Yes, *dear* Serjeant Armstrong,' added Caithlin emphatically, 'I *so* much enjoy his company!'

Her eagerness seemed to generate further unease. Michael O'Mahoney looked away; and his wife, who had said next to nothing throughout, began poking the contents of the fire-pot in a purposeful fashion. Caithlin looked down at her lap as silence descended.

'Well,' said Henrietta, never content with such pauses, 'we have a long ride back to Cork. Matthew, do you not think we should take our leave of these good people?'

Taking their leave was a protracted affair, however, since the rest of the village was intent on shaking the hand of the man in whom, quite simply, they had seen both their deliverance (the eviction warrants had been cancelled on grounds of public order) and a promise of equitable treatment in the future by the military. But, if a handshake was one thing, it seemed scarcely appropriate for Caithlin after her welcoming embrace. Indeed, Hervey judged it to be wholly inadequate. So as she, the better judge of prudence, held out her hand, he took her by the shoulders to kiss her cheek, and so innocent and natural a gesture might have passed unremarkably had not Caithlin's own unease suddenly manifested itself in coyness. And in that instant Hervey finally, though with chill confusion, sensed the delicacy.

As they left the village Henrietta was mute, and she continued thus as they took the road to Ballincollig, the chill now beginning to numb his faculties. Yet something from deep within told him what he must do to explain his former insensibility, to lay to rest what had blighted their time together these past weeks, to put an end to any concerns she might have about Caithlin. 'I should like to show you a special place near here,' he said after what seemed an age of silence.

'Is that not where we have just been?' she replied with a hurt that left him in no doubt what he faced.

They rode to the ruins of Kilcrea friary. The place had lost nothing of its peacefulness, though the wind now whistled constantly through the lancets. As he helped Henrietta down from the saddle she would not meet his eyes. She seemed almost lifeless, like one of Elizabeth's childhood dolls whose horsehair filling had been lost. There was no sign of the self-possession which had drained him of his own confidence so many times that summer in Wiltshire.

They walked round the ruins, he recalling their history as it had been told to him by Father O'Gavan, though she showed scant attention and even less enthusiasm. He pointed to the stones and their inscriptions, and he told her how Caithlin had taught him Irish there.

'And what did she want from *you*, Matthew?' she asked with a directness he had never imagined of her.

He could give her no answer. In truth he had never supposed Caithlin had wanted anything but an increase in learning. And had they not always been chaperoned by Father O'Gavan? No, they had not of late. But nothing had ever passed between them, had it? Hervey found himself quite unable to think clearly, and even began to shake his head as if to deny the doubt. But, if he had anything in his heart for which to beg forgiveness, there were no *deeds* for confession. 'I taught her a little Greek,' he replied, and even as he said it he knew it sounded absurd.

'Greek!' exclaimed Henrietta.

Hervey took fright, losing all remaining perspective. 'Yes,' he replied, in panic almost, 'she already has some Latin.'

Henrietta began to laugh. She covered her mouth, so loud was her laughter, yet it scattered the starlings beginning to roost in the lintels. 'Greek!' she exclaimed in another peal of giggling.

Hervey looked at her hopelessly.

'Oh, Matthew, you are so . . . That girl adores you: it is as plain as can be. What do you really suppose has passed between you?'

He opened his mouth, but nothing emerged. At last, though, his instincts began to speak, for he saw at once quite clearly – indeed with *absolute* clarity – that the resolution of their separate months of confusion and despair lay within his grasp in this moment. He took her shoulders gently in his hands. 'Marry me, Henrietta,' he said, and he was surprised by his own words, for he had been trying to formulate the proposal with what he considered due refinement.

She looked up at him and shook her head, and it seemed as if a cold blade were piercing him. But then a look of absolute contentment came about her: 'I want nothing else,' she said clearly. 'I do not think I have at heart wanted anything else since the schoolroom!'

'So, my dear Henrietta, you are to marry a man of no fortune, a man very likely to be cashiered, disgraced and cast out from society. You will be dishonoured. And all this for *love*?' asked the duke with so grave an air of dismay that Henrietta was almost abashed.

'Yes,' she replied defiantly.

The duke smiled. 'What great things might I do if I had such a wife!'

Henrietta smiled, too, a smile of relief, and with it sprang back her spirit. 'Then take unto yourself some Hervey blood. Do not you have any feeling for Elizabeth?'

'Permit me, Henrietta, but I know a woman's heart well enough. Miss Hervey's would not open itself to me – of that you may be assured. No, not even for a coronet!'

'William, *that*—' But the duke bade her stop.

'There are more felicitous matters to discuss, madam,' he began. 'Your affianced's court martial – I think I may have news that will be pleasing.'

'Truly, I am all ears, sir,' replied Henrietta intently.

The duke rested an arm on the chimney piece in his voluminous library and began the news that he supposed must bring her such happiness: 'It seems to me too risky to let this case proceed to trial. What must needs be is that proceedings are abandoned.'

Henrietta looked dismayed. 'Forgive me, William, but is not that what everyone has been trying to do? You said the news was *felicitous.*'

'Felicitous – yes. But, on the contrary, it is *not* what Mr Hervey's attorney has been about. What he has quite properly been doing is addressing the issues – the case for the defence

– in anticipation of its coming to trial. And it is a clever case, too, turning on a most elegant point of law. But *so* elegant, I fear, and so momentous in its implications, that it runs the gravest danger of defeat – though I for one would take it to the House of Lords come what may.'

'Then, why seem you so sanguine?' she asked, perplexed.

'Because, dearest Henrietta, these several past weeks I have been canvassing my fellow landlords and have secured a remarkable concordance so far as this case is concerned. What do you suppose would be the implication if your Mr Hervey were to be acquitted in open court – remote though the chance may be?'

'I cannot think,' she replied, more perplexed.

'Well, let me suggest to you, as I have to my fellow land-lords, that the whole question of forcible evictions might subsequently be adjudged dubious in law. Every land-lord in the country would then be in the very devil of a position.'

'But', began Henrietta, grasping well enough the prop-osition but remaining unconvinced, 'you have said that there seemed but little chance of Matthew's being acquitted?'

'Indeed,' smiled the duke wickedly, 'but in the question of rights of eviction none of them would wish to wager, even against such long odds. None would ever want to see it subjected to a judicial ruling. I think it is time that I wrote to Sir Dearnley Lambert and went to see Mr Magistrate Gould, and perhaps the agent, too.'

'Oh, William, you are cleverness personified!' gasped Henrietta as she threw her arms round him.

'Let us just say that honour and self-interest are for once in accord.'


A Cavendish, and a descendant of the great Boyle, if only through marriage, was enough to put the Ballinhassig magis-trate into a state of mild panic. For his part, he declared on hearing the duke's proposition, he would be content to leave things entirely to the military and, on second thoughts, he would also rescind his submission to the Lord Lieutenant. William Devonshire was especially relieved at this latter since it saved him the journey to Dublin to argue his case at the Castle.

Fitzgerald, the agent, was altogether less pliable. Only the threat of using the Cavendish name with his employer shifted his stubbornness. At first he protested that there were no grounds on which to press for his removal: the wider implications of the legality of forcible evictions were not his concern, he argued. Whereupon the duke simply smiled and agreed, adding that, although it would give him no pleasure to use his title to coerce a baronet, he would have no hesitation in doing so on this occasion.

These two, were, however, the easier of his antagonists. There remained one enterprise of especial delicacy, for if this business with Hervey did indeed comprise an element of vindictiveness (and his instincts told him it did), then he would have to make sure that General Slade abandoned any proceedings when the magistrate withdrew his complaint. Buoyed by his success at Ballinhassig, the duke therefore journeyed to Fermoy to pay what he announced as an introductory call on the startled general, and invited him to dine at Lismore the following evening. He then left Fermoy as soon as he decently could, but would have been heartened to learn that, such was the enthusiasm for dinner at Lismore, Slade's staff spent the rest of the day sending messages throughout the county to cancel the invitations which the general had issued to dine at his own headquarters that same evening.

Henrietta took much persuading to be at dinner the following day, and Elizabeth even more. The duke insisted, however, that in his scheme of things their being there was of the essence. For he had surmised that a ward of the Marquess of Bath would tend further to overawe Slade, and that, when he learned she was in Ireland at the express invitation of Matthew Hervey, the seeds of doubt as to the wisdom of proceedings against him would be sown. Elizabeth's connection need not be revealed until it was propitious, he added, and if the general possessed the least degree of acuity there might be no mention at all of the . . . *difficulties.*

And so, at the end of that dinner into which Slade had entered as an unwitting enemy enters an ambuscade, Henrietta and Elizabeth retired with the general's lady. The Duke of Devonshire poured out his best port (as Slade was quick to recognize) and broached the question of the charges laid against Lieutenant Hervey. Slade professed but an imperfect knowledge of them but looked disconcerted by the volley. The duke bade a footman bring cigars, thereby allowing the general a little more time to appreciate the extent of the danger he was in. Though no soldier, the duke was now warming to his work and judged it the moment to fire a volley from, as it were, the second rank: 'Oh, by the by, General, you know, I presume, that Lady Henrietta Lindsay and Mr Hervey are to be married?'

Slade reeled visibly at this intelligence.

Now was the time for ruthlessness, the duke knew, and his third volley was decisive – a model of artfulness, of fox-cunning, even. The words were so deft that, later, Slade would not be able to recall them with any precision. Yet firmly in his mind, now, was the awful notion that he was laying charges against the brother of the future duchess. He could barely hide his discomposure. 'If this magistrate is to withdraw his complaint,' he began, his voice transposed by half an octave at least, 'then there is no reason whatever why this young officer should be kept in anguish a moment longer. I shall send instructions, first thing tomorrow morning, that all charges against him (if indeed there be any) be dismissed. I am right grateful to you, Duke, for advising me of the matter.'

Now, if the Duke of Devonshire had any reservations as to his stratagem, any doubts as to Hervey's integrity in the matter, any fears that Slade might be too much maligned, they were largely allayed by the general's quite evident disingenuousness. And when they joined the ladies the doubts that remained were entirely dispelled by Slade's great show of discovery that Elizabeth was the brother of 'one of my officers – a most active and engaging young man!'

The duke raised an eyebrow as he glanced across to Henrietta and Elizabeth. And in that he managed to convey the intense satisfaction of a man who had comprehensively outmanoeuvred a knave of the blackest kind.

Serjeant Armstrong hitched up his sword and fell into step beside Lieutenant Hervey. Picket duty came round frequently when there was but one troop in barracks – and only one officer and a handful of serjeants. But there were worse things on a cold January morning than inspecting the lines.

'Will Miss Lindsay and Miss Hervey be paying another visit to Ireland, then, sir?' he asked with a distinct twinkle in his eye.

'I hope so, but not before the summer, I should think,' replied Hervey, non-committal.

'It was good that they were able to stay longer to make up time for your confinement.'

'*Arrest*, Serjeant Armstrong, *arrest* – I'm not a woman with child!'

'Forgive my lack of learning, sir,' Armstrong retorted with heavy irony.

Hervey returned the fire-picket's salute as they passed the hay store. 'Learning be damned! You were fishing!'

'I was no such thing! I merely asked if we were to see the ladies again.'

In the feed store Hervey checked the quartermaster-serjeant's ledger to compare it with the figures he had been given at the orderly room. Armstrong began counting the sacks of oats, opening several at random and prodding the contents with his whip.

'Sixty-seven, sir,' he called at length.

'Thank you. All correct, then, quarm'serjeant,' said Hervey, signing the ledger.

Taking up the conversation again as he and Armstrong left the store, Hervey decided there had been enough beating about the bush. 'You will see plenty of Lady Henrietta because, as you very well know, we are to be married – that is, if her guardian consents.'

'Now, how did I know that, sir?' was Armstrong's almost convincing protest.

'Because Johnson told me you had already collected your winnings from Serjeant Harkness! Really, Armstrong! Betting on your troop lieutenant's marriage stakes!'

Serjeant Armstrong was momentarily, and uncharacteristically, silenced, giving Hervey further opportunity to discomfit him. 'Tell me how in heaven's name you learned of it,' he pressed.

'I can't say, sir.'

'What do you mean, you can't say? This isn't a game of charades!'

'Would that be like brag, sir?'

'Armstrong!'

'Well . . . all right,' he began reluctantly, halting in mid-stride. 'Miss Lindsay told me 'erself.'

'She what?'

'She came to riding school just before leaving for England – while you were away in town – and told me.'

'Whatever *for*?'

'She's *your* intended! How should *I* know why she wanted me to know?'

'Serjeant Armstrong, if she confided in you that day there must have been something earlier. What had you been saying to her before then?'

'Nothing.'

'Don't lie.'

'I . . . I just put in a good word for you from time to time. You'd do the same for me!'

Hervey laughed. 'I just have!'

Armstrong's expression lost its remaining assurance. 'What do you mean?'

'I *mean* last week. While you were with my intended at riding school, I rode over to Kilcrea to see Michael O'Mahoney. And he asked me if you were good enough to be a son-in-law.'

Armstrong was struck dumb, though he recovered after some self-conscious shuffling. 'Ah, well, right enough. I've been on duty at that place for the best part of two months off an' on since the trouble. I got to calling on the O'Mahoneys and walked out with Caithlin once or twice. I never thought I'd be asking an Irish lass to marry me, an' I never would 'ave thought she'd have me – they may be dirt-poor, but she's full of learnin'. I think the old man's pleased enough but I couldn't speak for them two brothers. She's a grand lass, though. She'll make a soldier's wife right enough!'

Hervey agreed wholeheartedly. But whether she would be happy the other side of the barrack-room curtain . . . Well, it was none of his business now. However, if that was where she was to live, then Hervey was certain of one thing: she could not live more happily or, it would seem, more cherished than with this man.

'An' so will that Miss Lindsay make a soldier's wife,' said Armstrong, who could never be troubled with titles. 'An' it was me as told you as much in England if you remember!'

'Indeed I do, Serjeant Armstrong; indeed I do!'

The orderly trumpeter, passing on his way to the middle of the square to sound 'Watering', was bemused by the sight of both men shaking hands and smiling. His call interrupted their mutual congratulations, however, demanding a further round of mundane inspections – a half-hour in the stables checking that buckets were full and clean. Afterwards Armstrong, his customary wile and composure restored, took advantage of the earlier *bonhomie* to probe on the question that occupied so much of 'A' Troop's canteen talk. 'The word in the mess is that "C" Troop will be wanting a new captain in a couple o' months,' he began.

'Since you know so much, Serjeant Armstrong, you ought to know that I will not be eligible to apply!' Hervey answered, sounding more than a little sore.

'That I did not know, sir. How is it, then?' asked Armstrong with a frown.

'Because – and I do not wish this to become commonplace in the mess or the canteens – General Slade has in his dispatches declined to endorse any recommendation for promotion.'

'What! An' after all that business at Kilcrea?'

'*Because* of the business there apparently. It seems my judgement is questionable!'

'In God's name! Can't you appeal?'

'I am not even meant to know! It is only because Lord George Irvine is acting as military secretary in Dublin that I learned about it. He recommends we let sleeping dogs lie for a while.'

'Sleeping dogs be damned: you're as good as finished in peacetime with a mark like that against you. That Gen'ral Slade 'as 'ad it in for the regiment since T'loos – that's what this's about! Can't your grand friend the duke help?'

'No, I think not. Something will up, peace or no. All we can do – as Major Edmonds would say – is be stoical.'

Armstrong looked puzzled: 'Well, it's all Greek to me!'

# PART TWO

# ONE HUNDRED DAYS

---

The Tiger has broken out of his den
The Ogre has been three days at sea
The Wretch has landed at Fréjus
The Buzzard has reached Antibes
The Invader has arrived in Grenoble
The General has entered Lyons
Napoleon slept at Fontainebleau last night
The Emperor will proceed to the Tuileries today
*His Imperial Majesty will address his loyal
subjects tomorrow.*

Paris broadsheet, April 1815

# CHAPTER TWELVE
# 'EVIL NEWS RIDES POST'

*Cork, 12 March 1815*

*The Times* arrived in Cork each morning two days after leaving the new steam presses in Printing House Yard, unless strong contrary winds delayed the Bristol packet. From time to time its news arrived sooner, by word of mouth of some traveller who had covered the 130 miles from London to the great sea-port faster than the mail-coach's twelve hours, and who had been able thereby to join an earlier sailing. But not often.

News of Bonaparte's escape from Elba reached Cork in this accelerated fashion, however, and for several hours on 12 March 1815 one Jeremiah Sharrow, manufacturing apothecary's agent, found himself the unlikely guest of the officers of the 6th Light Dragoons, who pressed him to every detail of the escape and the response of the government of Lord Liverpool. Without doubt Lord George Irvine, who had been retained in Dublin, much against his will, would have greeted the news with the pleasure that a sporting man takes in seeing a fine dog-fox break cover: with good hounds, and a huntsman who knew what he was about, the chase and prospect of a kill promised capital sport. Major Joseph Edmonds received it differently, however: '"Evil news rides post, while good news baits!"'

'Milton, I think, sir,' began Hervey, 'but I cannot quite place it—'

'*Samson Agonistes.*'

Hervey had watched the major's spirits ebb throughout that winter. Command seemed a trial to him now, with nothing of the energy of those days before and after Toulouse. He no longer seemed to lose his temper even. Hervey had thought the news might somehow invigorate him when, as picket officer, he had brought it to the mess: instead it received only the melancholy quotation from Milton. Here, indeed, was the heavy heart of a family man who had spent practically every one of his thirty years in King George's uniform on active service. He had no personal wealth to speak of, and although he had accumulated a little prize-money he had lamented that he would never be able to buy the lieutenant-colonelcy of even an infantry regiment now that peace had come to Europe. He was too old, he knew, to seek preferment with the Honourable East India Company. In truth he had privately become reconciled to going on to half-pay and to joining his wife and three daughters in Norwich. Hervey was puzzled none the less why this news of the flight from Elba was not greeted with more enthusiasm: surely it was cause for hope in one respect, for the fortunes of war were ever changing? The *Agonistes* seemed apt indeed – Samson 'calm of mind, all passion spent'. It was not a heroic state – not a state fitting for this man in whom the regiment had placed its trust time and again, and who had never once failed them. 'Do you believe there will be war again, sir?' he asked (he would not be put off by the insouciance).

'Why in heaven's name would Bonaparte have left Elba otherwise? I doubt it was to pay a call on a mistress,' Edmonds replied tartly. 'Believe me, if they let him get to Paris the Bourbons will run like hares and the Old Guard will rally straight to him. There aren't but fifty thousand of our troops and Prussians in the Low Countries, and he'll have three times that number in the field within two months. Do you think the Austrians have any more stomach for a fight? The Dutch are treacherous, and the Brunswickers are finished. I doubt even the Prussians' resolve.'

Hervey was unabashed still. 'But we broke what remained of their southern army at Toulouse, and the other allies had crippled the northern ones. What can he achieve?'

'He can put the wind up that congress in Vienna, that's what – make them give better terms, a republic perhaps. They should have seen it coming. Elba was too close to home for him, in both senses. You remember the *Agonistes* – Samson's despair in his incarceration, of living "a life half dead, a living death"? How did they think they could cage such a beast as Bonaparte within scent of his old prey?'

Hervey decided on a prudent withdrawal: 'How indeed, sir! Shall there be any message in reply for the adjutant?'

'Doubtless Mr Barrow is at this instant relaying the tidings to the outlying stations. Be so good, Hervey, as to give him my compliments and send a recall to officers on furlough. But why we must receive this evil news from *The Times* and from some travelling man, rather than from Dublin, I truly despair. We may surmise that the Government has paid off all the telegraph-station lieutenants in their search for economies!'

One question alone exercised Hervey, however, one for which the officers' recall augured well. But he would put it to the adjutant, for he judged that Edmonds's melancholic humour would not admit of reason. 'What do you think be our chances of joining the duke's army, Barrow?' he asked after returning to the orderly room.

'As little chance as you have of no more picket duties this year!' was the perfunctory reply, though delivered with a smile.

And for a whole month it looked as though Barrow would be right, until on 20 April orders were received from Dublin to prepare six troops for immediate service in Belgium. Edmonds was at once transformed, throwing himself into the preparations, working with the punishing energy of a steam hammer. One morning he sat down after Muster and wrote, without drawing breath except to dip his pen, 'Directions for Carrying Camp Equipment,' specifying the means of securing every item a dragoon would carry: 'Mallets, tents, pins and hatchets to be carried in water buckets fixed to the near ring of the saddle behind. The powder bag to be carried by the Orderly

Corporal. Kettles to be fixed with strings upon the baggage, till straps can be provided. Canteens to be slung on the right side, haversacks on the left side. Picket posts strapped to firelocks. Corn sacks with corn divided between the ends, across the saddle. Hay twisted in ropes and fixed upon the necessary bags. Water-decks neatly folded and placed upon the hay. Nosebags fixed to the off-ring of the saddle behind. Forage cords upon the baggage. Scythes wrapped with hay-bands and strapped with the handles to the firelocks. Sneeds, stores, &c, to be carried by the same men. Old clothing, hats and spare things not wanted at present to be properly packed and lodged at the regimental store . . .' And so on and so on, until every last detail had been arranged.

'Really, Hervey, there is no need of an adjutant with the major so,' rued Barrow one morning as he gave him his orders for picket. 'He is riding to each and every outstation to inspect for himself every horse! Heaven alone knows when he sleeps.'

On the 27th, Lord George Irvine arrived from Dublin to take command, which Edmonds relinquished with not a sign of the intense disappointment that he must have felt, and on the 29th 'A' and 'B' Troops marched from the barracks to the Cove to begin embarkation. Nine days later, including re-shipping at Ramsgate, they landed at Ostend. Or, rather, the officers and men landed – by lighter: the horses were pushed overboard to swim for the shore. This not unusual method of disembarking always meant delay while the two groups were reunited, and almost invariably occasioned injury to both parties. On this morning, however, Lieutenant Hervey was able to hand over 'A' Troop to Captain Lankester, who had rejoined them at Ramsgate, at exactly the Irish establishment of 66 horses, less chargers, and 71 other ranks – and all fit for duty.

Ostend harbour itself was all activity. Officers on home leave who had made their own way to Belgium were hailing comrades as their regiments disembarked, or greeting old friends in others, and the scene resembled – as one India hand put it – a Calcutta durbar. Laming, now the Sixth's senior cornet, who had been in Ostend for over a week, grasped

Hervey with unrestrained enthusiasm. 'D'ye know, it's like the first day of the summer half at Eton. I have not seen so many old friends in years! What a turn-up, eh? And we all believed that half-pay or selling out was all that beckoned! Have you heard that Lord George is to get a brigade? Dutchmen mostly, though – he'll have no brigade after the first shot is fired!'

'Who is to command us, then?' asked Hervey, warily.

'Edmonds, of course. And right glad of it I am, too – you'll see soon enough that things here are not as they should be. Now's not the time to be foisted with an extract.' He paused and then frowned. 'Why are you looking so?'

'Nothing, nothing at all. It is just that the major has not been himself these past few months, although he has worked like a black since orders for here came. Whose brigade are we to be in?'

'Grant's for the time being, with the Seventh, Thirteenth and Fifteenth, so I understand. They arrive only now. But have you heard who is to command the cavalry?'

'You mean it is not to be General Cotton?'

'Uxbridge!'

'Great heavens,' replied Hervey, reflecting Laming's smile of satisfaction. 'But I thought that he and the duke could not speak with each other – after that business with his sister-in-law, I mean?'

'That is as maybe, but I hear tell the Duke of York himself was adamant, and that Wellington has accepted with good grace. And so he deuced well should – Uxbridge is the only general with cavalry genius!'

Hervey smiled. But then, why should not Laming make so precocious a judgement? He himself would not hesitate to voice such an opinion, especially in respect of Uxbridge. 'On that we can all be agreed, and yet had not Le Marchant fallen at Salamanca—'

'Floreat Etona, Laming!' came a call from the press behind him. Hervey would have walked away, leaving Laming to yet another Fourth-of-June encounter, but something in the voice made him turn instead. 'By heavens, *Jessope*!' he exclaimed, and there followed much vigorous handshaking and mutual expressions of delight.

'But why, my dear Hervey, do you sound so surprised on seeing me thus? You do not suppose Lord Fitzroy Somerset would have sallied hence without me?' said the ADC, with the same solemn self-mocking that had so endeared him to Hervey in Spain.

'No, I did not suppose it for one minute. You are quite charming enough to flatter any assignment out of the Horse Guards, of that I am sure! To tell the truth, my dear Jessope, I had not given it a moment's thought: we have been uncommonly busy in the Line, you know! But now that I see you here I am full of confidence at last in this campaign! Shall I suppose that Lord Fitzroy is to be military secretary again?'

'Verily he is,' began Jessope, ignoring Hervey's earlier irony. 'But listen, my dear fellow, this campaign ought to be a very fine summer's sport indeed! Hardly anyone believes that Bonaparte will survive long: his marshals and generals will throw him over now that he has been declared an outlaw. Brussels has become quite like London – so many of Mayfair's hostesses have set themselves up here. And we are hunting in the forests just outside. I tell you, it is capital, sir, capital!'

'I think it will come to a fight,' replied Hervey, refusing to endorse Jessope's dismissiveness.

'My dear fellow, so do I, so do I. And so does the duke. But there will still be plenty of sport!'

'Then, who is it that does not suppose there will be war?'

'Those fools in Whitehall, to begin with. I tell you, they think this thing so trivial that Slender Billy was at first to be made commander-in-chief.'

'Who is Slender Billy?' asked Hervey with a frown.

'In heaven's name, where have you been these past months? The crown prince of Orange, that is who!'

'But was he not one of the duke's own ADCs in the Peninsula – *surely* he was?'

'The same, the same! In any event, I am given to understand that some arrangement has been concluded. I think the young Dutchman is to be given command of a corps. Your esteemed

Lord George is to be a liaison officer at his headquarters.'

'Lord George? But I thought he was to command one of their brigades,' said Hervey, intrigued by this turn of news.

'Lawks, no! They will not even give the duke direct command of Dutch troops in action, let alone make one of our officers a brigade commander. No, he is to go and keep an eye on Slender Billy! But look, we've been here nearly a month and the duke rides out each morning with Lord Fitzroy. You may accompany if you wish – he is the most engaging of company on a good day.'

'I am very pleased to hear it!' said Hervey with a smile, amused at Jessope's familiarity. 'But it does not sound as if the duke is having too many good days by your accounts.'

'Nought without his capability, I assure you, my dear friend. But how say you to riding with us?'

Hervey smiled again. 'I should be honoured to ride with you – both!'

'Capital! Then, I shall send word as soon as is expedient. Now, I must go and collect the dispatches which that frigate yonder should have aboard,' Jessope said, nodding to the single-decker about to drop anchor in the outer harbour.

No sooner had he gone but that Hervey was confronted by a figure who excited every contrary emotion to those inspired by Jessope's unexpected company. Under a helmet resembling that of an ancient Greek hoplite was the face of Hugo Styles, the flesh more than usually loose but the complexion now florid. The broad gold braid down the front of his scarlet jacket shone as if new from his tailor that morning. 'Well, Hervey, a far cry this from Wiltshire. And by the look of ye y've come even further than from there.'

Hervey chose to ignore the reference to his well-worn field dress and instead returned the greeting – such as it had been – formally but briefly: 'Good morning, Styles.'

'I am given to understand that I should congratulate you on winning the esteem of Lady Henrietta Lindsay,' continued Styles with disdain.

'I cannot say what you should or should not do.'

'You are an extraordinarily favoured man, Mr Hervey, extraordinarily favoured,' he went on, his tone changing to one of reproach.

'I count myself so,' replied Hervey, holding to the clipped speech that betrayed his impatience.

Styles, sensing perhaps that he would force no change in Hervey's humour, reverted to his former condescension. 'I understand this business here might be tedious in the extreme. The talk in London is of peace. I do hope we may be allowed a little recreation – they say Brussels is a tolerably fine city, not at all provincial. How many horses have you brought?'

'Two.'

'My dear fellow, do you think that two will be enough?'

'I managed in the Peninsula well enough.'

'Yes, yes, but if we are to race and hunt every day you will need more than two.'

'I would not gainsay your logic, only your supposition.'

'Well, we shall see. I fancy that you in the light cavalry will all be sent on picket to the frontier in any case.'

Hervey thought this the only sense Styles had spoken throughout the exchange. The heir to Leighton Park – lieutenant of yeomanry and now cornet of Life Guards – seemed more than usually gifted with foolery. 'Very possibly, Styles,' he sighed. 'And it would be a most welcome duty, too, shaking off the flotsam hereabouts! Now, you must excuse me – I have work to do.' And he strode off towards the corralling area.

The effects of this unwelcome encounter did not last long, however, for in the corralling area, the park-like gardens in front of the harbourmaster's house, he found the perfect antidote: Joseph Edmonds, positively transfigured by the news of his command.

'And with pay, too, no less!' Edmonds laughed.

Hervey could not recall how long it had been since he had heard Edmonds laugh so. Months, many months. The major restored to good humour *and* in command – by his reckoning it would make the difference, perhaps, of two troops!

\*     \*     \*

In the days that followed, there was little to sustain them in that humour. The provision of forage was not good, the commissaries protesting that all their attempts to consolidate supplies were to no avail. They cited any number of reasons – none of which enraged Edmonds so much as the price of corn. 'As if book-keeping were to be admitted to the arts of war,' he complained. As a consequence of this failure to establish any form of supply, his six troops were scattered about the farms over a wide area around the town of Drongen, outside Ghent, so that local arrangements for forage might be made. And as one morning he was despairing of ever getting them together for regimental drill Lord Uxbridge arrived unannounced.

The commander of the allied cavalry, and the duke's presumptive second-in-command, sympathized. 'It is not only regimental drill that might be wanting: *brigade* drill is my most pressing concern,' he confided. 'My regiments are scattered the length of Flanders to keep them fed. Unless we may work up as brigades we shall be at a most trying disadvantage in this open country.'

'I wonder that you will have any opportunity to form divisions, then, my lord,' the major enquired.

'Just so, Edmonds, just so!' replied Uxbridge. 'I despair of assembling even one division for but a single field day.'

'Well, General, we shall drill as best we can – you know we shall – but I have so many new men: I hope that is not the case with the rest of the army.'

'Ha! But I fear it is, Edmonds. I am *certain* it is! But it is worse with the infantry. The duke is not in the least sanguine, and matters are not as they should be with the allies. There is even difficulty with the Prussians. Still, *we* shall be well, of that I am sure! At least my brigade and regimental commanders are old Peninsular hands. How I wish I had been with you in the second campaign! Do you remember Sahagun, Edmonds? Of *course* you do! Well, we shall not freeze this time: if this heat continues, we shall drop like recruits in the Indies! But we may, I fear, see a good many Sahaguns before Bonaparte is back in his box!'

Yes, here was a cavalryman with the surest *coup d'œil*. All would be well; but, even so, Edmonds had not liked what Uxbridge had said about the difficulties with the Dutch and the Prussians. Never had he trusted anyone but an English regular, yet now they must rely on allies close on both flanks. Was not this what he had warned of that very day in Cork when the news of the escape from Elba arrived? And it would be no Peninsula this time – no Fabian campaign of advance and withdrawal on Wellington's terms, no game of cat and mouse. This was too close to Paris for the French, and Bonaparte himself would be in the field. It would take the whole weight of an allied army – an army of unity – to defeat him, not one of rifts and suspicions.

Later in the morning Hervey rode into Ghent to see d'Arcey Jessope, whose invitation to dine with his regiment he had received the day before. 'But, first, my dear friend,' said the ADC as he greeted him enthusiastically, 'I want to show you my new charger. I am excessively pleased with him, I must admit. He is the most beautiful creature!'

They went to the château stables where Jessope had lodged his new horse, and an orderly led him out under a magnificent saddle-cloth. 'There!' exclaimed the captain of Guards. 'Tell me your opinion – is he not the most magnificent steed, fit for an aide-de-camp to the duke's military secretary!'

Hervey smiled; Jessope had such an attachment to looks! This gelding was, however, as fine a looking thoroughbred as Hervey had seen. An inch short of sixteen hands, he guessed, there was a pleasing symmetry to his conformation. His lean head, indicating the real quality of his breeding, was well set on. He had a kind eye, betokening a generous disposition (and that, Hervey judged, was what Jessope needed above all else). He had a nice length of rein let into sloping shoulders, putting the saddle in the right place. He stood on good legs, not too spindly as some thoroughbreds had, with enough bone below the knee. His quarters were well let down, and his hocks were well under him. His summer coat, a deep liver chestnut, shone. And – which Jessope no doubt found most pleasing – he carried his tail well. Hervey had but one reservation: he was a shade too short-coupled for his liking. True, Jessye had a short back, but he always believed this to be less a concern in non-bloods. But, he had to admit, this gelding was a picture, and he congratulated Jessope.

'Let us ride together a while, then, and I can show you his paces: he trots as if on air!'

Hervey readily agreed. The tacking was called for and, after a little difficulty fitting the saddle ('He is somewhat cold-backed,' Jessope explained), they set off for the park near the great cathedral of St-Bavon.

To Jessope's frustration, however, he could not keep his gelding on the bit.

'Is he green?' asked Hervey, trying not to make too obvious a suggestion that Jessope's hands might be wanting.

'Well, he was warranted eight years old. I think, perhaps, I have not been able to give him quite sufficient exercise since coming here.'

Hervey was sceptical, however, and he observed the gelding intently as they trotted along the sandy ride that bisected the park. The horse would not relax its back, seeming instead to hold it stiffly, and there looked to be too little activity in the hind legs for so well bred an animal.

When they returned to the château Hervey asked if he might look him over more closely.

'Do you think there might be some ailment, then?' asked Jessope, with more than a note of concern.

Hervey paused before making any reply, running his hand along the horse's back, feeling for obvious sore points. But there were none: the back was as clean as could be. 'Look,' he began, 'I know only a very little about these things. But I am always a trifle uneasy about short-coupled thoroughbreds. I like more room for the lungs, though I must say that yours seems to have not too shallow a chest. You say he is eight years. Has he done much?'

'I don't rightly know,' said Jessope, a might uncomfortably. 'I bought him at Tattersall's, as the property of a gentleman.'

Hervey looked in the gelding's mouth. The groove in the crown of each incisor was gone, and the star was present in

245

the central ones. 'Well, he is eight at least. Beyond that I cannot tell.'

'What do you suppose is the trouble, then?'

Hervey let out his breath and raised an eyebrow. 'Look, Jessope, he is a handsome thing, but . . .'

Jessope had by now braced himself. 'Tell me what you suppose!'

'I fear he may have a kissing spine.'

Jessope looked puzzled.

'I have seen it only a couple of times before, and there is no sure way of knowing, but each time it has been a thoroughbred with a short back. A kissing spine is when the vertebrae impinge, invariably in the middle back.'

Jessope looked crestfallen. 'And what may I do about it?'

'The first thing you must do is seek the opinion of someone better-qualified than I. There must be a staff veterinary officer with the duke's headquarters.'

'Yes, there is,' replied Jessope. 'And what if he confirms your diagnosis?'

Hervey paused again. 'I am very much afraid that at his age you can do nothing. But in any event, you must have a horse that you may rely on in the field. You do have others?'

'Yes,' he replied, 'of course, but they are not one bit as magnificent as he.'

'Jessope, my dear friend, believe me,' urged Hervey, 'I understand that it is necessary to be turned out magnificently on the staff. But when it comes to fighting you know full well that it's "handsome is that handsome does".'

Dinner comprised both agreeable company and good fare, the Guards having paid handsomely for the contents of a market garden nearby and for venison from their château's deerpark. There was champagne brought that day from Rheims by traders of resource, its cost inflated, however, by the 'tolls' paid to French patrols near the border. In respect of champagne, at least, even during the late wars, neither the allied blockade nor Bonaparte's edicts had ever quite extirpated trade. But Jessope had been curiously reserved throughout dinner. And afterwards, walking in the formal gardens of the château, he revealed why. 'You must not breathe a word of this,' he began, in almost a whisper, 'but matters are looking very grave indeed as regards the Prussians.'

Hervey committed himself to absolute discretion.

'There might even be a thorough rupture in the alliance,' he continued, Hervey's expression of surprise encouraging his conspiratorial manner. 'It would seem that earlier this year, at the congress in Vienna, there was some *impasse* as regards the future of Saxony and Poland. The Prussians appeared to want to incorporate the greater part of both into Prussia itself. It would seem that a secret treaty was signed in which we agreed to side with Austria and France against the Prussians – and with the Russians, too, I believe – in the event of its coming to a fight.'

'Great heavens!' sighed Hervey, 'and I suppose you are going to say that the secret is now out?'

'Bonaparte discovered it – naturally – and is now most skilfully driving a wedge into the alliance.'

'What shall happen?'

'I know not. Lord Fitzroy considers that it will not make a deal of difference in so far as the congress is concerned. Bonaparte must be dealt with – the Prussians know it well enough. And the only way is by concerted action. But in Vienna they may have their stately dance: the difficulty will be in the field, for it seems there is much resentment already amongst the Prussians. Gneisenau, their chief of staff, can be trying at the best of times – so hearsay has it.'

'But is not Prince Blücher to be their commander? He has a reputation as a seasoned soldier, has he not?'

'Yes, indeed. But you with all your study will know that the Prussians have a most curious system. The chief of staff answers direct to their king in many matters – principally in the strategy of the campaign. So even though Blücher is the field commander he is bound by Gneisenau's orders in certain circumstances.'

'It is a curious system for sure; it evidently works, however.'

'Evidently so, though it is untried in coalition. Oh, and by way of adding to the discord,' said Jessope almost as an aside, 'they are shooting the Saxons!'

'*What?*' gasped Hervey.

'Several Saxon regiments have mutinied, and the Prussians are shooting the ringleaders. Altogether, then, not everything on our left flank is as the duke would have it be!'

Hervey raised his eyebrows and then shrugged. 'And what does headquarters think Bonaparte will be about next?'

'The duke believes there will be no attack in the north – at least, to begin with. He believes Bonaparte will strike first at the Austrians on the Rhine.'

'And what of us here, then?'

'Oh, there will be some offensive to hold us in Belgium, that is for sure. But look, my good friend, I have to be back at headquarters ere long. I will tell you all as I hear it, but it must go no further. I tell *you* because I cannot trust anyone else to keep silent and, in truth, I must talk with someone – the confidences are all but intolerable. Now, riding out with head-quarters – shall you be able to join us tomorrow?'

'You may be sure of it.'

'Then be there by eight: the duke will be very prompt.'

# CHAPTER THIRTEEN
# DESIGN FOR BATTLE

*Flanders, 2 June 1815*

When Hugo Styles had raised an eyebrow at the supposed inadequacy of Hervey's equipage – 'do you think that two will be enough?' – he had scarcely fancied that one of those two horses would be an unprepossessing little mare. And had it been Styles about to ride out in the company of the commander-in-chief, albeit no doubt at the back of a large field, that ornament of an officer would for certain have ridden the poorer-looking charger to the headquarters, his groom leading a finer one, and there he would have changed horses – just as at home he might take a hack to a covert, and thence change to a blood for the chase. But Hervey had chosen to do the contrary, though acutely aware that the Sixth's officers had at one time scorned Jessye as a covert-hack. Not that he feigned to consider, for the briefest instant, the alternative. He dismissed it, however, on the grounds that the Duke of Wellington would not engage himself in the sort of Hyde Park ride that Styles might have envisaged. And if there was to be anything tricky, then he wished to be on that handy little mare – indeed, the handiest in everyone's judgement now. Perhaps if Harkaway had not thrown a splint he would have chosen him instead, but the gelding was gorging himself on the lush green grass of east Cork, making whole again in anticipation of Hervey's return to the hunting field in that glorious county.

The headquarters party that morning was not as big as he

had expected. The duke himself, wearing a plain blue coat and hat, and riding a big grey, was accompanied by Lord Fitzroy Somerset. This, Hervey's first sight of the duke's military secretary, greatly took him aback, for the man looked no older than he.

'That is because he is *not*!' said Jessope. 'Well, not by more than a year or two. And a lieutenant-colonel to boot!'

Hervey studied him, fascinated. Twenty-six or twenty-seven, a lieutenant-colonel in the Grenadiers and one of the duke's principal staff officers. A son of the Duke of Beaufort (no doubt this had been instrumental to his first being appointed ADC to Wellington in Spain), but there were many similarly connected officers who failed to win so signal a favour. Patronage could be but an incomplete explanation. And here was *he* – a lieutenant with hardly the means to buy a captaincy, and a stop on promotion even if he did have. It would have required the attributes of a saint at that moment not to feel at least some particle of resentment.

'Did you know his wife is with child – their first?' added Jessope, as if Hervey might have any idea – or, indeed, interest. 'She is in Brussels at this time.'

'I was not even to know he was married!' he replied flatly.

'Why, yes,' began Jessope, unperturbed, 'last August, to the duke's niece. It was a deuced fine wedding, I may tell you!'

Hervey smiled to himself. The duke's niece – how these threads wove tight together! And he wondered who these other three in the party might therefore be. Perhaps they, too, were officers of like affinity. He began to feel uncomfortably out of place. Maybe, had he not been so conspicuous (he was wearing field order, so that he looked not unlike the two staff-dragoon orderlies accompanying the duke), he might have felt more inclined to ease, for the others wore plain clothes of black, blue or green which would serve them equally well in the hunting field. And they seemed intent on keeping their own company, though apparently on nodding terms with Jessope.

'Where is the escort?' he whispered.

'There is no escort. The duke keeps his field small and relies on quality,' replied Jessope, likewise *sotto*. 'What do you think of that entire he rides – *he* is quality, is he not?'

'Truly he is, though more a youngster than I would have supposed.'

'The duke has a stable of near two dozen, counting drivers. And most of them bloods!'

'Then I shall be sure to remain a respectful distance behind with Jessye!' he smiled.

'What of the Hanoverian you bought of me? Was he not a more meet companion for a ride such as this?' asked Jessope, puzzled.

'I rode him here – did you not see? In truth he would, I agree, have set me off finer in a parade. But my mare, here, is the fleetest little creature God made.'

Jessope frowned.

'Believe me,' insisted Hervey, 'in a squeeze I would be with no other.'

A fast trot south and west took them through villages full of British, Dutch and Belgian troops, for the most part infantrymen. The duke stopped once or twice to exchange words with an officer he appeared to know, but there was no formality. The commander-in-chief's progress was, indeed, as brisk as reputation had it. Then, as they turned back in the direction of Ghent, crossing a hayfield which had taken its first cut a week or so before, a big buck-hare got up from almost under the duke's feet, startling his young horse and those of his nearest attendants. The duke, however, re-gathered his reins before any of them and was straight after it, hallooing loudly.

'Soho!' called Jessope to Hervey. 'We must be in at the kill!'

The hare led them in a huge circle over country empty but for a few labourers by the hayricks. They crossed three streams at a furious pace, and still there was no check – a full five minutes' galloping. A sunken road all but proved the hare's escape, too, for the duke's horse pecked on landing short of the top of the far bank and tumbled its rider. Two of the other officers, riding hard up close, went the same way.

The third pulled up before take-off, as did the staff dragoons and Lord Fitzroy. Hervey put Jessye at the hedge, where the others had gone for the gap, and she cleared the road in a soaring arc.

Ignorant of what convention demanded of him, and seeing the duke already on his feet and remounting, he galloped off after the hare. With no-one in front, now, to check his speed he pressed his legs to Jessye's flanks and closed steadily with the big buck. At twenty yards he drew his sabre and, pointing, pressed the mare to a final effort. The buck jinked to the left and Hervey came back to the recover, turning Jessye sharply, who did a neat flying change of her own accord to lead with the left leg. The hare continued running to the left, and Hervey knew he would not be able to get on its inside, so he leaned forward at full stretch and pointed down the nearside. A second or so later and he lifted the quarry on his sabre.

'Smart work, boy, smart work!' shouted the duke as he caught up, bringing the rest of the field with him. 'The smartest swordwork I have seen in many a year!'

They began circling in a walk to let the horses down, and Hervey presented the hare to the staff dragoons. 'For your pot, troopers!'

'Who's your hard-riding friend, Jessope?' called the duke as the ADC caught them up.

'Lieutenant Hervey, Sixth Light Dragoons, your Grace,' he replied.

The duke smiled, turning to him:

> '"A different hound for every chase
> Select with judgment, nor the timid hare
> O'er matched destroy."

Do you know that verse, boy?'

'Indeed I do, sir. It is Somerville's *Chase.*'

The duke nodded. 'Just so, and I think I should despise an Englishman who did not know it. Hervey – the name is familiar. We have met before, have we not? Toulouse?'

'Yes, sir; I was commanding a flank picket,' he replied, incandescent at the recognition.

'Indeed, you were,' added the duke, breaking into another smile. 'Lord Fitzroy, this officer accounted for a horse battery on his own. What sport there is to be had in the cavalry!'

'I sometimes wish I had remained a light dragoon myself, Duke!' added Lord Fitzroy, offering Hervey his hand.

'Well, I cannot say the same myself,' laughed the commander-in-chief, 'though I was only a dragoon on paper, as it were. It seems to me, though, that a light dragoon is something a man must be at some stage of his life but that he must move sharply on to more serious things! Consider the elder Pitt, Hervey – now, there's a dragoon who moved on to greater matters!'

Everyone laughed politely, as subordinates tend to when a senior officer attempts humour.

'I think it best if I first seek distinction as a dragoon, your Grace!' Hervey submitted.

'But you are almost *there*, my dear fellow!' countered the duke. 'You know how to handle a picket. Now, if you can do something to check this appalling habit our cavalry have got into of galloping at everything and then galloping back again, without note of the circumstances, you will achieve distinction right enough. I dare say you will be unique!'

Hervey smiled awkwardly, for he knew that, though the remark was in jest, an earnest particular underlay it, a particular on which the duke had expressed his disapproval many times. The commander-in-chief was in good humour, however, certainly none the worse for his tumble, and the party turned for home in high spirits.

'Come ride up alongside, Hervey,' called the duke as they set off back on long reins. 'Tell me, what is your opinion of what Bonaparte might do here?'

Though startled by the unexpectedness of the question, he answered at once, for it was a matter to which he had given much thought. 'I suspect that many will think he will envelop us by a drive around our right flank, cutting us off from

Ostend and the other Channel ports, perhaps fighting a holding battle on the border around Charleroi: he has made so many moves of this like before.'

'Yes,' said the duke slowly, as if surprised by the discernment of the reply and intrigued by the question posed by 'many will think'.

'But that is excessively risky,' Hervey continued, thoroughly warming to his subject. 'His strategic aim must surely be to knock us – the British I mean, sir – out of the fight, back into the sea, and to send the Prussians back across the Rhine. It seems to me, your Grace, that if he puts his effort into an envelopment, then what he is doing is trying to use sheer weight to achieve his design. He might not *have* enough weight, and he might also drive us *towards*, rather than away from, the Prussians – and then he would simply have too big an army to defeat.'

The duke was about to say something, but Hervey failed to notice and instead pressed on to his second conclusion.

'If, however, Bonaparte strikes direct for Brussels he might drive a wedge so deep between the two armies that each falls back along its own lines of communication, and he would thereby have achieved his strategic purpose by the indirect method. That I am sure is much more at the heart of what he seeks to do with his so-called "manoeuvre", yet everyone – excuse me, your Grace – *many* seem only to see the movement rather than the purpose.'

'Well, well!' replied the duke. 'Whoever would have thought it! I have officers in the cavalry who have studied Bonaparte rather than just Reynard! Do not take offence, Mr Hervey: the two have much in common!'

There was more laughter.

'So you are acquainted with Bonaparte's so-called "Strategy of the Central Position"?' continued the duke.

'Yes, sir; I have read much on the subject. It is the strategy that I believe would give the best chance of success here.'

'Well, then, describe it – briefly – for the benefit of my friends here,' he added, indicating the three staff officers who were now looking at Hervey with evident regard, rather than merely through him as before.

'Briefly, sir, *divide et impera.* His army, divided into two echelons, drives between the two opposing armies. He uses just sufficient force to fix one in place and then concentrates the rest to defeat the second. He does not have to destroy the second completely, just to destroy any hope of its assisting the other. He then turns to defeat in detail the first army which he has fixed in place.'

'And what are the prerequisites of the strategy?' asked the duke, his eyes now fastened on him, hawk-like.

'*Pre*-requisites, sir?' Hervey began, stressing the anticipatory so as to be wholly clear of what his answer was conditional upon. 'Surprise and security.'

'Just so,' nodded the duke pensively, and without another word he broke into a trot.

It was midday by the time they returned to the commander-in-chief's forward headquarters at Ghent. Hervey had fallen back to his original place next to Jessope, who was much amused by the 'strategic tutorial' as he called it. As they entered the courtyard of the inn which had been pressed into military service, the duke turned to them both. 'Thank you, Mr Hervey. I have much enjoyed your company,' he said warmly. 'Captain Jessope, you must bring your thinking friend out again. Yes, gentlemen, surprise and security: they are everything!'

It became even hotter in the days that followed. Supply, as far as it affected the Sixth, seemed to be much better, although the troops were still scattered about numerous villages in order to take forage direct from the farms rather than through the system of depots. And while this suited them in many ways it still made mustering for drill difficult: the brigade had only been able to hold two field days since arriving, although there had been yet another change of location, this time to the River Dendre around Grammont. Here, though, they were plagued by midges, and it was not long before sweet itch appeared, particularly in those horses billeted in the poorer, unkempt farms where there was little cover and scant waste-discipline. Never had the regiment suffered from it so badly. In 'C' Troop one morning sixteen horses could not be saddled, so abraded were their backs, and Edmonds became affeard of an epidemic. There was no agreement, even, as to its cause, for many believed the connection with midges to be circumstantial. Neither was there unanimity as to treatment. The new veterinary officer, young and active, had no doubts, however, and managed to procure large quantities of sulphur, treating all the cases with his own foul-smelling potion. It had unusually early results, although three of the worst cases had to be dispatched by the farrier's axe. Captain Lankester had sniffed when he heard of the losses, for each day he had had all his troop horses brought in before dawn, and again before dusk, when the midges were the most active, and had lit fires to smoke them away. As a consequence they had lost not one trooper, nor had any been unfit for saddling for more than a day. His own chargers he anointed with a most precious lotion he had bought the previous year in London on the recommendation of a tea-planter: oil of citronella, one of the East India Company's most exotic and expensive imports (the planter had sworn by it). It had a most pleasing smell yet was wholly repugnant to any flying insect, and Lankester had been able to enjoy his shooting and fishing unplagued after daubing his face and hands with it. And he had now been able to transfer exactly this protection to his beloved hunters.

But if the new billets did not favour the horses they certainly suited many of the officers, since it took less than two hours to get to Brussels. The capital had almost as many theatres as London, and dances and levees carried on apace. At one of these (and he had only been to the one) Hervey had met Lady Fitzroy Somerset.

'Are you the officer who courses hares with his sabre?' she had asked laughingly.

To which Hervey had replied that he could have done better with a lance.

'My husband tells me that your conversation with my uncle

set him thinking for several hours. *Quite* an achievement, Mr Hervey!'

'I am sure the duke is thinking constantly, madam,' had been Hervey's reply. It had been the best he could manage, for he was not as yet at ease in that company, and Lady Fitzroy Somerset put him in mind of Henrietta Lindsay and of his initial awkwardness in *her* company. It had been a charming enough exchange, no doubt the inconsequential talk of such gatherings, but even if there had been only a fraction of truth in the idea that the duke had found his discourse stimulating, then it was some comfort for a man whose prospects, still, were so comprehensively blighted by General Slade.

Then, in the second week of the month, Hervey received another invitation from Jessope to ride out with the duke. The party, a bigger affair than before, assembled in the courtyard of the Hôtel de Ville in Halle, on the Mons-to-Brussels high road, and it soon became apparent that its purpose was more than morning exercise. Standing beside a large map fixed to the double doors of the empty stables was Sir William de Lancey. 'He acts as the duke's chief of staff until Sir George Murray arrives from Canada,' explained Jessope. 'And those other two officers are the duke's artillery and engineer commanders, Sir George Wood and Sir James Smyth. I think we shall see good sport this morning!'

The duke duly appeared, walked to the map and, taking the pointing-stick which de Lancey proffered, began to address the assembled party. 'Gentlemen, I want today to complete my reconnaissance of defensive positions in the event of Bonaparte's making a direct move against Brussels – a move which I am still far from convinced he will make. Nevertheless I intend being ready for him if he does. If he should strike for Brussels, it will not be to take possession of the lace factories.' There was polite but restrained laughter. 'His purpose will be to divide the Prussians and ourselves. Although it may seem, therefore, that he has the initiative – in that he chooses the time of attack – he does not entirely choose the *place.* He must attack astride the junction of the two armies – and that junction is where the good General Blücher and I make it. And where we make it is as far east as we dare without exposing my right flank and Ostend. So we shall of course make plans to cover the Mons–Brussels road, but that is not his likely axis since the junction will be further east towards Charleroi,' he explained, pointing to the features on the map. '*Now*,' he continued, with a pause for further emphasis, 'we will not hold him forward on the border: there is little chance of our being able to concentrate there in time. But we will *delay* him there – make him pay the price of time – and we will *stop* him along this line *here*, through Braine-l'Alleud, Mont St-Jean and Wavre. And this morning we shall examine a defensive position astride the *chaussée* on this ridge at Mont St-Jean which, if these maps are at all faithful, promises to have capability – as that *other* landscaper might have described it.'

There was more polite laughter. 'Torres Vedras, Duke?' asked his engineer. 'Capability Brown would have approved of our landscaping efforts there!'

'No, Sir James, the effort is too great for so slender an eventuality. But, more to the point, we could never keep the enterprise secret – and in that lay half the strength of Torres Vedras.'

Colonel Smyth seemed disappointed.

'You will not allow me to raze any bridges, Duke, and now you do not want me to throw up any earthworks!'

'The bridges will be more use to us when we move against France than they will be to Bonaparte if he moves against us, and I am afraid that I cannot spare troops for digging!' he replied with an emphatic smile.

Soon afterwards they left the inn yard, preceded by a half-troop of hussars from the King's German Legion, and headed south along the Nivelles road and then east along a poor cart-track towards Mont St-Jean. Jessope and Hervey were soon covered in the grime of the road, and so fell back just far enough to escape the dust cloud.

'I for one should recommend he blow up all the bridges,' called Hervey when they were well out of earshot.

'Should you indeed!' replied Jessope with a smile.

'Yes. The duke's predicament is that he has no absolute

intelligence of where Bonaparte will strike, and so he must watch a considerable front. Before Bonaparte strikes you may be sure that he will have taken all manner of measures to deceive us, but the one thing which will reveal his hand is the location of his engineers and their bridges. It will be very difficult to mask such activity.'

'No doubt the duke has considered it.'

'Of *course*; I was merely expressing my judgement, that is all.'

'Your judgement made a great impression the latter day, you know. I should not wonder but that the duke will write to your colonel on the matter.'

'I wish he would write to General Slade!' replied Hervey with a resigned shrug, and as they trotted on towards Mont St-Jean he recounted to Jessope, for the first time, the events of the previous November.

It was a long day. The duke made the keenest inspection of the ridge running east to west, to the south of the village of Waterloo, astride the Charleroi–Brussels *chaussée*. Although low-lying it suited his purpose well, he told the party. Its reverse slopes would give his infantry protection from artillery fire, his supplies and reserves could move undetected and he could, if all else failed, withdraw into the cover of the Forêt de Soignes behind and continue the fight there. What he especially prized was the fortuitous situation of several clusters of buildings just forward of the ridge (the small château of Hougoumont to the west; in the east the settlements at La Haie and Papelotte; and in the centre La Haye Sainte farm) which, when garrisoned, might serve, in his words, as anchors for the whole line.

Throughout, the duke had not spoken to Hervey, but at the end of the reconnaissance, as they gathered on the crest of the ridge at the point where the *chaussée* bisected it, and just above one of the anchors – La Haye Sainte farm – the duke called him over. 'Now, Mr Hervey, what would you say was the principal weakness in this position?'

Hervey was even more astounded than the first time the duke had asked his opinion, for that time it had begun as mere banter: now the duke seemed wholly in earnest. 'Your Grace,' he began, pausing for no more than the fraction of a moment, 'it is a very advantageous position indeed – as strong as I have seen outside the mountains of Spain. The approaches in the centre and his left are so open that Bonaparte could scarcely attempt them without the most fearful loss. He will in all likelihood, therefore, seek to envelop your left flank – he has cover to move his troops a good way round, and the country beyond Papelotte is so trappy that—'

'*Yes, yes* – so what is the answer?' the duke interrupted impatiently.

But Hervey was not fazed. 'The Prussians must threaten that flank from the outset so that he dare not risk the manoeuvre – and two full brigades of cavalry will be needed on the left of our line as additional insurance.'

Hervey's confidence in his opinion, which brought smiles to the artillery and engineer officers, was at once vindicated: 'Hervey, if you had said anything else, then I should have written you off as a mere hare-chaser after all. Yours is *precisely* my appreciation, too, except that I would go further. If Bonaparte gets this far, and if the Prussians are still with us as you say, he will have surmised that our left – the east flank – is too risky an essay. Our *right* will be then his best course. But, look, I wager that he will be tempted by desperation to force his way straight through the centre – the high road to Brussels. I am not intimidated by all this talk of manoeuvre. He has never yet had to face a stubborn sepoy general – of whom he appears to think not a great deal – and I perceive that he might receive a very great shock in that respect here.'

No-one spoke. Not a word.

'Well, come then, gentlemen, we must survey our delaying position next. The crossroads at Quatre-Bras, I think – three leagues south. It should not take long!'

Hervey returned to the regiment's billets so late on 15 June, after yet another solitary excursion, that Captain Lankester and the other officers from First Squadron had left for the grand ball in Brussels without him. He toyed with the idea of riding there alone but gave it up: by the time he arrived the best part of the dance would be over, supper especially. It was not as if there had been a personal invitation: he would be one of the party comprising

The Officer Commanding
His Majesty's 6th Lt. Dragoons,
and Three Officers

as the card specified, whereas Lankester and most of the others had had their own cards. Edmonds had politely refused the invitation. 'Poor old Richmond!' he had said on receiving it. 'Comes out to Brussels hoping to get a corps and all he gets instead is the duchess spending his money! I'll not embarrass them: they were not expecting it to be *me* in command when she wrote it. I shall pass it to Lord George.'

Hervey had in any case kept his own company for so long during the preceding weeks that the notion of such a gathering at this time was unappealing. At the beginning of the month he had ridden into Brussels and returned – to the astonishment of his fellows – with a great sheaf of Ferraris et Capitaine maps which had cost him all of twenty pounds (over a month of his pay), and he had ridden out since, each day, not returning until after dark. When pressed by his fellow cornets and lieutenants to answer for what he had been about, he was invariably less than specific: he had been riding the country between Quatre-Bras and Mont St-Jean. Lankester, however, always insisted he recount his day's reconnaissance, and on one occasion, after Hervey had explored as far as the border, they had as a consequence ridden over to Edmonds's headquarters billet to apprise him of the duke's plan for that sector – the only plan, indeed, that they had the least knowledge of. Edmonds had made one remark only: 'Can't think why he doesn't blow the damned bridges!' And Hervey had smiled to himself.

When he returned, during this evening of the 15th, with

more to inform Lankester of than ever before, his troop leader's absence at the ball put him in a quandary. He rode to Edmonds's headquarters to tell him of the sound of intense cannon fire which he had heard from the direction of Charleroi: indeed, on returning to his own billet after the reconnaissance he had been surprised to find that there were no movement orders. Edmonds had asked if he had heard anything in the direction of Mons, but he could only say that he had encountered two of General Dornberg's Hanoverians taking routine dispatches to Brussels and they had reported that all was quiet on that front. The major decided nevertheless to send a report to the brigade commander with his evening returns, and a copy direct to Lord Uxbridge. He then stood Hervey down: 'All my instinct, Matthew, is that we are about to be tested as never before. I intend turning in early, and I implore you to do the same.'

Hervey woke abruptly, just after three o'clock, to the trumpeter's short reveille. It was a less insistent call than 'Alarm', but long experience said that the short reveille portended something. Almost at the same time Lankester and the others returned from Brussels with the news that the French were across the border at Charleroi and engaging the Prussians, the news having been brought to Wellington himself at the Duchess of Richmond's ball. A few minutes later Edmonds arrived in 'A' Troop's billet to find out what Lankester knew.

'I do not understand it,' the major began. 'We have just had orders to concentrate at Ninove – but that is north of here.'

'It makes no sense to me, either,' said Lankester.

'Great heavens, what a beginning,' groaned Edmonds. 'We have been here these two months and we are now caught napping. Lankester, send if you will a galloper – no, you can spare no officers – send an *orderly* to General Grant to verify those instructions for Ninove. He cannot have failed to appreciate, surely, that we are south of there while everyone else is north or west. Meanwhile I shall assemble the squadrons in Grammont.'

Corporal Collins and his coverman took off down the road

towards Grant's headquarters while the remainder of 'A' Troop mustered by the light of their camp-fires. The moon had set at midnight, and it was still pitch-dark. Lankester addressed his troop in the most composed manner imaginable: the French were on the move, he began; the troop would be likewise soon, but they should not expect any more intelligence since the duke himself found it in scarce supply. 'What I *can* promise you, however, with as much certainty as maybe, is that if you do not fill your bellies with something warm within the next half-hour there will be scarce the chance to do so in a week!'

By the time that Edmonds got the troops together from the outlying billets it was after five and there was reasonable light, but Collins had brought back a change of rendezvous and command, the purpose of which was not immediately apparent to the major. '*Vivian*'s brigade? Why the change? But no matter. Mr Barrow!' he called briskly to the adjutant, 'send an orderly to Sir Hussey Vivian's headquarters. The regiment will now march on Enghien – column of troops, if you please.' And, turning back to Lankester, he asked quietly: 'Why do you suppose we are changing brigades?'

'Well, if Hervey's own understanding of the duke's design is correct, I suspect Vivian's is going on to the left flank to keep contact with the Prussians and will need an extra regiment.'

'So you think Hervey's excursions all over Brabant these past few weeks will repay his efforts?' smiled Edmonds.

'He supposed better what would be the French point of attack than did anyone. I should have wagered a hundred guineas Bonaparte would strike towards Ostend!'

'He may do so yet! But I tell you this, Lankester: there is not space between here and Brussels to check them if things continue as they have begun. I cannot for the life of me think why Uxbridge has not formed divisions, even if there were no chance to gather for drill. There are just too many brigades loose, and we have not a clue as to our purpose. Thank heavens at least that we have brigadiers who know what they're about! Can you imagine Slade in such a crisis?'

Lankester could, only too well. But at Enghien, which they

reached soon enough, they were not enlightened much. Indeed, they became *materially* confused, too, since a large part of the army seemed to be trying to push south and east through the town, guns and waggons blocking the roads as completely as ever the enemy could. Vivian's orders, which now arrived by galloper, were to move on to Braine-le-Comte, twelve miles to the south-east astride the Mons–Brussels highway. It would have been an easy enough march under normal conditions, but the road was now jammed with traffic, the heat was intense and they were not able to water in the town. Even Hervey, who had ridden these roads often enough, knew of no easier way to Braine. There seemed no alternative but to push down the road, if such it could be called, taking to the fields when progress was altogether halted. In the event they did well to reach the town at four in the afternoon, but there was still no sign of Vivian.

By now the sound of gunfire was quite distinct, although from which direction it was uncertain. It seemed principally to be from the south-east, but at other times it seemed equally to be almost *due* east, towards Nivelles. Edmonds took a bold decision to alter their line of march, since gunfire due east (as he perceived the duke's design from Hervey's telling) threatened the worst. Scarcely had the Sixth got nosebags on their hot and hungry animals than Edmonds ordered 'Mount' to be sounded.

There was a sudden commotion in 'A' Troop. One of the horses, a fractious gelding that more than one rider had cursed as a rig, lashed out with both hind legs in the tight press and struck a mare in the rank behind. She squealed and threw her rider, who managed nevertheless to keep hold of the reins, and then stood quite still on three legs, the off-fore hanging uselessly like a rag arm. Her dragoon quickly recovered himself, took one look at the leg and saw that the cannon bone was shattered. Immediately, he primed his pistol and put it to her head, but he held it at too inclined an angle and with insufficient grip so that, when he fired, the ball scraped along the horse's skull and off to a flank, striking another dragoon in the thigh. The pistol flew from the dragoon's hand with the excessive recoil, breaking his wrist, and the flash and report sent the mare into a frenzy.

'Jesus Christ!' spat Serjeant Armstrong, springing from his own horse on to the startled mare's neck. 'Where's the farrier, in God's name!'

But the farrier was with the others at the back of the column, and still they could not calm the mare. Only a blanket over her head settled things. Hervey made his way through the press with his carbine as half a dozen dragoons got her down on her side and others made space. Seeing what must be done, he pushed a cartridge into the breech, put the muzzle in the fossa above her left eye and aimed at the base of the opposite ear – just as Daniel Coates had taught him. He pulled the trigger. The mare kicked out, twitched for a few seconds, and then lay still.

Armstrong began cursing all and sundry for their clumsiness before Captain Lankester rode up and took in the scene. 'Very well, then, gentlemen, first blood to the French. Let us see to it that they have no more here.'

'A' Troop resumed the march subdued, sheepish almost. And an even more difficult march it was, since the road was no better now than a cart-track, though it led straight to Nivelles, and then beyond to Quatre-Bras. They could see nothing of the fighting, however, as they approached Quatre-Bras about eight, the sun setting behind them. The village, and the important crossroads from which it derived its name, was screened by dense woodland. But the noise, louder though not as intense as it had been in the afternoon, was unmistakable, and cannon shot flew over from time to time. Edmonds was relieved nevertheless. Hervey's appreciation had been correct, for as they neared the trees he saw at last Major-General Sir Hussey Vivian.

'Well done, Edmonds! I am sorely glad of seeing you,' called his brigadier. 'What a beginning! I am only just arrived myself. Come, we must find what we are to be about up there,' he said, nodding in the direction of the village.

As Vivian and Edmonds entered Quatre-Bras they were

met by one of Uxbridge's gallopers in as great a composure as could be imagined. And his instructions astonished them further, for all that Uxbridge wanted was for them to bivouac in place, with just a field officer's patrol out on the left flank to make contact with the Prussians.

'The Sixth to take the patrol, then, please, Edmonds. I have still to collect the Germans from Nivelles somehow,' said Sir Hussey, his hussars of the King's German Legion having had a greater distance to march than even theirs.

Lankester made his rounds before taking the picket out. 'What did I say at muster?' he called here and there with a wry smile. 'You shall not see your baggage this side of Brussels! Plenty of green fodder to cut, though. Put your backs into it, boys!' Choosing a lieutenant for the patrol caused him no great thought: Hervey's German and his familiarity with the country were singular.

Indeed, both skills were to prove inestimable since the moon was low and, though they probed all the way down the road almost as far as Ligny, they could make no contact whatever with the Prussians. Working their way back to Quatre-Bras soon after midnight, the moon having set, was even more perilous than the ride out: Lankester would later reckon it to be among the most hazardous essays of his life, and more than once Hervey's German was the saving of them as nervous Dutch patrols beat about the country. At about three a Prussian hussar came into the outpost (which Lankester had finally settled one league from the crossroads) with intelligence of the Prussians' battle around Ligny. After Hervey had questioned him (the hussar's Brandenburg was the clearest German he had ever heard), he was escorted to Vivian's headquarters in Quatre-Bras.

'Ill news indeed,' said Lankester when he was gone. 'I had not expected to hear of such a reverse. Which way do you suppose the Prussians will retire?'

Hervey peered at his map by the light of the outpost's fire. 'Well, we must hope they *do* fall back on Wavre as they are meant to. Lord Fitzroy's ADC says the duke has consummate trust in Prince Blücher. He says the old marshal would die in the saddle rather than not keep his word to him.'

'And what will the duke do now?'

'Well, I spoke before of the defensive position at Mont St-Jean. Like it or not, with the Prussians unable to hold the French at Ligny I do not see that he has any option but to fall back there – and let us hope that that is where the rest of the army is already making for. He *must* maintain contact with the Prussians, though. If he does not, then I doubt he is strong enough to hold even at Mont St-Jean, and then there'll be the very devil of a fight in the forest behind. What I could not discern from that hussar was whether the Prussians have any fight left in them. If the French gave them such a drubbing that they cannot re-form, then even if they fall back in concert with us it will not be to any purpose. It looks forbiddingly as if Bonaparte may have achieved his first objective.'

'My dear Hervey,' said Lankester, holding out a flask of brandy, 'you have a truly remarkable grasp of campaigning. There is not one officer in a hundred in this army who would have any notion of strategy beyond brigade drill – though in fairness they know that drill well enough. I hope with all sincerity that you will have a brevet out of all this – I for one will recommend it, though you know Edmonds will always anticipate me in that regard. But frankly, in this army, I feel sometimes that you would do better to capture some absurd French eagle!'

Hervey had never received praise from Lankester before. Curiously, it felt better even than the rare praise he had received from Edmonds. The master at Shrewsbury who had taught him his Greek, the gentlest of men whose academic interest in battles would have made him envious now of Hervey's position, could have told him why: a Stoic's praise was worthy, but a Corinthian's was an inspiration.


A little sleep, in the few hours remaining before dawn, was all that Hervey was able to snatch, but it was satisfying enough. The outpost was called in soon afterwards, and they found the rest of the Sixth still in bivouac and making breakfast. That meal consisted of nothing more, however, than tea and biscuit from the troopers' haversacks, there being neither sign nor news of the baggage train. Other than the periodic crack of a Baker rifle from a picket, its sharp report easily distinguishable from that of a musket or a carbine, there was silence from the direction of the previous day's fighting. Rumour spread around the bivouac that the French had been decisively repulsed, that there would be a general advance and that the Sixth would be expected to lead it. Hervey was able to stop these fanciful ideas gaining too much of a hold, but it was a blow to them all none the less when orders came at about nine for a general withdrawal. The one mitigating detail was that their brigade was to cover the left flank. Hervey heard one of the younger troopers ask an older sweat if they would see any action there, and the sweat began to regale him with an account of Sahagun and the retreat across the Esla. Hervey remembered it well: it was more than apt – but God be praised that Slade had not command this time!

'Nothing new under the sun, is there, Mr 'Ervey?' Corporal Collins called as they took ground in front of General Picton's division on the left. Hervey checked himself: Sahagun was one thing – yes, they had faced a superior number of French cavalry there – but this was quite another affair. Upwards of two corps of infantry, by his recall of the commander-in-chief's assessment, with artillery *and* cavalry, were about to fall on them. He knew they had to buy time for the duke's infantry to struggle back to Mont St-Jean, and he reckoned that they themselves would be lucky thereby to make the ridge as a regiment.

It was nothing less than astonishing, therefore, when they found themselves sitting for three hours awaiting the supposed onslaught – three hours in which the duke's infantry and guns were able to march up one of the best roads in Europe to a defensive position which Hervey had thought one of the best he had seen. Was this really Bonaparte in the field? he wondered. Could it be a feint after all?

Captain Lankester rode along the front of the first

squadron, Edmonds having ordered squadron-grouping for the withdrawal (a move that placed Hervey in field-command of 'A' Troop). Lankester exchanged the odd word with his troopers in a manner so matter-of-fact that Hervey could not but admire the accomplishment, as if the owner of some well-run estate were hailing his contented tenants on his morning ride: 'I'm sorry, First Squadron – no breakfast, no rum, no Frenchmen, but I think we'll have all of them aplenty and in good time, if not in that order!' he called, to much laughter and cheering. 'It could be worse, though!'

'How's that, sir?' came a voice from the ranks.

'Well,' replied Lankester, wishing now that he had not said it, and trying to think of something, 'it could be *raining*!'

Half an hour later it was. An apocalyptic clap of thunder, at almost the same instant that the French guns opened up, precipitated a torrential downpour which continued throughout their withdrawal to Mont St-Jean. But, rain or no rain, the withdrawal proceeded as a model exercise, conducted as if on a field day. The squadrons fronted repeatedly, the horse-artillery troop unlimbering and engaging each time in support. Then it would be 'Guns, Cease firing; Out of action!' and 'Light Dragoons, Threes Right, at the trot, March!' It was repeated once, twice, so *many* times that no-one would remember precisely. Only once did they nearly come to grief, in Genappe when Third Squadron took a wrong turning, their captain unable to read his sodden map in the sheeting rain. Hervey, realizing the error, had galloped after them and brought them back on to the right road just in time for the horse artillery to deal with a squadron of *lanciers* pressing them hard. Even Barrow had been moved to remark on the address he had shown: 'It is my opinion, sir,' he exclaimed to Edmonds, shaking his head in disbelief as Third Squadron galloped back on to the *chaussée*, 'that the Service can ill afford to lose such a man for want of promotion.' It was the last place from which Hervey would have expected praise.

*     *     *

Thunder, lightning, rain in torrents and mud up to the fetlocks the instant a horse left the *pavée*: the conditions were a trial worthy of the most exacting reviewing-officer. But the enemy seemed unable to press to a decisive advantage. Three hours' delay before resuming their advance! It was all Hervey could think of – *three hours*! What a difference that unaccountable failure was now making. It had been the duke's deliverance no less! And dusk – earlier than the day before with so heavily overcast a sky – now began to envelop them in a blanket of safety as they reached Mont St-Jean, the lanterns of dozens of staff officers rallying the regiments to their collecting areas and thence to bivouacs near their battle positions. None of those officers could have expected the rearguard in such good order: soaked, exhausted, hungry – men *and* horses – but in formed bodies under perfect discipline. *Three hours!* What a price Bonaparte had paid already for that inexplicable stay. Had he not, himself, told his generals to ask of him anything but time? There was now a chance – *just* a chance!

# CHAPTER FOURTEEN
# A HARD POUNDING

---

*Mont St-Jean, Waterloo, 18 June*

Before dawn broke, the bedraggled troopers of the 6th Light Dragoons were roused from their sodden sleep by the hands of the inlying picket. The flattened corn, which had at first afforded some comfort to backs aching from long hours in the saddle, had also held the surface water as if in a honeycomb, so that saddle aches had given way to cold cramps. Everywhere men scratched at beards three days old, and felt the griping of empty stomachs. There was a rank smell about the place, worse than was usual even for such a rough bivouac. So dark and hurried had been their camp that latrine discipline was all but ignored. There was no breeze, and few fires had survived the torrents of rain to take away the fetid air. The Sixth had never liked to bivouac with others, whose legionary habits they deplored, and as the troopers moved silently to the horse lines they were further dismayed by a trumpeter some way along the ridge blowing reveille, soon to be echoed by others of neighbouring regiments in a cacophony of different pitches, and they cursed them for the racket which put their own stealth to nought. A drummer in an infantry battalion began beating emphatically. The rain had drummed all night; at least it had now abated to little more than a drizzle.

A hand shook Hervey's shoulder, but only a touch was needed to wake him. Except for the few hours he had snatched the night before, it had been over a year since he had slept on the battlefield, but the instincts of the previous five remained. In any case the rain had allowed no more than a fitful sleep. It had been near midnight when he had at last lain down (he had peered at Jessope's watch by the light of a provost marshal's lantern), and, looking now at the sky, with the first intimations of daylight over where he supposed, and prayed, the Prussians must be, he estimated it to be about four o'clock. The hand had moved on, but Johnson was there in its place with a canteen of tea. He wondered how he had been able to find a fire on which to brew it on such a night, and reckoned that not one officer in a dozen would be woken in this way. Yet in Spain no-one had wanted this little Yorkshireman. The canvas of Hervey's valise had kept out much of the night's downpour, but the thunderstorm which had accompanied the withdrawal from Quatre-Bras had been too much, and he had crawled into it already soaked to the skin. Now he shivered as he took the tea.

'Couldn't get no brandy or nothin',' Johnson said. 'A German 'ad some snaps but 'e wanted gold for it – gold!'

'We cannot go another day on liquor and tea, Johnson,' groaned Hervey. 'Where are the quartermasters?'

'Still progging, I expect, sir. I've been up 'alf t'night w't 'orses an' there's no sign of nobody.'

'Why is it so infernally difficult to bring food up to the army astride a high road?' he sighed despairingly. 'So there is nothing for the horses, either?'

'No.'

'Surrounded by corn, and no hard feed! Do you suppose there is *anything* to be had, Johnson?'

'Oh ay, sir,' chirped his groom. 'Artillery waggons 'ave been comin' in all night. There's plenty o' shot an' shell, by all accounts.'

Thank heaven for that at least, thought Hervey, though he could not fathom why it always seemed to be a question of alternatives – powder or shot, rations or fodder. They had snatched a hurried breakfast on the sixteenth, at Lankester's insistence, and there had been nothing since, only biscuit, geneva and tea – and green fodder. Now he was grumbling, and that vexed him even more. Could he not put up with an empty stomach for a day or two? There would be plenty enough to fill it after they had swept the French from the field. 'Damn it, Johnson, here's a guinea: go and buy anything we can get our teeth into!' he sighed.

The dawn's drill was routine, however, to be done on the emptiest of stomachs. The regiment stood-to just before five; and twenty minutes later, when the sky had lightened enough for Edmonds to be sure that there would be no attack at first light, they had stood down. As the order to dismiss was passed along, Serjeant Strange, who had again stepped effortlessly into the boots of the troop serjeant-major, came up to give the muster report: rank and file seventy-four, present-sick three, absent-sick three, missing two, horses sixty-eight.

'And the armourers, Serjeant Strange?'

'Corporal Ford is ready to begin now, sir. I shall get them to sharpen by half-sections.'

'And I suppose there is no sign of rations and forage?'

'Some barley has come up, but little else. Serjeant Armstrong has been foraging all night but he's not found much. He says the place is fair crawling with troops, never seen so many. We shall not be able to cut any of the corn, either, since it's all been flattened.'

There was nothing gloomy in Strange's delivery, simply matter-of-fact. Both of them had seen it often enough before, in the Peninsula, but half the troopers were new drafts who had seen nothing more arduous than a field day outside Cork or a review in Phoenix Park.

'They did well yesterday, though, think you not, Serjeant Strange?'

'The greenheads? Ay, they did well enough. But I can't say as we were pressed that hard, sir.'

'True enough,' agreed Hervey, and then he smiled. 'But the troop has stolen another march in getting the armourers. Heaven only knows how many times we hacked with blunt blades in Spain: we want none of it today.' He thought of Salamanca, and the repeated cutting to rescue d'Arcey Jessope.

'How many do you suppose the duke has here, sir?'

'How many what?' he replied, conscious that his thoughts had been elsewhere.

'How many troops do you believe the duke can dispose on this position?'

'How many can you see, Serjeant Strange?'

'Well, I have not seen this many tight-packed since . . .' He looked thoughtful.

'Exactly so! I would hazard you have *never* seen the like, even with *your* service! Well, I may tell you something: the duke can dispose of eighty thousand or nearabouts!'

Strange whistled, an uncharacteristic display.

'*But*', continued Hervey, 'he is so suspicious of Bonaparte's intentions that he planned to station one-quarter of these at Hal and Tubize lest the French march on our flank for the Channel ports. And I believe he will have done so even now.'

'Still, a goodly number – more than ever he has had before for a single battle, I should surmise.'

'*But* less than half are our own, and most of those are largely untried.'

'Mr Hervey,' began Serjeant Strange warily, 'you are not saying that you doubt the outcome today?'

'Not for one moment,' he replied without hesitating, 'but Bonaparte can dispose of so many – a hundred thousand, they say – that it would be rash to suppose we might spend a second night here. He will for sure have a superiority in guns, and he has the initiative so will be able to concentrate them. The duke's artillery amounts to a hundred and fifty pieces – no more – and he must dispose of them along a wide front.'

'But what a front, sir!'

'Indeed so, Serjeant Strange, and you will not have seen the half of it. It is a very handsome position to defend. There is a château at yonder end of this ridge which is a veritable fortress – or will be once the Guards have done with it.'

'And you have learned all this in riding with the duke, Mr Hervey?'

'Ay, we rode every inch of the ground. But I tell you, Serjeant Strange, the duke will come to rue leaving that corps at Hal, for with the forest behind he has little space to manoeuvre and he has a great want of reserves. Without the Prussians he runs a very close race indeed!'

Shots now rang out raggedly the length of the ridge as the infantry proved their cartridges and firing-locks, and the sentries, whose muskets had been primed for their night watches, discharged them rather than risk drawing the charges. Soon the cavalry would be doing the same with their carbines, and Hervey winced. Every time he had heard it in the Peninsula he had winced. 'How we do flagrantly tell the enemy of our position and strength, Serjeant Strange! Do we not break the most fundamental principle of war? And all because of a worry over damp powder. It is so needless, too, for with percussion-locks there would be no fear for it.'

'Well, that is true, sir: I reckon your carbine must be the only one of its like in the field today. Had I the opportunity I should have bought one for myself, whatever the price, for it might be the difference between the quick and the dead on a day such as this.'

'Exactly so,' said Hervey. 'The Rifles at least might have had them if His Majesty's Government and the Ordnance had shown a little more address.'

'Indeed they might: there is nothing those riflemen would like more than to load on their bellies!'

Hervey smiled with him. 'It is a mercy at least that Bonaparte never laid eyes on the patent, for he would have had it in the hands of every *tirailleur* by now.'

Camp-fires were burning soon after stand-down, primed by the same powder for which there was such a fear. In the quantities the troopers of the Sixth had used to light theirs the combustion was not an altogether reliable indicator of the absence of damp, but the flames augured well. The horses were unsaddled and given their few pounds of uncrushed barley. Slade would never have permitted that, thought Hervey, but Edmonds knew he could have them saddled up sharply enough in the event of an alarm, and Sir Hussey Vivian had yet to issue even a preparatory movement order.

'There's a stream just behind the ridge, Mr 'Ervey sir,' said

Johnson as he handed him another canteen of tea. 'It's a bit brackish but right enough.'

The downpour had not been without its advantages, then, for a want of water near the position would have delayed them sorely. 'Well,' replied Hervey, 'since that half-loaf of bread you bought will not detain us long, I shall shave. It can be a passable substitute for a good night's sleep.'

'I'll fetch thee some hot water, then. There's some on the boil for Serjeant Armstrong's potatoes.'

'Potatoes?' said Hervey with some surprise. 'How can it be that you found the most expensive loaf in Flanders and Armstrong finds potatoes? Where in heaven's name did he—?'

'There was a commissary officer pissing by the side of the road and . . .'

'Enough, Johnson; I can guess the rest,' he sighed. 'Fetch my razor, if you please.'

By the time the armourers had re-sharpened 'A' Troop's sabres it was almost seven, and Edmonds came walking through the lines with the RSM just as Hervey's men began their meagre breakfast of tea and parboiled potatoes. The older ones gave him a cheer and hailed him with easy banter. 'Thought T'loos was meant to finish 'im, then, Major!' called one old sweat.

'Well, if you remember, Harris, *we* were never permitted a crack at him that day!' Laughter and more cheering followed – and just a shade forced, Hervey thought.

'Not much of a choky, then, Elba, eh, sir?' called another sweat, an old Indiaman.

'And you of all people would know about chokies, Finch!' *Raucous* laughter and cheering erupted. Nerves were on edge, Hervey concluded.

'Could be worse, sir: it were snowin' at Sa'gun.'

'That it was, Smiler, and it seems an age ago. D'ye think we shall ever get a Christmas at home?'

'In my case, Major Edmonds, it's more a question of whether I'll ever get a 'ome at Christmas!' There were *peals* of laughter, and Hervey smiled at the black humour, the soldier's secret weapon. Edmonds had a way with these men, of that there was no doubt. Different from Lankester's – very different – but equally effective: *more* so, perhaps, for Lankester was held in respect and admiration whereas with Edmonds it was respect and affection. Hervey admired them both, though if pressed he would have owned to aspiring more to Lankester's patrician ease: Edmonds's obvious devotion to his troopers made him somehow more vulnerable. He seemed to know every man by name – nickname in many cases – including recruits who had only just joined. In the weeks before they had received their sailing orders Hervey had thought him worn out, beyond repair, but now his solidity seemed never more welcome, for though there was laughter in the ranks its nervous edge suggested a rawness which needed nursing.

'Well, Mr Hervey,' began the major with a smile, 'it has come to pass, and just as you foretold.'

Hervey had muttered but a few words of reply, and with no little self-consciousness, when a commotion behind made them turn. The sight rendered both speechless for the present. Indeed, it would endure in the mind of every man in the Sixth that day (they were all to witness it), to be recounted in drawing rooms and alehouses alike for years to come. For the commander-in-chief, on his favourite charger, Copenhagen, accompanied by a galaxy of senior officers and their staff – a veritable *troupe dorée* – was making his ceremonial progress through the lines. The duke's gelding, his sleek chestnut coat the picture of condition, was as well known as his rider to the old Peninsular hands. Though his breeding was good (Hervey had heard tell his dam had a line to the Rutland Arabian), he was not the handsomest of horses – certainly not one to have tempted d'Arcey Jessope. But the duke had told his staff many a time that though there were many handsomer and faster, he had never known Copenhagen's like for endurance and bottom. Handsome is as handsome does, smiled Hervey to himself.

But the rawest recruit could recognize the duke's own

profile, and it was as well, for he was not in uniform. He wore instead the same blue coat of that first morning's ride when they had chased the hare. His buckskin breeches and tasselled boots were, too, of a pattern that might have been perfectly at home in Piccadilly. His cocked hat was the only appreciably military apparel, set off by four cockades – the Hanoverian black of King George, and three smaller emblems in the colours of Portugal, Spain and the Netherlands, the four armies in which the duke held rank of field marshal. But, all would later recall, with what presence and authority did he make his inspection!

He acknowledged the salutes with an expressionless nod. Long acquaintance with his army had scarcely inspired love – on either side – but the duke had confidence in their steadiness in defence, and they in turn trusted his choice of ground and dispositions. There was no cheering: it did not seem appropriate and it would not have been welcome. Across the valley Bonaparte would soon be making the same procession, and at his approach drums would roll, bands would strike up 'Veillons au salut de l'Empire', his soldiers would cheer him to the heavens – 'Vive l'Empereur!' – and the sound would carry across to the Sixth not half a mile distant. *No*, the duke did not permit cheering, for if he allowed it once it might invite the opposite in other circumstances. As he neared the end of 'A' Troop he paused. 'Good morning, Major. Good morning, Mr Hervey. I trust the Sixth will guard the flank keenly. You shall see action enough even over there. We shall today show Bonaparte how a sepoy general defends a position!'

Edmonds made some appropriate reply, and Hervey swelled with pride at the duke's attention, but the nobility of the major's comportment could not hide the wound, and then Hervey felt meanly for his own pride while this officer of thirty years' loyal service received no more recognition than was indicated by his badges of rank. But the duke was never a one for flattery, and Edmonds might soon take comfort in that knowledge, for the Earl of Uxbridge, as conspicuously military-looking as the duke was otherwise, chose at that moment to test (albeit unwittingly) the fragility of their association. 'You had better apprise me of those sepoy-general plans, Duke,' he said with a smile, 'lest I be required to execute them.'

'Plans!' replied Wellington sharply. 'I have no plans, sir: I shall be guided by circumstances!'

Edmonds raised his eyebrows. And then Harris, Sir Hussey Vivian's brigade major, riding up with orders to proceed to the flank, took the duke's second barrel before he could utter a word: 'Ah! Harris, you may tell Sir Hussey that I will have his hide if the brigade so much as *thinks* of leaving that flank for a minute!'

'Well, Mr Hervey,' said Edmonds at length, when the duke had passed by and Harris had relayed his brigadier's orders, 'the commander-in-chief seems a trifle liverish, but no matter; let us go and mark our ground. We are indeed to be the left-flank brigade, as you supposed, though I confess to being surprised that we are to be the directing regiment.'

That much at least was a compliment to Edmonds, thought Hervey, for it would have been easy enough for Vivian to relegate them to the supports. 'The duke's plan' – he cleared his throat as he realized his difficulty – 'that is to say, the duke's *dispositions*, are as he anticipated them to be during his reconnaissances.'

'Good God, man – not you, too!' Edmonds snarled. 'Don't you damn well turn into another of those arse-licking fops that go by the name of staff officers in this army of ours. Say what you damn well mean! The duke has *plans* – of *course* he has plans, or else he's even more of a— Look, Hervey, he won't confide in Uxbridge because of all the trouble with that strumpet of a sister-in-law. I am impressed – no, I am *greatly* impressed – that you are so much in the mind of the commander-in-chief, but I am truly dismayed that Uxbridge, his own second-in-command, should appear to know so little!'

Hervey thought to make some amending remark, something that might restore the major's bruised pride, but nothing came to mind that might escape another tongue-lashing. 'Indeed, sir,' was all that he judged prudent.

But Edmonds could not leave things unresolved. 'Well,' he barked, 'what do you suppose are these damned "circumstances" the duke refers to?'

Hervey considered it was all-or-nothing time. 'Sir, the duke is relying on a rapid junction with the Prussians: they must come to his support here or he knows he may be too sorely pressed.'

'Yes, yes, go *on!*' demanded Edmonds.

'Sir, the duke has disposed his line along this ridge with three strong positions forward as . . . *anchors.* These are the château of Hougoumont on our right' – he pointed to the distant roofs – 'the farm called La Haye Sainte just below us here in the centre, and the farms at Papelotte and La Haie over on the left below where we shall take post.'

'Yes,' replied Edmonds, this time more measured.

'Sir, the French will not make a frontal attack: their strength is in manoeuvre. They would be unwise to manoeuvre against our left, however, since that is the direction from which the Prussians must come. They must therefore be expected to mount an attack which might envelop our right. Hougoumont will thus be of prime importance.'

Edmonds paused for a moment. 'Admirable, Hervey, quite admirable,' he said, almost inaudibly.

'Thank you, sir.'

And then, with a sigh, he turned to him again. 'I am put in mind of the late Lord Chesterfield's dictum.'

Hervey was unaware of it.

'There is a silly, sanguine notion, his lordship said once in the house of peers, that one Englishman can beat three Frenchmen, and this encourages, and has sometimes enabled, one Englishman, in reality, to beat two.'

Hervey smiled broadly. 'Those may indeed be the odds here, sir – two to one. All should be well, then!'

Edmonds smiled, too. 'Come, let us repair to the flank. We may have nothing to do there but at least we know what we are *meant* to be about!'

Hervey saluted and returned to his troop: Cornet Seton

Canning, his only officer, and Serjeant Strange would be expecting orders.

Canning looked more boyish than ever that morning but, other than listening to his troop leader with intense concentration, he showed no signs of anxiety. The *first* courage was always the greatest, Hervey recalled, yet he rued that the duke would have to depend on so much of it in this battle. If only the American war had not taken the first battalions, the Peninsular veterans . . . But Canning had been steady enough the previous day, as had the others new to battle, and Hervey had made up his mind that, boy or not, he could trust him. By heavens, he himself had been only a year older at Corunna! Next he sought out Armstrong. A few words of appreciation for his night's foraging seemed in order. He found him sitting on an up-turned camp-kettle, the reverse of his sabretache serving as a writing-slope, and scribbling hurriedly. Hervey could not recall seeing him with a pencil in his hand before, and it brought to mind the teacup in the garden at Horningsham. A smile came at the thought. 'Serjeant Armstrong, is it not a little early to be writing a memoir?' he called.

Armstrong acknowledged the jest but with some reserve. 'Nobody would be wanting a mere serjeant's account when all you officers is so eloquent with the pen.'

Hervey frowned.

'No, sir, it's me last will and testament. Never 'ave 'ad cause for one before now, and I've always thought it tempting fate for a soldier to write one.'

'Heavens, man, you're indestructible! You'll be seeking absolution next!' said Hervey with genuine surprise.

'Ay, that an' all, Mr 'Ervey! If I could find a priest, I might very well do so.'

'Serjeant Armstrong,' he replied resolutely, 'if you could find one priest who would not envy your dutiful record, I should at once become a papist myself!'

'Well, tell that to my Caithlin if I stop a musket ball with my vitals today. And be so good as to witness this will meanwhile.'

Hervey smiled again as he put his signature to the document. 'You know, of course, that I cannot be a beneficiary and a witness, too?'

'Well, I cannot very well leave my *wife* to you, can I? Though she is my only possession of any worth. But I know you wouldn't see her fall on the parish.' Armstrong fixed him with an unyielding look.

'You may depend on it,' he replied, and there was a second or so of intimate silence before Edmonds's trumpeter sounded 'Stand to your horses'. 'Very well, then, Serjeant Armstrong, to your post – right marker, right-hand troop, brigade right-regiment!'

'Thank the Lord we are not with General Grant on the right of the Line, eh, sir?'

Hervey looked puzzled. 'Why?'

'Because if the duke ordered the Line to right-wheel I should be marking time for three whole hours!'

They both laughed. 'That was a real *Joe Miller*, Serjeant Armstrong! But you took me by surprise nevertheless! Away with you – and good luck!'

Private Johnson answered the trumpet with Jessye. She looked uncommonly good, with not a scratch from the day before. Johnson had even made quarter-marks. But still Hervey had second thoughts: 'No, Nero, I think, please.'

For once his groom did not argue. 'Take 'er for the minute, then, sir, an' I'll bring 'im up.'

The Sixth mustered quickly and without ceremony. Edmonds's brisk commands moved them to the left at the halt in column of squadrons. There was a minute or so's wait to allow several ammunition waggons to clear their line, and then it was 'Walk-march', by the trumpet, along the unpaved Chemin d'Ohain towards their vigil on the flank. The Scots Greys, with the rest of the Union Brigade, trotted by in the other direction, towards the crossroads at the centre of the line. They were a rare sight. They had scraped off most of the mud which had covered them from head to foot the day before, but the rain had caused the dye of their red jackets to run over their white belts, as if the sanguinary work they were about to begin was already completed. 'Guidbye, Lights; ye'll be unco' palled over there!' they called. The Sixth's troopers were happy enough to return the banter and trade good-humoured insults, but they had more than a suspicion that the Greys might be right, that they would indeed see nothing of the fighting which these Scotsmen craved so much. But Hervey was first astonished at the impertinence, for here was his regiment, with all but eight successive years' campaigning, and yesterday was the first action the Greys had seen in a quarter of a century! Their spirit could not but be admired, however – the 'first courage' again. They meant to make up for those years, and knew they would have every opportunity of doing so. And he knew, too, that afterwards they would never let anyone forget it!

'Why are they so particular about ridin' greys anyway, sir?' asked Johnson after a mutually incomprehensible exchange with one of their troopers.

'Well,' said Hervey, 'it is their name surely.'

'I mean why did they 'ave to 'ave greys in the first place?'

'I beg your pardon, Johnson. I mistook your meaning. It had nothing to do with their horses: their uniform was grey cloth when first they were raised.'

'I wouldn't want one of them 'ats, that's for sure,' Johnson scoffed, certain that the bearskin must topple over in the charge.

'No, nor I. They are uncommonly attached to them, though. I think they captured many from the French grenadiers in the Duke of Marlborough's wars. What is most vexing, though, is that they must now dock their tails. I envied the Heavies the days when they had long tails. I think it the most abominable thing still that we must do it. I thank heaven that chargers are exempt: I could not bear to see Jessye plagued by flies as I have seen others.'

'Well, if dealers would stop docking 'em before they was remount age we wouldn't 'ave to buy 'em. It's because all them fashionables wants 'em that way.'

'Yes, you're right of course, Johnson; I don't think many believe any longer that docking strengthens the back.'

The Chemin d'Ohain took them past an extraordinary patchwork of uniforms. The red of the British infantry, the backbone of Wellington's campaigns, predominated; but there were lines of blue coats, too, of the Dutch-Belgian corps, with the distinctive orange facings of their militia battalions. And then the more familiar green of the King's German Legion – exiles whose hatred of Bonaparte would mean no quarter to any Frenchman hapless enough to fall prey to their bayonets. Of the Dutch, Hervey was not so sure. During his reconnaissance the duke had confided his concern at having so much of his army made up of untried allied contingents, and for that matter untried British battalions. But his own infantry were well drilled, at least, whereas the Dutch-Belgics had until recently been drilled in French methods. There had been many sneering asides – Hervey himself had made some – but word now was that they had given a good account of themselves yesterday at Quatre-Bras. Perhaps, then, the concern would prove unfounded? Hervey prayed that it would be so, for if they were to face Bonaparte in the strength that the Prussians had felt yesterday . . .

And then for once, just for an instant, as he watched a company of Rifles doubling along the road, he wished that he might be elsewhere than with the Sixth. 'D'ye see those riflemen, Johnson? I'd give a deal to be with them today, for they will be in the thick of things, come what may!'

'Can't say as I would,' Johnson replied with a shrug. 'They're as big a bunch of roughnecks as you'd find!'

'That is as may be, but you should have seen them six years ago on the retreat to Corunna. I tell you, had it not been for their discipline and marksmanship in that march over the Galician mountains . . . Well, let us just say that more than one corps owes its survival to those men.'

'What are they meant to be about today, then, sir?'

'They will take up positions, out in front of the brigades, to counter the French *tirailleurs* and then to harry the columns of infantry. I tell you, they may rely on being in the thick of the action, come whatever. And did you hear what those infernal Greys were saying – that we were riding to the flank like ladies withdrawing after dinner!'

But then a voice called him back from his thoughts – 'Hervey! Hervey!'

The sight of Lieutenant Hugo Styles, with a detail of the 2nd Life Guards, was almost too much, and he would have turned Nero away but that Styles suddenly spurred towards him like a man demented, grabbing his arm after almost colliding with him. 'Hervey, my *dear*, *dear* fellow, is this to be a real battle?'

Hervey's jaw fell. 'I think that is the general idea,' he replied in his astonishment. He had not meant to sound scornful, but Styles in any event seemed in no condition to detect scorn, intended or not.

'Hervey, I am given command of a troop; I cannot do it!'

Hervey's first instinct was to express himself not in the least surprised that Styles did not count himself able – that he was a pompous, self-important ass, that he was about to get his come-uppance and that it was no good whining now, having looked down his nose for so long. But, for all his desire finally to cut him down to size, Hervey hesitated (for what of the wretched troopers of the Life Guards, who were equally new to the battlefield and in need of steadying?). Instead he de-loped: 'Of *course* you can do it, Styles. You are an experienced officer, and your men will follow you,' he said staunchly, hoping he might sound convincing.

'But that is it, you see,' Styles returned quickly. 'I cannot recollect myself; I do not know what I am about!'

Hervey suppressed another urge to speak sharply, to demand that Styles stop snivelling and take a hold of himself. Instead he continued with his quiet reassurance. 'Styles my dear fellow, that is how we all feel,' he lied. 'You will do your duty well enough; you *will* be capable, I tell you.'

'Is that really so, Hervey? You, too, have doubts? Thank you, *thank you*.' His eyes were now wild with alarm. 'Let us dine together at Westbury when this is over. I shall tell Henrietta Lindsay of your composure!'

'Yes, indeed, we shall dine together.' Hervey knew it to be unlikely, and he cursed him in his heart for bringing Henrietta to mind. Styles would forget this exchange soon enough, he warranted. He was glad of the excuse to rejoin his troop when the squadron trumpeter sounded the trot.

The repeating 'C's of that call never failed to thrill. They spelled action. They signalled an urgency to close with the enemy, or to put some distance between them. And the snorting of the troop horses, who knew the call as well as their riders, and the jingling of bits added to the exhilaration. But this morning Hervey found no thrill. The flank was, by the rubrics of the drill-book, the appointed place for light cavalry, and he himself had recognized the wisdom of doubling to two brigades on this occasion, but he knew nevertheless that they were leaving the seat of action far behind, for Bonaparte would not attempt anything on *their* flank with the Prussians so close. Even the duke's dispositions seemed to confirm it, for as they trotted along the road atop the ridge, bordered in places by thick, high hedges, or sunken by as much as a man's height, he saw less and less of the familiar and reassuring red and more of the blue coats and orange facings of the allies: Wellington would not have so disposed his weakest forces had he expected them to face any determined action. Hervey's heart sank further, yet he saw that the Dutch-Belgics were setting about the position with a will, cutting gaps in the hedges so that cavalry could pass through, digging out embrasures for the guns and making loopholes for the riflemen. They even cheered heartily as the Sixth rode by.

After three-quarters of a mile they reached their appointed place, opposite the hamlets of Papelotte and La Haye a few hundred yards across the valley to their right, and they executed a smart evolution from column into line, coming to a halt on the forward slope with the warm sun on their faces, Hervey's troop in the second line forming the support to 'B'. Lankester at once called him forward. 'How do you suppose this conforms with the duke's intentions?' he asked.

The senior captain – and also, thereby, Edmonds's second-in-command – was remarkably free from pride to enquire thus of his junior, thought Hervey. 'I think it very exactly as the duke intended, sir,' he replied. 'See, in that scattering of farms below us – mark the roofs yonder – he intends disposing his Nassauers. They may be there this minute. And if you stand in the stirrups you can just see La Haye Sainte below the cross-roads close where we bivouacked last night. That, he has garrisoned with some of the German Legion and the Rifles. We cannot see the château at Hougoumont, for it is perhaps a mile beyond the farm at La Haye Sainte. Here, see, I have a sketch of the position. The duke said that he intended to place four companies at least of the Guards there. And he will need to, for it will by now be nearer the French lines than our own.'

Lankester studied the sketch-map intently. 'And there is nothing to our east but the Forest of Ohain?'

'No,' replied Hervey warily. 'A couple of leagues or so beyond the forest will be the Prussians – on this side of the Dyle river, we must hope, for I believe the duke will want for a junction with them ere too long.'

It was still not eight o'clock, but everywhere steam was beginning to rise – from the ground, the horses, the saddlery; from the men themselves, and from the roofs of the dwellings in the hamlets hastily abandoned by their occupants and now garrisoned by the Duke of Saxe-Weimar's Nassauers. Only a year or so ago these men had fought for Bonaparte, but Wellington must surely be confident of their steadfastness to trust them to such a position – even on this flank?

'Would that *I* were able to find such faith,' replied Lankester sceptically, and Hervey nodded as, with growing despair, he surveyed the sodden ground, a gun team nearby struggling fetlock-deep in mud to drag a nine-pounder along a rutted farmtrack.

Major-General Sir Hussey Vivian rode along the front of his brigade, calm, assured and exquisite in the hussar field dress of his old regiment, accompanied by his black trumpeter.

That he ought, by regulation, to have been wearing general officer's uniform mattered not to Vivian, who cared only, and jealously, for his hussar brigade. Even Lord Fitzroy Somerset, on the duke's behalf, had chided him, as he had the other cavalry brigadiers, though to no avail, especially since Uxbridge himself insisted on wearing the dolman. But if Vivian was at all dismayed by the appending of the 6th Light Dragoons to the hussar brigade he had never once shown it: he had even placed them on the right of his line.

'Good morning, General,' said Lankester as the brigadier reached First Squadron, he and Hervey saluting together. 'I think it may be another Toulouse for us, by all accounts.'

'Ha!' laughed Vivian, 'you will recall that I was in a field hospital with a damned ball in my shoulder – along with Lord George. But I doubt you will be inactive here today. Bonaparte is in the field and he is sure to manoeuvre against us. In any event, I do not think that we shall long remain in this position: the Prussians are marching to us, and I fully expect them on this flank by noon. I do not suppose Lord Uxbridge will keep us idle thereafter.'

'Let us hope not, General,' Lankester replied, 'but I am surprised the French have made no move yet. Not even their artillery has begun harassing fire.'

'Sir George Wood believes it is too wet – their guns would have no ricochet fire, and since Wellington has placed most of his infantry on the reverse of the crest their shot would have limited effect. He believes, too, that they have few howitzers: we should not forget that Bonaparte is first an artilleryman, and will not join battle until he is sure of his guns! He must be deuced confident, though, to be awaiting the ground to dry out, what with the Prussians about to fall on his flank at any moment.'

'We are sure of the Prussians, then, General?'

'We had better be! I dined with Müffling some days ago, and he swore that Blücher had given his word. That ought to be enough!'

'Well, I for one would be content with a Prussian's word.'

'Exactly so, Sir Edward. But to more pressing matters.

Uxbridge has recalled Mercer's troop to the centre – temporarily, I would hope. There is a Dutch foot-battery making its way hither in its stead – though with little enough haste, I'll warrant. I do not suppose, however, that artillery will be a requisite for some while at least. But good luck to you, gentlemen; I must now have words with Sir John Vandeleur.'

Vivian gave them a cheery wave in response to their salutes as he spurred into a canter towards the adjacent brigade.

'Well,' sighed Lankester, 'what think you of taking away Mercer's guns?'

'The duke will have an inferiority of them, it is sure, and will make up for it by wheeling them about. Sir George Wood says our horse batteries are the envy of all, the French included.'

'That is as may be, Hervey, but what use is a foot-battery to us? It cannot support any manoeuvre. Perhaps that is why it is sent to us, to anchor us to the spot!'

'Then, it would have been more expedient to remove our horses!' smiled Hervey. 'But what chance do you give our manoeuvring in this soft going even had we Mercer's troop still?'

'Nothing faster than a trot without risk of losing formation. But at least the French will find the going as heavy. Look, Hervey, if we *do* go forward, then you *must* keep up close and check the pace: you will not be worth the name of supports otherwise. We have drilled often enough. I am confident of "B" Troop's handiness in the rally, but holding "A" Troop as supports at the right distance is of the essence. *Heavens*, but these are difficult evolutions to accomplish at the best of times!'

'Indeed, sir,' replied Hervey, 'and I have seen so many regiments' drill in the weeks since we arrived that I have my doubts that all will be capable in this regard.'

'Hervey, I have not the slightest doubt that some are wholly *in*capable. I saw the Union Brigade at drill less than a fort-night ago: a real Dutch ball it was! The Scotch Greys are as handy as a Thames barge without a rudder! And if any run on today they will pay dearly – as, indeed, may the poor souls who will have to recover them.'

A rattle of distant musketry, towards the centre of the line, or perhaps beyond, and the first that morning, stayed further reflection on the state of the cavalry's drill. Hervey looked at his watch. 'A little after eleven,' he said.

'Curious that musketry should open a battle such as this,' replied Lankester.

'I think it must be skirmishing around the château,' suggested Hervey.

'Then it seems he is to force that flank after all,' conceded the captain, turning his charger round and making back for his place in front of the squadron.

But the sound of skirmishing did not distract them long, for across the valley there came the first sign of activity in three hours. A troop of horse artillery trotted on to the opposing ridge, and fluttering lance pennants just visible two hundred yards or so to their rear indicated sizeable supports – unlike that memorable day at Toulouse which had given Hervey opportunity and tribulation in equal measure. He took out his telescope and studied the troop as it began to unlimber, the gunners, dressed in hussar fashion, manhandling four burnished-brass cannon into line, with the sun, now high over the French lines, glinting on the barrels. '"And the Lord said unto Joshua, Stretch out the spear that is in thy hand toward Ai."'

'Beg your pardon, sir?' said Hervey's trumpeter.

'Book of Joshua,' he replied absently. 'Joshua waved his spear, and it glinted in the sunlight, the signal to spring the ambush on the Canaanites.'

The trumpeter nodded.

'Joshua was my first hero,' Hervey continued, still peering through the telescope. 'I remember, as if yesterday, the first time I heard my father read that lesson. It is strange, is it not, to think of those fearsome acts of war recounted in so tranquil a place as a church?'

'Strange indeed, sir. A very contrary thing can the Bible be,' agreed the trumpeter readily.

Hervey lowered his telescope with a sudden thought: it was the Sabbath – his father would be in his pulpit this very minute, and Henrietta, perhaps, in his congregation . . .

But before he could indulge his thoughts of Horningsham too deeply his trumpeter cried out excitedly: 'Look, sir, a galloper!'

Lieutenant the Honourable Charles Dawson, the distinctive blue busby-bag of the 18th Hussars flying horizontal as he sped along their front, called to him as he passed: 'Sport, Hervey! I'm off to bring Mercer!'

'Yes,' he sighed, '*well* may he gallop after Mercer, with *still* no sign of that damned Dutch battery!'

Sir Hussey Vivian, with whose summons for Mercer's guns Dawson now sped, was contemplating the courses now open to him. There was but one of any aptness, however, for launch what he might at the guns they would be overwhelmed by Jacquinot's lancers beyond, their red and white pennants now unmistakable in the clear morning air. And any cavalry would first suffer sorely from the battery's fire as they advanced in such heavy going. No, he would have to wait for Mercer – or the Dutch, wherever they were. And he was certainly not prepared to retire behind the ridge so soon, for it would sorely try the Nassauers in the hamlets below, steady as their reputation might be, if they perceived the line to be withdrawing. But, curiously, no fire came from the troop. They merely stood, like the rest of the French line, in eerie silence.

Hervey turned to look at his own command. He saw the apprehensiveness of the new troopers, and the impassiveness of the older ones, who were mostly chewing tobacco. At the end of the first rank, the flanker, Armstrong, sat with the faintest trace of a smile on his lined face, like some seasoned foxhound waiting patiently at the covertside, assured of the good sport to come. Not Serjeant Strange, though – not that Hervey was able to see him behind the rear rank. *His* face would reveal nothing whatever. He then looked over to the other squadrons, noting with pleasure the congruity of the horses within troops, which long custom – and attention since their return from Spain – had ensured. There was his own troop, consisting entirely of dark bays. There was 'B' with blacks, 'C', like 'A', with bays. 'D' had lighter browns, 'E' (the smallest, but smartest) were all chestnuts, and 'F' were mainly blacks with some dark bays. All were compact, active types, mainly Irish; few were over 15 hands at most. And although the practice had been discontinued by an Army Order of 1799, the Sixth, in common with most other regiments, still mounted all their trumpeters on greys. No, he thought, the regiment did not disgrace Sir Hussey's brigade. And if they had to ride at this battery, well . . .

After what seemed an age, but which the adjutant's journal would record as one quarter-hour only, the sound of Mercer's troop returning broke the silence – the thud of hoofs pounding on soft ground, the clatter of running gear and, above it all, the jingle of harness. The six gun-teams galloped straight through the gap between Vivian's and Vandeleur's brigades on to the forward slope and deployed in two sections, the faster way of coming into action than by the usual three divisions. As they did so a thunderous fire erupted far over to the right.

'I think it has begun in earnest, then,' said Hervey to his trumpeter coolly. 'Eleven-thirty, by my reckoning.'

But before the man could make any reply the French battery opened up, ripple fire so that the gunners could better observe their fall of shot and correct. The rounds went high, but one gun at least needed to make no corrections, its shell slamming into the ground and exploding five yards in front of Edmonds. His horse, a fine black mare bought the previous summer at Banbridge, and Edmonds's pride and joy, was thrown screaming on to her back, legs flaying frantically for several seconds before falling still. The major lay motionless by her side, his body riddled with splinters, his neck broken.

The Sixth let out a groan the like of which Hervey had never heard. One trooper close by threw up noisily; another fell out of the saddle in a dead faint. He himself was frozen with uncommon horror.

'Mr Hervey, take command of the squadron, please,' he

heard Lankester saying as the captain rode forward to assume Edmonds's place. RSM Lincoln and the major's trumpeter, himself bleeding from the lacerations of a dozen splinters, were already dismounting to carry their commanding officer to the rear. Lankester had to think quicker than ever before, as, with dismay, he perceived that his first order in command might be to retire – as shameful to him as it was perilous to the unity of the line. The French gunners, with the range thus established, would now be loading solid shot rather than shell, or even double-loading both. In open order the round-shot would go through each of the four ranks like a hot knife through butter, but they were at least drawn up in line of squadrons (by Vivian's prudence, or the need to show a wide front? – he could not know which). Was there enough time, even, to go threes-about to get behind the crest? But then, if the French corrected high, there might just be . . . Lankester had it! '*Dismount!*' he shouted.

No reviewing officer could have faulted the steadiness with which the Sixth executed that command. It was as if they saw Edmonds himself observing the movement, and they rendered it precisely as required in the 1801 manual, as he would have wanted it. In open order they did not need to make ready. Taking the time from the man in front, each trooper threw a lock of his horse's mane into the left hand, at the same time quitting the right stirrup and placing the forefinger and thumb of the right hand on the pommel of the saddle. Then a pause before the second motion. Bearing on the left stirrup, assisted by the right hand, each man brought the right leg clear over the cantle, many a trooper repeating to himself the orders his rough rider had barked at him so many times in training: 'In this position the body is to be kept perfectly upright, the shoulders well back, the breast out, the belly in, without constraint, the back hollow, the thighs and legs together, and the head turned to the front over the left shoulder!' The third motion brought the right leg to the ground and the left leg from the stirrup. Scarcely had the left foot touched the ground than the four guns fired in unison. Three roundshots whistled just above head-height to go bouncing harmlessly down the reverse slope. The fourth slammed into one of Mercer's guns, now unlimbered and being aligned with the handspikes. It turned the big nine-pounder over as if a toy, crushing the layer beneath the barrel. He screamed so loud that Mercer's own fire order could scarcely be heard.

'*Shell*, one thousand, three degrees!' he called through a speaking trumpet, while the ammunition-numbers ran forward to the stricken gun. The other layers worked as calmly as if at drill on Woolwich marshes, calculating the angle of the forward slope with the plumbline in order to offset the three-degree elevation on the tangent sight. But Hervey heard the range – one thousand yards – with surprise, and hurriedly pulled out his field sketch.

'No, sir!' he called to the astonished artillery captain as he dropped his reins and sprinted towards him. 'I have *paced* it. Eight hundred!'

Mercer turned with a look like thunder, but Hervey's confidence was unshakeable. 'Truly, sir, I have *paced* it: it is no more than eight hundred yards – that slope is deceptive.'

Mercer's profession was not about being deceived by slopes – sixteen years an artillery officer, most of them on active service, and this boy from a cavalry regiment was correcting his fire orders in front of his troop! The layers stared at him, frozen for an instant. Yet something in Hervey's manner was so compelling that, for the first time since leaving Woolwich, Mercer accepted a correction. 'By heavens, boy, you had better be right!' he shouted menacingly. '*Eight hundred*, two degrees, two guns ranging!'

Number 1 Section's lead gun fired, followed by the second section's. Hervey watched with admiration, but anxiously, as the crews worked with mechanical exactness. The ventsmen had their leather-stalled thumbs over the touch-holes in an instant to prevent the ingress of air (blow-back from smouldering powder was ever the risk) while the number sevens swabbed the barrels with sponge-staves. Both shells arched faithfully across the valley to strike their target squarely. The first exploded between two of the guns, felling most of the gun-numbers. The other set light to an ammunition limber, and the secondary explosions at once threw the remainder of the battery into confusion. Mercer confirmed the settings as the number eights were loading the bagged charges and their fixed projectiles. The number sevens turned round their staves and rammed home the charges with the solid end. The ventsmen stuck prickers down the touch-holes and primed them with quills of gunpowder, the lead-gun numbers struggling to re-position and re-lay their pieces after the violent recoil.

'*Fire!*' shouted Mercer. The gunner-layers ignited the primers with portfires, and the four remaining nine-pounders belched their explosive shells at the horse battery. Twenty seconds it had taken, by Hervey's reckoning – faster even than a rifleman might re-load!

They wrought a woeful havoc, too, the French gunners who were not yet casualties of the ranging salvo cut down almost to a man by the splintering metal. Cheering erupted from the ranks of the Sixth, but Mercer's work was not finished. 'Number One, shell, carry on! Remainder, three rounds shot, three degrees, *fire!*' he called, adding the extra degree's elevation for the heavier roundshot. Having killed the gunners, he intended completing the battery's destruction. It was as much vengeance as military necessity: the French might have killed the Sixth's commanding officer, but they had also killed three of Mercer's gunners and destroyed one of his guns.

In two more minutes the gleaming French cannon and limbers were a wreck of shattered wood and twisted metal, the drivers having decided on prudence rather than on bringing their teams forward with shell continuing its ruinous work.

'Stop! Cease loading!' ordered Mercer, and his gunners began making safe again, sponging barrels and returning charges to the limbers, while the captain, grim-faced, turned and rode up to Hervey's squadron.

'Well done, sir. Hervey, is it not?' he asked, raising his hat.

'It is, sir,' said Hervey, returning the salute and wondering how it might be that Captain Cavalié Mercer should know his name.

'If we had fired at one thousand yards, the rounds would have fallen unobserved beyond the ridge. The French had our range and would have fired off three salvos before we could have corrected on to them. I think they would have broken us,' said Mercer gravely, before adding with a sigh: 'That is why Adye's *Pocket Gunner* condemns contra-battery fire.'

'Except where the infantry are suffering more than the enemy's,' Hervey added on an impulse.

'Upon my word! A cavalryman who has read the artillery manual. I thought you read only French novels,' replied Mercer without the trace of a smile, and he reined about and trotted away to lead his troop out of action.

Hervey now looked about for the RSM, praying that there might be news that Edmonds would somehow live, though knowing there could not be. Had he but died *gloriously*, sword in hand, going for the enemy. Not *this* way, unceremoniously, with the opening shot. Even though Hervey had seen men beheaded by shot, or disembowelled by shell splinter, Edmonds's death was still . . . *unseemly*.

Lankester called him over. 'Hervey,' he began, with a shake of the head, 'I have not time to begin to express to you my regard, for there is immediate business to be about. You are not the senior lieutenant, but Strickland is new to us and, besides, I do not wish to take him away from Third Squadron at this time. So you will keep First Squadron for as long as we are in action this day. But remember this: First has always been the directing squadron, and to re-order that now would be imprudent. It will come to action soon enough, and when we go forward keep the pace steady, or else the supports will take off and there'll be the very devil of a mess.'

'Yes, sir,' replied Hervey resolutely.

Lankester smiled. 'You will do your duty well enough, Matthew.'

But it did not come to action as promptly as Lankester had expected. Midday passed with the noise of battle continuing to their right but still nothing of consequence to their front. Hervey sat motionless before his squadron. It was not the first time he had seen clear air between himself and the enemy, but hitherto behind him had been no more than a picket, a half-troop at most. He wished profoundly, however, that the circumstances had been different – that in front of him, two horses' length, and to his left, there might have been Edmonds. He raised a hand to wipe away the moistness in his eyes. 'Mr Canning!' he bellowed.

Cornet Seton Canning closed up from 'A' Troop and saluted. 'Sir?'

'Mr Canning, if we are to advance, you will keep the pace steady and remain within strict support distance, do you understand? There must be no bunching or running on to "B", and in this heavy going it will not be easy. I do not wish to be bumped!'

'I shall do my best, sir; you may depend upon it,' he replied eagerly.

'I know you will,' said Hervey encouragingly; and then, as if they were at some field day, he began examining his cornet's understanding of the battle. 'Canning, why do you suppose that battery came into action against us?'

'To test our strength, sir?'

'Perhaps, yes. But what did it achieve?'

'Nothing, sir, in the larger scheme of things.'

'Are you sure?'

'Well . . . I . . .'

'Let me put it to you that it has told the French two things. First, that they cannot tempt us from this flank too easily; and, second, that the duke will send guns here if we are threatened.'

'I see, sir. But to what use would the French put that intelligence?'

'How do you suppose Bonaparte will fight this battle? He would not risk manoeuvring against this flank with the Prussians close enough to take him in *his* flank as he did so. And he is too much of a general to attempt a frontal assault.'

'So he will manoeuvre against our right?' suggested Canning.

'That is what *I* should do, having first tried to tempt the duke to reinforce elsewhere along his line at the expense of that flank. So do you now think there might have been purpose in that battery's otherwise imponderable action?'

'Yes, sir,' replied Canning, in evident awe of his senior's grasp of strategy. Yet not long after Cornet Canning's admiring response, at about one o'clock, there began a series of events which astonished them both – astonished them all. A cannonade like the crack of doom erupted from the massed batteries in the French centre, so loud that it made the horses start even on this distant flank. Nero all but threw his rider, who had dropped the reins to record some detail in his sketch-book. Though Hervey could not see the guns because of the lie of the land and the smoke now drifting across the valley – nor, indeed, any fall of shot – he concluded somehow that the cannonade was directed on the centre of the line. To what purpose, however, he could not immediately discern. Canning, too, thought they must be directed at the very place they had bivouacked. 'Why do they pound the centre, sir? Do they expect the duke will reinforce it?'

'That could be so, yes, but it is now so late in the day that Bonaparte is chancing much by doing so. It will be telling with what he follows, for it is the very devil of a hard pounding.'

'Will not all the infantry in the centre be carried away by shot?' asked Canning incredulously.

'If they were to stand in its way, yes,' replied Hervey, 'but the duke will have disposed them on the reverse of the slope. They will be sorely plagued there, but by no means as ill as if on the for'ard.'

Canning nodded, feeling foolish for not having come to that conclusion for himself. But the cannonading continued longer than ever Hervey had supposed likely – for a full half-hour or more. And the sound of the guns carried to Brussels, where the doors and windows shook, and to Antwerp. And even across the Channel to Kent where two days later, before news of the battle reached England, the *Kentish Gazette* would report that 'A heavy and incessant firing was heard from this coast on Sunday evening in the direction of Dunkirk'.

'Hervey, how will the French attack?' asked Canning at length.

Hervey at first confessed himself puzzled. 'Yet if they *do* assault the centre they must first break up the duke's line, for the musketry of those battalions would be too great for advancing infantry to withstand. He may suppose, of course, that his artillery has shaken our infantry so badly that they will not stand. Bonaparte has, too, a fairish quantity of heavy cavalry, and if these move against the centre, then the brigades will have to form square, thereby reducing the number of muskets that can be brought to bear. He must support them with horse batteries, of course, or our own cavalry and artillery would frustrate him. But if he followed up at once with infantry in large numbers he might gain the crest.'

'And what should *we* do then?'

'Our orders are to stay in this place,' replied Hervey cautiously. 'And, indeed, if we abandon it, the French might very well take advantage and turn our flank, though I still cannot see how they dare risk doing so with the Prussians so close.'

'Where *are* the Prussians, then, sir?' asked Canning ingenuously.

'We may be sure they are making best speed towards us, Canning. Do not be affeard of that.'

'But, sir, if the French were about to gain the crest in the centreI, what would be the good of our remaining here? Surely—'

'Canning, your shrewdness does you credit, for that is the very question on which the battle might turn. And that is why we have generals.'

'I see, sir,' replied the cornet, reassured, while Hervey merely lapsed into thoughtful silence.

A quarter of an hour passed. Little could they make of what was happening in the centre because of the dense clouds of smoke drifting across the valley. But then, between the thunderous volleys, there came a different sound: cheering, shouting, drums, and soon, quite distinctly, although almost a mile away, cries of 'Vive l'empereur!' And as the cannonading fell away the distinctive beat of the drums could be made out: *rum-dum, rum-dum, rummadum dummadum, dum, dum.*

'What is that, Hervey?' asked Canning with a look of alarm.

'It is called the *pas de charge*,' he replied ominously, peering through his telescope, though still the powder-smoke was too thick to see whence the drumming came. And then the smoke cleared enough for there to be no doubt. 'See there, Canning! *That* is how the French will attack – nay, *do* attack!'

Canning put his own telescope to his eye and gasped. 'But . . .'

'But what?' said Hervey briskly.

'But they come in great columns, like Greek phalanxes. And the cavalry – I can see lancers and cuirassiers – they are on the flanks. You said they must first make our infantry form square!'

'Then, if our centre is intact, they will pay dearly. How fast can our infantry volley?'

'I confess I do not know, sir, for I have never seen them,' Canning replied sheepishly.

'Twice in a minute. And they do so in two ranks only, instead of three, unlike every other army in the field: hence the duke can dispose of such a long line. How many do you count in those French columns?'

'I cannot rightly see, for there are so many . . .'

Hervey peered even more intently through his telescope as the clouds of smoke cleared, the massed battery having halted its bombardment. 'Well, Canning, unless I am very much mistaken those are not battalion but divisional columns. They will be even more susceptible to fire.'

Canning continued to study them. 'But there seem to be hundreds so tight-packed that—'

'That ball and case would ravage them. Ay, indeed, and our infantry will enfilade them, too. In those French divisions there are probably eight battalions – six hundred men to a battalion. They'll front two hundred, twenty-five ranks deep or more.'

'But why . . . ?'

'Suppose yourself for a moment to be standing in the path

of one of those columns. Might you not be intimidated?'

'Yes, sir, I fancy that I might.'

'Well, that is how Bonaparte has swept so many from the field these past years. I tell you, Canning, it takes nerves of steel to stand your ground before such a machine!'

Hervey and Canning (every man in the Sixth, indeed) now watched with a mixture of exhilaration and dread as three divisional columns – all of fourteen thousand men – marched up the slope, astride the Brussels high road, towards the strongest part of the duke's line, while a fourth veered towards Papelotte farm and the Nassauers below. Hervey could not at first believe it – a frontal assault, no manoeuvre, and this from the greatest proponent of that art in Europe! He felt somehow cheated that in their first direct encounter with Bonaparte they faced the tactics of the battering ram.

But with what magnificence did that assault unfold! The drums kept up the *pas de charge*, almost as intimidating as the cannon fire, which had now ceased. The solid ranks of Bonaparte's blue-coated infantry, with their whitened cross-belts, forced their way through the uncut rye which covered the slopes. The duke's guns began now to play on them, and gaps opened, to be sealed almost at once as the ranks closed up and pressed resolutely forward. A furious fire erupted from Papelotte farm below where the Sixth stood, as the Nassauers poured volley after volley into the column as it engulfed the buildings. Further towards the centre, Bylandt's Dutch-Belgian brigade broke and fled, but the Cameron Highlanders, behind, rallied and met the French with a storm of musketry which kept them from making any progress beyond the crest. Not a man in the Sixth could have relished the situation of the duke's infantry, yet their enforced in-activity made them fretful once more. Might they not have harried the columns at least? The dragoons began cursing, and even the horses champed at their bits.

But it seemed to Hervey, as he peered ever more intently through his telescope, that the momentum of the French attacks was broken. Some of the columns were at a standstill, and he could even see red-coated infantry on the forward slopes by La Haye Sainte. And then came a sight that at once both thrilled and agonized him in equal measure, for at that moment there was nowhere for a cavalryman to be but with the dense host of scarlet-coated horsemen, the Union and Household brigades with Uxbridge himself at the head, as they poured over the crest and down into the valley to set about the reeling columns. In an instant the greatest of battles would be over, and without the Sixth so much as drawing swords!

The ground shook with the thundering hoofs of heavy horses. He saw the Greys, their mounts so conspicuous amongst the browns and blacks of the other regiments, the tall bearskins of the dragoons themselves distinctive even at that distance. They were having the best of it, scything through the disintegrating ranks of French infantry and over-running an artillery battery which had misjudged its withdrawal! He saw their heavy sabres rising and falling – again and again and again – as they cut the gunners down. But then beyond he saw also what the Greys evidently had not – lancers and cuirassiers, in prodigious numbers, moving to the counter-charge, and he cursed the unfledged heavies, blind in their ardour. They would hear of the duke's displeasure soon enough if they ran on without rallying! But then he saw, with mounting horror, that few would live to hear that rebuke, for their horses were so blown by the heavy going of the hollow beneath the ridge that the French must surely catch them before they might retire. Sir Hussey Vivian came galloping across the front towards where Sir John Vandeleur sat with his staff equally transfixed by the Greys' perilous situation. 'You had better go to the heavies' aid, Sir John,' he shouted. 'Take the Sixth as supports, if you will.'

Lankester smiled: the words were keenly judged, for Vandeleur was Vivian's senior. Hervey smiled, too. *That is why we have generals*, he had said to Canning. It was indeed, for he had heard the duke's words plainly enough, and woe betide Vandeleur if he misjudged it! Lankester smiled again, more obviously this time; for they would sit in contemplation no longer. 'Sixth Light Dragoons, *Draw swords!*' he ordered.

The rasp of metal on metal set Hervey's teeth on edge as the sabres, 1796-pattern, with their wide, curved, slashing blades, were drawn from steel scabbards. Rasping meant blunting, but this time he welcomed it as the sound of grim resolve, and he knew that not one of his troopers, new or old, would be satisfied to return his sword unbloodied.

'Form a third support line for Vandeleur, then, Sir Edward,' called Vivian as he rode back. 'Keep them up close but hold them tight to the rally; for if you, too, fall foul of the French I cannot come to your aid.'

'Ay, Sir Hussey,' replied Lankester, 'we shall at least sweep the French out of the farms below.' And then, as Vandeleur's front line took off at a brisk trot, Lankester gave the order: 'Sixth Light Dragoons will advance, First Squadron directing, *Walk-march*!'

By the time the Sixth had cleared the Ohain road and angled right towards the grand battery, Vandeleur's regiments were into a steady canter, the falling slope giving them additional impulsion. Lankester increased the pace to a brisk trot, but still the regiments were opening too great a distance, and he had to press into a canter, although the ground was so bad that dressing was soon lost. By the time they reached the bottom of the valley he had given up the struggle and they, too, were in a gallop before ascending the far slope.

Every gun in range now seemed to turn on them. Men and horses began to fall, bowled over like rabbits. There were all manner of profanities after each new explosion: '*Close up, close up!*' Hervey called continually. Then a shell burst not ten yards to his left, the blast tumbling Nero so quickly that Hervey could not leap clear. The big black gelding fell heavily, snapping its neck and dropping stone-dead on top of him. Riderless horses galloped by so close he marvelled he was not trampled. When they had run clear he struggled to free himself, though every bit of wind seemed knocked out of him, but his leg was pinned fast by Nero's dead weight and there was no shifting it. Searing pain shot through his head – and then darkness.

\* \* \*

# CHAPTER FIFTEEN
# VOILÀ GROUCHY!

*Near La Haye Sainte, 2.30 p.m.*

'Allez, vite, fouillez-les!'

He lay in fetlock-deep mud, pinned fast by Nero. The horse's bulk obscured his sight of all in the direction of the shouting. In the other lay the blue-jacketed bodies of his troopers.

'Fouillez et tuez-les – chacun, vite, vite!'

He could just make out a lance pennant over Nero's flank, thirty yards away, perhaps nearer. Then a pistol shot as, unseen, a *lancier* dispatched a half-dead trooper before searching him.

He was closer to panic than he had ever been. He had nothing but his sabre to fight with, for Nero lay with the saddle still in place and Coates's carbine trapped in the holster beneath. The nearside holster was empty, but even had the pistol fallen within reach he knew it would be useless after lying in the mud. And now there were more hoofs and a different voice – better French, a voice of authority rather than of mere rank. He stopped struggling, and strained to listen.

'Les Prussiens vont . . .' – the Prussians were making for the left flank of the English, said the lancer officer. 'The emperor is at this very moment strengthening his flank at Plancenoit, but there is little he can do to prevent the Prussians joining the field. We must not let our brave soldiers lose heart when they appear. The emperor wishes it to be known, therefore, that he expects Marshal Grouchy's men at any moment on that flank: the marshal is marching even now from Genappe where they have beaten the enemy. Whoever appears on that flank are not Prussians but Grouchy and our countrymen. Voilà Grouchy! Comprenez-vous, mes braves?'

So Bonaparte would deceive his own soldiers! Yet how might they be deceived for long? he wondered. Because the battle would be a close-run affair. Even perfidy might have its reward.

He heard the lancers moving off; but his relief was short-lived, for one of them had dismounted and begun searching a trooper's body not three dozen yards away. He now had but one means of escaping the same fate as the wounded man – the carbine. No matter how much he heaved he could not pull it from the holster, though. He fell back in the mud, almost despairing, but his sabre lay still attached to his wrist by its knot-leather, and he could at least die sword-in-hand.

Only then did he see how simple it was to release the carbine, for it was the holster itself which was trapping it: if he could cut it free, he could then pull both from beneath the horse. He set to work on the holster straps with his newly sharpened blade, and in a short time managed to pull it free from the saddle.

The carbine had been more thoroughly immersed in the cloying mud than even he had been. A flintlock would now misfire for sure: could he rely on this percussion lock? He eased himself up on to an elbow again to fumble for a cartridge from his small-pouch, wiping it clean and praying once more that water had not permeated the gut casing. Still pinned fast under Nero, he fumbled to unfold the carbine's butt. The click of the retaining pin seemed as loud as a pistol shot. He lifted open the breech and inserted the precious cartridge. He cocked the firing-hammer and brought the carbine up into the aim, steadying the foresight as it bisected the horizontal between the upper arms of the 'V' of the back-sight. His aim wavered, for he could not lie fully prone. He waited for the lancer to come closer, until, at twenty yards, the man was now larger than the 'V', and the bisection was level with his chest. He breathed in and then held his breath to freeze the aim, taking up the play in the trigger. 'Please God . . .' he prayed (such long odds – a percussion cap from the Kirk and a cartridge from a sheepfarmer). 'Please God . . .'

The crack was deafening, and a curtain of powder-smoke billowed before him. Death or deliverance awaited its clearing, yet he did not doubt his aim, and the curtain parted to reveal his skill – the lancer lying stone dead, his chest a frothing crimson. Hervey now pulled himself upright. The freeing of the holster allowed him the extra reach to cut through the girth straps and, with the saddle loose, there was enough play for him to struggle from under Nero's dead weight at last. He sprang up, half-surprised that his leg, numbed after its constraint, was in one piece, for he had seen many a leg shattered in lesser falls. The lancer's horse stood obligingly still by its erstwhile rider. He seized the reins and leaped into the saddle despite the pain now displacing the numbness. Only then did he see Serjeant Armstrong galloping back down the hill towards him.

'Oh, thank Christ, Mr 'Ervey! I thought you were done for! Come on, quick, sir – the regiment's gone back, there're lancers everywhere!'

'You don't have to tell me that,' said Hervey with a grimace as he spurred after him.

The French horse was sluggish, and he had to use the flat of his sword to move him apace through the mud, knee-deep in places.

'How did we fare?' he called to Armstrong.

'We saw 'em off, sir,' he shouted back, 'but, Jesus, that lance is a fearsome thing. We need that bloody weapon ourselves. Some officers went down. I saw Captain Elmsall and Captain Roberts fall, an' I think they're dead.'

Lankester dolefully confirmed as much when Hervey and Armstrong reached the depleted ranks of the Sixth back on the ridge above La Haye. 'Hervey, I am doubly relieved at seeing you,' he called as they galloped up and saluted. 'There is but Nall left of the troop leaders, and no more than a half-dozen other officers.'

'What of Cheney, sir?' asked Hervey in dismay, 'and Laming?'

'Laming is right enough, but I think he will lose an arm. Cheney was set about by lancers while he was trying to rally Second Troop. Canning brought First out – with Strange's help; the "boots" did well!'

Hervey would have heard the entire muster roll, but Bonaparte's intrigue was the more pressing, and instead he rattled off his intelligence.

Lankester listened intently and, even with an incomplete knowledge of Wellington's design for battle, comprehended its significance at once: 'Very well; go immediately to Lord Uxbridge – if he is still with us, that is, for he was at the head of the heavies and in the thick of things when we reached the Greys.'

Uxbridge had returned to the place whence he had led the heavies in the fateful charge against d'Erlon's columns. Behind the crest of the ridge, astride the *chaussée*, he held, as it were, the tollgate to the Brussels road. The French infantry had paid a terrible price attempting to force that gate, and would do so once more, but there was now a change in the pace of the battle – if not quite a lull, then a perceptible slackening. Yet despite his earlier exertions the Earl of Uxbridge looked just as he did at a field day, his pelisse off the shoulder in true hussar fashion, his dolman immaculate, his shako set square. Hervey was discomfited by his own mud-spattered appearance, thankful at least that he had not lost his own shako. Uxbridge seemed not to care in the slightest. 'Well done, Mr Hervey,' he replied on hearing his report. 'I am only gratified that your French was sufficient – and that you had some notion of the implication of such a ruse. But we must waste no time trying to find the duke. Marshal Blücher's liaison officer – Baron Müffling (you will remember him, I think, from our review last month) – has this hour set out to discover what is happening with our gallant allies. Ride after him; take the Wavre road. Inform him that— No, *go* with him in person to the Prussians! I myself shall tell the duke.'

Hervey thrilled at the commission. He was no mere galloper but an emissary – and from the duke himself to the dauntless Prince Blücher. He gathered his reins as calmly as he could, saluted and then sped back to the Sixth. Gone was the mare's sluggishness, and instead she bucked for the best part of a hundred yards while he tried painfully to apply his leg to pick her up. How in God's name did the French school their horses? he wondered.

'Next time, Mr 'Ervey, sir, I'm gooin' with yer,' called Johnson as Hervey reached the regiment; 'It's not right gooin' off in a charge an' leavin' me. Where's Nero?'

'Johnson, it's as well that you *did* stay here or you might now be lying down there with Nero, and a lance in your back,' he replied curtly. 'Look, take this French trollop; I will have Jessye from you now. Where is Serjeant Armstrong?'

'Here, sir!' came the confident reply from behind.

Hervey turned and saw his broad smile – and his sword-arm in a sling. 'I had not appreciated that you were bloodied, Serjeant Armstrong,' he exclaimed. 'Is Serjeant Strange fit?'

'Ay, sir. But what do you want of him?' asked Armstrong suspiciously.

'I have a dispatch for the Prussians and need of an escort.'

'This arm will not fail you,' Armstrong declared, pulling it from the sling.

'No, I cannot risk it. Fetch Serjeant Strange, if you will,' replied Hervey sharply, bringing a welter of protests from his covering-serjeant, which were only silenced in the bluntest of terms. Johnson attempted likewise to protest, and he, too, was silenced only with difficulty. When Strange came up, Hervey explained their assignment and then instructed Armstrong to tell Lankester of it, receiving a surly salute in reply as he and Strange took off down the ridge-road after the baron, Jessye bucking as violently as had the French mare.

Half a mile beyond the flank picket of Vivian's brigade they saw at last General Müffling and his escort, the same distance again and about to enter the Forêt d'Ohain. Hervey quickened the pace still more, though Strange's horse was beginning to tire, and it seemed that they might close the distance before the Prussians were too deep into the forest. But he had gambled on speed alone to keep them safe, and the gamble now looked like failing; for suddenly, as if from nowhere, there came a check to their progress – perhaps even an end. Three or four hundred yards away, and trotting towards them, red tunics and tall *chapkas* vivid against the background of green, was a lancer patrol. Their red-and-white lance-pennants fluttered a full fifteen feet from the ground, and Hervey might have admired them had they not been standing between him and his mission. He counted a dozen (unpromising odds, to say the least) and he knew he had but two options. He might run back to the security of the allied line: it scarcely *was* an option, though, for Strange's horse would soon be outpaced. He tried instead to judge the angle between them and the French, and the point where they might gain the cover of the forest, but it was so acute that a gallop in that direction offered little chance of success, either. Yet he must make a decision.

Strange had already made it: 'Go on, sir; I'll stop them!'

He had never before heard such urgency in Strange's voice. *Stop* them: Strange said 'stop', not delay. Both knew what that meant, for stopping could only be at one price.

'*Go on*, sir!'

Hervey unclipped the carbine from his crossbelt and thrust it and the cartridge-pouch at Strange. 'Here, you know the mechanism well enough.'

*That* he did, for the carbine had been the talk of the Sixth in Ireland, and he had fired it. He took them without a word but reached inside his tunic and pulled out what looked like a leather tobacco-pouch, though Hervey knew he did not smoke. 'Here, sir, take this for later, *and go on, now*!' he urged, spurring his tired gelding towards the patrol. 'And good luck, Mr Hervey,' he called over his shoulder.

'Good luck to you, too, Serjeant Strange!' said Hervey beneath his breath as he, too, spurred into a gallop. There was no show of sentiment: the formality was exaggerated even. Hervey knew he would have done the same himself had their circumstances been reversed, and that Strange was only doing his duty as countless other serjeants were doing at that moment. But it made it no less gallant. He reckoned Strange would be able to get off four or five shots before the French closed with him, but this was no guarantee that the *lanciers* would be dissuaded from pursuit, for the patrol (if it knew what it were about) ought to divide – one group to deal with Strange, the other to intercept *him*. But he guessed they would not, for he had never thought much of their patrolling. Knee-to-knee in the charge, *yes*, but not this sort of work. And pride would surely get the better of them when the first lancer was hit.

He gambled well. Even against the continuous thunder of gunfire a mile away he heard Strange's first shot, then after a few seconds another, then another and another – then nothing. With fifty yards to go to the trees he looked back. The French had made straight for Strange, and there was an evenly spaced line of four dead or dying lancers. Each shot, which Strange fired mounted, had told, and now the best marksman in the regiment was parrying a lance with his sabre. Hervey looked away for an instant to fix his opening into the forest. When he turned again Strange was no longer visible, overwhelmed by the French. '*Stop* them', indeed: Strange had known precisely the price he would pay.

The forest swaddled him in leafy silence as he slowed to a jog-trot, then a walk, for Jessye was blowing hard. First Edmonds, now Strange – he wondered who might live to recount this battle. His head hurt sorely. The trees were a blur, and he was all but overcome by the urge to lie down, dropping the reins and letting Jessye take him along the rutted track, oblivious now to his surroundings.

A pistol exploded. He felt the ball kiss his cheek. Bark splinters flew as it struck the tree behind, magpies and jays scattering in noisy flight, making Jessye shy.

'Votre épée, monsieur! Rendez votre épée!' shouted the *chasseur à cheval*.

Hervey touched the graze, curious that there was no pain – nor then any blood on his fingers. His gut tightened, his mind raced, the plume of the *chasseur*'s busby changed from a blur to sharp detail, and he saw that neither flight nor resistance was prudent in the face of two cavalry pistols not ten yards ahead.

'Je dis encore, monsieur: rendez votre épée.' But the voice somehow lacked assurance (though the escorts – five, six, or even more – looked solid enough).

'Eh bien, lieutenant,' replied Hervey, measured, thoughtful; 'qu'est ce que vous faites ici?'

The lieutenant looked surprised. It was for *him* to ask that question, he stammered. What was an Englishman doing, speaking this way?

Hervey felt himself trembling uncontrollably, yet he did not know if he were. His voice almost broke as he now grasped his chance: 'Alors, messieurs: je ne suis pas Anglais. Je suis l'agent de l'empereur.'

The lieutenant looked anguished. 'C'est pas possible—'

But Hervey would not let him finish, instead piling on his doubts. He reached into a pocket (the escorts gestured with their pistols) and took out the de Chantonnay ring. 'See this: it is the seal of the de Chantonnays – *my* seal. No Frenchman can fail to recognize it!'

The lieutenant rode up closer and peered at it. 'Do you not have papers of authorization, monsieur?' he asked sceptically.

'What? To be found by the English or the Prussians! Do you take me for a fool?' rasped Hervey in his most imperious French. 'I have papers well enough, but you will find them only with the emperor's staff. Now, if you please, I have business to be about.'

The lieutenant shifted uneasily. 'What business is this, monsieur?'

'I am not about to disclose the emperor's business to a lieutenant!' gasped Hervey, 'even to a lieutenant of *chasseurs*!'

'Then, I am afraid, monsieur, that you must accompany us so that we may verify your identity,' said the lieutenant.

Hervey was now fired by the deception. 'Imbecile!' he shouted. 'What in the name of France do you think we are about this day? You have seen my seal, have you not? You recognize it surely?'

'Yes, of course, monsieur, but—'

'Then, let me put to you this for your consideration, which only those in the emperor's confidence must know. The Prussians – they are expected hourly upon this flank, are they not? Mais Prussiens, monsieur? Jamais! They are Grouchy's men, no? *Voilà Grouchy!* n'est-ce pas?'

The lieutenant was at a loss . . . and then profoundly relieved. 'Oui, c'est ça; *voilà Grouchy!* Truly, monsieur, that is so. A thousand pardons for delaying you: I was only doing my duty, you understand. May I provide an escort for you?'

'Indeed you may not!' thundered Hervey. 'You will fly from here this instant and leave me to dupe the Prussians. Away, at once!'

The thrill of so outrageous a bluff turned rapidly to cold dread as he pondered the consequences had he failed – shot out of hand as a spy. Sister Maria had said, 'You could pass for a Frenchman,' and he had. How he wished she might know of the providence of that ring. He pushed it deep into a pocket as Jessye extended her trot. The forest was cool, soothing – and silent still, the thunder of cannon fire to the south no more here than a rumble. He began to doze in the saddle again . . .

'Halt!' came the command, unseen.

He pulled up at once and looked around. He could see nothing.

'Wer ist das? Wohin gehen Sie?'

But before he could make any reply there came another voice: 'Nein, verflucht! Es ist ein Engländer!'

He did not hesitate a second time. 'Herr General!' he called, the Prussian's vast bulk unmistakable in any light.

Half a dozen mounted figures emerged from the trees. Two of the general's cavalry escorts kept their pistols trained on him as he rode straight for Müffling and launched into his dispatch with a fluency that took them aback.

'Teufel! Gefährlicher als ich gedacht hatte!' exclaimed the baron. '*Much* more dangerous than I had imagined. Come; we must make straight for Prince Blücher.'

Hervey sighed, relieved that Müffling had grasped the danger and was prepared to act. Indeed, he was first relieved that he took him at his word, for he had no written authority, nor was he an ADC. And, as they quickened on, the general's eyes widened in astonishment when Hervey recounted how he had discovered the ruse. The general kept repeating his assurance, however, that all would now be well just as soon as they found Prince Blücher. Hervey believed him.

But his confidence faltered on first seeing Blücher's men a half-hour later, for where he had been expecting to see a military machine, the legacy of Frederick the Great, he saw only . . . *disorder* (some would say *chaos*). *Never* – not even during the worst moments of the long retreat through the Astorgias to Corunna – had he come upon anything so disheartening. Was 'rabble' too extreme a word for this mass of soldiery, guns and waggons toiling through mud axle-deep? It was as if the entire army had become stragglers. Müffling, however, knew both his countrymen and his allies, and perceived well enough Hervey's dismay. 'It is true,' he conceded, 'we were evilly mauled yesterday at Genappe. But do not underestimate the hardiness of these men, Mr Hervey. "Alte Vorwärts" has given your Duke of Wellington his word, his *sacred* word, that he will come to his aid. You do not suppose that these men will be unworthy of it?'

This pledge of constancy, and of the spirit that animated the Prince, was heartening, but it seemed unlikely. Yet soon it proved true, for when they found Prince Blücher he was encouraging his weary infantry in person. 'Kommt, meine Kinder, noch einmal!' he exhorted them, slapping his thigh and waving his hand. His intent could be in no doubt, and his energy was at once imparted to the jaded foot-soldiers. When he saw his old friend, however, he turned his horse and rode up in a welter of earthy opinion. 'Mein Gott, Müffling, es ist Scheisse, reine Scheisse!'

Hervey fought hard not to laugh. Field Marshal Blücher, the veteran hussar and fighter of the French: warm, emotional, with a soldier's vocabulary – and reeking of onions and gin. What greater contrast with the duke could there have been? Blücher even apologized for smelling so rank (having dosed himself, he explained, after a fearsome fall at Genappe), and shook Hervey's hand so vigorously that he thought his wrist must crack.

'This officer bears extraordinary intelligence of a ruse by the French,' said Müffling. 'I consider that you should hear it before my own.'

The marshal listened to Hervey's report in frowning silence and then turned to one of his ADCs, instructing him to hasten General von Ziethen's corps to the duke's flank.

'And, sir,' ventured Hervey in textbook German, animated by Blücher's determination to foil this stratagem, 'may I propose one additional order? May I suggest, sir, that General von Ziethen opens fire as soon as his men debouch from the forest, for although they will be half a league or more from the French the firing will signal hostile intent and should therefore confound Bonaparte's ruse.'

'Ja, ja, richtig; das ist eine exzellente Idee,' replied the field marshal excitedly. 'Vieles Schiessen!' he shouted, slapping his sides as if about to take off after hounds. 'Vieles Schiessen, Lutzow!' he called after the ADC.

Hervey was as anxious to be away as the ADC (for, his business concluded, he wished to search for Serjeant Strange), but he saw that his progress would be quicker in the company of Baron Müffling. Yet Müffling showed no enthusiasm for an immediate return, Blücher and he withdrawing for a full quarter-hour to confer alone. He dismounted and fed Jessye some corn which a commissary was content to give him, and as he sat on a fallen tree holding her reins he began to study more closely the men who filed by. And what he saw began to encourage him; indeed, inspire him. These men – as a body – looked as if they had had a mauling, and yet they had with them all their personal equipment. What was more, it was as serviceable as he had seen – *more* serviceable even. And the faces of the musketeers of the Silesian Regiment trudging past, though tired-looking, had a fearsome aspect: Hervey thought he saw in them a positive lust to be at the throats of the enemy.

The cavalry carefully picking their way around the infantry were even more convincing. They, too, bore the signs of battle, but they carried themselves with the same grim determination. These hussars knew what they were about. How proudly the black-and-white shako-cockades bobbed with their horses' action. And what horses!

'Zey are fine, are zey not?' said one of Müffling's ADCs, who had come over to share his tree, handing him a silver flask.

'Yes,' said Hervey. He could not say other, for they *were* fine horses, in the finest condition – and this despite their exertions of the past week. 'Trakheners?'

'Ja, Trakhener. Do you know ze breed?'

'No, I have heard much of them but I have never before seen one.'

'You admire zem, ja?'

'Very much. They are bigger, I think, on the whole than our troop horses – half a hand, I should say. Plenty of bone, and beautiful heads, too,' he smiled, thinking how much Jessope would approve of them.

'You do not have a cavalry stud in England, I understand?' continued the ADC, offering his flask again.

'No, we buy from dealers. There never seems a want of good horses.'

'Ja, I admire much your zoroughbred. Ve are using some zoroughbreds now at Trakhenen Stud, I am hearing. To give more speed. But your horse is not a zoroughbred, I zink?'

'No,' replied Hervey with a wry smile, facing the hopeless

task of explaining Jessye's breeding. 'Her sire was a thorough-bred, but her dam was a Welsh Cob, an old breed from —'

But the ADC needed no priming. 'Ze Velsh Cob I am admiring very much!' he said in delight. 'Ze hardy native pony und ze Andalusians make zis cob four or five hundred years ago, I zink. Ze ambassador in Berlin has von of zese ponies for his son, und it is – how do you say? – ze handiest little horse in ze Grünewald.'

'And I fancy that mine, too, is the handiest in *this* forest!' laughed Hervey.

When at last they began back for Mont St-Jean it took them all of two hours through the mud, and the press of men, horses and waggons, to reach the edge of the forest. Yet in that time he became confident at last that the Prussians would assail the French, as they had promised, with all vigour and dispatch. It only remained to see how soon this would be.

But searching for Strange was not possible, for as they emerged from the tree-line they saw more French cavalry, forcing them on a wide detour. 'Herr General,' began Hervey as they reached Vivian's flank pickets, 'may I ask you the favour of reporting to Lord Uxbridge that I have done what he commanded: I believe my duty now is to rejoin my regiment.'

'Of course, Mr Hervey; you have done your duty admirably. And I must apologize again that my hussars mistook you for a Frenchman,' he smiled. 'Do not concern yourself about Prince Blücher. He is above seventy, you know, but still he is a tenacious soldier, *ein treuer Husar* as we say. He will never give up!'

Hervey had half-expected to find the Sixth gone from above La Haye. Instead he found Vivian's same pickets on the flank; but although the regiment had dressed a little towards the centre, as the brigades had tried to close the gaps, they held the same ground as four hours before. 'Has, please God,

Serjeant Strange ridden in, sir?' he asked, hoping against hope that he had somehow made his escape.

'I fear not,' replied Lankester, holding out a flask. 'You had better take a draw on this brandy and tell me all that has passed.'

When Hervey's account was ended the captain turned to Adjutant Barrow who, though Hervey had not observed it, had been active once more with his pocket-book. 'Is there anything more for the record, Barrow?' asked Lankester.

'No, sir,' he replied, 'except that, if I might be allowed to say so, this seems uncommon service. I am sorry for Serjeant Strange; but Mr Hervey should not, in my judgement, let it rest upon his consciousness, for it was noble necessity.'

Hervey might have resented so cold a dismissal of Strange, but he recognized the adjutant's purpose well enough. And Lankester voiced the same: 'Indeed so, Barrow, and very aptly put,' he nodded. 'Well done, Hervey. You cannot grieve, for there has been no deficiency in your conduct. And now, if you please, I desire that you resume command of your squadron, for there will soon be hot work to be about.'

Hervey was grateful enough for their solicitude, yet it did little to reassure him as he rode over to his squadron. Cornet Seton Canning greeted him with evident relief as he resumed his place at the head of First, for Canning had joined the regiment just before they had left Cork, and after only the first field day he had grasped for himself the extent of his inexperience. Command of a squadron had sat uneasily with him for the past few hours.

Armstrong's relief stemmed from a different impulse, however, for he counted his lieutenant more than a mere squadron leader. 'Thank Christ, Mr 'Ervey,' he exclaimed. 'This is worse than Salamanca!'

'Tell me of it, Serjeant Armstrong! For I do not wish to dwell any more on *my* past hours. Serjeant Strange is dead – I am certain – and I had to leave him in the field.'

Armstrong paused, but (and Heaven knew how much he wanted to know of the circumstances) he held his peace, and began instead to rail against their own inactivity. 'Not fewer than twelve Frog charges in a row!' he thundered, recalling with startling imagery the attacks on the centre by the masses of *cuirassiers* and *lanciers*. 'They 'ave tried to break them squares all afternoon. Every time they came on they've been seen off by the guns or Lord Uxbridge's men in the middle. The 'ussars on the other flank 'ave been all over the place – and yet we 'ave sat 'ere idle as a monk's prick. One paltry gallop in the whole day!'

'The duke's express orders, Serjeant Armstrong,' Hervey sympathized. 'We are rooted to this flank until relieved by the Prussians.'

Armstrong shook his head in despair. 'And what good might that do? Look yonder,' he spat, pointing to La Haye Sainte. '*There!* The French 'ave taken it at last! What's the sense of us sitting here, then, with the centre about to give way?'

Half a league hence the Duke of Wellington turned to the Earl of Uxbridge and said calmly: 'Night or the Prussians must come!'

## CHAPTER SIXTEEN
# NIGHT OR THE PRUSSIANS

---

*Overlooking Papelotte and La Haye, Evening*

Hervey took out his watch. The smallest of shell splinters was embedded in its face, neatly piercing the letters *d'A.J.* on the cover and arresting the hands.

'Aren't you the lucky one, Mr 'Ervey,' said Armstrong. 'That would've made the eyes water!'

How *was* Jessope? he wondered as he examined the watch, puzzling whether the mechanism was still intact. How he envied him his situation, in the thick of the fighting, with Lord Fitzroy and the duke.

'Half after six,' said Armstrong, looking at the watch he had found at Vitoria. 'Where are them Prussians, then?'

Hervey had no answer. Then Brigade-Major Harris came galloping along the line, the tails of his red staff-coat flying like an express boy's.

'Hallo, somethin's up!' said Armstrong hopefully.

Hervey agreed, and rode up to Lankester in anticipation.

'The flank pickets report that Prussian hussars are approaching. Both brigades are to move to the centre as soon as relieved,' said Harris.

Lankester merely looked at Hervey for an acknowledgement, confident that there was no need of elaboration. Hervey nodded, saluted and trotted back to his squadron, his broad smile at once conveying the intention through the ranks.

'Are we to 'ave at 'em at last, Mr 'Ervey?' someone called.

'Yes, boys, now's our time!'

Later he would ponder on that familiarity. It was what Edmonds, for sure, would have said, and Lankester, too – although the captain would more likely have said '*my* boys'. But Hervey had done so unaffectedly, and the squadron accepted it – as an unbroken horse at last accepts the bit.

Ten minutes later, with the first green jackets of the death's-head hussars coming on to the ridge, Vivian's brigade began its move. Lord Uxbridge rode up. 'Well done, Vivian,' he began. 'You have anticipated the duke's intentions precisely. A gap is opening in the centre, and some of the foreigners are beginning to waver. I may tell you, it is damned hot work there!' Hervey's mare squealed suddenly as his trumpeter's grey fly-kicked and threw his rider, causing Uxbridge to turn. 'Mr Hervey!' he exclaimed, 'we must speak of certain matters when there is opportunity – if your trumpeter leaves you in one piece, that is!' And Hervey flushed bright red as the wretched dragoon attempted to remount in a profusion of apologies.

They trotted all the way to the centre. 'Guns may gallop, Captain Lankester,' Vivian had called as they began. 'Cavalry proceeds at a trot lest those that do not know us should conceive that we might be affeard. Lord Uxbridge says the Cumberland Hussars have already left the field – and they supposedly steady Brunswickers!'

'There is no-one better than Sir Hussey for a show such as this,' said Lankester, falling in alongside Hervey and First Squadron. 'He will handle the brigade as if on review. And I should do so myself, mark you, for I warrant that such a show will be all that keeps some of those Dutch in place.'

A harsh judgement, thought Hervey, for it soon became apparent that even the King's Germans were shaken. As the brigade reached the crossroads above La Haye Sainte they formed into line, the Sixth extending in two ranks on the right behind General Colin Halkett's Hanoverians, just to the west of the crossroads, with the remainder of the brigade to the rear of Colonel Ompteda's ravaged German legionaries. The Dutch battery which had been working feverishly as they arrived fell silent, smoke obscuring their line of sight; and then, as the acrid black fog cleared, Hervey had his first glimpse of the inferno which the slopes had become, a sight which horrified the recruits and veterans alike. And not only the sight, for every sense was assailed. It was hotter here by ten degrees or more. The powder-smoke was so thick he could taste it, and the noise was truly deafening. Horses went rigid with terror. Even Jessye would not respond to the leg, Hervey having to dig in his spurs for the first time he could ever remember. Had they been fretting on that flank for want of this? He could scarcely credit it. Cannon shot flew thicker than he had heard even musketry before. And there were so many bodies – men and horses – that he could but marvel at the steadfastness of these men to his front. How had they borne it? He thought of waves beating against a sea wall – breaking, receding, but each time washing away more of the wall so that the time must come when it would be gone, and what lay beyond inundated. The smoke cleared again, and he raised his telescope. The tall bearskins were unmistakable: the Garde Impériale were advancing.

Lankester trotted along the Sixth's front, as cool as if he were at morning exercise. 'Once the infantry have fallen clear of us to the rear we shall charge those columns,' he called to each of his squadron leaders, still certain the Hanoverians would break at any moment. 'Keep an eye on their cavalry supports,' he urged. 'Nall is hit, Hervey: you are now the senior, mind.'

'The fortunes of war,' sighed Hervey. A cornet less than a year ago, a stop on promotion – and now within a mere stunning-shot of command of the regiment. And Lankester, by exposing himself thus, was doubling, perhaps trebling, the chance of such a shot. *Must* he place himself broadside to the enemy? But what, then, was the alternative – a covered approach along the rear of his squadrons, trusting his orders to the trumpet? That was not the way.

Hervey saw the roundshot hit the ground five yards to Lankester's off-side as he rode back. It threw up a fountain of earth, bounced with barely diminished velocity and struck the captain's bay, easily the finest-bred horse in the regiment, squarely in the flank with an audible thud. The third of the four men Hervey most admired in the regiment went down like a skittle at a fair. He shut his eyes and groaned, just as when Edmonds had fallen, but this time he hesitated for barely a second before pressing Jessye towards where the manual told him the commanding officer must stand: centre, one horse's length in front of the regimental guidon, and a place he never dreamed he would know except in the pages of that drill-book. But how long might it be before Rook, commanding Third Squadron, would in turn have to ride up to take that place? Would he at least remain long enough to lead the charge to stop the waves? What should he now do? What orders should he give? The instinct to grasp at the familiar was strong. One order, at least, might be useful – if unorthodox. 'Shorten stirrups!' he called. They could at least have the benefit of reach if they were to go at these infantry-men. The order was repeated along the ranks, for it had no trumpet call (besides, seconds before, his trumpeter had slumped forward in the saddle, his shoulder carried away by a bullet from the cloud of *tirailleurs* preceding the Garde).

Jessye scarcely moved a muscle as Hervey pushed his left leg forward, lifted the sheepskin and felt for the buckle. Two holes would do (he was already riding one hole shorter than the adjutant would have approved). Then the same on the off-side, all the time without taking his eyes from the field ahead. He leaned forward to check the girth, hoping it would need no tightening – he had pushed her hard, and she might well be tucked up. But, no, it was tight enough, though he need not have worried about her standing still if he had to take in the girth a hole, too, for she was as steady as he had ever known. Indeed, she seemed in some kind of trance, and so did the rest of the regiment's horses as he glanced behind him. There was not even the usual napping that accompanied any parade in close order. It was as if they were paralysed by the abyss into which they looked. Would they answer to the leg when the time came?

He waited. It was all he could do now. Nor was he sure whether he was meant to charge when he judged it the moment, or whether the order was to come from Vivian. But if he did not charge, *then* what . . . ? He resolved to trust his judgement and answer for it later – if there *were* a later. Better a rebuke from Wellington for excess of ardour than to be remembered as another Sackville (would the cavalry ever expiate the shame of Lord George Sackville at Minden? Even the Marquess of Granby, going bald-headed for the French days later, had not expunged the stain). But how might he lead a charge with this shaken infantry brigade in front? And it was not only the living who barred their way: for a hundred yards beyond the Hanoverians the field was strewn with dead and wounded – men and horses. No momentum could be had through such a charnel house surely. All he might do was keep his gaze fixed forward, lest looking about should weaken his resolve, and trust that he might have a right instinct in this.

The Garde were magnificent. They marched for so long astride the high road, straight towards the weakest part of the line, that it seemed nothing could stop them – not grape, not musketry, not the boldest cavalry charge ever. But then, astonishingly, they veered to the left so that the main weight of the attack must pass to the west of La Haye Sainte and to where the Guards stood, backed by Vandeleur's brigade. But *was* that where the Guards were? It was where they were *meant* to be, yet he could not see them. They had surely not withdrawn? Must Vandeleur face the attack himself? Could this account for the Garde's change of axis, the threat of the sabre preferred to the volleys of the infantry? But the Garde's flank battalions were still bearing down steadily on the Hanoverians, and the Legion now began pouring volley-fire into the densely packed columns of bluecoats. Each discharge felled them in whole ranks, like a scythe through corn, but still they came on. It was impossible that the Hanoverians, whose own ranks stood sorely depleted, should hold once they clashed bayonet to bayonet. Hervey steeled himself to the order: 'Sixth Light Dragoons, Draw swords!' he shouted, his voice stronger and clearer than he expected. Then, quietly, he nodded to the trumpet-major beside him (all of whose trumpeters had been carried from the field, and his own trumpet-arm was bound to his chest): '"Walk-March" as soon as the Germans have cleared our front, please!' And the trumpet-major took up his bugle, knowing he would need its extra octave to sound the call above the noise.

But the Germans stood. *How*, he would never know, especially once Halkett himself had fallen. Their last volley tore into the blue files point-blank and, like a prizefighter swaying after a body-blow, the columns wavered. A reserve brigade of Dutch-Belgians, in the short blue jackets that made them look as if they were his own regiment dismounted, marched resolutely forward to the left of the remains of the Hanoverians and added their muskets to the curtain of fire that prevented the élite of the Grande Armée from gaining the ridge. He felt shame that he had ever joined in the scorn heaped on the allies before the battle. But, glancing across to where he supposed Vandeleur must soon take the main weight of the assault, something seemed amiss. 'What is that, Trumpet-Major?' he gasped, peering through his telescope. 'The smoke is so bad. Is it the duke?'

'I can't tell sir,' replied the trumpet-major.

'Yes, yes – it is the duke. He waves an arm, but I cannot see whom he beckons . . .'

Hervey saw soon enough, for as if from nowhere, from out of the ground even, appeared the Guards. There must be a thousand – no, *more* – a red fortress not twenty yards in front of the French! Maitland's brigade had lain concealed until this moment. 'Oh! the steadiness, the nerve!' Hervey cried aloud.

Their fire was continuous for half a minute. Never had he seen drill so rapid: *Load . . . present . . . fire!* Again and again. The French fell in their hundreds. Then the guardsmen were rushing forward, bayonets glinting in the evening sun which filtered through the smoke, and he saw the duke waving his hat in the air. He looked towards Vivian, in front of the brigade, the general's voice audible even above the musketry which the infantry were still pouring after the recoiling French columns: 'Come now, my boys, will you follow me?'

And then loud cheering, with 'Ay, to hell, Sir Hussey!' along the length of the brigade. They surged forward, gingerly at first, picking a way through the standing remains of the King's Germans and the dead and dying of both sides beyond, until the slope began to give them impulsion.

At the bottom they set about a reserve battalion of the Garde trying desperately to form square. Their sabres made light work of the attempt, and Hervey rallied them quickly to push on to the batteries beyond, for the guns had begun a brisk fire again now that the Garde had cleared their line. As they raced up the slopes he knew it was over, with nothing in sight but a few *chasseurs* scarcely capable of defending themselves let alone mounting any counter-charge. Half a mile beyond La Haye Sainte, astride the high road, he led his squadrons straight at a battery of big 12-pounders – 'les belles filles de l'empereur'. He could see the gunners had no fight left in them: they ought to have been able to get off a round of grape in the last fifty yards, but instead they raced for their horses or cowered under the guns. The Sixth fell on them with rare savagery, the drivers – mere boys – crying and hiding their faces as the sabres cut at them, the troopers standing in the stirrups to put extra force into the downswing. No-one who did not raise his hands in complete surrender was spared, and some who did found it too late.

Hervey still had the regiment in hand (by some marvel, for blood had brought them to a frenzy), and they rallied quickly to the trumpet. Horses were blowing hard as they pushed on up the slope through what remained of Bonaparte's army swarming from the field. Everywhere there was shouting – 'sauve qui peut'. And 'trahison', too. Why? (He could not imagine what part treachery had played in their defeat.) As they broached the crest, whence Bonaparte had surveyed the field for much of the day, he could see the solid blue line of Prussian infantry sweeping over the ridge to the east and down into the valley that had almost seen him dead. He quickened the pace yet further, for he could see Prussian hussars nearing and he was determined to gain the crest first.

There was no sign of Uxbridge, nor of Vivian even. Smoke

drifted everywhere, and the light was fading. Should he now drive on down the road towards Rossomme? Every instinct was to do so, but with no-one following him up . . . ? It was as well that he hesitated, for Sir John Vandeleur would have need of him. 'Where are the Prussians?' shouted the general as he emerged from the smoke.

Hervey pointed to the hussars approaching from Plancenoit to the north-east. 'I think they will be from General von Bülow's corps, sir.'

Vandeleur looked surprised by his knowing. 'Lord Uxbridge is wounded. Are you the foremost squadron?' he asked.

'I fear we are the foremost *regiment*, sir,' replied Hervey to the new commander of the duke's cavalry.

'Great heavens! I had not supposed Vivian's brigade to be so thinned. Hold here; we are all blown. I have not the slightest idea what has become of Vivian himself. I must have the Prussians take on the pursuit.'

'I speak German, sir, if it would help,' said Hervey hesitantly.

'Help? I should say it will!' replied Vandeleur, turning to his staff. 'None of *us* have a damned word of it!'

Help it did, for Vandeleur would no more have recognized Prince Wilhelm at the head of von Bülow's cavalry than he would an officer in another brigade. And now was not the time for discourtesies (Sir John was notoriously short on ceremony). He managed to give, with Hervey as interpreter, a passable account of the last hour's fighting, and the prince agreed to take up the pursuit.

'One more matter, General,' said Wilhelm, his hard Berlin consonants commanding absolute attention. 'Marshal Blücher and the Duke of Wellington must seal this arrangement. I propose they rendezvous in this very place, at this inn – La Belle Alliance – an apt name for the battle itself, think you not?'

Vandeleur looked at Hervey, who did not wait to translate for him: 'We may arrange the rendezvous, your Highness,' he began instead, 'but the duke is very particular about naming his battles.'

The army slept that night where it halted, on the battlefield itself, surrounded by the dead and dying, their exhaustion utter. The campfires which, as a rule, lit up after battle, like so many stars in a clear sky, were few and far between. Everywhere men just lay down and slept.

Not so in the Sixth. They could not claim to have suffered as the infantry, and Hervey had two thoughts only: to recover their dead and wounded, and to make ready for the advance on Paris, which he knew must follow soon. Making-ready he could, with confidence, leave to RSM Lincoln and Assheton-Smith, the senior of the other three lieutenants still in the saddle, but recovering the dead and wounded was another matter. 'Mr Lincoln,' he began thoughtfully, 'we have but a half-hour of twilight. Scour the slopes in front of the battery we overran, but no further. I myself shall search for Serjeant Strange.'

'As you wish, sir,' replied the RSM, his voice for once muted, 'but I urge that your cover-serjeant goes with you.'

Hervey was more than content to take the counsel, since there was no-one else with whom he might begin to relate his sense of guilt at this time.

In failing light, and against the flow of Prussians, they trotted north-east, the sights and sounds all about them reducing even Armstrong to silence, for never before had either of them re-crossed a battlefield. And never, for sure, one as bloody as this. What therefore made Hervey check in front of La Haye Sainte he could not tell: the ground was everywhere covered with the dead and dying. But one body lying face-down, sword still clutched in an outstretched hand, even among all the others drew his eye (perhaps the uniform looked too pristine compared with the muddy, gory remains all around). He dismounted and turned the scarlet-jacketed body over. The wild, staring eyes, which he had last seen on the ridge that morning, rolled upwards, yet there was no other life.

So Styles had reached the slopes in front of the batteries,

dying with sword drawn, going for the enemy. Whether those eyes stared in wild fear or with the exhilaration of the charge mattered not: Hervey would be able to tell his people that their son had died among the enemy. And that was all he would need to say.

It was after midnight before they found Strange. Hervey had prayed so fervently that they might not, but his body they found easily, alone, and where he had last seen him, contorted in the agony that the dozen or more lance wounds had inflicted (for that was the number the lantern revealed).

'Jesus, Mr 'Ervey,' cursed Armstrong, 'it's an infernal weapon; it's . . . *unchristian.*'

They wrapped him gently in a blanket, as if wounded, and then Armstrong caught one of the loose horses roaming even this remote corner of the battlefield – a chestnut (Strange had always liked chestnuts). Unmarked by the battle, she stood patiently while they lashed his body into the saddle.

They picked their way back to La Belle Alliance, in silence once more, across a moonlit landscape where ghostly figures shuffled or darted in and out of the shadows. At times they were accompanied by a press of riderless horses seeking the security of the herd, some barely able to walk so appalling were their wounds. It was past three o'clock when they reached the inn, and burial that night was unthinkable. Hervey had resolved that Strange would have the rites of the Wesleyan service, so they wrapped his body in a velvet curtain (blue – the colour which had clothed him in life) and laid him in one of the rooms. Soon afterwards, Assheton-Smith and the RSM came with the regiment's parade-strength. Hervey studied it through eyes that already ached, and which now filled with tears. He could scarcely believe the order of their loss, for they had been so late engaged. Only five officers and 123 other ranks would be ready for duty at dawn.

'I have posted an inlying picket only, sir,' said the lieutenant. 'Do we stand-to as usual before dawn?'

Hervey checked his irritation at the suggestion they might do otherwise. 'Yes,' he replied simply.

\*    \*    \*

His leg ached, his head pounded, and he felt weak for want of food. He ought to do his rounds of the squadrons – that was what Edmonds would have done, was it not? But surely he had done sufficient of his duty, and was it not now his duty to rest? The RSM insisted it was, and Hervey yielded. Johnson had already taken Jessye, who had carried him through so much that day without once even stumbling, and he now brought his valise. Hervey put his hand on his groom's shoulder. 'I am glad that you at least . . . ,' he began, but then stayed his sentiments and went instead to the next-door room in silence. He lay on the floor by Strange's body and struggled to think of a prayer. But sleep came quicker.

## CHAPTER SEVENTEEN
# THE AUDIT OF WAR

*Before Dawn, 19 June*

At his headquarters, the inn on the Brussels *chaussée* at the village of Waterloo, the Duke of Wellington slept. He had returned after dark, eaten some supper with those of his staff who had survived, and then sat down to write his dispatch to the prince regent. When he had finished, he had instructed the headquarters physician, Dr Hume, to bring him the casualty list at first light so that he might attach it. One of his ADCs, Sir Alexander Gordon, had lain mortally wounded in the duke's camp-bed, so he had, instead, lain down in an adjacent room, wrapped in his cloak. Hume crept in silently and placed the list by the sleeping commander-in-chief. When he returned after daybreak he found the duke up, studying it intently. His face was still grimy from the previous day, and there were traces of tears.

On the other side of the battlefield, Hervey, wrapped also in a cloak, slept, too. And death, in the shape of a comrade, was likewise but a few feet away. Johnson roused him as late as he dared before the squadrons paraded for stand-to.

'Are there no orders for the pursuit?' he asked as he took the canteen of coffee (the beans were Johnson's sole find in the inn's cellars).

There were none. And RSM Lincoln had disquieting news: there had been no contact during the night with Sir Hussey Vivian or his staff.

'Very well, then, RSM,' said Hervey resolutely as he rose

(stiffly), 'We must stand-to with extra vigilance lest there has been some unaccountable reverse since last light.'

'Shall I detail parties to search for our wounded, sir?'

Most of their losses had been on the ridge at Mont St-Jean: they would surely by now have been recovered. 'No, Mr Lincoln,' he concluded, 'I cannot spare even a dozen. We must trust to the medical services.' Had he but known that these were already overwhelmed, that the wounded were yet lying on the ridge – and that some would do so another night – he might have dispensed with all caution and taken the whole regiment back to scour for their fallen. 'Ask the RM to get the squadrons collecting loose horses, if you please, but not to venture beyond carbine-range: we shall need all the prize money we can lay in for widows' pensions.' The RSM saluted and made to leave, but Hervey had one more concern. 'Is Corporal Sandbache fit, Mr Lincoln?'

'Yes, sir,' he replied dubiously.

'Then, I wish him to read the burial service over Serjeant Strange; he is a preacher, is he not?'

Hervey made his rounds in silence, except for the briefest word here and there to warn for an outlying picket, and he held the squadrons a full quarter-hour beyond first light, for without knowledge of who else was about he would not risk an encounter with stragglers. There was a mood of numb relief about the Sixth. All they wanted to do was get away from this place, for never before had they halted where they fought, so that the sights, the sounds and the smell of the battlefield had remained with them as they lay, recruits and older hands alike unnerved by the strangeness of it. All night long there had been moaning and shouts for help. Those of the regiment who had not been called for duty, and who had slept soundly, had indeed been fortunate. Those who had stood sentinel would tell of the moaning, the cries, the screams, and the ghoulish sights which the moon had shone upon. They had seen men sitting clutching at a stomach ripped open by a sabre slash or a piece of shrapnel, one by one succumbing to death as their life-blood drained away. Others, less dreadfully injured, or possessed of some last strength, had risen and staggered off into the darkness, only to fall down again after a few steps. There were horses, too, that suffered no less, and claimed more pity by their helplessness. Some still lay with their entrails hanging out (and yet some of these would live), attempting to rise from time to time, only to fall back again in the manner of their fellow, human sufferers. And then, all strength spent, their eyes would close gently, there would be one last convulsive struggle, and their suffering would be at an end. All this as close, in places, as a dozen yards. Yet few, even the usual Samaritans, had dared to venture out of the lines that night, for there were too many roaming the field intent on evil business, and shots had punctuated the small hours as the wounded who tried to resist the looters were sent to join the dead.

He walked through the lines of tethered troop-horses, casting an eye over each to gauge their condition, and exchanging a word here and there with a dragoon who felt the need of something to say. It amounted to little, however, since the exhilaration of the gunfire and stirrup-charges had passed, and the reality – thinned ranks and lost comrades – was grimly apparent in the daylight. As he neared the in-lying picket-post the corporal (the ubiquitous Collins) rousted its troopers for a salute. 'Picket! Commanding officer approaching. *Pree*-sent . . . arms!'

Hervey glowered at him, but Collins returned the look with defiant pride. As far as *he* was concerned Hervey was commanding officer irrespective of rank: arms would be presented, not a mere butt-salute.

He left the bivouac and crossed the rutted road to see the ground over which they had fought with such resolve. Smoke still drifted in places, but to his left and right he saw clearly the shattered remains of Bonaparte's folly. Where, the day before, there had been magnificence – proud *cuirassiers*, fine horses, burnished guns, fluttering lance-pennants, the bear-skins of the Garde, eagles, tricolours, and everywhere 'Vive l'empereur' – there was now only desolation. Even the silence was melancholy. No wind, no rain – not even the skylark was tempted to song. Here and there a single shot rang out as a horse, too badly injured to be worth hobbling with to the meat-market, was put out of its protracted misery. And long, chilling screams, ending as abruptly as they had begun, reminded him that death, were it to come, were best to come quickly in his profession.

In the distance the sight was no less doleful, for on the slopes of the ridge at Mont St-Jean – the sea wall against which the French-blue waves had battered all day – was the red of Wellington's dauntless infantry. But they lay in lines rather than standing upright in squares. Was there so great a difference 'twixt a battle lost and this?

'De l'eau, monsieur – pour l'amour de Dieu, de l'eau,' cried one of Bonaparte's gunners, propped up against a limber wheel. His pipeclayed-white breeches were blood-darkened from the oozings of the slash across his chest – a slash which one of the Sixth's own troopers must have made. Hervey stooped to pick up a water-canteen from a gunner who no longer had need of it, and put it to the man's lips. The water trickled down his tunic, for he had not the strength to swallow, and he slumped to one side, eyes open in a look of bewilderment – yet stone-dead. Hervey closed them with his thumbs. 'Into thy hands O Lord . . . ,' he murmured.

He opened a pocket of the man's tunic to see who this soldier of France might be. Gaspard Juvenal, said his papers, from Saintes in the Charente-Maritime – a provincial Frenchman whose blood had flowed into foreign soil. Had he served these guns in the Peninsula? Had they met before in battle? Or had Gaspard Juvenal ventured even further from the Gironde, perhaps to Muscovy, and seen the basilicas of the tsar's capital?

'That 'un dead an' all, sir?' called an orderly, examining each body in what remained of the battery.

'Yes, just,' replied Hervey, more than ever conscious of the slender divide.

'No, I 'aven't found any alive this side of the road, either. Whoever caught these poor beggars was 'orrible neat with the sword. I reckon some over there is nought but into their teens.

What in God's name is Boney doing fighting with slips of boys, d'ye reckon, sir?'

Hervey almost sobbed, conscious that this was indeed the Sixth's handiwork. Instead he turned his remorse against the orderly, angered at being touched thus. 'They were old enough to fetch powder and put a portfire to a touch-hole if needs be,' he snapped.

'Ay, they were right enough, sir,' replied the man readily. 'Found ought worth anything on that one, sir?' he continued breezily.

The orderly would never know how close he came at that instant to knowing the same sabre that had made its accounts at the battery. Hervey bit into his glove. 'I have not searched him with any thoroughness,' he said curtly.

But still the man was not put off. 'Then, I'll have a look for meself, sir, if that's right by you.'

There was no regulation of which Hervey knew that prevented an orderly of the medical services from relieving the dead of their worldly possessions. It was, indeed, a consideration to many, who might otherwise have sought a less sanguinary billet with the commissaries.

'Wonder if this did him any good, sir,' said the man after a deal of rummaging, holding out a rosary.

Hervey cursed beneath his breath as the orderly threw it aside. 'I will have that, if you please,' he snapped.

'Right enough, sir,' came the cheery response, 'but it's not worth a ha'penny.'


When the orderly had finished his work Hervey walked over to the furthest gun and sat on the trail of its abandoned limber. He put his head in his hands and searched for a prayer that might transport him from the death and despoiling, and from the monstrousness of the orderly and his work. 'Lord, now lettest thou thy servant depart in peace . . .' he began. But his thoughts wandered. Which of these thousands lying before him had been His servants? 'For mine eyes have seen thy salvation,' he continued resolutely. Serjeant Strange had been his servant. And Lankester. And Edmonds, too, though he would never admit it. *Edmonds* – the major had been more to him than his own kin these past six years. He shuddered at the lonely prospect of soldiering without him. But Strange had been worthier than any, in the sight of the Almighty, surely. And yet he had not departed in peace. Would his death torment him for ever?

Only then did he remember the oilskin pouch that Strange had thrust at him on parting, and reached into the deep inner pocket of his jacket where it rested securely with his other keepsakes: Sister Maria's signet ring, d'Arcey Jessope's watch, and the prayer-book his father had given him. He took out the pouch and unfolded it carefully. There was a lock of grey hair in the first fold – Strange's mother's? Then a letter (Hervey would not open it), and then a miniature, whose likeness was obscure since water had at some time permeated its case. Small enough tokens of sentiment, he concluded, but perhaps no surprise from so taciturn a man as Strange. The doubts began to gnaw at him again. Had there been *no* other course but to leave him and gallop for the trees? He took out the prayer-book, hoping for some relief in its formularies (in the Thanksgiving perhaps) – 'For Peace and Deliverance from our Enemies'. 'O Almighty God,' he began, 'who art a strong tower of defence unto thy servants against the face of their enemies,' ('servants' again – service, obligation, duty: the words came crowding), 'we yield thee praise and thanksgiving for our deliverance from those great and apparent dangers wherewith we were compassed . . .'

'Mr 'Ervey sir!' The voice was its usual insistence. He turned to see Serjeant Armstrong striding towards him, looking to neither left nor right. 'The brigade-major's come. I told 'im to wait and said I'd fetch you meself. What are you doing out here? Who are you talking to?'

'Merely taking time to think, Serjeant Armstrong, that is all,' he replied.

'You don't want to be thinking. What's past is past – gone,' he insisted. ''Arry Strange did 'is duty, and that's it. We'll say some prayers over 'im in a minute or two with Preacher

Sandbache and then it's *on* for us. There's no place for contemplating till everything's over.'

Sir Hussey Vivian's new brigade-major (Harris had all but lost an arm after they had moved to the centre) seemed rattled. 'I may tell you, Hervey, that we have a brigade in name only,' he began, 'and the butcher's bill is prodigious. Uxbridge will be lucky to live, by all accounts: his leg was taken clean off. Vandeleur is given command, but there is to be no pursuit, for the army is not up to it. We are merely to follow on the Prussians in the event that Bonaparte turns, although I wager he is making for a ship this very instant. America, they say, will give him sanctuary.'

Hervey said nothing. Instead he rued his own ill-fortune: Uxbridge close to death, a man who might help him. And then he cursed himself for his thoughts.

'So the brigade is to march for Nivelles,' continued the BM. 'The Sixth are to lead – and none too quickly, if you please: as I said, we are not pursuing the French but following the Prussians. All we must do is get to Paris ere they break every window in the city!'

If Hervey had never before seen a battlefield the day after action, neither had he followed in the wake of a full-blown pursuit. The road to Nivelles was a trail of abandoned equipment, some of it no doubt jettisoned purposefully – baggage-waggons and the like, which could only hinder an orderly withdrawal. But much else betokened rout: small-packs, powder-horns, muskets and side-arms, the odd field-piece even. Nothing of value, however; for, vigorous though the Prussians must have been in their pursuit, all the signs of a systematic harvesting of booty were there – chests broken open and empty, bodies stripped and waggons like-wise. Occasionally they came across a clothed body – a Prussian dragoon or hussar – his sword thrust into the ground and his helmet on its pommel, the minimal honouring of the dead before the needs of the pursuit had driven his comrades on. In Nivelles that night the Sixth sold the prize-horses to a livery stables at well over the official price. Twelve hundred pounds for the relief fund. Hervey was well pleased, and the regiment's spirits began to revive with the issue of salt-beef and coffee (and the modest purchases of wine) as at last the commissary waggons caught up with them.

Subsequent entries in the regiment's journal would read like milestones along the high road to Paris: Charleroi, Maubeuge, Laon, Soissons. Sometimes there were unhurried halts; other times they marched through the night. But never did they see a Frenchman offering resistance. Except once. And for weeks afterwards their gallant allies were, in consequence, held in some disregard by the regiment. Already, indeed, the Prussians' wanton destruction *en route* was occasioning resentment. The duke's instructions for his own troops had been most particular in this respect, as they had been after the Pyrenees: he had even ordered that troops should only of necessity cross standing crops, and in single file. Yet the Prussians had put the torch to anything and everything.

And so, in the late afternoon of the last day of June, fewer than ten miles short of St-Denis in the very outskirts of Paris, the plight of a lone Frenchman brought the Sixth to anger. They had seen the small château some distance off. It stood in the middle of open pasture, a handsome-looking house but without any sign of life. Had it been later in the day the Sixth might have made their billet there, but instead Hervey determined only on a watering halt. As the point-troopers rode into the yard, however, a shot rang out from a lower window, devoid of all glass and shutterless. Both men turned at once for the cover of the walls, dismounting and snatching their carbines from the saddle-boots in which they had rested idly for all but a fortnight. Scarcely had they pulled cartridges from pouch-belts, however, than out from the doorless château came an old man in his nightshirt raving like a madman and waving a sabre wildly. The pointmen, sensing this was no serious resistance, clipped the carbines to their pouch-belts and drew their sabres instead. Disarming the defender of the château took but seconds, so that by the time Hervey and the forward detachment rode into the yard the old man was simply raving harmlessly. 'Je suis Bourboniste! Pourquoi vous me persécutez?' he was shouting.

Hervey dismounted. No one meant him any harm, he said: 'Est-ce que vous êtes seul ici, monsieur?'

The wild eyes darted about as more of the squadron came into the courtyard, and he glanced anxiously more than once towards the house, which bore the scars of what appeared to have been a brisk fight. 'Oui, oui!' he replied.

Hervey asked what fighting there had been around the château.

'Rien, monsieur, pas du tout,' he replied, and then his brow furrowed. 'Monsieur, vous n'êtes pas Prussiens?'

As soon as Hervey had convinced him that they were not, the old man relaxed visibly. The surgeon was summoned, and Hervey asked how he had sustained his head-wound, for blood matted his hair. 'Les Prussiens, monsieur,' he began: they had attacked him, taken everything that could be taken, destroyed the rest and then tried to burn the house down.

'Them is nowt but bloody fiends!' protested one of the troopers when Hervey translated.

He and Armstrong went into the château while the surgeon attended the old man. 'Christ, Mr 'Ervey,' gasped the serjeant, 'there's not a piece of glass not broken!' The shards were almost ankle-deep, the remains of fine chandeliers and mirrors shot to pieces. Furniture – evidently the less portable pieces – was now merely gilded matchwood. Velvet and brocaded curtains hung in tatters, flame-blackened, and the carpets were ingrained with excrement. In every room it was the same: from the top of the house to the kitchens, nothing remained undamaged, not a window or a door even. Except the door from the kitchen to what Hervey thought must be the cellar, which was firmly fastened though it looked as if it, too, had been off its hinges. 'Looks like the Prussians weren't partial to wine then, sir,' said Armstrong, shaking his head in disbelief.

'That hardly seems likely after what we have seen, do you not think?'

'Why's it locked then?'

'Well, I wager it was not locked, when they left.'

'You reckon the old man's hidden something in there, then?'

'Not some*thing*, Serjeant Armstrong, some*one*. Or more than one. Where is his family? Perhaps he sent them to Paris for safety, but how would he know there was any danger? No, I think the Prussians took him by surprise.'

Only with the greatest reluctance did the old man give up the keys, and he remained close by as they unlocked the heavy oak door. A light was burning below – more than enough to illuminate the occupants.

'Jesus Christ!' exclaimed Armstrong. Hervey shouted for the surgeon.

The terror in the girls' eyes was enough to relate what must have gone before, and their soiled white shifts testified to the violence of their ordeal. Hervey checked his instincts: he wanted somehow to reassure them, but he knew it was better to leave them to their father and the surgeon.

He and Armstrong picked their way once more through the debris of the great hall, this time without a word, but then Hervey grabbed him by the arm. 'See there!' he called, peering up at one of the corner bosses on the ceiling. All were peppered with bullet holes, but the decoration on one was still recognizable.

'See what?'

'See the device on that corner boss, and see here this,' he replied, taking the de Chantonnay ring from a pocket.

'It looks the same. Does that mean anything?' asked Armstrong indifferently.

'Well, a fleur-de-lis within a laurel wreath: it is the de Chantonnay seal, and I should say therefore that we were in a residence of the de Chantonnays.'

Armstrong shrugged. 'That didn't save them two lassies, did it?'

*  *  *

342

The vicomte de Chantonnay-Fougard fell to his knees, even amid the broken glass. 'Monsieur, c'est le travail du grand Dieu.' Gaining then his composure, he explained how he – the entire de Chantonnay family indeed – knew that the ring had been passed into the hands of an English officer after Bonaparte's defeat.

It was a little enough undertaking, replied Hervey.

But the family was indebted to him, protested the vicomte. And now he – a widower and cousin of the comte de Chantonnay – must impose once more on that Englishman and ask protection of him for his two daughters, for their safe conveyance to their aunt in Paris, 'au nom du roy et de Dieu, monsieur!'

Hervey thought a while. It was not possible for himself to escort them, he explained: there was not even a carriage in the mews. But he would leave a cornet and quaternion at the château, and once they reached Paris he would see that a carriage was sent for them.

'Vraiment les Anglais sont gentilhommes. Je vous remercie, monsieur. Je n'oublierai jamais cette gentillesse.'

But Hervey hoped he would forget soon enough what had occasioned the need of his gratitude, and resolved to make a beginning at once. 'Mr Lawrence!' he called into the court-yard, and up the steps came running the junior cornet, his fresh face and fair locks betraying barely seventeen years – fewer, even, than the younger of the daughters. 'Mr Lawrence, you will choose three of the steadiest troopers – married men, if you can – and Corporal Sandbache, and you will make these people as comfortable as you can. Do you have any French?'

'A little, Hervey . . . *sir*, I mean.'

'Then, speak softly to the vicomte, here, and clean up a room so that his daughters at least may try to regain some modesty. Place each man upon his honour and that of the regiment. They are to be as your own sisters, Lawrence – do you understand?'

'Perfectly, sir. I am sorry you doubt me,' he added, more puzzled than offended.

Hervey sighed. 'I am sorry, William. It is just that an outrage such as this . . .'

Armstrong, however, did not scruple: 'Mr Lawrence sir, just tell whichever bastards you pick – and that goes for Preacher Sandbache, too – that they'll have me to answer to if one of them so much as looks at them lassies!'

*Paris, 20 July*

Hervey had remained in command a full three weeks. The regiment had arrived in Clichy at the beginning of the second week in July, and he had at once put them to the routine of a garrison, where comforts were bought only at the price of tedious proximity to headquarters. He was not, in most respects, greatly exercised, but one concern in particular was beyond his capability to deal with: the speculation in commissions to which the casualty lists had given rise. Indeed, he was convinced that the regiment might soon have officers on paper only, so brisk was the trade purported to be. His relief, therefore, when Lord George Irvine resumed command was palpable. And he welcomed even Adjutant Barrow's return from his sickbed in Brussels ('I were getting nicely used to it,' Barrow lamented. 'Silk sheets and fine ladies with china teacups. Treated as quite the gentleman, I were'). Lord George would know how best to spike the trade, and all Hervey now hoped was that his conduct during his brief tenure of command might be deemed worthy for the stop on promotion to be removed. Of the army's prize-money his share as a lieutenant amounted to about £35, of which half, by custom, would go to regimental alms, leaving just enough to replace his losses of uniform and camp-stores. He still had not the means to purchase a captaincy.

But *would* his command be deemed worthy? Who might know that he had led the squadrons in the final hour, that he had brought them to Paris? Vivian and Vandeleur would have seen nothing out of the ordinary; Lord Uxbridge was already invalided home, and replaced once more by Sir Stapleton Cotton. The fortunes of war seemed perverse in the extreme.

The summons to Cotton's headquarters (or, rather, to Lord Combermere's, for so he had been ennobled after Spain) came therefore as a harbinger of hope. Yet what might Combermere have to say to him that Lord George Irvine might not? All that Lord George knew was that Combermere apparently wished to question him on some aspect or other of the battle.

'Mr Hervey, how our paths do cross!' began the general, holding out his hand. The room, in the Place Vendôme, had a more spartan look than Hervey had imagined on entering the building. 'You have had quite a time these past few weeks, I understand.'

'I think all would say that they have been momentous weeks, sir,' he replied guardedly, for there was not enough in Combermere's proposition from which to infer that he judged *his* time to have been singular.

'Just so, Mr Hervey; just so. And I may tell you how keenly I feel the want of those weeks: it was by no choice of mine, however, that I remained in England. But that is no matter,' he continued, handing him several sheets of paper. 'Here, my boy, I wish you to read this and tell me if in general terms it is accurate. Sit down, if you please.'

Hervey took the papers and began to read. The first paragraph made his heart pound. By the end it was racing, and he struggled hard to maintain an even tone in his reply. 'It is completely accurate, sir – in its facts, that is. The opinions expressed are, of course, Lord Uxbridge's.'

'They may be Lord Uxbridge's, my dear boy, but I warrant they would be shared by any who knew the facts,' said Combermere with a smile. 'Wait here one moment,' he added, leaving the room by a side door.

Some minutes later he reappeared, still smiling: 'The duke wishes to have words with you. Come!'

The commander-in-chief's room was, if anything, even

more spartan than his cavalry commander's; but he, too, smiled readily as Hervey entered, and stood to offer his hand. 'Sit, if you please, Mr Hervey. Will you have some coffee, or chocolate – or perhaps you would prefer Madeira?' he asked, gesturing towards an ADC standing by for the purpose.

Hervey saw no reason for restraint: 'Chocolate, if you please, your Grace.'

'Now,' began the duke, after waiting for the ADC to leave. 'Lord Uxbridge has sent me a long dispatch from his sickbed, and in it he recounts the signal part that you played in bringing the Prussians to the field at Waterloo. And Baron Müffling has acquainted me with the advice you gave to Prince Blücher. It was well judged, Mr Hervey – very well judged, for their opening fire, even at so extreme a range, gave notice of hostile intent and thwarted Bonaparte's stratagem.' The duke paused and took a sip of his coffee. 'What you do *not* know, in all probability, is that the French will to fight appears to have been dealt a mortal blow thereby, for since they believed the firing to be coming from Grouchy's men the word spread rapidly that Grouchy had turned traitor. Bonaparte was hoist well and truly with his own petard. You may have conceived, on your own account, that the battle was a near-run thing, Mr Hervey. Well, indeed it was – the closest-run thing you ever saw!' The duke paused again to sip some more. Hervey was transported with pride, scarcely able to contain his anticipation of the recognition which this audience must be presaging. '*Now*,' continued the duke, with a cautionary inflection which brought up short Hervey's flight of fancy, 'this all amounts to a situation of some delicacy. You may be aware that although Prince Blücher and I share the very best of relations, it is not quite that way with General von Gneisenau. Indeed, in the very highest matters of state things are not as they should be.'

Hervey nodded his understanding.

'I very much regret, Mr Hervey, that I dare not make any recognition of what transpired with the Prussians at Waterloo, and therefore of your part in it. We must not say anything which in the least part suggests that the Prussians did not make all speed, and of their own volition. And that they fired on debouching from the forest entirely out of their ardour to engage the enemy. I must swear you to absolute confidence in this matter: it is known to but a handful of people.'

'I understand, sir,' he replied, almost choking on the words.

'One more thing, Mr Hervey,' continued the duke, his expression now as intense as when they had first exchanged those few words at the convent in Toulouse. 'Your service to the de Chantonnays. I am well pleased to learn that my instructions to protect the civil population have been so punctiliously observed.'

Hervey returned the look quizzically.

'The de Chantonnays are staunchly Bourbon. My chief of intelligence, Colonel Grant, has much cause to praise their assistance these several past years. Am I to understand, too, that you have in your safekeeping a ring for the count?'

'That is so, sir.'

'And do you bear it with you, this instant?'

'I do, sir,' he replied.

'Then I think you may soon be able to discharge your obligation in that respect. Colonel Grant will be able to take you to the count: he is here, in Paris. And now, my boy,' he declared, rising and holding out his hand, the smile once more returned, 'you have my thanks again, and I wish you good fortune: I am certain you shall have it!'

In Lord Combermere's office, with more chocolate, Hervey tried to reconcile his exhilaration and disappointment.

'What precisely did the duke say at the end?' asked the general.

'He thanked me – and wished me good fortune, I think, sir.' He could scarcely remember the flow of things, let alone the exact words.

'There was no mention of . . . *reward*?'

'None that I recall, sir; no, none whatever.'

Lord Combermere looked surprised, though Hervey did

not notice. 'Lord George Irvine tells me he is to send you back to England with papers for your colonel. I should be very much obliged if you would deliver this to the adjutant-general at the Horse Guards: it is of a routine but sensitive nature, as I understand,' he said, holding up a sealed dispatch, 'and this other to Lord George, please. I will apprise you generally of its contents: it commends your service at Waterloo, without mentioning anything of the Prussians, and expresses the duke's hope that you might be advanced in regimental seniority or suchlike. I am sure these things augur well for the future, Mr Hervey.' And with that, and a warm handshake, Lord Combermere bade him farewell.

Hervey rode back to Clichy more thoroughly confounded than he supposed he had ever been. He presumed this express wish of the duke's must annul all bars to his captaincy, but Combermere had not mentioned anything of field promotion. And, since he was no nearer possessing the amount required for its purchase, the prize looked distinctly hollow. He had never expected garlands for what he had done, but their absence after the promise implied in the duke's eulogy he felt cruelly.

### The Following Day

Colonel Grant was an unlikely-looking spymaster. His features seemed too distinct, his gait too obviously military and his voice too loud. But of his business there was, by all accounts, no greater practitioner, and if the duke had felt himself humbugged by Bonaparte's essay into Belgium, then not one portion of blame would he allow this gallant officer to bear. The colonel arrived at ten o'clock at the billets of the 6th Light Dragoons and, to intense speculation among those officers who recognized him, he and Hervey left by carriage for the house near the Tuileries which was the Paris residence of the comte de Chantonnay. Footmen attended their arrival, and Hervey was at once spellbound by the sumptuousness – the fine paintings, hangings, crystal, and gilded furniture, unaccountable survivors of both the revolution and the recent occupation. And he could not but wonder at Sister Maria de Chantonnay's willing exchange of all this for her frugal orders. There was champagne, Neapolitan confections – and music.

'Do you like Soler, monsieur?' enquired the count in the clearest of English.

'If this be his music, then, yes, but—'

'Spanish – he was Spanish, and a Franciscan. Perhaps that is why he writes with such beauty and lightness of touch. Better even than Scarlatti, do you not think? Do you hear those *appogiaturas*?'

Hervey nodded admiringly as the bewigged musician ran breathtakingly up and down the scales of the eight-octave harpsichord in the corner of the *grand salon.*

'My daughter would approve only of Bach, however,' added the count with mock despair. 'His music is *much* more attuned with her Carmelite austerity!'

'Well, Mr Hervey,' interrupted Colonel Grant, 'perhaps it would be appropriate now for you to return the ring to the count?'

Hervey made to take the ring from his pocket, but then paused. He looked at the two men awkwardly and swallowed hard. 'Forgive me, monsieur,' he began, 'but I swore a solemn oath that I would give it only into the hand of the comte de Chantonnay himself.'

The count looked puzzled, and Colonel Grant impatient. 'Mr Hervey, do you suppose that I, as the duke's—?'

'No, sir, I do not suppose anything. And that is why I must not suppose an identity without its first being reasonably established.'

Colonel Grant flushed with anger, but the count stayed him: 'No, no – it is well that Mr Hervey is so conscientious in the discharge of his oath. I may assure you that my daughter will have placed the heaviest of obligations on him in this respect. What may I do to convince you that I am my daughter's father, sir?'

Hervey hesitated. 'I, that is . . .'

'Perhaps you might take her own assurance?' suggested the count.

Hervey looked blank at the notion.

'Be so good as to ask mademoiselle to join us,' said the count to his footman.

A clock began chiming the eleventh hour, and, before it had finished, the footman returned.

'Good morning, Mr Hervey!' Sister Maria's voice commanded an end to their polite talk. She smiled full and warm as she strode towards him across the *grand salon* and embraced him unselfconsciously. 'I am glad to see you safe. From all that we have heard your life has been in very great danger.'

He did not suppose that she could have had any notion of the particulars, so he replied with a simple 'We were fifty thousand in the most grievous danger, Sister'.

She smiled again: that was what she would have supposed him to say. It was a smile he had seen many times in Toulouse. And at first, indeed, there seemed nothing about her appearance different from that morning at the Convent of St Mary Magdalen when they had said their farewells. She wore the same habit of black homespun. There was the same stark white wimple that framed her face at their every meeting, and the veil that fell around her shoulders, in the way that Caithlin O'Mahoney's hair fell about hers. And yet there was about her a different sort of composure from that which he had formerly admired.

'*Ma fille*,' the count interrupted, 'perhaps Mr Hervey would like to see the garden.'

The garden, or gardens (for there were three distinct ones: an Italian – geometric, with elegant little fountains; another owing something to the south of the country, with terracotta pots everywhere; and one decidedly English), was uncommonly quiet. The noise of the street was excluded and, at this time, with the sun high and its heat growing, there were few birds with any inclination for singing. Hervey and Sister Maria walked for a quarter of an hour, first in the Italian and then in the Provençal garden, she pointing to some feature and then he to another. They spoke little of the year that had passed. There was so much that might be said, yet Hervey sensed their time together was short, and for his part he could not thus aspire to relate anything of substance. When they reached the English garden he thought it time they should return to the house, conscious that Colonel Grant remained there waiting.

'Well, Sister,' he began, 'I am gratified that I have been able to discharge my obligation to you, and to find you in such manifest good spirits. I believe, however, that I must now take my leave of you: you will understand that there are pressing matters to be about.'

Sister Maria evidently did not consider any matters to be ultimately too pressing. 'You are right,' she said, 'I am in good spirits. I am at peace with God and restored to my family: there is nothing more I could desire. But you, I perceive, are not in such spirits. Something troubles you.'

Hervey recoiled at the intrusion, just as he had the first time in Toulouse. 'Nothing troubles me, Sister,' he said briskly, making some unnecessary adjustment to his sword-slings and turning towards the house.

'Mr Hervey,' she insisted, 'I am sorry that one year has put this distance between us.'

Her words halted him in mid-stride. He did not wish to share his thoughts with anyone now that he had been able so firmly to place them at the back of his mind (or so he thought he had placed them). Serjeant Armstrong had upbraided him for brooding that morning after the battle, and he had been careful since to avoid any such occasion for censure. But he could not pretend that this woman had no sensibility of his disquiet when she so clearly had, nor that their former vocal intimacy was erasable. He sighed. 'Sister Maria, there is hardly time to begin to explain the circumstances, but I have on my conscience the death of a brave man. My head tells me that it should be otherwise, but not my heart. I should wish, perhaps, to tell you more, but I sail for England shortly. Time is truly pressing.'

'Very well, Mr Hervey,' she conceded, turning with him for the house, 'we cannot speak of it, but I urge that you do so when you return to your country. I have been studying your prayer-book – the one you gave me. It is – how do you say – *très contestataire*?'

'*Disputatious*?' suggested Hervey.

'Yes, *disputatious*. But no matter. In its exhortation before mass – or *communion* as you say – the priest invites him that cannot quiet his own conscience to go to him for absolution. Do you know such a priest that might, as well as pronounce absolution, give just counsel in this?'

'Yes, I do,' he replied wearily.

'Then, you must see him with no more delay than is strictly necessary for your other duties.'

Hervey agreed.

'And now, before you go,' she smiled, 'my father wishes to make some small gesture of our gratitude. Come!'

Later he would regret, much, that their tryst was so brief. Yet in that brief meeting she had again given him a certain peace, and strengthened his resolve on a course additional to priestly absolution (though she could not know it). And he was glad when she said that she would be remaining in Paris, for when he returned he could take up her invitation to visit at the Carmelite house in the city whence she was appointed.

### That Afternoon

'You appear to have made a most felicitous connection, Hervey. Grant tells me that Count Chantonnay has more influence with Louis Bourbon than Condé even,' said Lord

George Irvine as they sipped Madeira after a light luncheon of calf's tongue followed by early strawberries brought from Provence. 'Let me see that bauble again.'

Hervey handed him the velvet-covered case.

'A fleur-de-lis within a laurel wreath – and those are without doubt the finest emeralds. And prettily fixed on that sky-blue ribbon, too. It should set off your levee dress handsomely!'

'It is a family order, sir, approved of the Court by long custom, the count informed me. He was insistent that I should receive it.'

'Of course, of course,' smiled Lord George. 'I am sure the prince regent will not be ill-disposed to the notion of a foreign decoration's adorning one of his officers. Envious, perhaps, but not ill-disposed. And a touching reunion with your nun was had, I understand?'

Hervey would not be drawn. 'She is a remarkable woman.'

'And you will leave for England this night?'

'Immediately after the service of memorial for Captain Jessope,' he replied, at once heavy.

'Jessope? Lord Fitzroy Somerset's aide-de-camp? He is killed too? I did not know it. I wish in God's name we might see a list soon. Lord Fitzroy himself is not long for this world, too, by all accounts. Jessope dead! I cannot say I knew him well – I met him but infrequently at White's – but an engaging officer, though. And you knew him?'

'Imperfectly,' replied Hervey softly, hoping that Lord George would not dwell on it – which he did not.

'Your captaincy, however,' demanded his commanding officer peremptorily. 'What are we to do?'

'As I said, sir, it is wholly beyond my means; it would not do to delay selling any longer – Anson's widow will need an annuity.'

'Be that as it may, Hervey, I will not send the papers to Craig's Court until we reach England. Have you *no* prospects, of *any* sort?'

'None, I am afraid, sir!'

Lord George sighed pointedly. 'Mr Hervey, let me speak

plainly with you. Are you not to marry the ward of the Marquess of Bath?'


*Whitehall, 27 July*


The troopers of the Blues, standing mounted sentinel at the gates of the Horse Guards, brought their heavy-cavalry-pattern swords from the shoulder to the carry as Hervey got down from the carriage and walked between them, returning the salute with his right hand. He would have preferred the anonymity of plain clothes but he had thought it fit to wear undress instead so that he might gain entry to the Duke of York's headquarters with more expedition. He touched his forage cap to the two dismounted sentries at the inner archway and entered the building through an unimposing door in the side-arch. Within, an orderly directed him up the stairs to the adjutant-general's department where he was received (rather distantly, he thought) by a civilian clerk. 'Please be seated Mr . . . ahm . . . Hartley. We shall attend you forthwith.'

Hervey sat on a bench comfortably upholstered in buttoned green leather and picked up the copy of *The Times* of that day which lay on an adjacent table. He turned to its inside pages and studied the consolidated list of officers who had died at, or since, the battle. He knew more names than he did not. He read reports by special correspondents on the movements of the Militia along the south coast, the condition of the forces in Canada, and the occupation in Paris. He read a summary of the parliamentary debates on flogging, and his bile rose on seeing the persuasion of so many as to its supposed efficacy. All news and opinion devoured, he then turned to the front page to amuse himself with the personal notices: 'A SINGLE GENTLEMAN wishing to domesticate in a genteel private family. . . ; A RESPECTABLE young person WANTS A SITUATION as BAR-MAID . . .' (he had to read this a second time); 'RESPECTABLE officer's daughter wishes for a situation as a companion . . .' (a fate he feared for Edmonds's daughters). And when even these had exhausted his attention he looked at his watch – the same which Jessope had given him, restored by the skill of a Paris horologist – and enquired of the clerk why there should be such a delay in accepting a dispatch from Lord Combermere.

'I beg your indulgence, Mr Harley, we have so much to be about in the wake of events on the Continent,' the clerk replied.

He turned to the back-page sales: 'A PAIR of handsome BROWN CHARIOT or CURRICLE GELDINGS, 15 hands 2 inches high . . . ; THIRTY very clever, active, well bred, seasoned MACHINE HORSES, in high condition, mostly young . . .'

Up and down the columns he went, from 'valuable collection of paintings' to 'singularly elegant gothic cottage'. They occupied him another half-hour, and still there was no activity in the clerk.

'Now, see here,' he began, putting down the paper noisily, 'I have urgent regimental business to be about. Will you kindly present that dispatch to the adjutant-general now so that I may be released to attend to it.'

'Mr Hurley,' replied the clerk, with an indulging smile, 'papers arrive from Paris every day, hourly at times. If your letter were urgent, it would be marked as such. You are merely a courier, sir!'

'Courier be damned!' he stormed. 'I have the welfare of brave men's widows, and much else besides, to be about. If you will not so much as have the courtesy to read the letter, then I shall not wait hereabouts!'

He stalked out of the headquarters and marched angrily across the parade ground even as guardsmen were drilling there, reaching the middle of St James's Park before his anger began to subside. What had become of things? he railed. The nation seemed driven by self-important clerks for whom tallies and ledgers, copying and filing were ends in themselves.

It was early evening, almost a week later, that he stepped down from the Yarmouth-to-London stage at the crossroads near Southwold. So much had passed since his dismal time at the Horse Guards. The Earl of Sussex, whom he had called on shortly afterwards, had been solicitude itself. The earl, not yet an old man but whose service with the Duke of York in Flanders twenty years before had ended with a broken hip, had been at once animated by the prospect of finding new officers for his regiment. And in Norwich, where it was his business to settle the regimental estate of Joseph Edmonds, he had found the major's widow and two daughters in uncommon spirits and a very safe distance from destitution. But, unappealing though the prospect of Norwich had been, he anticipated that Southwold would be an altogether more formidable ordeal.

There should have been a chaise, or at least a van, from the town waiting at the crossroads, but there was not another soul in sight. As far as the eye could see in the direction of Southwold there was desolate marsh, and the forlorn calls of the curlew accentuated the eerie emptiness. In the other direction there was open heath, with scarcely a tree, and those that there were leaned to landward, bent half-way to the ground by the wind which often as not drove in from the sea. The coach-driver, anxious because hay-waggons had made him almost thirty minutes late on this stage, asked if Hervey would take charge of some packages for merchants of the town. 'Daren't wait no longer, zur,' he explained in Suffolk vowels more pronounced than Serjeant Strange's. 'Anything from Southwold'll 'ave to wait till tomorrow. There should be summat along soon.'

Hervey understood the driver's impatience full well: his pay would be docked if he were late at Ipswich, and there would be little chance of making up any more time along this road, as yet unmacadamized, and with a team already blowing. In truth he was glad of the peace of this lonely crossroads for a while, where he might compose his thoughts in respect of

Widow Strange. Not that she would have been aware of that status; for, while Margaret Edmonds might learn from an express or even *The Times* of her husband's death, Strange's widow would have no such notification. He had contemplated writing to her, but with no knowledge of whether she might be capable of reading he had demurred and resolved on this call.

A mile or so across the marshes, in the direction the stage now took, stood Blythburgh church, rising from the wetlands with all the grandeur of a cathedral, testimony to the county's former wool-wealth. Wealth long past, he knew. Now it was fishing and little else, although the war had brought additional business by way of the new naval establishments along the coast – victualling yards, hospitals, signalling stations. But he did not suppose the Strange family would have much of it.

After a quarter-hour a growler came up from the direction of Southwold and the driver began a litany of apologies before even the brake bound on. Immense was his relief when Hervey assured him that it mattered not at all and that he had the packages from the London coach. Minutes later, the parcels and his portmanteau safely stowed, they set off at a trot towards the little fishing town. 'Only a couple of miles, that's all, zur,' began the driver, 'but it's a bugger when the tide's 'igh 'cos the stream 'tween us and the town gets up and the old 'orse 'e doesn't always like it!'

Hervey sympathized. 'Do you know of a family called Strange?' he added. 'A fisherman, I believe.'

'Peter Strange?'

'I do not know his Christian name. He had a son . . .' Hervey checked himself. 'His son enlisted in the Army.'

'Well, there is but one Strange in Southwold, zur – or, rather, there *was* one Strange. Old Peter died last month. Have you come all this way to see 'im then?' he asked in amazement.

'Not exactly.'

'Terrible sad, it were. Alice Strange, old Peter's wife of nigh on fifty years, died in May an' old Peter just seemed to give up all will to go on. That daughter-in-law of theirs never left 'is side these past three months, but weren't to no avail: she 'ad to bury 'im, too.'

'Where is Mrs Strange now, then?' asked Hervey.

'Bless me, zur, in 'eaven for sure – an' Peter, too, for they were fine God-fearing folk.'

For all the solemnity Hervey found it hard not to smile.

'I meant their daughter-in-law,' he explained gently.

The driver looked at him quizzically. 'You know the family, then, zur?'

'No, I do not, but I have news of Serjeant Strange.'

'*Serjeant!* By, that young lad 'as done well. Oi knew 'e would, mind: never a braver man on an oar with a gale blowin'. Reckon 'e would 'ave joined the Navy 'ad 'e not seen 'is two brothers drown out in the bay. Said 'e wanted t'ave nothin' to do wi' the sea after that, did young 'Arry. Oi'm glad 'e 'as done well, though.'

'Yes,' said Hervey softly, 'he did well. Where might I find Mrs Strange?'

The driver's directions were precise, and Hervey tipped him a half-crown after alighting at the Swan hotel in the centre of town – a place, the driver was anxious to assure him, that was most appropriate for someone of Hervey's rank. And in exchange for this handsome tip the driver swore not to reveal the purpose for which Hervey was in Southwold, and to be outside the Swan at nine the following morning to take him the mile or so to the Strange cottage at the harbour inlet.

He slept better at the Swan than perhaps he had since those exhausted few hours at La Belle Alliance. The sea air was clean and invigorating. At Yarmouth, where he had spent the previous night, there had been a stench of putrefying fish which had forced him to close the windows of his room, and his doubts about leaving Strange to the French lancers had again returned to haunt him through the small hours. Armstrong had absolved him from all blame, as Lord George Irvine had. Even RSM Lincoln had given him his opinion that no other course had been possible. But ultimately there was, he knew, but one power to absolve (excepting, of course his Maker, to whom he must answer in the final account), and that was the woman for whom his widow-making had the most direct consequence. Would she comprehend anything of military necessity, though? Throughout the journey from Yarmouth he had turned it over and over in his mind. The closer he got to Southwold the greater was his dread, and the heathland through which the coach trundled, its scrubby bushes and sparse trees reminiscent of the landscape of Flanders, did nothing to quieten it.

At nine the following morning the growler drew up at the Swan, and in ten minutes he was in the little estuary harbour which was abuzz with the activity that high water brings. The Strange cottage was even smaller than he had imagined, and smoke rising from the chimney told him there was now no escape from his self-imposed act of contrition. He dismissed the driver with a shilling, saying that he would walk back to the inn, and then looked about him for a moment or so before approaching the door. He was glad that he had decided against presenting himself in uniform, for though it would have given him some . . . *authority*, some status of disinterest perhaps, it would surely have alerted so insular a community to the Widow Strange's misfortune (she might at least enjoy the liberty to reveal her unhappy news in her own time). His dark-blue coat might, however, make him pass harmlessly for any profession.

He had thought carefully during the weeks since Waterloo about what he should say. With Margaret Edmonds there was the consolation of knowing that, as a loyal follower of the drum, she would understand. Of wives of enlisted men . . . he simply had no knowledge. Those few who had been in Spain had, like the gypsies and squatters on Warminster Common, been inhabitants of another world, and the regiment had been in Ireland scarcely long enough for the picked men to bring wives into quarters there. Yet there was something about his expectations in the case of Strange's wife that he could not fathom, though it had exercised him to no little degree. For in the pouch which Strange had handed him, just before turning to face the lancers, there was a letter, and though he had not read it he saw that the handwriting was very fine. There was, too, a miniature, but water had at some stage permeated the oilskin and the likeness was obscure.

He knocked at the door. It was opened by a woman of thirty years (perhaps fewer) in a black crêpe dress, her long black hair tied up with a black ribbon and jet slides. All his preparation was suddenly to no avail. 'I . . . that is, would you be Mrs Strange?' he stammered.

'Yes,' she replied, with the rising note which turned the simple affirmation into a question.

'Mrs Strange,' he began, trying hard to recall the sequence of information he had practised, 'I am Lieutenant Hervey of the Sixth Light Dragoons, your husband's regiment.'

He paused. She looked at him coolly. Would any officer bring ought but bad news? 'He is dead?' she asked simply.

Standing in the open door of a cottage on a busy quayside was not how Hervey had imagined this would be. 'I am very sorry but it is so, Mrs Strange. May I come in?'

She listened in silence as he recounted the events of 18 June. He had resolved beforehand that he would attempt to explain the significance of what her late husband had done, notwithstanding his oath of silence to Wellington, for surely a widow deserved no less. And, further, if she did not grasp the significance of their mission that day, then she could not be expected to understand why he had abandoned her husband. And without understanding how might she be expected to absolve him?

'Would you like some tea, Mr Hervey?' she asked at length.

He was pleased to accept, for it seemed that such a gesture might indeed betoken some understanding. It offered him, too, the opportunity to consult the notes he had made previously, yet without which he had so far had to conduct this most difficult of counsels. Her calmness, her dignity, had all but dumbfounded him. He had heard of soldiers' widows seizing knives and having to be restrained from doing themselves injury. But Mrs Strange had received the news as well – better even – than Margaret Edmonds. And she had called him *Mr*, not Lieutenant. Here, indeed, was a sign of some . . . cultivation, some knowledge of affairs. She spoke, too, without Strange's Suffolk accent. She spoke without *any* accent. An educated, rather than a refined, voice but alien, surely, to the fishermen's wharf? Strange had been a fine-looking man, of that there was no doubt. What might he have been – forty? forty-five? But she was *so* much younger, and in different society Hervey might even have called her beautiful. She had cheekbones as high as the most fashionable of the ladies he had seen in Paris – as high as Henrietta Lindsay's. Large brown eyes, set perfectly apart, had the look of warmth and intelligence. Her hair, though he thought it certain never to have had the attention of a lady's maid, shone with hale condition.

He found his place in his notes. 'There will be a little money, Mrs Strange – not a lot, I fear. It is customary when a soldier dies for his companions to auction his personal effects, and they by tradition bid generously. Many of his possessions are still in Ireland, of course, but those he took with him into the field have raised a little over forty pounds.'

'That is a worthy sum,' she conceded.

'There is also the prize-money for Waterloo.'

She looked puzzled.

'After a battle the Army's agents assess the value of the enemy's equipment which has been captured,' he explained, 'and this is divided *pro rata*, that is to say—'

'I understand *pro rata*.' She said it kindly, though it did not prevent his feeling awkward.

'This amounts to £19 4*s* 4*d*,' he hastened, looking down at his notebook. 'There is regimental prize-money of £37 3*s* 8*d*, and arrears of pay amounting to £42 2*s* 3*d*. With various other payments, your late husband's estate amounts to £189 7*s* 8*d*. There is a full account here, Mrs Strange, and, if you feel able to sign this certificate, I have a banker's draft which will enable you to withdraw the money at any time.' He did not, however, explain that the 'various other payments' were his own share of the Waterloo prize-money.

'Mr Hervey,' she began, 'I am most touched that you yourself should have troubled to make this journey. I sense that you feel responsible to some degree for my husband's death, and that this might in some measure account for your coming to Southwold. I know nothing of battles, of course, but I do understand that judgements must be made in an instant and that afterwards there is infinite time in which to reappraise them. Is there any purpose in such reflection, though? I am greatly touched, too, that my late husband's fellow men should have been so generous in raising such an amount, and I should like very much to write and express that gratitude. Would you be able to take such a letter?'

'Yes, of course I would, ma'am.' *Ma'am* seemed as appropriate as if she had been—

'Oh,' she then added distractedly, 'but I have no writing paper.'

'There is writing paper at the Swan hotel, where I am staying, Mrs Strange. You would be most welcome to dine there and to write your letter before, or subsequently, in peaceful surroundings.'

She seemed relieved. It was curious, he thought, how things of little consequence assumed such importance at these times (Margaret Edmonds had been likewise distressed at having sent away her cook for the day).

'I shall dine at three, then, for I intend walking by the sea a while, with your leave, ma'am.'

He walked by the sea for three hours. And he swam, too. It had been close on eight years since he had swum in the sea, and on the last occasion – at Corunna – he had done so for his life. The peace of the day (for the beach was empty but for seabirds), and Mrs Strange's absolution, now contrived in him such contentment that he could not otherwise remember, and he lay in the warm sun and thought of Henrietta (and a homecoming that few could hope to enjoy) until it was time to return to the Swan.

At five past three the chaise he had sent for her drew up to the inn, and Mrs Strange stepped down. Hervey met her at the door, and they went straight to the Swan's dining room, a place of some elegance, if a little old-fashioned by the standards he had lately seen in Paris. Mrs Strange made some admiring remark of the furnishings: though she had lived in Southwold for fifteen years, this was her first essay to the hotel. This intrigued him, for it seemed likely that a woman of her refinement might at least have taken tea there even if money for anything more substantial had been wanting. 'It is only that temperance denied us access, Mr Hervey,' she revealed when he pressed her.

She studied the bill of fare intently, and, with her eyes so occupied, Hervey found himself admiring her form. She wore a dress of cotton velvet (green, not mourning), even though the day was warm. Its waist was lower than was the fashion – lower, indeed, than had been the fashion for some years – yet it was unquestionably a dress made by a skilled seamstress. Its neck was high, and she wore a necklace of jet. She was fuller-bosomed, fuller-mouthed than Henrietta, and she put him in mind of a portrait on the grand staircase at Longleat House, a painting he had many a time gazed at as a boy – Reynolds's subject a picture of inaccessible allure.

'Do you have any family, Mrs Strange?' he asked as she looked up.

'No, Mr Hervey; my mother died many years ago and my father likewise almost seven years past, just after Corunna.'

'Why do you say Corunna, ma'am? It is an uncommon reference, is it not?'

'It was after Corunna that Harry came home to Southwold on furlough. He was a devout worshipper at the chapel of which my father was minister, as was his family. When my father died . . . well, I was quite alone; there was nowhere for me to go. Harry was a corporal and asked me to marry him. I think he did so out of kindness: we hardly knew each other.

He was the finest of men – strong, gentle, dutiful. I came to live with his parents and continued to teach at the school. These past two years, though, both his father and his mother have been largely unwell and I have spent all my time, in consequence, nursing them both. They were so good to me, it was no hardship – well, perhaps a little tiring.'

Hervey paused before putting to her the concern that now troubled him as a man as much as an officer. 'Forgive my directness, Mrs Strange, but how straitened will your circumstances be?' (With only two hundred pounds she might purchase an annuity of, say, fifteen pounds at most – hardly enough to keep even the cottage roof over her head. And it would go intolerably hard with such a woman.)

'I have some savings, sir: Harry sent home the major part of his pay, and there was a little family money. But I should not remain inactive even with sufficient income – though I will *not* be a governess. I used to keep my father's school before he became ill. I might do likewise again.'

To Hervey the solution was at once manifest. Not a fortnight before, he had received a letter from Elizabeth expressing her anxiety for her father's school, at her own inexpertise and the exhaustion it wrought in him. 'You find being a schoolma'am not objectionable, then, Mrs Strange?' he enquired.

'No, indeed, though there is little opportunity of an opening hereabout.'

'Just so,' he agreed. 'See here, Mrs Strange, my father is vicar of a small parish in Wiltshire. He is having great trouble in maintaining his school for the village children. My sister helps but cannot spare all the time that is needed. There is a cottage set aside for a schoolmaster, and although the stipend is very small I think it might be adequate. You are, I believe, the very sort of person my father has need of.'

'Mr Hervey,' she smiled, 'you are most kind, but you forget perhaps that my father was a dissenting minister. I hardly think it fitting for me—'

Hervey was undeterred, and stayed her protest. 'Mrs

Strange, my father has need of someone to instruct the children of the village in the elements of reading and writing, and in those of mathematics. I am sure that you can contrive to do that without offending against too many of the Thirty-Nine Articles!' he laughed.

'But I should be obliged to attend his church, should I not?'

'John Wesley would have approved of piety wherever he found it, think you not, ma'am? But there is, indeed, an independent chapel in the village if the parish church were not fulfilling.'

She laughed. 'I think we need not be so solemn! And how shall I apply for this position?'

'That much I can do for you myself,' he replied. 'When might you be able to take up those duties, ma'am?'

She thought for a moment. 'It will take me a week or so to conclude all that needs be done here,' she said, 'but then I should be ready. Sad as it will be to leave this place after so many years, it has now more unhappy memories than I should wish.'

' "Thou hast left thy father and thy mother, and the land of thy nativity, and art come unto a people which thou knewest not heretofore!" '

'The Moabitess?' she said, returning the smile. 'But Ruth had a Naomi from whom to draw strength, whereas I have not.'

He smiled again. 'You will at least find my sister agreeable, but I am afraid that for Horningsham it will be a long drive, Mrs Strange – first London, then Salisbury.'

'Or a pleasant cruise from here to Portsmouth perhaps?' she replied.

He laughed again. 'You are right, ma'am. I am but a landsman, and regard the sea only as a barrier.' He liked this keenness of wit. It reminded him of Caithlin. 'Mrs Strange, the day is warm and I have taken much exercise: would you find it offensive if I took a little hock?'

'Not in the least, sir,' she replied at once. 'And I, if I may, shall join you, for it was never by my own pledge that we were a temperance household, only out of respect for my family and then for Harry – which, I may assure you, is no less diminished now.'

'I did not suppose it for an instant, ma'am,' he replied.

# CHAPTER EIGHTEEN
# THE INTERESTS OF THE SERVICE

*Horningsham, Wednesday 9 August*

It was a little before ten o'clock, and the morning was already hot, when a coach drawn by two quality middleweight greys drew up to Horningsham vicarage. The horses were not fresh, their shoulders were in a lather and the dappling on their quarters was accentuated by prodigious sweating. The coachman himself looked no fresher, his face grimy and his shirt almost black with the dust of the road. Down from the carriage stepped a tall man in his mid-twenties wearing white breeches, court shoes and the long-tailed coat of a Foot Guards officer, for all the world looking as if he were alighting in St James's Palace yard to attend a levee. After stretching stiff limbs, brushing the dust from his shoulders and placing his cocked hat under his arm, he exchanged a few words with the coachman and walked towards the house. Vexed that no servant had appeared to assist with the horses, he was already disposed to some disdain of it. Here was no classical architect's expertise, for sure; rather, was it the haphazard work of successive country builders. The oriel window was quite fine, he conceded, and there was about it a quaint charm, but the house did not betoken a well-endowed living: of that he was certain. He pulled the bell rope at the door, self-consciously adjusted the aiglets on his right shoulder and waited for an answer. At length (too *great* a length, he considered), it was opened by Francis, stooping more than usually, who after the officer's introduction, which he did not fully hear, showed him into the vicar of Horningsham's modest library.

Francis was now in something of quandary, for the Reverend Thomas Hervey was at the school and his wife was with him. Elizabeth was taking a walk, and the only member of the family at home was engaged in what Francis judged to be an affair long overdue. This visitor from . . . (he had not quite heard) could not, in calling unannounced, presume upon him therefore. 'It may be some time before anyone is at home,' he said. To which the officer replied that he would wait indefinitely.

Meanwhile, in the drawing room, the overdue affair was reaching some conclusion. 'And that is why I am late in coming here,' explained Matthew Hervey. He was seated on a long settee, with Henrietta a further distance along it than he would have liked, and he was recounting, though not without interruption, his movements during the past momentous six weeks. 'Believe me, I should not have been spared from garrison duties in Paris had it not been for these other necessities.'

'Well, Matthew dearest,' began Henrietta with a wry smile, 'I should never have supposed that the profession of arms brought such intercourse, and with so *many* ladies of evident charm and accomplishments. It seems such a pity that the unhappy circumstances of these encounters should otherwise mar the enjoyment of them.'

He hesitated. There was no mistaking the challenge that her smile belied. 'Madam,' he began (for her name was still not habitual with him), 'do not think for an instant that . . .' But it would have been better had he hesitated a little longer before beginning, and then he might have finished his protest with resolution.

'Think *what*, sir?' she demanded, her eyebrows arched high. 'Think that you might take some pleasure in feminine company?'

'No . . . well, that is . . .' he stammered.

'*No*, you do not take such pleasure? Or *no*, I should not *think* it?'

There was a knock at the door, and Hervey could not conceal his relief when Francis appeared. 'Begging your pardon, Master Matthew and your Ladyship, but there is an officer waiting to see someone.'

'An officer?' asked Hervey uncertainly. 'To see me?'

'I don't rightly know, sir; I'm sorry as I didn't quite discern what the gentleman said.'

Hervey looked at Henrietta, who smiled. 'Perhaps, Matthew, if you were to receive him, his purpose might be revealed? I do not suppose it will be any great mystery.'

Francis announced their visitor with as much recall as he was able. The name 'Howard' was all that Hervey could glean from this fumbled introduction, but he knew him at once to be a lieutenant of Foot Guards and general's aide-de-camp. But he could not begin to imagine what might bring St James's to Horningsham. 'Good morning to you, Mr Howard,' he said, offering his hand, though the officer seemed a trifle reluctant to take it. 'How may we assist you?'

And equally reluctant did he seem to reveal his purpose, so that Henrietta, losing patience, felt it necessary to reassure him: 'Sir, do not suppose that I shall reveal the secrets of the Horse Guards to the French – or even to the people of Wiltshire!'

The officer cleared his throat awkwardly. 'Mr Hervey, you will recall delivering a dispatch from his grace the Duke of Wellington to the Horse Guards two weeks past?'

'Of course,' replied Hervey.

'And you did not await an acknowledgement.'

'No – I did not expect one.'

'*You* did not expect one, Mr Hervey? Were you not on his *grace's* business?'

'Not so; that is . . . not directly.' Even as he answered he felt a gnawing doubt. At the time his business seemed clear enough; now he was less certain. 'I was on an assignment as regards regimental affairs and carried the dispatch as a supplementary duty. The clerk at the Horse Guards showed no urgency to attend to it. I had other matters to be about.'

'Just so, Mr Hervey,' replied the officer coolly. 'I am

commanded to request that you accompany me to the Horse Guards immediately.'

A request by a senior officer, conveyed as it was by an ADC, was to all intents and purposes an order. A moment's impatience with the headquarters clerk and it had come to this: for an instant he supposed he might next be asked for his sword. Was it, he wondered, the curse of Slade?

'Immediately, did you say?' snapped Henrietta, making Hervey start almost as much as the officer. 'You must understand that it is quite impossible!'

'Madam,' he began, 'I understand that it might not be to your convenience, but I have the most explicit instructions to insist that Mr Hervey accompany me. The adjutant-general himself—'

'Sir, it is indeed no little inconvenience, for Mr Hervey and I are to be married this coming month!'

Hervey was dumbfounded. He looked at the officer with blank astonishment, and then again at Henrietta.

'Is that not what we were speaking of this very moment past, Matthew?' she challenged.

A minor commotion in the hall signalled the return of the vicar of Horningsham and his lady. Hervey's mother bustled into the drawing room with loud protests that her absence at the school had been in the ignorance of her visitor's calling. 'My dear,' she gushed to Henrietta, 'why did not you tell us you were to call – and today of all days when cook is at her sister's?'

'It is of no moment whatever, Mrs Hervey,' began Henrietta with a smile and a touch of the hand upon her arm. 'Matthew and I were met to discuss our arrangements.'

'Arrangements?' asked his mother.

Another commotion attended the return of Elizabeth, who swept into the room, pulling off her broad straw hat and throwing it on to a chair. 'Arrangements, did I hear *arrangements*?' she laughed.

The Reverend Thomas Hervey protested: 'That is what was said, and I dare say they are entirely private arrangements and no business of ours!'

Elizabeth, most unusually, now giggled. Her eyes twinkled, her mouth parted and her ringlets danced. The sun, despite the hat, had worked its usual way with her face, and freckles dotted her cheeks. The officer was staring at her when first she noticed him. Not awaiting any introduction she strode five full paces over to him and held out her hand. 'And you will be one of Matthew's friends?' she beamed. 'Only his serjeants call on us as a rule!'

The officer caught his breath as best he could, but not before Henrietta spoke to her enquiry. 'No, my dear – not a friend; for sure not a friend. He is come to take my future husband from me, and forcibly if necessary.'

Elizabeth hesitated (though showing no surprise at Henrietta's notice of marriage), and then narrowed her eyes to a fearsome challenge.

The officer who had at first disdained this provincial household was routed. He blushed and stammered an apology. 'I hope you will understand, ma'am,' he concluded.

'I have never heard of such a thing!' said Elizabeth, and with so much indignation as to make Hervey himself wince. 'I had always thought us too far ashore for the press-gang. Why must you take him?'

At which point Hervey's father thought fit to re-assert sovereignty in his own vicarage. 'I am afraid, sir, that our manners here are not what they might be in London. I am the Reverend Thomas Hervey, vicar of this parish; and this is my wife . . . ,' he continued, turning to Hervey's mother, who frowned and made a small bow, 'my daughter, Elizabeth . . . and my son, and my . . . ah, Lady Henrietta Lindsay,' he said, indicating each in turn.

'I am obliged, sir. Lord John Howard . . .' And he in turn bowed.

'Well, then, sir,' resumed Elizabeth, 'upon what necessity do you take our brother, son and soon-to-be husband from us all?'

'I am sorry, Miss Hervey, you will understand that the interests of the Service—'

'Do not you tell me about the interests of the Service, sir!'

she replied sharply. 'Do not you presume us to be so country-bred that we know nothing of affairs! My brother is only yesterday returned from the Continent, where he might have been killed on the field at Waterloo. Were *you* at Waterloo, sir?'

'Oh, Matthew, he was a stuffed shirt, a real cold fish. "The interests of the Service", indeed. Who does he think we are? What can be so important about that dispatch?'

Hervey had chided her the instant Lieutenant the Lord John Howard had taken temporary leave for the Bath Arms (where he hoped to find a tub in which to soak, and horses for their immediate return). No entreaty by Hervey's father had been able to persuade him to take his refreshment at the vicarage. Instead it had been agreed that he would return at two to begin their journey to London – for such was the address, he insisted, with which he had been enjoined to act.

'I think it must be a serious matter,' conceded Hervey to his sister, though with little more than a frown. 'I have clearly misjudged things, but' – a smile overcame him – 'I do not much care, for Henrietta and I are resolved to marry the instant I return. She declares she will brook no more absence!'

'But *how* serious do you suppose it might be, Matthew?' asked his father. 'What could be the nature of the complaint against you?'

'Well, sir, what I suppose is this: that there is some message which waits upon my return to France. I dare say there will be another month or so's duty in Paris – that is all.'

'And for this their lordships would send an officer from London?' he replied doubtfully.

Hervey merely lifted an eyebrow.

The fresh pair of livery horses brought from Warminster took the carriage at a good speed along the turnpikes. Repaired in the spring and not yet rutted by the autumn rains, the roads admitted comfortable progress and, thereby, easy conversation, but neither of the occupants of the carriage spoke a word. By six o'clock they were in Whitchurch, and the coachman hove in to a posthouse to water his team.

As they stepped down Howard broke the silence. 'Look, Hervey,' he began with a warmth in stark contrast to his earlier cool formality, 'this is very unsatisfactory for you. I was sent by General Calvert after a great deal of shouting in the commander-in-chief's office when the Duke of Wellington returned. I allowed my own vexation at having to be about this business to intrude upon my courtesies with your family. I fear they may not forgive it, your sister especially, and I had no right to presume your guilt in the matter, either. I beg your pardon.'

'Thank you, Howard, but it is no matter,' replied Hervey with a shrug. 'I was unquestionably hasty in leaving the Horse Guards that morning, but it was not on my own account that I did so. And as for my family, well . . .'

'Will you be wantin' t'eat, m'lord?' called the driver.

'No, we must press on at best speed, Allchurch. I want to be through the Piccadilly bar by seven. We will need to change horses in Farnham, I would suppose. I'll sleep a little now and relieve you of the reins in the early hours if you wish. You are quite sure of the road?'

'Oh ay, y'Lordship: it's changed not a farthin'sworth since past years. This team'll get us to Farnham betimes. I'll prime the pistols now, though: it used to be a bad stretch here to Guildford in the dark.'

Their progress along the turnpike, with the fullest of moons, was faster even than by day, for there was little carting traffic until they reached the outskirts of London in the early dawn. Allchurch had stopped only once, in Farnham, to change the two bays, and by five they were in Chelsea village, slowed to a walk by the carting traffic into the city and by that already returning with horse dung and night soil, a convenient circular trade. Both passengers were now awake, Howard strangely animated by the bustle, in telling contrast with his languor at Horningsham. Along the King's Road he jumped out and stopped an ice-cart, empty but for one block under an insulating canvas. He bought three pieces the size of house bricks, throwing one up to Allchurch and then climbing back inside to give one to his charge. Hervey smiled at him for the first time.

In less than an hour they were passing the bar at Piccadilly and, turning into St James's Street, Lord John Howard could at last feel at home, for the coach halted outside White's. 'We shall use my club to dress,' he said airily, 'but first a barber to shave us and then some breakfast – you *will* have some breakfast?'

Hervey, for all the anxiety that had been mounting since they had entered the capital's environs, readily agreed. Indeed, he found himself wanting to talk, in part as distraction from what he now feared must come but also to return Howard's increasing warmth. 'It is only my second time here: d'Arcey Jessope once brought me,' he added.

'Ah, Jessope, poor man. I fear that I fill his empty boots at the Horse Guards. You knew him well?'

'He was an acquaintance in Spain.'

'He was a great friend of Lord Fitzroy Somerset. It was he who had Jessope appointed to Lord Wellington's staff, you know. I'm told that it was the same sharpshooter who accounted for them both at Waterloo. A cruel irony.'

'Yes, I understand that it was so. I did not see Jessope fall but I saw Lord Fitzroy walking back with his arm shot away.'

'You were *there*, at that *moment*?' asked Howard in some awe.

'We were many. It is just the way,' replied Hervey. 'Have you news of Lord Fitzroy?'

'He is recovering well. You have heard, I suppose, that he had his arm amputated without a murmur and called for it to be brought back so that he could remove a ring his wife had given him? But then, such bearing is perhaps only to be expected of a colonel of Foot Guards.'

Doubtless Howard was unconscious of his presumption, but Hervey thought none the less to deflate him gently. 'My dear Howard,' he smiled confidentially, 'he was first a cornet of light dragoons!'

And then both laughed.

They entered the Horse Guards through the unimposing door in the inner arch, the same that had admitted Hervey two weeks before, and climbed the stairs to the offices of the commander-in-chief.

'Good morning, My Lord,' said the clerk gravely – and bowing – the same clerk on whose account Hervey was now arraigned. Several officers about the place made inaudible asides and stared at him with obvious contempt. His stomach tightened, his eyes began to lose their focus, and the voices around him became strangely disembodied. And yet he remained sensible of his condition and of the proceedings. He had known no feeling like it before – not at Corunna, nor Salamanca, nor even Waterloo. Oblivion had stared at him there, but dishonour faced him now – infamy even.

'General Calvert wishes to see you the moment you arrive, gentlemen,' Hervey heard the clerk say as he hurried to the double doors of the adjutant-general's office.

And before either officer could plead a moment's pause he was announcing them. Howard beckoned Hervey towards the doors, but he stared back in confusion. Was he meant to surrender his sword and remove his shako?

'Keep them!' Howard hissed, all but pulling him into the entrance. They managed nevertheless to halt in step and salute in front of the huge mahogany writing-table.

Sir Harry Calvert was already on his feet, however, and holding out a hand. 'Mr Hervey, my dear boy, welcome; I am sorry indeed that you have been recalled so early. I do trust it has not been unduly inopportune – the interests of the Service, you know, the interests of the Service.'

*Recalled? Inopportune?* Hervey's astonishment was almost matched by Howard's, and both were apparent to the general. 'My dear fellows, whatever can be the matter?'

375

Howard motioned Hervey to say nothing, choosing to recount himself the circumstances of their return, which he now did in all its detail, and with unabated particulars of the offending instructions he had acted upon. Calvert was aghast. He walked towards a contrary door and opened it. 'Colonel Arnold, be so good as to come in here,' he called, and then, as his military assistant entered with pocket-book open, he turned back to the two lieutenants and frowned. 'Mr Howard, if you please, repeat for me the information you have this instant apprised me of.'

When Howard had done so the adjutant-general turned to his colonel and asked him if he did not think it the most shameful thing he had heard. Arnold agreed.

'Then, sir, be pleased to rid me once and for all of that infernal quill-driver. This is one liberty too many.'

And with that the adjutant-general's staff was peremptorily reduced. Indeed, such was the noisy relish with which Colonel Arnold carried out his instructions that Hervey began to feel sympathy for the unfortunate clerk.

'Now, gentlemen, sit down, if you please,' continued General Calvert. 'There is little time. Mr Hervey, you will recall bringing Lord Wellington's dispatch two weeks ago. It did not require an acknowledgement but it is the procedure for the clerk receiving dispatches to peruse them at once and to interrogate the bearer if there be any matter for clarification. Mellor did not do so; indeed, it appears that he dealt with it with quite extraordinary laxness. I had begun to suspect as much. He has for some time been quite incapable of remembering his position. I fear his taking a lease on a house in Blackheath has given him certain gentlemanly propensities!'

Hervey smiled respectfully at the general's attempt at some levity, while suppressing a growing indignation at the inference that his presence at the Horse Guards was merely an instrument for the demise of the offending civilian.

'Only when the Duke of Wellington himself attended here on Monday was the import of the dispatch revealed, for in it he recounts – in some detail – your remarkable exploits at the late battle we are to know as Waterloo. The duke wished that your signal role be recognized but considered that to mark it by public honours would detract from the honour due to the Prussians. You will understand the sensibilities in these matters, Mr Hervey.'

Hervey bowed in acknowledgement, his pulse beginning to race.

'He did consider recommending a companionship of the Bath, along with all other commanding officers – since you had commanded your corps in the closing moments of the battle. But so many other junior officers had been required to do the same that he thought this impractical. He has therefore asked, and their lordships of the Treasury have agreed, that you be awarded *ex gratia* the amount of five thousand pounds.'

Hervey's face spoke of his utter shock. His pulse beat faster than he could ever remember, and he was thankful to be seated. He made to speak, but General Calvert lifted up a hand.

'This is, however, conditional on your absolute discretion in the matter. Not a word of the provenance of this sum is ever to escape.' Calvert's eyes searched Hervey's.

'You have my absolute assurance, sir,' he replied.

'But now to more urgent matters,' continued the general. 'You may know of Lord Fitzroy Somerset's incapacitation. The duke found him an indispensable aide-de-camp and secretary. Moreover, he spoke French with perfect fluency.'

With fluency, yes, thought Hervey, but with an abominable English accent! But what was this to do with—?

'You speak French with equal fluency, and German, too, it seems?' suggested Calvert.

'Yes, sir,' he replied cautiously. *Surely* he could not be suggesting—

'Well, it is the duke's wish that you be appointed to his staff forthwith as under-secretary and aide-de-camp. If you are in agreement, you will be given a brevet captaincy – *given*, mind – which in due season will be confirmed as regimental rank. How say you, Mr Hervey?'

Hervey sprang up like a flushed partridge.

'I . . . I am astonished, sir! I . . . I accept, *of course*!'

'Well, then, *Captain* Hervey, there remains but one difficulty. The duke has this day left for Paris, and there are pressing matters for him to be about with both our allies and the French king. Really, my boy, you are required there at once.' And, turning to his colonel, he asked if a frigate were still stood by.

'Yes, Sir Harry; she could leave Chatham on this evening's tide – about eight, I think.'

'Then,' said General Calvert, turning to Hervey, 'you had better lose no time in making arrangements. Mr Howard will lend you every assistance, I am sure. Now, you must excuse me since I have to attend on the Duke of York. Goodbye and good fortune, Captain Hervey. The Service is indeed favoured to have officers of your faculty. Do not suppose that this peace is an end to the requirement for such aptitude.'

'Thank you, sir,' replied Hervey simply, before replacing his shako, saluting and turning for the door.

Howard seized his arm the moment it was closed behind them. 'My *dear* fellow, no-one could feel happier with this than do I. I could gladly run through that self-important ass of a clerk who began it all, but for my over-hasty presumption, too, I am truly sorry.'

Hervey smiled and touched his arm. 'No matter, no matter.'

'See, then,' Howard pressed, 'we have but a few hours to catch that frigate by tonight's tide. I shall arrange a coach for Chatham. You will need meanwhile to see your tailor and agent, and look for other necessaries until your camp-kit is brought to Paris – though I hardly think you will see hard beds there any longer!'

'Yes, yes . . . thank you, Howard; it is all so . . . But see here, what I *must* do is write to Horningsham. Is there somewhere I may do so?'

'Of course: we shall go to the staff office here. But look, write only a brief account, and I myself shall take it for you. The rest I shall say on your behalf. I could do no other in the circumstances.'

'My dear Howard . . . ,' began Hervey, pleasantly taken by this warm act of contrition.

'No, I will hear no objection,' he insisted. 'It is the very least thing that I may do for a fellow officer. And, indeed, I mean to make some amends with your sister' – he faltered a fraction – 'I mean your family – with whom I seem to have made a disastrous beginning.'

But Hervey did not fully grasp this other aspect to his altruism, for his thoughts were with Henrietta once more. 'With the approval of her guardian, we might be married in Paris this next month,' he mused aloud.

'The approval of Lord Wellington might be the greater impediment,' suggested Howard with a smile.

' "And the child Samuel ministered unto the Lord"!' replied Hervey, smiling, too.

'What?'

'First Samuel, chapter 3, verse 1.'


His Majesty's Naval Dockyard Chatham, at seven that evening, was still bustling. Hervey's chaise and pair stopped at the huge gates, the driver took directions from the Royal Marine sentry and then trotted the team a further quarter-mile to the quay where the frigate was moored. Hervey had expected her to be riding at anchor in the roads, and he was pleased that he would not, after all, have to board her precariously from a jolly-boat. As he stepped down from the coach his eye was caught by the decoration of the gallery window high above the quay on the still-rising tide. A figure stared out at him and then disappeared. The gundeck's yellow side smelled of new paint, and the sail, even to his untutored eye, was furled to perfection. Efficiency itself, he sighed. The Marine sentry at the foot of the gangway which led to the upper deck presented arms, but Hervey hesitated: the conventions of boarding one of His Majesty's ships were ever a trap to an unwary landsman. And (he would truthfully admit) of men-o'-war and captains of frigates he was ever in thrall.

But the brevet captain swallowed hard. Fastening on his sword-belt and taking up the scabbard in his left hand, he touched his shako peak to the Marine and strode resolutely up the steep gangway. As he stepped aboard and turned to salute aft (the one custom of which he was certain) the same figure of the gallery window appeared on deck, immaculate in frock uniform. His face was a year or so older than Hervey's (but not more), and it remained motionless while returning the salute. Then it broke into a quizzical smile. 'Captain Hervey, we presume? We are glad you have at last arrived. I am Captain Laughton Peto.'

Even in the short time it had taken to exchange these compliments three seamen were down the gangway and bringing up Hervey's chests. He struggled to find some apt reply in deference to this courtesy. 'I am afraid my journey here has been in much haste, sir. I confess I do not even know your ship's name.'

Peto smiled again. '*Nisus*; you may have heard of her. Now, Captain Hervey, the tide will be turning any minute. You may come aft and watch as we get under way so that you will have something favourable to tell the duke of your time with the Service. Have you seen a frigate make sail before?'

Hervey glanced at the epaulettes on the captain's coat. The left one looked distinctly newer. By which he concluded that, since the 1813 regulations required two epaulettes irrespective of seniority (he did not wish to peer too closely at them to search for the crowns which would have settled the matter), Captain Peto had held the rank prior to Bonaparte's exile to Elba – when, indeed, Hervey had been but a cornet. Thus, it occurred to him that Captain Peto might have commanded *Nisus* on their Dover escort a year before, which had made such a show of sail on leaving them. But before he could allude thus Peto spoke again. 'I should tell you, too, that in my cabin there are sealed orders for you from Paris, to be opened only when we are under way.'

'Sealed orders – for *me*?' Hervey could scarcely contain his wonder at the change of circumstances: a few hours before and he had been staring oblivion in the face. 'What do you suppose they say?'

'My dear Hervey,' laughed Peto, 'I have not the beginning of an idea. I am a mere frigate captain; *you* are aide-de-camp to the Duke of Wellington!'

**THE END**

Brigadier Allan Mallinson is a serving cavalry officer. He originally trained for the Anglican priesthood, but joined the army in 1969 and served with the infantry in Malaya, Cyprus and Northern Ireland. He commanded the 13th/18th Royal Hussars in Cyprus and Norway, and has since worked in the Ministry of Defence and for the Foreign Office. The author of *Light Dragoons*, a history of British cavalry, and a regular reviewer for *The Times* and the *Spectator*, he is currently the British Military Attaché in Rome.

*A Close Run Thing* is the first book in Allan Mallinson's series featuring Matthew Hervey. The next two novels, *The Nizam's Daughters* and *A Regimental Affair*, are also available in Bantam paperback and the latest novel in the series, *A Call to Arms*, will be published in Bantam paperback in 2003.